DAVID GEORGE
CLARKE

REMORSELESS

A COTTON & SILK THRILLER

GW00806403

clarkeFiction

30127085414857

Suffolk Libraries

amaz   ¹¹/₂,

Copyright © 2017 David George Clarke
ISBN 978-1-912406-09-8
All rights reserved
This is a work of fiction. Any resemblance of any of the characters or places to real
persons living or dead or to real places is purely coincidental.
No part of this book may be reproduced in any form or by any electronic or
mechanical means, including information storage and retrieval systems, without
written permission from the author, except for the use of brief quotations in a book
review.

For Gail, with love.

Books by David George Clarke

The Dust of Centuries

Quincentenarian

The Delusion Gambit

Fatal Consequences

The Cotton and Silk Thrillers

Irrefutable Evidence

Remorseless

The Cambroni Vendetta

An Imperfect Revenge

Non-Fiction

Hong Kong Under The Microscope

A History of the Hong Kong Government Laboratory 1879–2004

REMORSELESS

Chapter One

Former Detective Chief Inspector Mike Hurst was not a happy retiree. It had been seven months since the total cock-up that saw serial killer Olivia Freneton avoid capture in what should have been a straightforward arrest; seven months since she evaporated into thin air, leaving behind her the mayhem of one officer dead, one severely injured and two others incapacitated. Seven torturous shitty months.

And it was down to him: he had been the boss.

As the Board of Inquiry had been all too keen to point out, if Mandy Gwo, the diminutive Chinese prostitute the team was meant to be protecting, hadn't launched herself at Freneton like some crazed martial-arts fighter and stabbed her in the hand, the body count would almost certainly have been higher. Without the girl's frenzied attack, Freneton would probably have systematically worked her way through all of them. Whenever he thought of that scenario, which was often, Hurst would shudder and reach for the whisky bottle, an increasingly frequent companion since he had been more or less forced to retire.

In the soulless interview room used for the inquiry, the unfailing brilliance of the twenty-twenty hindsight dished out by the prat of a chief superintendent from Internal Investigation Branch was as galling as it was smug. Of course it could have been handled better, of course if the armed response unit had been contacted five minutes earlier they would have been on hand, of course they could have … what? Could have what? There was much they *could* have done differently, but in the heat of the moment with the girl's life at stake, snap decisions had to be taken, and no one on the team had hesitated. What none of them had foreseen was the extent of Freneton's brutality.

Hurst put down his fishing rod and shifted his bulk on the thin plastic cushion tied to his rowing dinghy's wooden seat. He had never fished in his life before retiring; now it was part of his routine. Not really a passion, since he never caught much, more of a time-filler, the hours spent bobbing on the waters of one of the Lake District's many meres and tarns were his way of trying to put the ignominious end to his otherwise noteworthy career behind him.

Thirty-three years; a working lifetime of policing, most of it as a detective. He was old school, he didn't deny it, but his methods had still got results even if they hadn't involved hours glued to some screen. DI Rob McPherson had been the same. A dyed-in-the-wool no-nonsense copper; tough as old boots, but ultimately, not tough enough. It had taken Freneton just one savage blow with a side-handle baton to McPherson's nose, followed by another to his head, to cause so much internal cranial bleeding that he died within minutes.

Hurst lit a cigarette — he'd started smoking again after several years of abstinence — and retrieved his hip flask from his rucksack. He took a swig from it and shivered. What the hell was he doing sitting in a rowing boat on a bleak day in March? Why was he putting up with temperatures in single figures and a stiffening wind that made it feel like Siberia? Wallowing in self-pity, that's what he was doing. And declining into a sad old fool. He wasn't even sixty and yet he looked washed up, his vitality drained.

He needed to get a grip; he wasn't the only one whose life had been wrecked. Neil Bottomley, the detective sergeant Freneton whacked in the teeth, had not recovered his former easy-going manner, while Jennifer Cotton, the bright young detective constable against whom the bulk of Freneton's wrath had been aimed for unmasking her as a serial killer, was still convalescing. At least she was in Sardinia, soaking up the sun no doubt, even in March. The girl had a number of things going for her, not the least of which was a doting and mega-rich stepfather.

Jennifer was a bright girl with the potential to become an excellent detective. Currently she had been poached by The Met's Art Fraud Squad in London, or at least that was where she was going once she'd recovered. Hurst didn't think much of the idea; too airy-fairy. Jennifer needed good, solid, on-the-ground experience as a detective if she wanted to get on. Then again, she was young; there was time. A couple of years checking out paintings and traipsing around auction houses should be enough to make her see sense and bring her running back. He'd give her a call, see how she was getting on, extol the virtues of being a real detective.

He shrugged in defeat as he stowed his fishing rod — the fish seemed to have migrated to somewhere warmer and he didn't blame them. His wife Lynda was of the same mind; she'd been on about a winter holiday somewhere in the sun. Hurst wasn't sure he fancied it: always too busy with one investigation or another, he'd never been much of a one for holidays. There was no denying he owed it to her; he'd been even more difficult to live with than usual since his retirement and she had stoically borne the brunt of his introspection as she let him try to work his way through it. She had seen it all before — police officers' wives frequently got the thin end of a frustratingly uncompromising wedge — but she was devoted to him and he knew it. When he got home, he'd go online and find somewhere warm for them to go. He'd heard Thailand was good, and cheap too. Time to spread their wings and explore farther afield than their usual Skegness.

Rather than start the outboard, he decided to row the half mile to the moorings. The exercise would warm him up. As his muscles began to complain, he thought of Derek Thyme, the young, black detective constable who had been the fourth person in the car that awful night. Derek had been next after Rob to gain Freneton's attention. He'd hauled the Chinese girl out of the car from in front of the bitch's nose, but Freneton was unfazed. Having seen to Rob, she'd sprung from the car and faced up to Derek, taking him by surprise with a well-aimed kick to his crotch. He'd recovered in time to use his brilliant sprinting skills to race after her, knowing she was hunting for Jennifer, and it was only his speed that prevented her from kicking Jennifer to death. And that speed had been noticed: Derek was currently shortlisted for the UK squad for next year's Olympics in Rio. Recognising this, the force had given him what was effectively a desk job in a fraud squad in London. Mixed blessings, thought Hurst. Thyme was no desk jockey, but the hours would help his training. He shivered; he certainly didn't envy Derek pounding the track in the current temperatures.

When he reached the moorings, Hurst was breathing heavily from the exertion. He attached the mooring rope to his buoy and waved to Jock, the weather-beaten boatman who ferried owners to the jetty. Now he was up in the Lakes once or twice a week, Hurst had taken to leaving his boat on moorings rather than go to the effort of hauling it out of the water. It made sense and the fees were negligible.

"Catch much, Mike?" said Jock, eyeing Hurst's rucksack, his Glaswegian accent as harsh as the cries of the screeching gulls.

"Nothing left to catch, Jock. You buggers have fished the place out."

"Ach, there's plenty if ye know where ta look," said Jock, tapping the side of his craggy nose. "I'll come out wi ya next time, if it'd please ya. Show ya a few tricks o' the trade."

"I'll hold you to that," said Hurst, nodding his delight. Jock wasn't known for his willingness to pass on his skills. "I'll be up next week."

Otley in West Yorkshire, where Hurst and his wife had moved to four months previously to be closer to Lynda's relatives, was about an hour and three quarters' drive from the Lakes. Hurst was a skilled driver, having taken all the police courses, and although the A65 was a fast road with some notorious black spots, he knew them all and was instinctively alert to them. The idea of calling Jennifer Cotton had lifted his spirits. He was fond of the girl and still remembered with embarrassment when Freneton, still a police superintendent and as yet undiscovered as a killer, had insisted to the boss, Chief Superintendent Pete Hawkins, that Jennifer be hauled across the coals for not revealing she was Henry Silk's daughter. Henry Silk, TV star and number one suspect in the murder investigation that had shattered lives and put Hurst where he was today. Jennifer had stood up for herself well, but her world had collapsed around her.

Eleven miles west of Otley, the A65 curves gently southwards before running along the south side of Chelker reservoir, a man-made lake several hundred yards long. As Hurst approached it in the gloom of the overcast March evening, the traffic was light, enabling him to stay just above the 60 mph speed limit. Glancing in his Ford Explorer's rear-view mirror, he saw the single headlight of a motorcycle that had caught up with him and was following too closely. Why doesn't the idiot overtake? he thought, irritated by the invasion of the personal space around his speeding vehicle, there's plenty of room and no lights coming from the other direction.

His phone rang, distracting him. It must be his wife checking on where he was. He pressed the button on the steering column to engage the hands-free set.

"Lyn, I—"

"Hello, Mike. Do you recognise my voice? I'm sure you do. It's in all your nightmares."

Hurst frowned, trying to process the information while still distracted by the damn motorcycle. "Freneton?" he said after a second's pause. "What …? Where …?"

"Ah, DCI Hurst, the last time we spoke you were trying to persuade me to give myself up. Do you remember? I'm sure you do. Well, let me congratulate you; you should feel privileged."

"What the hell do you mean, Freneton? Where are you?"

"You're the first on my list, Mike Hurst, a list that is about to get shorter. Goodbye, I hope you can swim."

The motorcycle accelerated round Hurst's car, cut in sharply and braked hard. Hurst reacted instinctively, whipping the steering wheel to the left in the direction of the reservoir wall. As he did, there was a muffled bang from beneath his car. He jumped on the brake pedal, but it hit the floor, as useless as the now unresponsive steering wheel in his hands. With no brakes and no steering, the Explorer careered on its course, crashing through the low, dry-stone wall separating the road from the reservoir and plunging into the deep water. Mike Hurst made no attempt to escape: he couldn't — the force of the car hitting the water had deployed his airbag, but with the unnatural angle of the impact, his head hit the driver's door window sufficiently hard to knock him out. As the car sank into the freezing water, he drowned without regaining consciousness.

After pressing the button on the remote detonator, Olivia Freneton twisted the powerful BMW's accelerator. Glancing in her nearside mirror, she saw the out-of-control Explorer crash through the wall and begin its plunge.

One down, she thought, as the motorcycle roared over the slight rise at the reservoir's eastern end and headed south to Birmingham.

Chapter Two

THE SAME DAY

Mandy Gwo felt more secure than she had at any time since she left China, more secure in fact than she could ever remember. Instead of punishing her for selling her body, the gods had rewarded her, lifted her out of the grim downward spiral of debt and depravity that had been her life in the months since her arrival at Dover crammed into a filthy container with sixty others. Not just lifted her out of it but given her a new start with a new name, and it was all legal, approved by the authorities, initiated by them. England was certainly a wonderful place as far as Mandy was concerned; a land of plenty.

The lucky break for Mandy was being picked up by the crazy woman who wanted sex with her out in some dark woods. It hadn't seemed like a lucky break at the time; the woman had intended to kill her, although for what reason, Mandy still didn't understand.

According to the police, it was a close-run thing. They had been watching and moved in on the car just in time. Mandy could remember the silence of the eerie woods exploding into deafening screams and shouts as she was ripped from the car by a huge black man. Then the crazy woman with the pretty name — Olivia — had burst from the car, kicked the black man hard in the balls, and set about beating up the other men, policemen, who had arrived out of nowhere.

Once it had dawned on Mandy that the crazy woman had

meant to kill her, she went crazy herself. She pulled out the stiletto knife she always kept hidden in a sheath sewn into her belt and charged at her. The woman was quick; she blocked Mandy's arm with her own, diverting the knife away from its target and into her hand. But despite the blood and what must have been a lot of pain from the deep cut, the woman managed to hit Mandy under the chin with some sort of cosh. After that, Mandy knew nothing until she regained consciousness in the back of an ambulance where a young policewoman with a pointy face like a rat was bending over her.

"Ah, Mandy, you're back with us."

"How you know name?" she croaked.

"ID in your handbag in the car, love. Looks a bit dodgy to me; you could be in a spot of trouble, but we won't worry about that now. How's the mouth feeling?"

"Mouf feel funny," said Mandy through her swollen gums and tongue.

"Not surprised. You lost a few teeth and took a bloody great bite out of your tongue, so the paramedic said. He's given you plenty of painkillers, so you shouldn't be feeling too much pain right now. We'll soon be at the hospital; they'll sort you out."

What puzzled Mandy was how friendly the police were to her. If she'd stabbed someone in China, even in self-defence, which it sort of was, she'd have taken a few beatings from the police in addition to the one she'd had. Here, they treated her like she'd done a good thing; saved several lives, they'd said. And no, she wasn't in any trouble, just as long as she told them everything that had happened.

After that, there had been visits from a social worker, an immigration officer, a lawyer who said she was representing her without wanting any money, and some other police officers who wanted to know all about the gang she worked for, how they ran her, where they lived. They said if she cooperated, since she'd been so brave and stopped the crazy woman from killing anyone else, they'd not only let her stay in England, but also they'd give her a new name, a new passport and find her a job so she didn't have to work on the streets. They'd even find her a place to live in another city.

So Mandy Gwo had become Kitty Lee. They moved her to Birmingham, housed her in a small clean flat in a high-rise council block and found her a job entering data onto a computer for a marketing company. It was boring work, but anything was better than the streets, and the company paid her for it without beating her up. Her social worker told her that because she was a bright girl, once her English had improved, they'd look at getting her something better, something more challenging.

The new Kitty sat back from her keyboard in the large office where she now worked and took a small mirror from her handbag to admire her new teeth, something she still did several times a day, even now, months after her life had changed. The crazy woman had done her a big favour when she hit her in the mouth. Mandy's teeth had been twisted and yellow; Kitty's were perfectly straight and white: beautiful, like a movie star.

She pulled at her hair, which was now cut by a proper hair-dresser, not hacked at by one of the other girls. She smiled into the mirror. She'd never be beautiful, she knew that, but now her face wasn't regularly swollen from black eyes, and with everything else she'd had done, perhaps she'd even find a proper boyfriend.

The smartphone in her handbag pinged. It was a text from her sister in Shenyang in north–eastern China where she came from. The smartphone was the first thing she'd bought with her new income, a prized possession. She'd proudly shown it to Dawn, her social worker, who'd admired it and then, for the tenth time at least, reminded the new Kitty how essential it was she had no contact with anyone from her previous life in Nottingham. No one, not a single person. She kept on and on about it every time they met. Kitty understood; she owed none of them anything and had no reason to contact them. As far as they were concerned, she'd been deported back to China. That's what the newspaper reports had said and none of the women she'd shared her life with in and around Forest Road West had any reason to doubt it.

Except one. Except Apple Chan. Apple was different; Apple had arrived after Mandy and was even plainer, skinnier and more mousey than she was. How was she ever going to get decent clients looking like that and with almost no English? Mandy had taken her under her wing and they had commiserated with each other, swapping stories of brutality and meanness from their clients, planning to get away, or at least find clients who gave them a tiny bit of respect.

Apple would be totally lost without Mandy. None of the other women took any notice of her; it was like she wasn't there. Despite the rules, Mandy simply couldn't let her friend down. She'd thought of telling Dawn about her, but that would probably have resulted in Apple being picked up and deported, a death sentence given the money she owed. No, the newly created Kitty couldn't risk telling Dawn.

However, she did contact Apple. She called her to tell her about her good fortune, tell her she'd bring her to Birmingham as soon as she could. Apple of course swore secrecy, swore she'd die rather than reveal Mandy's secret.

The March evening was wet and cold as Kitty walked back to the high-rise in the suburb of Nechells, north–east of Birmingham city centre, that was home. She glanced at the new watch on her wrist. Nine o'clock. Later than she'd intended but it didn't matter; she felt buoyant. Her English was improving and she'd found herself chatting to her workmates more and more. None of them was in fact ethnically English, rather they were their own United Nations of nationalities, although all of them had the local nasal twang Kitty had initially found difficult to understand.

There had been cake during the afternoon tea break — one of the girls was celebrating her birthday — and Kitty's supervisor, Nadine, had suggested a few of them go for a drink after work. It had been fun, relaxing, and there was talk of a night out over the coming weekend.

When she got home, Kitty was planning to call Apple, encourage her to simply get on a train and leave. It had been seven months now and she felt increasingly confident. Apple could hide out in her flat for a while until she thought of something to do with her.

Although when compared to Shenyang, the twenty-storey apartment blocks in Nechells dominating the surrounding streets of two-storey semi-detached houses were small fry, they helped Kitty's sense of feeling at home. Living on the tenth floor was perfect for her since it not only gave her a good view, but also the comfort of knowing no one was going to break into her flat through the windows. As for the front door, Dawn had arranged for it to be well secured with three different deadlocks to give her peace of mind.

As Kitty pushed open the door after releasing all three locks, she bent to pick up her bags — after leaving the bar, she'd been food shopping in a large Chinese supermarket that stayed open all hours, an Aladdin's cave of a store that stocked every ingredient she could possibly want, a small part of China in central England.

"Cooking up a storm, Mandy?" said a voice from behind her as she walked towards the kitchen counter. The person must have been hiding behind the door.

Kitty spun around, still clutching her bags.

"My name's Kitty," she said, "not Mandy. You're in the wrong flat. Please leave."

"Very cool, Mandy," said Olivia Freneton, clapping her hands slowly as she kicked the main door shut. "Surely you know who I am, don't you?" she added, her smile so cold Kitty felt she was being stabbed with icicles.

Then the smile disappeared. "I certainly know who you are, *Mandy*." She held up her left hand and waved it slightly. "This has never been quite the same since you plunged your little knife into it, and it aches like hell in cold weather."

Kitty wasn't really listening; she was too shocked by the intrusion into the flat she'd thought of as secure by this strange woman with tattoos on her neck, a black headscarf that made her look like a pirate, black lipstick and leather motorcycle gear. Who was she? What did she want?

She watched the woman's lips move, saw the dark intent in her eyes, and suddenly she knew. She was the crazy woman. The bitch had found her. All her muscles tensed as she thought rapidly about where the nearest thing to a weapon was.

As Kitty's face hardened, Olivia uttered a scornful laugh. "Thinking about where the knives are, Mandy?" she sneered, as if reading the girl's mind. "Well, you can forget it; I've moved them. Nothing important is where you left it."

"What you want?" growled Kitty, as she slowly adjusted the position of the shopping bags so her hands and arms could propel them more effectively.

"That's a simple enough question to answer," replied Olivia, her eyes fixed on Kitty's as if trying to hypnotise her. "I have a list of names I'm working my way through until no one's left. And you, Mandy, I'm delighted to say, are on it. You see, until I saw your friend Apple's phone, I thought you'd gone back to China. Big mistake telling her about your new identity, Mandy. A fatal mistake, in fact."

"Apple …?"

"Oh, she's fine. I would have killed her, of course, if she'd come back when I was searching her room. Lucky for her she didn't and she's none the wiser about my visit."

Kitty frowned. She didn't understand what the crazy woman was talking about, and she didn't want to be distracted by trying. She was waiting for her moment.

Olivia's eyes were still fixed on her. She knew exactly what the girl was doing from the minuscule adjustments of her body, so she'd help her along. She let her eyes leave Kitty's and seem to look towards one of the kitchen cupboards. The instant she did, Kitty burst into action, flinging the two shopping bags hard at Olivia, but Olivia was ready. She took two rapid skips sideways to her left, blocking the way to the main door, and stood poised as the bags and their contents crashed to the floor.

"Whoops, that was careless, Mandy," she said as she shifted her weight onto her left foot.

Kitty hunched slightly, the disappointment of her failed move crushing her. She was now expecting the crazy woman to launch herself at her, grab her around the waist and pin her arms. What she didn't anticipate was the full-extension kick as Olivia's right leg lifted and snapped straight, her foot driving into Kitty's windpipe.

The girl collapsed on the floor, clutching at her throat. Olivia watched her struggling to breathe, in no hurry to finish her off. The little bitch deserved no better than to die in terror. Perhaps she'd crushed her thorax, in which case she'd probably just choke to death as she lay there.

But Kitty's thorax wasn't crushed, at least not completely. Her desperate gasps became slightly easier as she forced air down into her lungs. She tried to move. She needed to get into a crouching position so she could defend herself. Olivia watched her with almost detached interest, as if she were watching some violent movie and not personally involved. She sighed and glanced at her watch. Better get on; she'd other fish to fry.

She launched another powerful kick, this time at Kitty's temple, feeling the bone break as she connected. There would be no returning from that, but for good measure, she took a short length of rope from her pocket and wound it around the girl's neck, pulling it tighter and tighter. There was little resistance; the kick had severely compromised a number of Kitty's brain functions and in less than a minute her body was limp. As Olivia pushed the lifeless body away from her, she gave the rope one final pull for good measure.

Chapter Three

Detective Constable Derek Thyme finished his extensive routine of warm-up stretches and headed for the track, pulling his balaclava over his head and slipping on his thermal gloves as he emerged into the frosty evening air. With the temperature hovering around three degrees and threatening to go lower, he had to be careful: cold was the enemy of the sprinter. If his powerful leg and back muscles weren't fully warmed, they could pull with alarming ease. He could have trained indoors; there was a top-class indoor track at the east-London centre he and dozens of other prime athletes used, but there was an outdoor meet in Bristol at the weekend and he wanted his body to be prepared for the expected conditions.

Tonight's routine would consist mainly of light jogging — light by Derek's standards, not the average mortal's — with a few short sprints thrown in. Nothing too extreme and comparatively speaking, almost a night off. In little over an hour, he'd be back on the Tube heading for the warmth of his small apartment near Edgware Road Station and some longed-for sleep.

After having been shortlisted for Team GB's Rio squad, Derek's training schedule had gone from gruelling to punishing, and trying to work it in with a day job in the Met's Fraud Squad was wearing him down. The posting had been designed to give him the time for his training, a generous gesture on the part of the force, but he couldn't appear to be skiving, to be a part-time police officer on full-time pay.

The problem was he disliked the work: fraud inquiries simply weren't his thing. He had quite a mathematical brain, so it wasn't the numbers or the complexity, nor was it the nature of the criminals he was investigating — he was appalled by the shameless cunning and deceit apparently law-abiding citizens would employ to cheat their fellow man, all with smiles on their charming, trustworthy faces as they squirrelled away fortunes of other people's money. They were everywhere, rats in a sewer, and he loathed them. Yet, even though catching them and putting a stop to their activities was important and should feel rewarding, try as he may, the enthusiasm wasn't there. He missed the SCF, the Serious Crime Formation in Nottingham, and the buzz that went with the hard graft of tracking down a murderer, a rapist or a kidnapper.

However, the SCF as he'd known it would never be the same again. It had been decimated by the Olivia Freneton case, literally. Lives lost, reputations ruined. And it was still continuing. Only that afternoon, he'd heard from one of his ex-colleagues in the SCF that their old boss, Mike Hurst, had been found dead in his car at the bottom of a reservoir late the previous evening. It wasn't clear what had happened, although they knew he'd been having a hard time coping with retirement.

For Derek, that fateful night in Harlow Wood, the night Rob McPherson died, replayed constantly in his head. It had been so horribly close; he had only just arrived in time to prevent Freneton from killing Jennifer Cotton. Even now, months later, his buddy and inspiration was still convalescing from her injuries, the worst of which was the result of the one vicious kick that Freneton had managed to deliver to Jennifer's head. In his recurring nightmares Derek was always delayed by another thirty seconds, giving Freneton time to pound Jennifer's head repeatedly with blow after blow. As it was, Jennifer's survival had been a miracle, and Derek had literally wept for joy when it was clear she was going to recover fully, albeit slowly. The medics had prescribed a long period of convalescence and her stepfather had insisted this would be in his Sardinian villa. Jennifer's new bosses in the Met's Art Fraud Squad were patiently letting her have all the time she needed, knowing she would be a strong asset once she reported for duty.

Jennifer had remained enthusiastically supportive of Derek's training and new job, listening to his doubts and encouraging him to put aside his worries and think of all the positives that would arise when he was chosen for the Olympic squad. Their frequent and lengthy calls on Skype were peppered with their usual banter, all designed to raise Derek's spirits and keep him motivated. Truth be told, he loved her, and not just as the mate she had been for nearly a year. However, he had no illusions as to his chances. Even though he didn't know what sort of bloke would fit Jennifer's bill when the time came, he doubted it was him.

As he pounded the track at the end of long days at work, or pumped iron in the gym, or tuned his muscles with the arcane punishments his physio delighted in inflicting on him, it was thoughts of Jennifer that kept him going.

Things were reaching a head in the training, the final selection for the prime squad was to be made within two weeks. Everyone was on edge and the book was wide open, full of amazing talent. Derek knew he had a good chance, although he worried about being up to it psychologically. But then again, he knew everyone else felt the same. The pressure was huge, and while there would be no shame in not being picked, he would be gutted if he weren't.

It was with these thoughts running through his mind that he made his way home. A short walk to Stratford Station and the Central line, a change at Oxford Circus to the Bakerloo line followed by a brisk ten-minute walk from Edgware Road.

In older parts of the Underground, like the Central line, he found the limited space claustrophobic. At six foot two, his broad, muscular frame seemed too large for the curved, low-ceilinged tunnels that weaved through the earth under the heart of London as he made his way from one platform to another. Claustrophobic too because there were always so many people, all in a hurry, all tired after long days at work, all lost in their smartphones, earbuds and whatever worlds they inhabited inside their heads.

It was almost impossible to hurry when the tunnels were crowded, or to dawdle. You had to go with the flow as the human droplets streamed along the pipes and burst out onto the platforms, spreading in either direction from the entrances but held back by an invisible barrier from spilling over the edge onto the electrified track — very few stations in the system had platform screen doors. On the older, narrower platforms, like those in Oxford Circus, it was a miracle how seldom people fell, given the crowds. People were wary, generally careful, resorting to jostling only once a train had arrived at the platform and its doors were open.

Derek considered the entire system antiquated and dangerous. The electrified track terrified him and whenever he could, he hung back from the platform edge. It would be one thing to fall onto the tracks if the power were from overhead lines, but there was no space for such luxuries, the trains only just fitting as the ancient tunnels sleeved around them. By necessity, the power was in the third rail, and if you touched that, you were dead.

Tonight, even though it was after eight o'clock, the Tube was crowded and the platform packed. An earlier breakdown had blackened the mood of the jaded commuters and everyone wanted to get on to the increasingly infrequent trains.

Every train arrival was preceded by a build-up of air pressure and a rising rumble of wheels as the train pushed a column of air ahead of it. Like a pounding migraine, the sensory overload would grow and grow until the front carriage burst from the tunnel's mouth at what seemed to be recklessly high speed. Derek would try to position himself where the front end of the train would stop, coming to a halt as it drew alongside him. Tonight he'd failed. Tonight, owing to the flow of the crowd, he'd had no choice but to turn the other way as he emerged onto the platform, soon finding himself near the point where the train would blast from the darkness.

He was two people back from the front of the crowd as the first increase in pressure from the next arriving train was felt and the roar commenced. The rattling made it sound as if the train were bouncing off the tunnel walls as it pounded towards the station. The noise rose to a crescendo and the crowd tensed as one, involuntarily moving forward a fraction, preparing for the squeeze into the carriages. When the train burst from the tunnel, Derek sensed a movement behind him, as if someone had tripped. He half-turned his head and as he did, he felt a prod in his side from something firm and unyielding, something propelling him towards the platform edge. The sudden movement shifted the rucksack on his back, pulling him onwards, and he stumbled. He took a short step to steady himself, but it wasn't enough; he needed another. When he took it, he found himself treading on thin air. In horror, he dipped forward, falling straight into the path of the oncoming train.

Chapter Four

Jennifer Cotton reached out of the water to tap the end of the twenty-metre heated pool and glanced up at Alicia, her personal trainer.

"Dieci secondi, Jenni! Dieci secondi!" yelled Alicia as she scrutinised her stopwatch, her Italian laced with her soft Umbrian Cs, her face beaming encouragement. "You were ten seconds faster. That's brilliant; you're improving every day. At this rate it won't be long before you're getting back to the times you were logging before last August."

She bent down towards the full-time client who had become a good friend.

"'igh five, cara! 'igh five!" she squealed in English.

"It felt good, Ali, really good," replied Jennifer in Italian as their palms connected, her refined Milanese accent in marked contrast to Alicia's strong dialect. She sprung out of the pool and grabbed a towel to brush the surplus water from her arms and legs before putting on her robe. She felt energised by the swim and thrilled with the time. After months of slow recovery, she was at last feeling she had turned a corner, that she was on the way to regaining her full health and strength.

She walked to the end of the pool where they had left the sliding acrylic winter dome partly open to the crisp but sunny March day.

"I can't wait for the sea to warm up," she said, pointing over the low stone wall to the emerald waters lapping onto the Fabrelli family's private beach sixty feet below. "I'd love to swim to the point and back. The way I'm feeling today, I'd leave you standing."

Alicia laughed. "You're on, although I think we'll have to wait a few weeks. The cold water wouldn't be so good for your muscles."

"You're the boss," shrugged Jennifer. Then with a sly grin, she added, "But take your chance soon before I'm fully fighting fit."

She sat down on the pool's edge and dangled her feet in the water. An array of solar panels ensured that even in the coolest Sardinian weather the water was deliciously warm, while the acrylic dome cut down heat loss as well as providing a perfect shield against any wind. Her stepfather Pietro Fabrelli, the internationally renowned fashion designer, often joked that the system was actually superfluous given the amount of heat Jennifer must generate as she powered through the water.

She stretched and worked her neck muscles.

Seven months. It had been seven whole frustrating months, with very likely a few more to go before she would be given a clean bill of health. At times the healing process seemed so slow she thought she would go crazy. It wasn't just the blow to the head, which made her irritatingly cautious doctors warn constantly against overstressing her body in case there were permanent weaknesses, there was also the injury to her chest. She had suffered an enormous blow to her ribs from Olivia Freneton's perfectly timed attack with her elbow as Jennifer had launched herself at her from the bushes in Harlow Wood. Her diaphragm had been weakened, and in addition to broken ribs, there had been internal bleeding from damage to her chest cavity. The outcome of all this was her journey back to health could not be hurried, no matter how much she protested.

Once he had been allowed to fly her to Italy, Pietro ensured Jennifer received the best available treatment private clinics could provide. She had gone first to Milan, where after only two weeks she complained she was claustrophobic from the over-the-top pampering and threatened to walk out. Leaned on by Pietro, her doctors quickly declared her well enough to continue her convalescence at the family villa in Sardinia, with weekly check-ups from a consultant flown over from the mainland.

However, his stepdaughter's health wasn't Pietro's only priority; he was also paranoid about security.

"That madwoman Freneton is still at large, tesoro," he had declared to Jennifer as soon as she arrived at the villa the previous December. "No one knows where she is, not your English bobbies, not the so-called experts at Interpol. No one. She has disappeared off the face of the earth. Because of that, we cannot take any chances. I've increased the number of personnel patrolling the house, the grounds and the surrounding area. It must be impenetrable to anyone who isn't invited."

Jennifer shook her head. "You worry too much, Pietro. She doesn't even know I'm out of England. The press has been told I'm recovering in a private hospital in Sussex. Anyway, what makes you think she'll come after me or anyone else on the team from that night? She's got too much to lose if she shows her face. My guess is she's gone to ground somewhere far from here, somewhere there's little chance of her being recognised. We'll probably never hear from her again, or if we do, it'll be because she's been picked up somewhere else entirely, like Australia, for a murder spree there."

Jennifer was convinced she was right; it would be foolhardy of Freneton to seek revenge. As the weeks and months passed, she more or less put the psychopathic ex-policewoman out of her mind until, a few hours after her encouraging fifty-lengths' swim in the pool, a call from her former boss, Chief Superintendent Pete Hawkins, changed everything.

"Jennifer, good evening. DCS Hawkins. It is evening there, isn't it?"

"Er yes, sir, it is," she replied, cautiously. "We're only an hour ahead of you. This is rather a surprise."

"How are you, lass? Still recovering well?"

"I am, thank you, sir, although it's frustratingly slow. But—"

"Of course," interrupted Hawkins. It was clear he wasn't listening. His voice was serious, strange, full of tension. Worried, Jennifer stopped and waited.

"Listen, Jennifer," he continued after a pause. "What's the security like where you are? I'm concerned it might need reviewing."

Jennifer suppressed a chuckle. "It couldn't be better, sir, I can assure you. I'm embarrassed by how much there is, considering it's just for me. It must be cost—"

"That's good to hear," interrupted Hawkins again. There was another pause, this one unnaturally long. When he continued, his tone was even more serious. He seldom joked and now his voice resonating through the phone made him sound like a messenger of doom.

"Look, Jennifer. I'm afraid I've got some bad news."

"What is—"

"There's been an accident, well, hardly an accident, it was bloody deliberate."

Jennifer felt her stomach tighten as she gasped involuntarily.

"Sir," she insisted, Hawkins' habitual prevarication now irritating her. "Please, just tell me. Who is it?"

There was another pause, the silence on the line torture as Jennifer waited.

"It's Mike," Hawkins finally replied, his voice hardly audible. "Mike Hurst. I wish …" There was a deep sigh. "He's … dead." His voice cracked as he said the words. Although he'd known since the previous night when he'd been woken with the news, the shock was still a raw wound.

"What … what happened?" Jennifer's voice was now little more than a whisper.

Hawkins told her the details of the incident, where and when it had happened, told her they were sure it was murder and who they were convinced was behind it.

"How did she do it?" asked Jennifer, more to herself than Hawkins.

"Don't know yet, but it was clearly bloody well planned. It would have taken pinpoint timing to get the car to go off the road exactly where it did. She must have been following him for days, weeks even. Learning his movements, his timing, his habits. Everything."

"If that's the case, sir, then none of us is safe. Not you nor anyone else from the team. And probably not Henry either, although he's in the US at the moment. Freneton's hardly likely to go there."

"It goes beyond the team, Jennifer, which is why I'm calling now. I was going to leave it until the morning but there's something else, another murder."

Jennifer shuddered, wondering what Hawkins was going to say.

"Who?" she whispered, when she couldn't stand the waiting any longer.

She heard Hawkins take a deep breath. "The Chinese prostitute, Mandy Gwo," he said.

"Mandy Gwo? How? I thought she'd been sent back to China."

"That's what everyone was supposed to think. In fact, it was a smoke screen to keep the press off her back and take Freneton's attention away from her. She was given full witness protection: a new identity and passport, a job and a new place to live down in Birmingham. But it didn't work. Freneton clearly wasn't fooled and went digging, at least that's what we're assuming. There was another Chinese girl, Apple Chan, who worked from the same address on Forest Road. We picked her up and interviewed her this afternoon after Mandy's body was found by the Birmingham police. She was reluctant to say anything to start with; you know how these women are. Eventually she admitted Mandy had kept in touch with her. Stupid little tart put Mandy's new name alongside her old one on her phone, along with her address."

"How did Freneton get it?"

"Presumably she broke into Chan's room and found the phone. She said she often leaves it behind in the daytime if she goes out. It's an old one, apparently, doesn't hold its charge too well."

"You're sure it was Freneton? How did Gwo die?"

"Oh, it had Freneton's name written all over it. The girl was kicked to death and just for good measure, throttled with some sort of cord, although the pathologist reckons the kick to the head would have killed her."

Jennifer found herself massaging her temple where Freneton's shoe had inflicted so much damage on her.

She was still puzzled. "How does the timing work? I mean, did she kill both Mike and Gwo yesterday?"

"She did, yes. It must have been very carefully planned. From Chelker reservoir, where Mike was killed shortly before six p.m., it would take about two and a half hours to get to where Gwo lived. The pathologist puts the time of death around nine p.m., so it adds up."

"She must have forced her way in. Did nobody hear anything?"

"There were three deadlocks on Gwo's front door and the SOCO found scratches, signs they were picked. So Freneton must have let herself in and been waiting."

"Three deadlocks? Christ, she must be good."

"That's why I wanted to know about the security where you are. She could just as easily strike in Europe as in England."

"Well, as I said just now, sir, it couldn't be better. You needn't worry about me; it's the others who need to watch their backs. And anyway, I assume the story about me is still that I'm convalescing in England, so she won't know I'm here."

"I wish I could be confident of that," muttered Hawkins.

A thought occurred to Jennifer. "Has Derek Thyme been told?"

"Not yet, no. My secretary's been trying to raise him since we heard about Gwo, but his phone appears to be switched off."

"He's probably training. He's got permission from his boss in the fraud squad to turn it off, or at least to leave it in his locker. Apparently his coach blows a fuse if anyone's phone rings during a training session. He's been known to smash them."

"I know the feeling," commented Hawkins. "Look, Jennifer, the assistant con's light's flashing on my phone. I'd better answer."

"Sir?"

"What is it?"

"I'm so sorry. About Mike, I mean. I know you went back a long way."

"Thank you, Jennifer." Hawkins paused, clearly fighting his

emotions. She heard another deep sigh before his voice came back on the line. "There'll probably be some more details in the morning. If there are, I'll call you then. Take care, and tell that stepfather of yours to ensure everything around you is secure."

As the line went dead, Jennifer dropped the phone in her lap and buried her face in her hands. "No!" she wailed as she rocked back and forth, her body shuddering as the reality of the conversation hit her.

Jennifer was still in the villa's large sitting room four hours later, staring out through the huge picture windows at the invisible sea. There was no moon and cloud obscured much of the sky. Whatever stars were visible, Jennifer didn't see them. After endless attempts to contact Derek, the same irritatingly jaunty voice had just told her once again the person she was calling was unavailable. She shook her head in frustration. She'd give him a bollocking when he did turn his phone on, tell him to have an excuse ready or his boss would hang him out to dry. It was one thing to turn the phone off during training; he was pushing his luck way beyond the limit by leaving it off.

At three thirty, Jennifer was sitting in the same position staring at the same nothingness, her mind far from the room as memories of Mike Hurst filled her head. When her phone's ringtone cut through the silence, she jumped in shock. The phone was sitting on the arm of her chair and in her haste to answer it, she knocked it onto the floor. Swearing at it, she bent to pick it up, her eyes widening when she saw the caller's number. It was the same one as earlier; it was Hawkins. Why was he calling again, in the middle of the night? She tried to repress the wave of panic jolting through her. Her finger hovered reluctantly over the answer button as if the action of pressing it would cause an explosion.

"Sir?"

"Jennifer. Did I wake you? Sorry, stupid question. I must have done."

"No, sir, you didn't. I couldn't sleep." Haven't even tried, she thought. "What is it? Has … has something happened?"

Hawkins was silent.

"Sir?"

"There's been another one, Jennifer. It has to be connected." Hawkins' voice croaked, as if he was being strangled. "I thought I'd better let you know as soon as possible. I didn't want you waking up and seeing some news report."

Jennifer's eyes widened as her mouth quivered.

"Another one?" she whispered, her chest heaving in fear of what Hawkins was about to say.

"Another … incident, yes."

"Tell me, sir, whatever it is, just tell me, please. Is it Derek? Don't say it is, I couldn't—"

"I'm afraid it is, Jennifer."

"Is he—"

"There was … It happened at Oxford Circus Tube Station in London. The platform was crowded and—"

"Sir," she pleaded, interrupting him. "Please, just tell me. Is he … is he dead? Please don't tell me he's dead. Please—"

"No, Jennifer, he's not dead. It's a miracle, but he's not. He's injured, broken his leg quite badly, but he's alive, stable and able to talk. He's convinced he was pushed."

No one on the platform was sure whether it had been an accident, an attempted suicide or an attempted murder. Certainly no one saw anything. Later, when it was reviewed, the CCTV footage showed little of value, no faces that even came close to resembling Freneton's. Eye witnesses all said it happened so fast it was over before they had time to register anything. Derek, however, had no doubt in his mind. He was quite sure he had been pushed. He had felt something dig into his side and shove him hard, just as the train roared from the tunnel. It wasn't a hand; it was something harder. But shove him it did, right into the path of the oncoming train. If it hadn't been for the lightning reactions of an ox of a man standing at the platform edge who not only grabbed Derek's flailing arm but also had the strength to pull him back, he would be dead. As it was, his right leg had shot out as he desperately sought solid ground, and the train hit it below the knee, causing compound fractures of both his tibia and fibula. His dreams of competing in the Olympics shattered with his bones, but at least he was alive.

Chapter Five

The early morning ferry from Dover to Calais was quiet. Most of the professional drivers were snatching some sleep while the trickle of early-season tourists sipped tea, coffee or beer as they flicked through screens on their phones. Dressed in biker gear and a black headscarf, with heavy metallic earrings, black lipstick, fake neck tattoos and a snarl to match, Olivia Freneton was guaranteed a wide berth from all of them. Regardless of this, she had still chosen her seat carefully, wanting to ensure she wasn't pestered by chancers from the bar or irritated by over-tired children on the rampage.

Her eyes were unfocussed as she replayed the events of the last two days over and over in her mind. Her long-planned killing spree had started so well, with Hurst and Gwo disposed of efficiently and ruthlessly. But the pleasure of those killings was overshadowed by her failure to kill Thyme. And failure wasn't something that Olivia took kindly to. It flew in the face of her precise planning, the endless hours spent covering every eventuality, every contingency.

The trip had been the culmination of seven long months that had seen Olivia sequestered in her hideaway in the remote Tuscan countryside, a renovated farmhouse set centrally in a two-acre plot at the end of an unpaved track. The only passers-by were locals in search of the many species of mushrooms that grew beneath the wild oak trees in the hundreds of square miles of woods surrounding the plot. However, the locked gates, 'Proprietà Privata' signs and notices announcing the fence around the property was electrified left any inquiring minds with no doubt of the owner's requirement for privacy.

Seven months of planning, seven months of searching the online UK newspapers for information, seven months of waiting, biding her time. Seven months in which ending the lives of the seven people who had turned Olivia's life on its head had never been far from her thoughts, their continuing existence a festering wound whose flesh needed excising.

Although online information on her former squad in the SCF in Nottingham had been scant, from the snippets she had found, she knew the Board of Inquiry had sat, deliberated and pronounced, and she knew Hurst had gone, retired. Of her other former colleagues, Hawkins was still the chief super and Bottomley was back on active duty in the SCF. But she could find no trace of Thyme, while Cotton was apparently still recovering at some anonymous location in the south. As for the civilians, the gossip glossies put Henry Silk mainly in the US and therefore inaccessible to Olivia, while according to the newspaper reports soon after the fiasco in Harlow Wood, the little whore Gwo had been sent back to China.

Olivia hadn't believed the reports about Gwo. She knew the girl would have been a useful source of information for which witness protection might have been offered in return, especially since she'd shown courage by attacking her assailant. Sitting at her computer in the farmhouse, Olivia often absently flexed her left hand when she thought of the girl. The scar tissue from the stab wound still gave her trouble and she wanted retribution. If, contrary to the press reports, Gwo was still in England, she shouldn't be too hard to find. She certainly hoped she was there; that particular piece of revenge would be most enjoyable.

However, Olivia's main target was Cotton, the smart young bitch whose dogged persistence had nearly led to her being caught, and Cotton was off the radar. Wherever she was, convalescing or otherwise, she needed to be drawn out, and the best way to achieve that would be to dispose of one or more of her colleagues. Cotton would be bound to attend the funerals.

With this in mind, Olivia's plan of action had slowly evolved as she gathered what information she could, until she finally felt ready to strike. She had returned to England in late February, driving up from Italy on her large BMW, the workhorse of a bike she loved to ride, and heading for the caravan she kept on an anonymous site near the Kent coast, conveniently close to the cross-channel ferry ports. As well as being where she stored a second motorcycle, a large Kawasaki, the caravan was one of three locations where she kept her essential supplies: spare sets of clothing, tools, fake foreign number plates, carefully packed and sealed explosive charges, remote detonators and untraceable mobile phones. The other locations were the lock-up garage and its attached flat in West Bridgford, where she had hidden after escaping from Harlow Wood, and her farmhouse in Tuscany. Duplication of resources was important to Olivia, a matter of eggs and baskets. If one of her hideaways was compromised, there must always be an alternative available.

Starting her killing spree with the softest of her seven targets — the three former colleagues who lived in or around Nottingham — was the obvious way to go. And of the three, Hurst would be the first, not only because he had been a more major player in her downfall but also because he was now retired, his daily routine more predictable. He would be the easiest to follow and kill.

In addition to her first three police targets, Olivia had also been determined to pursue her hunch about Mandy Gwo. It would be an easy task, one she decided to undertake once she had located Hurst and established his routines. She had to know whether the little whore could be part of her scheme or forgotten about. She planned to head for the house in Forest Road West in Nottingham where Gwo had lived. The other women there must know where she was: whores like Gwo were stupid; it was most unlikely she would have kept her mouth shut. If she was still in England, Olivia would get her name and address, find her, establish her routine and add her to the disposal timetable.

The first obstacle Olivia had encountered when she arrived in Nottingham was the discovery that Hurst no longer lived there. However, his new address in Otley, Yorkshire, was quickly established from a conversation with the new owner of his old house. Olivia introduced herself as a former school chum of Hurst's wife visiting from Australia, hoping to catch up, and the friendly new owner willingly obliged.

She had followed Hurst for several days, discovering where he went, what he did, how he came and went from his trips to the Lakes. When she learned he regularly headed out onto the lake in his own little boat, she was tempted to plant a larger bomb somewhere below the water line and watch him drown or freeze to death as his boat went down. However, having analysed all the variables, she came to the conclusion that there were too many unknowns: she would have to relinquish more control than she was prepared to. The goal was Hurst's death, and the car was the way.

The path to finding Mandy Gwo was as easy as Olivia had anticipated. She drove to Forest Road West not far from the centre of Nottingham, parked the motorcycle in a back lane and found the building where Mandy had lived.

It was shortly after eleven in the morning, too early for the occupants of the house to be up and about, given their night-time activities, so she resigned herself to waiting. After nearly two hours there was finally some activity. Two women wrapped in cheap raincoats headed out of the house, heads down, deep in conversation. They were followed ten minutes later by a Chinese girl in her early twenties who was even uglier and skinnier than Mandy, if that were possible. This was a bonus: a Chinese girl; she must have known Gwo. Olivia made her way into the building and quickly discovered it was empty — only the three women she had seen lived there — and a quick check of possessions in the rooms told her which was the Chinese girl's.

Once in the room, Olivia was prepared to await the girl's return and extract the information she needed before throttling her. However, as her eyes scanned the unmade bed and discarded clothes, they fell on a mobile phone on a chair, a charging cable attached to it. When she called up the address book, she couldn't believe her eyes. The stupid Chinese whore, whose name was Apple Chan, had listed Mandy's name and alongside it, her new name, Kitty Lee, together with her address in Nechells, Birmingham.

A fatal mistake, thought Olivia, but only for Mandy: Chan's stupidity had saved her life. Olivia put the phone back where she'd found it, quietly left the room and returned to her motorcycle. Apple Chan would never know she'd been there, certainly not until the police came knocking with the news of Mandy's murder.

There followed two days in Birmingham watching Mandy Gwo, after which, having learned she had a job and what her hours were, Olivia was able to fit Mandy's disposal into her evolving timetable.

With two definite disposals now scheduled, Olivia returned to Nottingham with the intention of adding Bottomley and Hawkins to her plan of action. But she didn't get that far. As she drove through the city centre, she was amazed to see Derek Thyme's distinctive scarlet Mini Cooper ahead of her in the traffic. Derek had been visiting his mother on a day off. Not believing her luck, Olivia immediately followed the car, hoping Thyme would take her to Cotton. He didn't, but he did take her to London and his tiny flat near Edgware Road. A day of watching Thyme gave her what she needed: he went to and from his work and his training on the Tube. The Underground. What a good way to dispose of someone: a crowded platform and a firm shove.

With Derek Thyme now in the equation, Olivia decided she would put Bottomley and Hawkins on the back burner and turn her focus to Jennifer Cotton. Cotton and Thyme were close; she was bound to be at Thyme's funeral. And when she appeared, Olivia would either strike immediately or follow her to wherever she lived and kill her there. Cotton's funeral would then expose another of her targets: Cotton's father Henry Silk. He would be there and Olivia would be waiting. Everything was lining up perfectly. If all went according to plan, she would complete at least five disposals in one trip before heading back to Italy, perhaps even all of them.

However, while the disposal of Hurst had gone perfectly,

followed three hours later by Gwo's, Thyme's had failed. He had survived. It had been so close, so very close, but all the brilliant contingency planning in the world couldn't have allowed for the presence of the massive oaf on the edge of the platform, a Viking warrior with shoulders to make the average buffalo envious. He had yanked Derek's arm so hard it was a wonder it wasn't ripped from its socket. At least Thyme's leg had been badly damaged, and his Olympic hopes quashed. For now, that had to be satisfaction enough, but if she ever chose the tube-train method again, Olivia would be sure to push considerably harder with her retractable truncheon, as well as to scan for bovine.

It had been fortunate for Olivia that there was so much confusion on the platform. She had been able to slink away to her BMW and return to the caravan to close it up. From there she hurried to Dover and the ferry, anxious to leave the country before some bright spark found her on the station CCTV and a stop list was issued.

As the ferry ploughed its way across the choppy English Channel towards Calais, Olivia continued to stare into space, forcing herself to be calm, forcing herself to focus her thoughts on the two disposals she had achieved. When she did and she thought of Mike Hurst's, she allowed herself a flicker of a smile. It had been impressive, a brilliant reflection of her skills.

Planting the bomb next to the most vulnerable spot in the hydraulics in Hurst's car had been easy. He always parked for the day in a quiet car park near the moorings, well screened from the road by trees and nearby buildings, a gift as far as Olivia was concerned. It had been the work of seconds to slip under the car and reach up to place the device. She had studied the model in detail and knew exactly where to put the bomb.

It had taken split-second timing to ensure everything was in place when Hurst's car reached the spot on the road she had chosen so carefully, perfect judgement to be confident of his reaction when she pulled in front of him and braked, and expert technical skill to include just enough explosive in the pack to take out the car's hydraulics at the predetermined moment. Nothing had been left to chance; everything was planned.

That was her forte. Planning. Sorting through the scenarios, predicting the outcomes, allowing for all contingencies. She excelled at it, and, fond of self-congratulation, she frequently lavished herself with praise, immensely proud of her skills.

Chapter Six

Jennifer's first instinct on learning from Pete Hawkins of the attempt on Derek's life was that she must return to England. She had to; he needed her. He was more than a colleague; he had become a very dear friend, one who had not only saved her life but also in the days and weeks following the near-fatal attack had spent every possible moment at the hospital by her side. She owed it to him; it would be the least she could do.

However, she also knew she was far from fully recovered herself and that her doctors would be unlikely to sanction a visit to England. She would have to talk to Pietro, persuade him.

She checked the time; it was still only four thirty, too early even for Pietro, who was nearly always up by five. She thought about calling Henry in California, but although there it would be early evening, his packed schedule often saw him filming until midnight. She sighed in frustration and headed for the shower. Ten minutes later, she was back on the huge sofa, a large mug of coffee nestling in her hands. She waited, watching the minutes tick by until she could call Pietro.

"Jennifer, tesoro, what is it? You're never around this early. I've only been up for a short while myself."

"Something terrible's happened, Pietro. We need to talk."

She went through every detail of her calls with Hawkins,

bursting into tears when she recounted how close Derek had come to being killed.

"I've got to see him, Pietro," she sobbed, "he's hurt badly and he'll be gutted by this; the Olympics meant so much to him. I can't just sit around here while he's in hospital."

"We'll work something out, tesoro," said Pietro, his tone reassuring but without any indication he was in agreement. "At least he's alive, a true miracle if ever there was one. Someone was looking out for him. Those other two didn't stand a chance. Do you think the police will have a guard at his bed in case this mad woman tries again?"

"Without question, yes. I'd imagine the others from the squad will have protection for a while too, Hawkins and Bottomley, I mean. Henry's probably OK; he's out of the country, and I …" Her voice trailed off as she realised she was developing an argument for not being in England.

Pietro was ahead of her. "The thing is, tesoro, apart from your recovery, which the doctors will probably say is still not sufficiently far on for you to be allowed to travel, there is the security aspect. This crazy woman cannot be anticipated. If you are in England, especially going to and from the hospital to see Derek, even with the team of guards I'd insist on providing, you are vulnerable. It's exactly what she'd want. You'd be playing into her hands. At least in Sardinia, you are safe. She'll have no idea you are there and even if she did discover your whereabouts, I'm confident she wouldn't get near you."

"So you're saying I can't go."

"I'm not exactly saying that, no. I can't, obviously; you're a grown woman. I'm simply saying I think it would be unwise. And surely the final decision must rest with the doctors."

"But I feel fine, Pietro, I do, really."

"That's not completely true, tesoro, is it? Your fitness is not yet back to what it was and you still get headaches if you overdo it. There is no shortcut, Jennifer, and your body, not your mind, must be the best judge. If you go against the needs and present limitations of your body, it will let you down. You know how it is."

She knew full well, but she refused to accept it.

"Tesoro," continued Pietro, his liquid tones beguiling, "let me talk to the consultant in a couple of hours when he's up. I'll explain it all to him, every last detail. But you only had a check-up a few days ago, I don't see how things can have changed much since then."

As soon as he'd rung off, Pietro called Henry in California, fully aware that he might have to bulldoze his way through a petulant director. Fortunately, Henry had finished relatively early for once and was driving home. Pietro rapidly explained everything that had happened and what Jennifer wanted to do.

"That's absolutely shocking news, Pietro, Jennifer must be gutted."

"She is, which is why she wants to take this foolish step. I'm hoping you will support me in explaining how unwise it is."

"Certainly I will," replied Henry. "With Jennifer, saying no would be like a red rag to a bull; she'd go charging ahead regardless. We need the decision to come from her, or perhaps from Derek when he's able to talk to her."

"Yes," agreed Pietro, "the doctors' opinion won't be enough; she'll be quite prepared to ignore them. However, when she calls, it would be better if you didn't mention we've spoken, don't you think?"

"Of course. I think I can act suitably surprised and I have no need to fake the horror I feel over the whole thing. This Freneton woman has to be stopped."

Within minutes, the hands-free unit in Henry's car pinged with another call.

"Jennifer! What a lovely surprise. It's very early for you; couldn't you sleep?"

"Oh, Henry," cried Jennifer, and she burst into tears again.

After sobbing through her story, she told Henry what she intended to do. "Pietro's clearly against it, and I know he'll lean on the doctors, so regardless of what they really think, they'll agree with him."

"I'm not so sure they'll need to be leaned on, Jennifer. Their opinion was clear in the latest assessment, the one you told me about a couple of days ago. They don't think you're ready."

"They're being ridiculously conservative. I'm sure Pietro is behind that as well. He'd rather I didn't go back to police work at all. Ever. You know, I was convinced Freneton was long gone, that we'd never hear of her again. I can't tell you how much of a shock this has been."

"Of course, and that's why you shouldn't rush into any decisions. You'd be exposing yourself unnecessarily if you went to England."

"You sound just like Pietro. Actually, I'd be pretty safe since I'd have a team of his heavies trailing me everywhere."

"You make him sound like a mafia don."

"Sometimes I wonder."

"Don't you think it would be better to wait until you've talked to Derek? You'll be in a far better position to judge once you've spoken to him, perhaps even seen him if they let him use Skype."

Henry hesitated, thinking through his tactics. Then he said, "He means quite a lot to you, this lad, doesn't he?"

Jennifer's voice was distant when she replied. "Yes, he does. He's someone very special. I think … He's very special." She stopped, not wanting to say more.

Henry smiled to himself. "OK, then," he said. "Let's do it this way. I finish the filming part of the movie tomorrow. The voice-overs in editing won't be for ages so if you're going to England, I'm going with you."

"You can't! Anyway, I thought you said last week you'd got an exciting new project coming up. A TV series."

"Ah, the Renaissance artist who's still alive today. The 600-year-old man who doesn't age beyond around forty because his gene structure precludes it. It's a great plot and since the books are a trilogy, it could spin on to several seasons."

"If it's about a man who never ages beyond 40, aren't you a bit—"

"Now, now, dear daughter. There's such a thing as make-up in acting, you know. Apparently my features are what they're looking for, as well as my brilliant acting skills, of course."

"And your modesty, no doubt. Didn't you say the filming starts soon?"

"You're more important, Jennifer. I'll get them to delay or let them go for someone else."

"You can't do that! You said it was the most significant part you'd ever been offered. You're now saying you'd give it up if I went to London. That's blackmail!"

"Oh, I wouldn't go as far as that—"

"Well I would, Henry Silk. I appreciate the gesture but it's out of the question. Anyway, while you're in the US, you're safe from Freneton, I reckon, since it would be too risky for her to try to travel there either on her own passport, which has been stopped, or on a stolen one."

"You realise the hole in your argument, Jennifer. You saying that while it's OK for you to put your head in the lion's mouth by going to the UK, it isn't for me. Doesn't compute I'm afraid. She's after both of us."

When Derek was eventually allowed to make a call on Skype from his hospital bed, Jennifer was still insistent she should be with him in the UK.

"Jen," pleaded Derek, once he'd let her give vent to her frustrations, "listen to me. I'm fine, really. Stop worrying about me and get yourself better, you prat. I don't need you here to hold my hand; I'm surrounded by dozens of nurses who are queuing up to do that."

Jennifer could see from the haunted look in Derek's eyes he was anything but fine, and more importantly she could see her intransigence was upsetting him.

Pulling a face, she said, "OK, you win, but I want you to promise me that as soon as you can, you'll get your backside out here. No, I can't trust you to do that, I know you'll only keep delaying it. Here's the deal: I'll make all the arrangements to get you here once the doctors give you the nod. This is the perfect place for you to convalesce. I've got a brilliant personal trainer, Alicia, whose hands I wouldn't advise you trying to hold, given her gorilla of a boyfriend, but otherwise I'll let her work her magic on you, and there'll be access to the best orthopaedic doctors."

"Jen, I—"

"No, Derek, you have to agree, otherwise I'm going to get out of here even if it means digging a tunnel to the mainland."

"Thanks," said Derek softly, his voice breaking. He gulped back his emotions before continuing. "I think it'll be a while until they let me go."

"I know it will, so we'll Skype. Every day if we can. I'm worried about you, you idiot."

Jennifer was right in her assessment. Derek's brush with death had unnerved him more than he thought possible and in the weeks following the incident at Oxford Circus, he hit many lows. Their daily Skype calls became a lifeline.

Unbeknown to Derek, Jennifer also commissioned her specialist to talk to his doctor to persuade him to release Derek earlier than he would otherwise have done on the understanding he would be in the most capable of hands at the villa.

During the first week of April, the villa was abuzz with deliveries of equipment for fitting out a room suitable for Derek's convalescence, and in mid-April, just five weeks after the attempt on his life, Derek arrived at the villa in an ambulance, embarrassed by all the attention being heaped upon him and not even daring to think what it might be costing.

Already mobile enough on his crutches, but with his leg still in plaster, he was soon standing by the pool looking longingly at the water.

"Christ, Cotton, is this your idea of a joke? It's going to be torture standing here watching while you swim up and down."

"All the more incentive to keep that healing process in top gear so the plaster can come off ASAP," replied Jennifer. "Alicia has put together a special diet for you as well as a bunch of daily exercises.

We're lucky she trained as a physio before going into personal training; she's linked up with our specialist and they reckon you'll be charging around in no time."

Derek lowered himself onto a lounger. "I hope the diet includes a glass or two of the wine you keep telling me about."

"Not for a few weeks," said Jennifer, her features clouding over with regret. "I'm afraid you'll have to sit and watch Alicia and me enjoying our evening glass of prosecco while you sip your sparkling water."

"You're joking, right! The doc in London said it shouldn't be a problem."

Jennifer pulled a face. "Our specialist is something of a traditionalist—"

"This is Italy!" cried Derek indignantly. "Wine's a tradition. I take it your specialist is Italian?"

Jennifer poked her tongue out at him and laughed. "Never difficult to wind you up, Thyme, is it? Of course a glass or two of Pietro's finest is on the menu."

Derek narrowed his eyes at her. "Score all your points while you can, Cotton. I won't be on these crutches for ever."

Chapter Seven

By the time she reached her Tuscan hideaway, Olivia Freneton's self-congratulatory euphoria over a job well done in killing both Mike Hurst and Mandy Gwo was once again becoming eclipsed by anger and frustration at her failed attempt on Derek Thyme's life. She had misjudged the density of the crowd; she should have stood closer to Thyme and pushed the truncheon harder. The presence of the huge man who saved Thyme was just bad luck, but she should at least have noticed him. It was sloppy, and she refused to accept sloppiness.

Having reviewed the situation more objectively as her BMW soaked up the miles back to Tuscany, she was increasingly angry with herself for scuttling away like a scared cat. There was no need for her to have left England; she could have gone to ground in her caravan for two or three weeks — she had enough food — and once the initial impetus of the search for her had diminished, she could have carried on with her disposals, ticked both Hawkins and Bottomley off her list and perhaps even visited Thyme in his hospital bed. If she'd managed to complete his disposal, who knows what other opportunities may have arisen?

It was true that all those scenarios would have incurred risk — everything she did when back in England was a risk. Just being there was a risk. But she was good enough to minimise the risks: she had all the disguises she might need sitting in the caravan's wardrobe, she had explosive packs, a comprehensive set of tools and even weapons, should she need them. And she had pencils, paper, notebooks and newsprint with which she could brainstorm her plans, formulate scenarios, consider and resolve problems. It was what she did; it was her very being, and she had let the opportunity slip in a moment of ill-considered … What? A look of disdain flashed across her face as she sat astride the BMW outside the farmhouse, watching the electric gates close behind her. The word 'panic' had flitted across her mind. Had she panicked? Olivia Freneton didn't panic, she simply chose the best path given the options of the moment. This time she had made the wrong choice. Why? There must have been something in her subconscious mind pulling her in that direction, something distracting her.

As the gate clicked shut, sealing once again the barrier of the strong fence surrounding her property, she considered the option of turning round and going back, and quickly rejected it for two reasons. The first was the inevitable increased surveillance at the ports, mainly focussed on people leaving the UK, it was true, but greater vigilance in passport checking of those entering the country was also a danger for her.

However, the second reason was far more serious and as she allowed herself to think of it, she realised this was what must have been niggling at her, controlling her decision-making: she was close to being broke. If she'd stayed in England much longer, she would have had to resort to petty theft for the resources to continue her killing spree. That spree would now have to go on hold while she addressed her finances.

She had bought her ancient farmhouse, her motorcycles and the caravan in Kent while she was still a police officer, long before her posting to Nottingham and the SCF, her capital outlay including a basic restoration of the farmhouse to bring the services, utilities and comfort into the twenty-first century. It had all been part of her brilliant planning; and now her isolated bolthole had come into its own. She had even had the foresight to steal an ageing VW Golf to run around in. It was inconspicuous, unlike the large BMW motorcycle, and with its fake Dutch plates, it was effectively off the radar to the Italian authorities. If she wanted to go farther afield than the local towns, she would go by train, leaving the car with a back-street garage owner in nearby Castiglion Fiorentino she had made an agreement with — for a nominal sum, he was prepared to let her park the car in his yard for as along as she liked, months if necessary. He knew nothing about the stern Dutch woman, not even where she lived, and he cared even less. However, while the capital items were bought and paid for, day-to-day living expenses couldn't be ignored and were proving to be a continual and irritatingly large drain on her dwindling cash reserves.

After parking the BMW in an out-building and letting herself into the main house, Olivia threw her bag into the corner of the large kitchen, kicked off her motorcycle boots and opened one of the wall cupboards to retrieve a bottle of Scotch. She never drank during an operation: she needed a totally clear mind to guarantee all her finely tuned faculties were optimal, from her instinctive timing to her anticipation when outmanoeuvring someone in a fight, her nanosecond reflexes and her brilliant ability to adjust and adapt in any scenario. Nothing was permitted to compromise any of that in any way and so alcohol was totally off limits. But when she returned to base, returned to review her performance, to adjust, revise and improve her plans for the future, relaxing in a scalding bath with a large whisky on ice was the perfect way to unwind.

And on this occasion perhaps more than any in the past, she needed to unwind. As she settled in her bath with her second large whisky, she consoled herself with the thought that ultimately all her targets would die. It may take some time, but they would, and at her hand. The months would go by, they would become more complacent and her task would become easier and easier. Right now, the SCF and other units would be buzzing with activity aimed at bringing her in, but the fire under that operation would soon die down and when no leads were found, it would burn itself out within weeks.

The whisky slowly soothed her jagged anger. Perhaps she had made the right decision after all given that her face would be everywhere. The caravan site may be a quiet, forgotten spot, the few occupied vans the refuges of forgotten losers, but even losers could read, watch TV and sometimes put two and two together. It could have been dangerous to hole up there for a protracted period.

She stretched in the water and took another sip of the delicious blend along with a chunk of ice, rolling them both around in her mouth, luxuriating in their smooth persuasion.

Sitting at the desk in her study the following morning, Olivia took a sheet of paper and made a list of potential sources of income. She divided the sheet into two columns headed short term and long term. Under the former she wrote: passport, ID and other document theft, theft of other saleable items, honeytraps. She tapped the paper with her pencil, uncertain whether or not to include her next idea. Burglary. There were plenty of well-appointed villas within a thirty-mile radius, many of them only occupied part-time. She wrote the word, pondering over it for several minutes before finally putting a line through it. The risk factor was too high for the potential rewards. She'd stick to what she did best.

And what she did best was good basic thievery. She was a skilful pickpocket and harvester from unsecured handbags. For her, gathering a crop of passports and wallets at airports and railway stations was simple, sometimes yielding as much as one or two thousand euros of an unsuspecting tourist's holiday money. Other theft took a little more cunning — a mobile phone here, a camera there — it was all small stuff, and to justify a trip to Amsterdam to where her tame receiver of stolen goods, Luuk Ackerman, sequestered himself in his damp rathole of a basement like some latter-day Fagin, she had to accumulate several thousand euros' worth of negotiable stock. The bastard drove a hard bargain, partly because he knew this weird Englishwoman was in trouble, partly because Olivia always over-valued her wares. But normally she returned grudgingly satisfied with whatever deal they'd struck.

Her other short-term income strategy was the honeytrap: the

one-off snaring of some gullible male, usually a British or American businessman, although she had occasionally picked up other men whose English was good. She had refined her technique over the years, culminating in the series of brilliant framings of the five fools convicted of killing prostitutes while she had been a police officer in England. Well, it would have been five had it not been for the dogged persistence of Jennifer Cotton: Henry Silk would definitely have gone down had it not been for her. All the more reason why the damn girl had to die.

The targets were everywhere, all she had to do was select them carefully, choosing the ones with plenty of cash or access to it. The rest was child's play. She still had a good stock of roofies — the powerful sedative Rohypnol used illicitly as a date-rape drug — that she had acquired while she was still a police officer, and a set of six different disguises, enabling her to repeat the stunt over several days in different hotels in the same city. Her best haul, on a trip to Turin, had been ten thousand euros in four days, thanks largely to one idiot who kept the passwords to his ATM cards in his wallet. However, she enjoyed the feeling of power less each time, finding the process increasingly sordid and not without personal risk, even given her unarmed combat skills. She certainly didn't want to do it forever.

She turned to the second column. Long term. This was harder and would require patience, planning and a certain amount of luck, initially at least. She had to find the right person — a woman almost definitely — and become her friend, maybe more than a friend, and steer her in the direction of trusting her, relying on her, allowing her access to her money before she disposed of her and disappeared, ideally with enough profit not to have to repeat the process ever again.

It was a new venture for Olivia, an exciting one guaranteed to stretch her mind and skills. She would need to be charming over a long period, never giving her target cause to question her. She would be projecting a personality so different from the Olivia Freneton the SCF team in Nottingham had known they would not believe it possible. That thought alone amused her, although in her heart she knew it would be a considerable challenge given her intolerant nature.

Everything about the project would require money, from the places she needed to frequent to the make-up, the hotels and the afternoon teas. The occasional spree of petty theft to top up the coffers would therefore be a necessity. She had already equipped herself with several designer accessories lifted with ridiculous ease from their rightful owners to augment the wardrobe of clothes she'd accumulated over several years, timeless fashions of the sort that would appeal to the targets she had in mind.

It would require patient observation of likely targets in and around the locations where such people moved. Plush hotels, restaurants and famous bars in the smarter cities like Rome, Florence and Milan. Sit, watch and wait. A spider in her web; observing, calculating, ready to pounce.

Chapter Eight

The crowd was suffocatingly dense, shoulder packed against shoulder, face against face, and yet faceless to a man. But it was never still, writhing instead in slow motion, ripples flowing through it like a snake on the move, even though there was no room to move, no place to go, no chance of separating one body from the next, no chance of moving back from the gaping hole of darkness beyond the platform edge. Yet despite the logjam of humanity, no one came close to slipping over that edge, an invisible barrier protecting them and preventing them from falling.

And the noise! The noise was incredible. Not the crowd; the crowd was silent. It was the roar from the tunnel as if some terrifying mythical creature were about to bound from the darkness into the station, consuming everyone in its path.

There was a cackle of laughter from behind him. Derek looked around and saw her. She was so close the sneer of satisfaction distorting her face almost enveloped him. Freneton. She was there, behind him, pushing towards him, accelerating towards him despite the crowd, her huge hands outstretched, linked together; an unstoppable battering ram.

Suddenly there was no one around him; the crowd had disappeared, evaporated. There was just Freneton on the otherwise deserted platform as the noise from the tunnel rose to a deafening siren, the sound reverberating cruelly, painfully around the empty void. All he could see were her hands bearing down on him, getting larger and larger, closing in, but he couldn't move, couldn't duck out of their way, couldn't use his own hands to deflect them, to parry them.

They hit him full force in the chest, lifting him up, spinning him in exquisite slow motion, tumbling in a perfectly executed back somersault. Equally slowly the train burst from the darkness, expanding as it found the luxurious extra space of the station after the confining tunnel walls. There was no one to grab him, no Viking hulk with vice-like hands to grip him and tear him from the train's path. There was just the train, a wall of metal now rocket-like as it slammed into him.

But it didn't obliterate him, didn't reduce him to a pulp, didn't separate him into a trillion molecules. Instead it shook him violently and screamed his name.

"Derek! Derek!"

"No!" he screeched, as his thrashing arms were gripped tightly and pulled to his side.

"Derek! It's OK! You're safe! You're safe. She can't hurt you. No one's going to hurt you."

A switch was flicked, flooding the room with light.

"Signorina Jennifer, is everything all right? The shouting …"

Jennifer turned from where she was holding Derek's arms against his body while Alicia was desperately trying to stop his plastered leg from pounding against the wall. "It's OK, Filippo, thanks. He was having a nightmare; nothing to worry about."

"Is there anything I can do, signorina?" The guard was concerned that this huge black man with his heavily plastered leg might run riot and smash the place up.

"We're fine, really." Jennifer smiled at him, hoping he'd be reassured.

"If you say so," said Filippo, still hesitant. He decided he would wait down the corridor, be ready, just in case.

He left, leaving the light on.

Jennifer turned to Derek, who was panting and sweating, the whites of his eyes beacons of fear, but he had stopped writhing. "That was some nightmare, Thyme. Where were you?"

Derek stared at her, not sure if she was real or part of the nightmare, and if she was part of it, was she really Freneton?

"Is his leg OK, Ali?" asked Jennifer, keeping her eyes on Derek's.

"No damage, but I'm worried that if this happens again and we're not here, he could hurt himself."

"I'll stay with him," said Jennifer, "until he's sleeping peacefully."

"Perhaps I should be the one," replied Alicia. "Your chest, it's still vulnerable. The damage isn't completely healed. If he starts lashing out, he could hurt you."

Jennifer looked down at Derek's face; he was peaceful now, almost asleep. She smiled. "I think it'll be all right. You're just down the corridor; leave your door ajar. If he starts again, you'll hear me if I yell for you. Help me move him over, will you. If I'm going to keep him quiet, I might as well be comfortable."

With Derek moved, Jennifer lifted the sheets and settled in the bed, sitting partly up as she put an arm around him, letting his head fall onto her chest. She stroked his hair and looked up to see an amused look on Alicia's face.

"What?" she said, grinning back. "I don't think he'll trouble us further, Ali. Try to get some sleep."

"Shall I close the door?" asked Alicia, her eyes still amused even though her voice was all innocence.

"I don't know, I might need protecting," said Jennifer. Alicia switched off the light and Jennifer smiled to herself as she heard the door click shut.

At six thirty the following morning, although the sun was still some minutes from lifting itself above the horizon, there was plenty of dawn light flooding into the room. Derek stirred as Jennifer tiptoed back in from a trip to the bathroom.

"Jennifer?"

"Go back to sleep," she said, slipping back into the bed next to him.

"What are you doing, Jen?"

"Looking after you, Mr Plonker. Trying to let the rest of the household get a good night's sleep."

He stared up at her, not understanding.

"You had a nightmare, Derek, a bad one. Ali and I had to hold you down to stop you wrecking the joint, and yourself."

A glimmer of recollection appeared in his eyes. "Oh. Sorry. You didn't have to …"

"Have you been having them a lot? It seemed bad."

Derek nodded slowly, his eyes now creased in rejection of the memory.

"Every night. Eventually the nurse gave me something; I was waking everyone up."

"Why didn't you say, you dummy? It's nothing to be ashamed of. We're mates."

"I thought with coming here, being in such a peaceful place, I'd be fine; that they'd go away."

Jennifer stroke his head gently. "You're an idiot. I'll stay with you tonight, make sure you're OK." She stopped and grinned. "Unless Ali wants a turn. She seemed quite keen."

Derek looked up at her, his face concerned. "Jen? I didn't, I mean, we didn't …? You know …"

She took his head in her hands and put her face close to his.

"Derek Thyme! Do you mean to tell me that after that night of passion you don't remember a thing! Huh!"

He looked sheepishly at her. "I just meant …"

"Derek, if you'd tried to sling your leg over me, the momentum of that cast would have thrown you out of the bed faster than I would. So, no, don't worry. You slept like a baby."

The April morning sun was warm on the sheltered terrace outside the dining room. Derek had got over the shock of discovering Jennifer had slept alongside him and was tucking into his breakfast.

"They don' feed you in the ospedale, Derek?" asked Alicia, her English strongly accented.

"Not enough, Alicia, no," he replied through a mouthful of egg. "And the food was crap. Jen wouldn't've approved. Not Paleo."

Alicia snorted. "I know. She say she Italian, but she don' eat pasta. You eat pasta, Derek?"

He glanced over to where Jennifer was pouring herself some coffee, her back to them.

"Love it," he mouthed, to giggles from Alicia. "But don't tell …" He nodded his head in Jennifer's direction and pulled a face.

Jennifer settled back down at the table. "Don't ever get arrested for anything, Thyme," she said, looking over to him.

"What do you mean?"

"Simply that you're not only transparent, which given you're a man is to be expected, but any interrogator worthy of the name would run rings around you."

Derek frowned. "What are you on about, Cotton?"

Jennifer smiled conspiratorially at Alicia and raised her eyebrows in question.

Alicia flicked her eyes closed in agreement and Jennifer turned back to Derek.

"One little innocent question and you spilled the beans."

"What?"

Jennifer nodded her head in Alicia's direction. "She's even more passionate about the Paleo diet than I am."

"Jeez, I'm surrounded by freaks," muttered Derek.

Alicia stood. "Freaks. I don' know this word but I think I get it. It's your first physio in one hour, Signor Thyme." She smiled malevolently. "I show you what freak is."

Two hours later, Derek was sitting on a lounger by the pool relaxing after his physio session and taking perverse pleasure in the tingling in his muscles. Jennifer finished a gentle fifty lengths and climbed out of the water.

"'ow was that, Signor Thyme?" she asked, mimicking Alicia's accent.

"It was great, Jen. She's mustard. I've really been missing the exercise. I think with the workout she's got planned for later and then more physio, my body will feel back on track. I need to get it moving. With any luck that'll mean I'll sleep the night through without dreams of being mashed by Tube trains."

"I hope so, the guards were about to throw you down the well."

"Is that what you do with all your awkward guests?"

"Only the noisy ones. It has to be the well; it's so deep you can't hear their cries for help."

Derek stretched and looked around, taking in the pool, the terrace and what he could see of the house. "This place is paradise, Jen, magical. But don't you get, I don't know, a bit stir-crazy here? I mean, there's not a lot to do, is there? You get waited on hand and foot; what do you do all day to keep those profound grey cells of yours ticking over?"

She smiled. "Well, Derek, this is Italy. I've got several lovers who come calling on a regular basis, and I've been spending quite a bit of time on Skype lately …"

"Yeah, sorry, I hadn't forgotten that. You've been brilliant. I couldn't have made it without you. But that still leaves you with time to kill, even if your Romeos are marathon men. I s'pose you're doing a lot with Alicia, of course, but …"

Jennifer laughed and tapped her head. "I know, the grey cells. None of that does much to stimulate them. Actually, you might be surprised to know I've been learning Russian. Not all my Skype calls are to you; there are almost daily ones to my Russian tutor, Irina. She's great."

"Russian! Why? Bit late to be a spy, isn't it? You know the Cold War's over, don't you?"

"I'm not so sure, but, no, I don't have ambitions to penetrate the inner workings of the Kremlin, and neither do I fancy Mr P. I was attracted by the challenge. Anyway, I'm not entirely new to it; I studied Russian for a year as a subsid. subject at uni; Nottingham's got a good Russian department."

"Wow! Impressivo."

"Same to you! You pronounced that well. I'll have to get Alicia to give you Italian lessons."

"She's already started, but I think it was mainly about whips and leather, from what I could get."

"Lucky for you you've got that cast on your leg, Thyme, or I'd push you in the pool on her behalf."

"Yeah, right," said Derek. He glanced down at a sizeable book Jennifer had left on a table by her lounger. "This your text book?" he said, picking it up. "How do you make sense of all those letters?"

"Not as difficult as it looks, you know. But no, it's not a text book. It's one of the greatest novels ever written."

"Really? What is it?"

"War and Peace. My goal is to read an original Russian version."

"You should get off this island, Cotton. You've got too much time on your hands."

Chapter Nine

Connie Fairbright put down the Italian newspaper she was attempting to read and moved her hand towards the Hotel Barchester's discreetly monogrammed coffee pot. But before she could reach it, an attentive waiter had spotted her need, materialised by her table and was bowing graciously as he poured for her.

She sat back in frustration. "Grazie, Mario," she said, her refined Bostonian tones sounding in her pronunciation of the Italian.

"Prego, signora," replied the waiter, with a slight tilt of his head, after which he switched to English to keep the assault on his beloved language minimal. "May I get you anything else, signora? Some more toast, perhaps?"

"No, thank you, Mario," sighed Connie, frustrated as ever that her attempts at practising the skills she'd spent the last three months trying to master were to no avail.

She'd thought it would be easier now she had all her time to herself. She would spend three hours every morning on one-to-one sessions with her language tutor struggling to mould her limited language skills into some sort of coherency, while in the afternoons she would luxuriate in the magical world of Renaissance art, her knowledge base expanded daily by her personal tutor, the fascinating Cesare Contorni.

At least that side of her ambition was being fulfilled. She had always loved art, Italian art in particular, and although in the early days of her marriage her acquisitive husband had indulged her with several works bought more for their inflated price labels than their merit, she had been frustrated. She had wanted to understand more, wanted to develop her tastes but was prevented from achieving her goals by a lifestyle that saw her as a perpetual society hostess flitting from one city to the next, one country to the next, according to the endless demands of her husband's personal goal of becoming the world's wealthiest man.

Brad Fairbright had come close to achieving his goal, probably would have achieved it if providence had granted him another five years on the planet. But an ill-advised flight in the poorest weather saw him and his ambitions die along with his three top aides as his jet became the plaything of a massive Midwest storm: tossed, flipped and finally flung into a mountainside.

Their marriage had long been a loveless façade without even the distraction of children to help paper over the cracks. The only tears she shed were for the memory of a short-lived time when, twenty years old to his thirty-three, she had been swept off her feet by his charm. Too late she had realised how that charm was all calculated, that she was just one more prize in a world of prizes. Brad had targeted her: she was good looking without being beautiful, from old money herself and therefore moulded from an early age into a mindset of compliance with her husband's demands for a submissive but impressive wife. He hadn't strayed, so far as she knew, and neither had she; he was just so driven by his ambition that any emotion had long been suppressed, rejected as irrelevant.

When Brad was killed and she took stock of her friends and family — her parents still ruled their own fiefdom in Massachusetts and her elder brothers were cast in their mould — Connie knew she had to break away, to leave. No one seemed to object so she closed up her various houses and walked away with the settlement she and Brad had agreed upon in the event of his death. She wasn't interested in his billions; they involved too much responsibility. But with a net worth still in nine figures and a dedicated team of advisers to manage it, she was hardly going to be roughing it. At forty-five and with her background of privilege, she had no intention of lowering the high standards of comfort in her daily life; she simply wanted to kindle her nascent ambitions. She knew that heading for Italy, learning the language and discovering art were all something of a cliché. She didn't care; she was finally in control of her own destiny. Except, it seemed, when it came to pouring her coffee.

She took a sip of her Americano, put down the cup and caught Mario's eye.

"Bring me another pot, per favore. This one's past its best."

When the coffee arrived, she put her hand on the waiter's arm, surprising him. "I'll pour it, Mario. When I'm ready."

She picked up her newspaper, determined to make another attempt at gleaning something meaningful from its columns, but before she had worked her way through two lines, her PA Caroline Monkton bustled onto the terrace, one hand pressed against her forehead, the other clutching her handbag, a ring binder, her phone and an iPad.

The diminutive grey-haired Ms Monkton sat down heavily in a chair that microseconds before the ever-efficient Mario had pulled out with magician-like finesse from under the table. Handing her baggage to him, she let out a loud sigh designed to inform occupants of nearby tables of the endless stress torturing her existence.

"Connie," she gushed, "I'm so sorry, I woke up with one of my headaches again. It's almost gone now, thank heavens; twenty minutes in a steaming shower certainly helped. Have you already had your breakfast? I hope you have."

All this was ejected from Caroline's mouth in a rush of British intensity, her forehead puckered in concern, her hands clasped together.

Connie looked up from the incomprehensible paragraphs. She was beginning to regret employing Ms Monkton, whose headaches she suspected were a product of too many late-night sips of gin taken in her room. It had been a moment's weakness: she had felt sorry for the sixty-year-old, been charmed by her English vowels and swayed by her penniless need. The younger candidates had all been better qualified, but, she suspected, gold-diggers. Caroline Monkton had reminded her of a music tutor she'd once had as a child. Rejecting her and her straitened circumstances would have been cruel.

"I'm done, thank you, Caroline, but let me pour you some coffee."

As she reached for the pot, she saw Mario react out of the corner of her eye. She turned her head and glared at him. He retreated in confused submission.

Connie put down the coffee pot and checked her watch. "You know, Caroline, I'm not in the mood for Signorina Grimaldi this morning; in fact I'm not convinced I want to continue with her. I'm getting nowhere with this damn language."

Caroline looked pained. "Are you quite sure, Connie? Your lesson is due to start in fifteen minutes. She'll be on her way."

Connie shook her head. "Tell her I'm not feeling well. I'll make a decision about her over the weekend. Heavens, there must be someone more dynamic out there, someone better equipped to knock something into my language-challenged brain."

"She came highly recommended," said Caroline defensively.

"I'm not blaming you, Caroline. It's just that there's no chemistry between us. She never laughs, you know. I should have let her go weeks ago. Get on to it, will you, rustle me up a shortlist."

"If you insist, but I must eat something first," said Caroline, the edge to her voice still there. She had negotiated a long-term deal with Connie's tutor in return for a cut of her fee; dismissing her now could prove expensive.

"Fine," said Connie. "But I think before you settle to your muesli, you should give the signorina a call, don't you?"

"Of course," replied Caroline, reaching for her phone, her nostrils flared in frustration. She needed to regain the moral high ground. "I'll go into the lobby; I don't think it's polite to call from a restaurant, do you?"

Connie shrugged. "I don't think it's a big deal, so long as you keep your voice down. But, hey, if that's what you want to do, go ahead."

Neither Connie nor her PA had noticed the woman sitting at the next table, her back to them. Nor had they noticed her the previous day, or the one before as she sat quietly watching. If they had noticed her at all, they would have registered little more than a tall, well-dressed solitary woman with shoulder-length chestnut-brown hair who appeared to be engrossed in a book as she slowly sipped at her coffee. She even turned the pages every minute or so, but nothing on them registered as she listened intently to the exchanges between the two women.

Olivia Freneton waited until Caroline Monkton had disappeared into the lobby before turning in her chair towards Connie.

"Excuse me," she said, her accent refined English, but more businesslike than Caroline Monkton's judgemental fluster. "I couldn't help overhearing; I hope you don't mind."

Connie turned to her. "Oh dear, I'm sorry if my PA disturbed your breakfast; she does get a little over-excited."

Olivia laughed, her eyes catching Connie's, her smile gentle reassurance.

"Not at all. It was what you were saying that caught my attention. It sounds as if you are looking for a good Italian tutor."

Connie raised her eyebrows in interest. "I am, yes, but you're … you're British, aren't you? I was really looking for a native speaker."

Olivia made sure her laugh was sufficiently self-deprecating. "Oh, no, not me, I'm very much a student. I just happen to have struck lucky and discovered the most wonderful man. He's full of fun and an outstanding teacher."

For this part of her scheme, Olivia was telling the truth. She had found Alessandro Rossi quite by chance as she trawled a number of language schools in Rome. She was unimpressed by many of them, as much for the prices they were charging for personal tuition as their quality. Her plan was to get to grips with the language while searching Rome's exclusive hotels for a suitable target; someone loaded she could befriend or work for, someone whose trust and confidence she could gain.

She knew it would be expensive: morning coffee and afternoon tea on well-appointed terraces were never cheap, and she had to look the part, even if at night she disappeared into the cheapest hostel she could find. But the language schools were likely to break the bank. She had almost given up on the idea when she noticed Rossi's advertisement pinned up in the hostel where she was staying. It turned out he preferred to work below the taxman's radar, cash only, and having sampled his style and liked it, Olivia proposed a long-term deal. With a fifty percent advance in his pocket, Rossi readily agreed.

Rossi's method was unusual. He rejected the classroom, rejected books and vocabulary lists. "Eyes, ears and this, signora," he said to Olivia, tapping the side of his head. "It's how children learn; we can too. I will correct you and correct you and correct you. I shall be merciless, particularly with your pronunciation since I don't want to hear the most poetic, exquisite and refined language in the world turned into a train smash, metal sheets grinding on metal sheets. So listen, copy, repeat and learn."

He was right. For three hours every day for the last three months, Olivia had walked the streets of Rome with Rossi, soaking up the scenery and history, but more than anything, soaking up the language. He fired constant questions, all structured to challenge without undermining her confidence, all aimed at teaching her to think in Italian, to work out alternative ways of expressing herself when one path failed. Rossi's method appealed to Olivia's love of contingency planning and she delighted in their time together.

Within a month of starting her lessons, not only had she improved more than she thought possible, but also for the first time in her life she was spending time with a man she didn't want to kill. She had never met a man like him: he was around fifty-five, totally at peace with himself and the world, never resorted to innuendo implying he wanted sex, and was always utterly charming. She knew he wasn't married, and when one day he introduced her to his partner Giorgio, an equally charming captain with Alitalia, Olivia felt a simple, undemanding enjoyment in the company of other human beings she had never before experienced.

Olivia was describing Alessandro Rossi's methods in detail to Connie when Caroline returned from the lobby.

"All settled, Connie," she said, ignoring Olivia. "Signorina Grimaldi isn't happy, but—"

"Remind me what she charges, Caroline, would you?" interrupted Connie.

Reluctant to commit herself in view of her deal, Caroline stalled. "Er, I'll have to check."

Connie waited while Caroline rummaged for longer than necessary in her bag.

"I'm still waiting," she said, finally, when it was clear what Caroline was doing. "You have all your files with you on the iPad, don't you?"

Now more than flustered, Caroline made a pretence of studying the tablet. The former police officer in Olivia could see guilt written all over her. She kept quiet and waited.

"Let me see," said Caroline, "Er, yes, it's, um, a hundred and twenty euros a session."

"Forty an hour, right?" confirmed Connie.

She turned to Olivia. "How does that compare with your Signor Rossi, er … oh my heavens, how rude of me, I haven't even asked your name, I was so interested in your story."

Olivia smiled. "It's Diana," she said. "Diana Fitchley."

"Pleased to meet you, Diana. It is all right if I call you Diana, isn't it?"

"Of course."

"Wonderful, I'm Connie. Connie Fairbright. And this is Caroline Monkton, my PA."

"Very pleased to meet you," said Olivia, offering her hand to

Connie. "And you too, Caroline," she added, turning her head and holding the PA's eyes with icy penetration. "And to answer your question, Connie," she continued, her eyes still boring into Caroline's, "Alessandro charges thirty an hour, although as I've said, I think he's worth far more."

An hour later, Connie and her new friend Diana walked into the Bar Napoli, Alessandro Rossi's favourite launching spot for his conversational walks. He eyed Connie suspiciously. He could tell instantly she was moneyed, but that didn't interest him. His strict criteria demanded simply that his students were willing to learn and be receptive to his unconventional methods.

"You will need to have a thick skin, signora," he explained without any further small talk once the introductions had been made. "No other language has vowel sounds quite like Italian, particularly English, whether it's British English or American like yours. I will require you to forget your vowels, forget them entirely, and learn them again as if they are something quite different, something totally new. I shall be relentless every time I hear a non-Italian vowel, correcting you and correcting you endlessly until you hate me. Believe me, it can work and if it does, the rest is easy. So, signora, I require a week to assess your potential for correct pronunciation. We shall walk the streets of this beautiful city seeking inspiration at every corner, reading signs, menus, advertisements, learning the vowels. If you achieve little or nothing, we shall go our separate ways, since I do not wish to waste your time or mine. However, I have confidence in my method and I am used to overcoming enormous resistance."

He waved an arm towards Olivia. "Diana announced her Englishness with every sound she uttered when I first met her. But after a few days of having her vocal cords torn apart and then rebuilt, she was starting to pronounce my exquisite language like a Roman, even if she didn't understand a word of what she was saying. Do we have a deal?"

Connie began her lessons that afternoon, having instructed a rather sullen Caroline to reschedule her art tutor. The first three days were as brutal as Rossi had predicted as he set about smashing her vowels into fragments before reconstructing them piece by painful piece; the following three days were merely painful. But Connie had a good ear and already by the end of the week, when she said anything in Italian, she now sounded far less American. When Rossi agreed to continue with her tuition, she was ecstatic.

During that first week and the three that followed, while Connie was with Rossi, Olivia gathered as much information as she could about the rich Signora Fairbright and her scheming PA. More than anything, she needed to know about their relationship; whether it was simply professional or whether there was a further, emotional side. How would Fairbright react to her PA resigning? Or being murdered? For one thing was becoming clearer in Olivia's mind: Caroline Monkton would probably have to die. The reason was simple: if Monkton returned to England, either sacked by Fairbright or having left of her own apparent accord once Olivia had read her fortune to her, there was a danger she might see Olivia's photograph on a police information broadcast, and although Olivia as Diana looked completely different from the photos the police had, Monkton might see enough of a resemblance to make the connection. That couldn't be allowed to happen.

Olivia's snooping into both Connie and Caroline's personal effects in their respective rooms, research as she thought of it, was exhaustive, but in the end, the matter was straightforward. The two women's relationship was purely professional, and from further observation of their interaction over the dinners Connie now insisted Olivia be a part of, it was clear Connie had had enough of her ageing and not-over-efficient PA. Monkton's personal papers, checked while she was out running errands for Connie, gave Olivia all she needed: the woman was a con artist like herself. Takes one to know one, thought Olivia. I was suspicious as soon as I set eyes on you.

The discovery saved Monkton's life since it was clear that whatever happened, she wouldn't be returning to England. She was on the run and destined to a life of drifting around Europe in exile trying to find people like Connie from whom she could extract a working wage while fiddling a little more on the side.

"Your problem, Caroline, is you're a petty thief who can't keep her hands out of the till."

Olivia had waited almost a month since she had first introduced herself to Connie, surprising Monkton one morning by knocking on the door of her room while Connie was somewhere on the streets of Rome with Alessandro Rossi and insisting they had a chat.

"You're a fool; you can't see the bigger picture. Connie has been paying you a generous salary for your inefficient services, but you couldn't resist, could you?" said Olivia as she sat down without being invited.

"I don't know what you're talking about, Diana. I don't think Connie would—"

"Would what, Caroline? Would like to hear about your arrangement with Signorina Grimaldi?" Olivia shook her head. "Very unprofessional. Or perhaps she would like to hear how, since that fiasco in Devon nearly ten years ago, you can't risk going back to the UK."

It was enough for Monkton; she crumbled.

"What do you want?" she whispered from behind the hands now covering her face. She looked through her fingers, her eyes darting, frightened. "I can't afford to—"

Olivia's snort of interruption was harsh.

"I don't want your money, you stupid bitch, I've got enough of my own. What I can't stand is seeing a crook like you taking advantage. Connie Fairbright seems to be a pretty rich woman whom I assume you were intending to fleece for all you could get."

Olivia's face fell into a snarl — she could only do supercilious for so long. "Your kind of low-life makes me spit. For two pins I would break your neck and toss you in the Tiber."

She paused to let the threat work its way into Monkton's consciousness. The woman was looking sick.

"I'll give you one chance, Monkton," continued Olivia. "You resign today, now. Then you bugger off out of Rome and never come back. Ever. In fact it would be safer for you if you left Italy altogether. Go and work your cons elsewhere; there are plenty of places to choose from. I know you've tried France and Switzerland in the past; try them again."

Caroline Monkton gulped, but she wasn't quite beaten. "And if I—"

She jumped as Olivia's fist hit the table in front of her.

"If you don't?" she growled. "If you don't, if I ever see or hear from you again, if you dare to try to contact Connie, even if you make it look accidental, I'll kill you. I'll break that scrawny neck. Do I make myself clear?"

Monkton's eyelids were batting up and down, her hands wringing together. "But … but I can't just leave. Connie wouldn't understand. You wouldn't tell her, would you, I mean, about …?"

Olivia's answer was to open her shoulderbag and retrieve a single typewritten sheet; a letter. She handed it to Caroline.

"Sign that and put it in Connie's room. Then take your things and go."

She took an envelope from her bag. "Here, I'm all heart. Take it."

The now-shattered PA opened the envelope to find a one-way train ticket to Zurich for that evening.

Olivia pointed to the letter. "Sign it. Now!"

Chapter Ten

The acrylic dome had long been removed and packed away, the intense Sardinian sun now more than sufficient to keep the large pool on the clifftop at an invitingly comfortable temperature. The languid days of summer had arrived, long afternoons for stretching out on a lounger in the shade of a sun umbrella the reward for more physically demanding mornings of exercise.

Derek had changed his mind about too much R&R being boring. Now his leg was no longer in plaster, he was working hard with Alicia to get his body back to the level of fitness he had achieved before Olivia Freneton put his ambitions on hold. However, while he knew his body was generally in good shape, his leg still needed treating with respect. The various titanium-steel pins holding it together were doing their job, the bone tissue was growing around them, the fractured bones knitting together, but he couldn't risk an awkward fall; not yet.

Alicia had not only put Derek on a version of the Paleo diet, much to his initial indignation —

"But I like bread, Ali, and spuds and—"

"Pizza, pasta and rice?" added Alicia, interrupting him as she chanted the words in her heavily accented English. "Sugar in disguise, all of them."

"Hmmm," grunted Derek.

— but also she had insisted on what she called her regeneration brew, a complex mixture she blended daily of herbs, spices, plant extracts and roots chosen to accelerate the healing process.

In a statistical sample of one person, it was hard to claim his speedy return to health was down to Alicia's brew or Derek's determination, but something worked and by the end of June he was ready to return to England and report for duty.

———

A week before his departure, Derek was sitting at breakfast with Alicia, her charts recording every aspect of his progress over the past three months spread out on the table in front of them.

"Look-a, Derek," she said, pointing to a steep upward curve, "The muscle function. See how it improve?"

Derek grinned at her. "No doubt about it, Ali, you're a genius. I'd like to put you in my suitcase and take you home, but I don't think Jen would be amused."

"Also not Carlo, my boyfriend. He remove the titanium pins one by one and grind your bones to dust," she said, smiling sweetly as she mimed using a mortar and pestle.

"Wow, Ali," said Derek, wincing. "You certainly have a way with words. When are you leaving for your week off to see him?"

"Two days," she said, a dreamy glint in her eyes. "I cannot wait."

"I can see that," laughed Derek. "Quick, put those charts away, Jen's coming."

Alicia hurriedly gathered the papers and slammed them into a file, but she was too late; Jennifer had seen them.

"Gloating over your performance again, DC Thyme?" she said aloofly as she set her coffee mug onto the table.

Unlike Derek's rapid progress, Jennifer's was far slower, the underlying damage to both her head and her chest still taking its toll. Every time she went a little too fast or put in a little too much effort, the headaches would start or her chest would complain. Neither were as bad as they once had been, but they slowed her down, frustrated her.

Initially, Alicia's obsession with logging every aspect of her performance had encouraged Jennifer, which was the intention. There was an upward trend to the curves, albeit a shallow one. But now, each time she saw Derek's charts, she felt her jaw clench with impatience.

"Jeez, Ali," she said, pointing at the file, "I thought I was making progress, but look at those figures. They blow mine out of the water."

"It's not the same, Jenni," said Alicia, her smile reassuring as she reverted to her rapid-fire Italian. "Derek's injuries were completely different. Yes, his leg was a mess, but that was it. Bone and muscle. Yours were far more complex. The brain is the most delicate of organs."

She put a hand on Jennifer's arm. "Look, I've been comparing your progress with others who survived injuries like yours, and it's excellent. You mustn't be discouraged."

Jennifer smiled at her friend. "I know, Ali, I'm grateful for all your work, believe me. It's just so frustrating. I mean, it's not as if I'm old. I'm twenty-seven, not seventy-seven; my body should be patching itself up faster than this."

"It's doing the best it can," said Alicia, "and it's doing brilliantly."

Derek hated to see Jennifer getting upset about her progress, wanting her to return to full fitness as much as she did.

"Got something that might interest you, Jen," he said. "Let me get my phone."

He stood and walked over to another table. As he returned, strolling towards them, the slight limp he'd been left with was hardly noticeable.

"Look at this, girls," he said with a grin as he held up the device. "I've discovered why I got off so lightly."

"I wouldn't call smashing your bones 'getting off lightly'," said Jennifer.

"Compared with losing a leg, it is," replied Derek. "Watch this video. One of my mates in the fraud squad got it from the team who were investigating my attempted murder. It was taken by some bloke just along the platform who was filming his girlfriend on his phone. Watch how Olaf reacted."

"Olaf?"

"That was the huge Swedish guy's name. Olaf. He came to see me when I was in hospital. Such a lovely bloke. He was in tears when I thanked him. The nurse had to stop him picking me up to hug me. I told him we'd definitely get together once I was fully operational again, have a few drinks. Anyway, watch it."

He pressed a button on the screen and handed the phone to Jennifer. Alicia leaned across to watch over her shoulder. The scene showed the girlfriend in the foreground, her face filling half the screen. Behind her, in the background, the tunnel at the end of the platform was clearly visible. As the train appeared, thundering towards the camera, the image jerked as the crowd moved as one. The huge Swede's body blocked the view of Derek falling towards the platform edge, but then his arms shot out and could be seen not only checking Derek's fall, but swinging his body round in the same direction as the train was moving, so as it hit Derek's leg, the impact was lessened since he was moving with it.

"Wow!" exclaimed Jennifer, "that's amazing."

"The team's DI had someone from a university look at it and they reckon the speed of impact was reduced by several miles an hour, which lessened its effect. Cool, huh!"

"Impressivo," nodded Alicia, standing up. "OK, I gotta some work to do with-a your schedules for when I not 'ere, and a programme for you for when you back in London, Derek."

As they watched her go, Jennifer turned to Derek. "Looking forward to getting back to work?"

Derek shrugged. "Yes and no. Actually, I wasn't at all until I had another email this morning along with the one with the video. It was from Hawkins."

"Hawkins! What does he want?"

"It's more what I want," answered Derek. "I really wasn't keen to get back to the fraud squad. As I've said before, the work didn't ring my chimes, important though it is. So I got to thinking about it and I reckoned that now I'm out of the Olympic squad, there's no reason for me to be in London. I mean, it was great of the force to find me a spot in fraud so I could do my training, don't get me wrong, but I was never happy from day one. So I wrote to Hawkins asking if I could go back to the SCF in Nottingham. He replied very quickly to say he'd support me and not only that, he'd put in a word with my bosses in London, smooth it over so it didn't look like I was ungrateful."

"You know," said Jennifer, "I think we all misjudged Hawkins, probably something to do with his miserable demeanour. Underneath, he's a very caring boss."

"Too right," agreed Derek. "In the email he sent this morning, he said it's all sorted. I report back at the SCF in ten days' time."

"That's brilliant, Derek," enthused Jennifer.

"Yeah," he said, a grin across his face. "So yes, I'm looking forward to getting back, now it's the SCF, and no, I'm not looking forward to leaving this place. It's paradise, Jen, and you've been amazing."

Jennifer smiled. "It's Alicia who's been amazing. Neither of us would have got to where we are without her."

"But it was you who sorted out my head, Jen, helped me banish those nightmares."

"All part of the service, DC Thyme," she said, the back of her hand brushing affectionately across his cheek.

The day before Derek left to return to England, after a lazy afternoon by the pool, Jennifer told him they should make his last night special by smartening up a little, rather than just wearing their normal shorts and Ts, after which she disappeared to her room to shower and change.

Martina, the cook, had prepared them a wonderful dinner of lobster freshly caught that morning, and, sensing something in the air, had discreetly retired to her small house in the grounds, declaring she was tired and would clean the dishes the following morning.

Derek was sitting on a sofa, occasionally glancing at a book but mainly staring at the golden light on the sea, when he heard Jennifer walk into the room.

"I hope a shirt and chinos are fine, Jen," he called, "it's a bit hot for a jacket."

When she didn't answer, he looked up and gulped. She was standing by the small bar wearing a close-fitting, black silk evening dress with a plunging neckline. The style was immaculate, the fit perfect. She had spiked up her short hair and replaced the stud earrings she normally wore with large gold hoops to match a gold necklace and bracelet. The three-inch heels on her black patent leather shoes lifted and accentuated her slim, lithe body.

"Drink?" she said, smiling to herself at the look on Derek's face. "There's some prosecco cooling in the fridge."

"Sounds perfect," said Derek, his tongue a soggy sponge. He put down his book and stood.

"Christ, Jen," he said, walking over to her, "you look amazing."

Jennifer put down the champagne flute she'd picked up and turned to face him. She smiled softly and took his hands in hers. "You look pretty cool yourself," she said, drawing him to her. "That colour suits you; you should wear it more often."

Derek looked down at his cream shirt. "If I'd known you'd be wearing an exclusive Fabrelli creation, I'd've made more of an effort," he said.

She laughed. "I wouldn't recommend Pietro's range for men to you. The current fashions are so tight it's better if you have no muscle on your bones, which kind of rules you out."

"So you can't see me on the fashion runway?" said Derek, revolving his shoulders slowly.

"Maybe as a surfer dude," she laughed. "Now, let me pour this prosecco and we'll sit and watch the sunset."

After deftly twisting out the cork, she poured two glasses and handed one to Derek.

"Every time I see you do that, DC Cotton, I'm most impressed."

"Practice makes perfect," said Jennifer as she took his hand and pulled him gently to the sofa.

"Look," she said as they sat.

"What?"

"The light on the sea. It's in that direction." She pointed past him. "Don't you think it's wonderful?"

"Wonderful," repeated Derek, but his eyes remained fixed on Jennifer. "Just as wonderful as every night in paradise. But right now, I'm enjoying the view on this side of the glass. I don't actually care if there's dense fog out there."

Jennifer tilted her head playfully as she bit on the end of her thumb, her eyes full of amusement. She put down her glass and held out a hand to him.

"Glass," she said.

He handed it to her and she put it on the side table next to hers.

Then she turned and this time held out both hands.

"Me," she said.

Derek took her hands and pulled her towards him.

Early the following afternoon, Jennifer went along with Derek in the car when Mario, the driver, took him to the airport.

"It's going to be quiet without you goofing around in the pool, DC Thyme. I'm going to miss you, and so will Alicia."

"I'll miss her too. Her workouts have been amazing. As you said the other day, Jen, she's a real find. Magic."

He glanced sideways at her, registering the quizzical look on her face, and grinned.

"I'll miss you too," he said. "Just a bit."

"How much?" she said, punching him on the arm.

"A pretty big bit," he laughed. He took her hand. "That was one amazing night, Jen."

"But?" she frowned.

"But nothing," he protested. "It's just, well, the whole ambience was pretty stunning, this whole place is so incredibly special. I mean, it's not Nottingham."

"I've noticed that," said Jennifer. "It's a bit farther to the sea in Nottingham."

"I don't mean that."

"I know what you mean, you idiot. You're worried the whole rose-coloured glasses thing has affected our judgement, that we're not in the real world."

"Something like that," he muttered.

"Look, Derek, you're my best friend in all the world and I love you to bits. Whether last night was just last night or whether it was the start of something bigger, I don't know, and nor do you. It's too early to say. For the next two or three months, all I'm probably going to see of you is your face on Skype, depending on when my dear dottore finally decides to give me a clean bill of health, so let's see how it goes."

She pulled his face close to hers.

"If when I get back to Nottingham we find we can't keep our hands off each other, I guess we'll know."

Derek grinned and kissed her lips. "I love you too, Jen. You know that, don't you?"

"Idiot," she said.

Chapter Eleven

Olivia didn't hurry to answer the insistent tapping on her door even though she'd been expecting it. When she finally did open the door, she was pretending to rub the sleep from her eyes.

"Connie?" she said, injecting surprise into her voice. "Sorry, I was having a doze. Is everything all right?"

It had been two weeks since, at Connie's insistence, she had moved into the hotel. They had already been spending every evening together, courtesy of Connie's tab, and as Connie put it, since the cost was loose change compared with the return on her investments, it seemed churlish to allow her new friend to return to some dive near Termini station.

Out of Olivia's earshot, Caroline Monkton had objected strongly, counselling caution with someone who until recently had been a total stranger. Her con-artist's antennae were quivering with alarm at this intruder to the world she had established with Connie; she didn't like or trust the smooth-talking Diana Fitchley an inch. But Connie was having none of it, and all Caroline's whingeing achieved was to increase the irritation Connie was starting to feel when around her PA.

"Caroline, over the last twenty-five years, I've met just about every kind of smart-ass smooth-talking con-man the business world could throw up, every type of snake-oil merchant, because that's all they are, even the ones with fleets of jets and limos. So I know when someone's trying to get one over on me; I can spot them a mile off. And Diana, no, she's the real McCoy. She's just a lovely person who's achieved more for me in a month than I thought possible."

Although angered at her boss's intransigence, Caroline had also felt perversely reassured by Connie's self-deception. Didn't detect me on your gold-plated radar, my dear, she thought.

But the reassurance had been short-lived, evaporating in a flash when Olivia put the boot in.

———

"May I come in?" said Connie. "I think I need a drink."

Olivia saw she was holding the letter that a couple of hours earlier she had thrust at Caroline Monkton.

"Come and sit on the sofa," she said, her voice all concern. "What can I get you?"

"A Scotch?"

"Really?" Olivia was now genuinely surprised. She'd only ever seen Connie drink wine.

"With some ice, if you have any," said Connie.

Olivia poured the whisky and a glass of spring water for herself before sitting down beside Connie. "Whatever's wrong, Connie? Have you had bad news? It is something from the States?"

When Connie didn't answer immediately, she added, "Is it to do with the paper you're holding?"

Connie looked down at the letter as if she'd forgotten it was there. She held it out.

"This was on my desk when I got back just now from my afternoon with Alessandro."

Olivia went through the motions of reading it and then sat back.

"Oh my heavens, how cruel. I can't believe it. I must admit I thought Caroline was, how should I say, a little self-righteous at

times, but to say things like that when you were so generous to her.
It's unconscionable."

Connie sighed deeply. "How could I have been so blind? I
thought I was a good judge of character. She's virtually accused me
of being a spoilt bitch, a naïve Yankee with more money than
sense. She hated me, Diana."

Olivia shook her head. "Classic tactic of a jealous mind, I'm
afraid, Connie. Do you know anything about her background,
what she was doing before you employed her?"

"Only what she told me, which wasn't a huge amount. Now I
think about it, she was quite evasive. She told me she'd PA'd on and
off over the years after she was let down by her shit of a husband
when he walked out with the maid, leaving her high and dry."

Olivia pursed her lips. "I wonder if it was true. Did she come
with references?"

"A couple, yes. I read them but didn't take them further. I
should have done, I know. I could kick myself, but, you know, I only
needed her to sort out my diary, run a few errands; I wasn't giving
her the keys to the kingdom. She had no dealings with my finances;
they're all dealt with through my brokers in the States."

Olivia nodded. "Do you think, perhaps, money was at the heart
of the problem?"

"What do you mean?"

"Well, I don't want to raise unfounded suspicions or even to
badmouth Caroline, but maybe she was looking at gaining access
to your money, relieving you of some of it."

Connie gave a resigned sigh. "It's possible, I suppose. It's one of
the hazards of being wealthy. In my position, you can't be too careful, hence all the care with my finances.

"But those accusations, they are totally unfair. I'm certainly not
what Caroline is suggesting; I'm no naïve Yankee and I'm not
spoilt. Yes, I was born into money, but that doesn't mean I don't
know the value of it. And you should see the charities Brad set up.
For the last ten years or so, it was about the only thing I respected
him for. He gave away tens of millions."

"He?" asked Olivia. "Don't you mean 'we'?"

Connie smiled and touched Olivia's arm.

"It was at his instigation, but it was a wonderful thing to be involved in, and in my view totally justifies the making of all the money, to be able to do something when tight-assed or corrupt governments won't step in. Maybe I'll take time out from my Italian studies and take you to see one or two of the foundations in action. Not yet, the learning curve's still steep and I'm loving it now I feel I'm getting somewhere. But in a few months. What do you say?"

"I'd be honoured," said Olivia, trying to look interested. Charitable foundations were the last thing on her mind; she had her own nest to feather.

She looked back down at the letter she was still holding.

"She doesn't say where she was going; only that she's always hated Rome and can't wait to leave. You know, from the way she's written this, she sounds a little unstable. I hope you don't mind my saying."

Connie laughed. "Say what you like. She's let me down, insulted me and run away. At least she hasn't stolen anything."

"You've checked your jewellery?"

"She never had the safe combination and it's not written down anywhere; it's etched in my brain. But just to be sure, I checked." She laughed. "All present and correct; the crown jewels are accounted for. Just as well; they're worth a pretty penny."

Olivia smiled, wondering as she did how much of a challenge the safe would be.

"So, what happens now? Another PA?"

Connie shook her head. "No, I don't think so. A PA's fine in an office situation, but I was never comfortable having one around in what are essentially informal surroundings. The roles get confused."

She raised her eyes to Olivia's. "I was wondering, Diana. You said you're on a sort of sabbatical of indeterminate length, taking time out from your real estate business in England, letting your business partners run it. Would you consider, hell, I don't want to say 'working for me', certainly not in a PA capacity. I mean, well, could you see yourself being a companion, someone I could share this Italian adventure with? After all, you're the one who's made it come alive for me. How would you feel about formalising things a bit; if, say, I paid you a retainer? Not to be a PA since I can get most things organised through the hotel. They'll get me someone to sort out the diary, make bookings and so on. Someone efficient who's not in her dotage."

Olivia touched Connie's arm to stop the flow. "A companion. How delightfully old-fashioned. That would be wonderful, thank you. But you don't have to pay me anything." She stopped and looked around her. "Well, the room would be nice, but …"

Connie giggled. "This is going to be fun. Here, give me that." She took Caroline Monkton's letter out of Olivia's hand and screwed it into a ball before tossing it into the air and batting it across the room with her hand.

"Up yours, Ms Monkton. You can rot in hell for all I care."

She stood and held out her hands to Olivia.

"Come on, Diana, let's celebrate our own special Anglo-American accord by going down to the bar and getting tipsy."

Chapter Twelve

With his return to the Serious Crimes Formation in Nottingham, Derek soon found himself immersed in work, with little time outside his long hours for much else besides following the rigorous training schedule Alicia had set him. And while he missed Jennifer, he also loved being back in the thick of things. Most of his mates from before the Harlow Wood case were still in the SCF; just the bosses had changed. Even Neil Bottomley seemed to have returned to his former sardonic self.

Thoughts of frequent Skype calls to Jennifer were soon put aside; there weren't enough hours in a day. But while their calls were limited to Derek's occasional days off, in between they kept up a flurry of text messages, mostly cryptic running commentaries on whatever cases he was following from Derek, while Jennifer's related to her now rapidly improving fitness and general condition, and her inroads into preparing for her new posting.

After a sea swim with Alicia one morning early in September, Jennifer was preparing for her daily call to her Russian tutor, Irina, when her phone pinged with a message from Derek. It was early, even for him. When she read it, her eyes widened in surprise.

'Big news, will Skype tonite ASAP after work x'

There was no way she was going to wait several hours without some information. Her thumbs hit the keys.

'Promotion'

'Haha'

'Sacked'

'Hahaha'

'What'

'Tell u later'

'WHAT!!!'

'Freneton hideaway found'

'Wow! Where'

'WBridgford'

'Call soon!'

'Going there now'

Five minutes into their Russian conversation, Irina commented that Jennifer seemed distracted. Was something wrong?

"Sorry, Irina. I've just had some interesting news from Derek in England, but I've got to wait until this evening to learn more. I can't go into it except to say it's very exciting."

"He has proposed?" Irina was an old-school Russian romantic.

"Ha! I don't think either of us is ready for that, and even if he is, if he did it with a text message, I think I'd kill him."

The afternoon seemed to be twice as long as usual, the passing minutes only made longer by Jennifer constantly checking her watch. She tried hard to immerse herself in revisiting her course notes on art history from her undergraduate days in Nottingham, all part of the preparation she had recently begun for the posting to the art fraud squad she hoped would be happening soon.

Finally, soon after nine in the evening, the Skype chimes sounded on her phone. She answered instantly.

"Derek. What took you so long? I've been climbing the walls waiting for you."

"Sorry, Jen. It all took longer than expected; you know how it is. The new DCI is keen to impress so he wanted everything he could get before he took it to the super and Hawkins. He's been hounding the forensic people all day."

"So impress me as well. What have you got?"

"OK, I'll run you through it. We got a call from a bloke called Clive Peters who's the owner of a flat in West Bridgford with a large lock-up garage under it. He rented it out long term a couple of years ago when he went off to Australia to work. The tenant was a woman who gave her name as Alice Morton. She paid him up front for three years, cash, so he didn't bother to check up on her, just happily pocketed the money."

"Nice bit of undeclared income."

"Exactly. However, Peters came back here a couple of weeks ago to visit his mother and at her house he was thumbing through a load of junk mail, old newspapers and so on — his mother's a bit of a hoarder — when he saw one of the police notices that were put out after Harlow Wood, the ones with the mug shot of Freneton, and he recognised her face even though the woman he'd dealt with had longer hair."

"Presumably she wore a wig when she met him."

"Must've. Nothing if not thorough, our Olivia. Anyway, instead of calling us immediately, the idiot called the flat, and when he got no answer, he went round there. After knocking on the door and getting no reply, he knocked on a couple of neighbours' doors and was told the tenant hadn't been seen for ages. So he let himself in, thinking perhaps he might find her body. He didn't, of course, although he did find a white van in the lock-up, but no sign of any recent activity in the flat, no food anywhere, empty fridge. Then it dawned on him that the place could be useful to our enquiries so he closed the door and called."

"Was this today?"

"Yes, this morning, just before I texted you. Anyway, Crawford, that's the new DCI, sent me and Bottomley round—"

"Bottomley and me."

"What?"

"Nothing. He sent you round …"

"Yes. We took a quick look and requested a full forensic team to search the place. It's so good having the lab in Nottingham now; they were round within half an hour."

"Impressive."

"Yeah, and they quickly came up trumps. They found traces of blood in the van which they've already done a preliminary DNA test on. It matched Freneton's, so this is definitely the right place. They're testing swabs from all over the flat too, of course, and they'll have the DNA on those tomorrow, but there's not much doubt it'll be hers."

"What about the van's plates?"

"The number's fake, not stolen but made up. Not in the system, never has been. So this afternoon, Crawford got everyone in on checking the videos from the traffic cameras that were taken on the night of the Harlow Wood case, checking for any sign of the van. And, ba-boom, there is."

"That was quick."

"It's amazing what you can do when you've got ten people determined to get a result. We can now put the van in several places near Harlow Wood and on the way back to Nottingham, all of it consistent with Freneton driving it back to West Bridgford after the incident. There's even a couple of shots that could show her face even though it was dark. Those have gone off for enhancement, but we're hopeful."

"Great stuff, but nothing we didn't already know."

"Right, but there's more in the flat. The forensic people found a modem attached to a webcam that activates when someone walks in front of it, but guess—"

"Derek, that's really worrying," said Jennifer, cutting in. "She'll now know the flat's been discovered and that you're back on the SCF team. You mustn't forget you're a target — how could you? — along with Bottomley and Hawkins."

"You too, Jen, and Henry, but—"

"Was there anything to indicate where she might be?"

"Jen, let me get a word in. I was trying to say that although the modem was there and plugged in, it wasn't working; the camera wasn't live. The techies reckoned it could've cut out in a storm — a power surge or something. Apparently there was one that hit a few places around here about a week ago. So even if she's checking the webcam regularly, she'll only know it's not working. She won't know it's been found."

"That's a relief."

"Yeah. What we're hoping is that when she discovers it, she'll risk coming back to check the place, since the flat is probably very useful to her. And she might want to retrieve the white van."

"How will you know?"

"Regular beat patrols; a uniform will drive past every three or four hours, plus someone from the SCF will look in several times a week. We're putting all her stuff back too, so she shouldn't know the place has been searched. You never know, she might even move in."

Jennifer grunted. "I shouldn't rely on it, and there should be two of you checking when you call in. She's dangerous, Derek."

"Don't worry, Jen, we've got it covered, and to answer your question, no, there was very little else in the place apart from some maps of places in the South West and Ireland."

"Interesting. Anything on them? Marks, indentations, a ring around the remote cottage she's holed up in and her phone number in the margin?"

"You wish. No, there didn't appear to be anything, but we've sent them to the forensic document people for checking."

"Weren't there any clothes in the place?"

"A few, yes, including some motorcycle leathers."

"Of course, there had to be. How could I forget the motorcycle she intended to escape on, the one I put out of action a few minutes before she put me out of action. Was there a ramp in the van for her to run a motorcycle inside?"

"Yes, there was, although of course she didn't get to use it since you buggered her bike for her."

"I wonder where she is. Has the van's number, fictitious though it is, been run through the UK traffic computers for records of any infringements anywhere in the country? Speeding, parking and so on?"

"It's under way, but nothing's come up so far."

Jennifer stared absently through the huge picture window as

she thought over the information, the moonlit view of the Tyrrhenian sea in surreal contrast to the mental images flashing through her mind.

"What's up, Jen?"

"Nothing, just musing. Look, I know I said this just now, but you have to be extra vigilant over your security. All of you. If by any chance Freneton has got wind of this, she might be more determined to finish what she started. You have been checking under your car, haven't you?"

"Of course I have, ever since I got back. It's become a routine, a compulsion almost. Some of the lads are referring to me as OCD Thyme instead of DC Thyme."

"And your flat?"

"Well, I've beefed up the locks, got an alarm, but I couldn't get all the stuff Pietro's security people recommended; it would be too expensive. If I installed it and anyone broke in, they'd be better off stealing the alarm system; it would be worth more than the contents of the flat."

"That's not the point. And Pietro would have underwritten the cost."

"Can't accept that, Jen, as you well know. It's different for you; he's a relative and therefore he can pay for things. Anyway, there are other things I can do that also come under the OCD umbrella. You know, like place stuff in a very specific way, stuff someone is likely to pick up and move. And as far as info about you is concerned, I've made sure there's absolutely nothing. Not on my computer, not in my desk, no written records. Nothing. As you know, I make all my Skype calls on my phone, and I have that with me at all times. And since I've turned off the cloud thing, nothing on my phone gets shared anywhere else."

"Just as long as she's not just sitting there waiting for you when you get home, like she was with Mandy Gwo."

"I wouldn't let her get the same advantage over me that she got the last time. I'd be ready for her kicks."

"Make sure you are." She ran a hand through her hair. "I wonder where she is, Derek. The West Bridgford flat could be one of any number of boltholes she's got. What about the maps? Is there anything in her force records to link her with the South West or Ireland?"

"Not that I know of, but she's got to go somewhere. And they would be good choices. Lots of remote locations."

"Yeah, but, you know, I don't buy into the idea of her sitting on her backside festering in her hatred. Even if she were broke, she wouldn't do that; she'd be doing something about it. Which does raise the question of what she's doing for money. It's not as if her income as a detective super would have left her with a fortune stashed away for a rainy day. She can only have limited resources. And probably no bank account, credit card etc."

"I don't know, Jen. After all, she had alternative IDs when she was on her killing spree, the Taverner and Doughthey ones. Perhaps she has others."

"Possible, I suppose. But I'm still finding it hard getting my head around her being holed up somewhere remote for months on end. She's got to be plotting our collective murders, surely. I mean, it's been months since she killed Mike Hurst and Mandy Gwo; I'm surprised she hasn't gone after Neil Bottomley and/or Hawkins. She knows where they are and from what you've told me they're doing nothing to hide from her."

"Well, at least you're probably out of her clutches while you're over there. Talking of which, any more news from your doc? You said last week you reckon he can't hold out much longer."

Jennifer laughed. "You're right. I'm convinced Pietro is leaning on him, telling him to keep me here for as long as possible. He's coming over to give me a check-up tomorrow and I intend to bully him into letting me go. I want him to show me all my charts and explain how they differ from a normal healthy person. And once I've forced my doctor's hand, I'm pretty confident I'll be given a clean bill of health, which is perfect timing."

"Why's that?"

"My new boss is paying me a visit in person to discuss my role."

Derek didn't even try to hide his surprise. "You mean he's flying over to Italy for a meeting with you? You, a DC? Unless they've made you a chief super and you forgot to tell me."

"Very funny. But, yeah, it's interesting. He made a point of saying it's important we meet here."

"P'raps he fancies a weekend away from the crap weather we're getting in the UK at the moment. September is normally good, but it's done nothing but rain for the last two weeks."

"We could do with some of that here."

"Yeah, I feel sorry for you. All that sun, sea and sand gets very boring, couldn't wait to get away from it myself."

"Well, I'll be leaving it behind pretty soon too, if I have any say in the matter."

"When's he arriving, your new boss? Who is he, anyway?"

"His name's Paul Godden and he's arriving in a couple of days' time."

Chapter Thirteen

In the two months since Olivia had contrived her meeting with Connie, things had gone well. The sensible and controlled Diana side of Olivia's personality had come to the fore and kept the wilder, angrier needs of her Olivia side in check. The lessons had helped. Both women were improving daily with their language skills, Olivia more so than Connie since her innate ability was greater. But Connie's determination and eagerness made up for much of the shortfall in her ability.

Every day after their respective language lessons from Rossi, and Connie's art class from Signor Contorni, they would sit down on the terrace of the hotel or on Connie's substantial penthouse balcony and talk through what they'd learned. Olivia would encourage Connie by getting her to explain in Italian what Contorni had shown her. This would inevitably result in peals of laughter from both women as first Connie and then Olivia invented words and phrases, followed by Connie impersonating Cortorni's liquid but serious tones while Olivia would reply with a passable take on Rossi's persistent and persuasive style. Connie was constantly adding to her substantial collection of art books, a large number of which would end up scattered around them as she dived from one to another showing Olivia an example of this artist's work here and that artist's there. Olivia would quietly and, she hoped, inconspicuously clench her jaw, resisting the desire to yawn, determined to mask her total lack of interest in art.

Dinner would follow, often in the hotel's superb restaurant, which was one of the finest in Rome, or at somewhere Olivia had discovered from discreet conversations with Lorenzo, the maître d'. She knew this was far more reliable than going online: the type of restaurants they visited were seldom written up by people like Connie — people who preferred exclusivity to sharing, people who had people to handle their computers for them rather than tapping on keyboards themselves.

They normally restricted themselves to a single bottle of wine, always a fine vintage, always Italian, while nightcaps in the bar or in Connie's room varied depending on how Olivia perceived Connie's mood. An exclusive limoncello with plenty of ice was a definite favourite.

There was occasionally a faraway look in Connie's eye as she said goodnight that made Olivia wonder about her physical needs. They rarely discussed men, except in disparaging terms, or women, and Olivia certainly wasn't inclined to make any move. If there were to be one, it would have to come entirely from Connie, and while she was prepared to accommodate Connie's needs if she perceived it necessary, Olivia doubted it was. She was fairly sure the faraway look was simply one of trusting friendship rather than a yearning for anything sexual. She hoped that was the case: she was concerned that if they did end up in bed together, the Olivia in her would take over and throttle Connie.

Connie's sessions with Cesare Contorni and Alessandro Rossi not only gave Olivia a welcome break from her target and her alter ego of Diana, but also the opportunity to plan possible scenarios for her yearned-for return to England to complete her disposals. She filled notebook after notebook, consolidating their contents onto her laptop using mind-mapping software. She delighted in immersing herself in the task of crafting one contingency plan after another, all of which she knew were brilliant, all of them flex-ible and dynamic. It was at these times, when she was using her considerable intelligence to process her schemes, that she felt most alive, the taut strings of her mind in perfect resonance with the flow of ideas.

Integral to many of her plans were her two boltholes in England: the West Bridgford flat and the caravan on the Kent coast. And because of the key role they played, it was essential to know they had not been discovered — the last thing she needed was to turn up at one of them to find a welcoming committee from the SCF.

To monitor them, Olivia had installed webcams. Of the two, the West Bridgford one should have been the more reliable: it had a good power supply, the bills were all paid up front and there was even a back-up rechargeable battery in case of mains outage. By contrast, power supply to the caravan was strung across several poles in a field, looping from van to van and always subject to the idiotic and unpredictable behaviour of occupants of other vans. It was, therefore, a shock when on a routine daily check of the feeds on her computer, Olivia discovered the West Bridgford webcam had failed the previous afternoon.

Given there was no indication of an intruder on the feed from the West Bridgford flat, the question was why had it failed. Living in Italy, where the power supply is capricious at the best of times and often destructively excitable in electric storms, Olivia was used to the inconvenience of power surges and she strongly suspected the failure was weather-related. The UK weather report for the previous afternoon confirmed her suspicions: violent thunderstorms had been recorded in the West Bridgford area as a mini-tornado wreaked havoc across the region. Several buildings had suffered direct lightning strikes with residents complaining of burnt-out modems.

Olivia sat back in her chair to ponder the situation. She was loath to implement a different, less convenient set of plans for the sake of a simple modem. It seemed ridiculous to discard the flat if its location hadn't been compromised, especially when it contained a well-hidden stock of explosive devices, some weapons and stolen identity documents. But without the live feed, she could no longer rely on its integrity. And while it was unlikely to have been discovered so quickly, she had to be certain. Which meant one thing: she must visit the flat.

She took a deep breath, a surge of excitement flowing through her. With respect to her disposals, she had completed her plans. She could go at any time, she just needed to contrive a situation where she could excuse herself from Connie for long enough. It would all be happening far sooner than she had expected, but that didn't matter. Her plan was logical and elegant, and with luck should result in her completing all five outstanding disposals.

The final piece of her plan had fallen into place two weeks previously while she was reviewing the problem of Derek Thyme and his whereabouts. It had now been five months since his brush with death at Oxford Circus Station and even with his extensive injuries, he should be well on the way to recovery, if not already back on active duty. Would he go back to the SCF? There was an easy way to check: call and ask. When she did, an obliging young lady had answered her request to speak with DC Thyme by telling her he was out of the office. If the caller would like to leave a name and number, she'd get him to call her back. Olivia had politely declined, saying she would call again later.

With this intelligence, she could act. She would dispose of Thyme, Bottomley and Hawkins on the same day, moving swiftly from one to the other, before retreating either to the flat or the caravan to await the funerals. Unless she was at death's door, Cotton was bound to go to Thyme's even if she didn't attend the others. But what if her attendance were perceived as a risk and she was barred from going? What if she were still too incapacitated? Thyme was closest to Cotton, probably in regular communication, and the answers to many of Olivia's questions about Cotton would probably lie in his flat. A minor adjustment to her plan now included two visits to Thyme's flat on the same day. The second one would be to kill him after she had disposed of Bottomley and Hawkins, while the first would be to check his computer as well as search for anything else that might lead her to Cotton.

All that remained was for her to make sure that Connie raised no objections to her being away. To do this, she invented an aged aunt who had just died, an eccentric old lady who for many years had lived in Brussels. They had seen little of each other in recent years, but the aunt had been good to Olivia when she was young when her mother was seriously ill. She was more than just obliged to go, she would explain, there could be complex legal matters relating to her aunt's estate to be resolved with her aunt's lawyer. She felt confident the gullible Connie would swallow the story.

Chapter Fourteen

Detective Superintendent Paul Godden arrived at the Fabrelli villa in the heat of the late afternoon as thunder clouds stacked themselves into soaring mountains over the Tyrrhenian Sea. Greeting Jennifer with an enthusiastic shake of her hand, he eyed the sky.

"Hope I haven't brought that lot with me from England."

Jennifer smiled. "It rains here too, sir," she said. "Most afternoons at the moment, and although it looks impressive, the storm won't last long. Very Italian, really."

"So the owners of paradise have control over the weather, do they," laughed Godden. "And it's so delightfully warm," he added, peeling off his beige linen jacket and removing his cream straw trilby. "By the way, I'm sure I've mentioned it before, but in art fraud we're not like the more routine crime squads. With us it's all first names. Much easier. So it's Paul, OK?"

"Might take some getting used to after the SCF," said Jennifer.

"I'm sure you'll manage."

He looked around. "What a wonderful place. Very good of you to send the car; I could easily have got a taxi."

Jennifer shook her head. "Mario doesn't have enough to do, so driving as far as the airport will have made his day. And anyway, it's all part of the security system. Unknown vehicles are not encouraged to come anywhere near here, and any that try get short shrift from our team of heavies."

"Yes, can't be too careful. I've been reading up about Freneton. Dreadful woman, incredibly devious and cunning. But resourceful, I'd say."

"Very," agreed Jennifer. "Contingency planning is her thing; she's obsessed by it and brilliant at it. And she has quite an intellect; it's just a pity she can't channel it beyond the hatred that seems to consume her."

Godden was head of a sub-unit of the Metropolitan Police Art & Antiques Theft and Fraud Squad that dealt exclusively with high-value theft and forgery of paintings. Jennifer had met him once before in hospital in the early days of her recovery when he'd called in to tempt her into joining his unit. Given her background in art history from her university days, she took little persuasion. Godden made the job sound anything but routine, with the added bonus of dealing almost daily with collectors and getting the opportunity to see their private collections. For Jennifer, it was irresistible.

At the time of their first meeting, only weeks after the Harlow Wood case, Jennifer was making such good progress that she hoped to be able to report for active duty within a month. But then the headaches began, along with debilitating nausea when she trained too hard. Alarmed by this development, her doctors temporarily banned all exercise and subjected her to a barrage of scans. The outcome was a revised convalescence plan designed to give her brain more time to heal. About a year was recommended, much to Jennifer's horror and disappointment.

She had spoken to Godden on Skype several times during the past few months when he'd called to ask about her progress, and each time she liked him more. Always polite, patient and never trying to bully her into hurrying back to duty, he was unlike any of the hard-bitten senior officers she had worked with in Nottingham. In his early forties, he had the air of a somewhat distracted academic, his lived-in corduroy jackets with obligatory leather elbow patches and his shock of unruly greying curls completing the picture.

Art was his passion. In every call he spent much of the time telling Jennifer about the latest exhibitions in London, or recounting a visit to a wealthy collector to see a recently acquired masterpiece that would never be likely to go on public view. If that painting happened to be from the Renaissance, he would talk excitedly and extensively about its comparative merit in relation to the artist's other works. His knowledge was extensive, particularly regarding the more minor artists from the period, many of whom he felt were underrated.

"Take Perini, for example," he suggested during one call that had already covered several fifteenth- and sixteenth-century Tuscan artists.

"Tommaso or Piero?" asked Jennifer.

"Er, Tommaso. Gosh, Jennifer, that's impressive. Few people have even heard of Tommaso Perini, let alone his son. Piero is almost totally unknown outside of a few dedicated collectors."

Jennifer smiled at his response. Tommaso Perini happened to be a particular favourite of hers. "I went to a wonderful exhibition of Tommaso's work in Rome a few years ago when I was on vacation from uni. I adore his work."

"If it was Rome, I'll bet I know where many of the pieces came from," replied Godden.

"Only one source, surely," laughed Jennifer. "They were from the art connoisseur and collector Corrado Verdi's collection. Do you know him?"

"I've met him a few times, yes. Amazing man. He has a profound knowledge."

"So I'm told. Ced Fisher, whom I met during the Freneton case, told me about him. They're pretty good friends."

"Ah, Fisher. Brilliant man; turned the art world on its head. There's hardly an insurance company worth its name who won't insist on having his program scan any high-value works they've been asked to cover. He's been of remarkable assistance to us on a number of occasions as well. Delightful chap."

"He is," agreed Jennifer. "His wife Sally too; they're quite a duo. But getting back to Verdi; does he ever come to London? I'd love to meet him."

"Shouldn't be difficult to arrange the next time he's over. Although I should watch your step with him, if I were you. Quite an eye for pretty young girls."

Jennifer chuckled; Sally had told her all about Verdi. "I think I can look after myself," she said. She puckered her lips ruefully. "At least I thought I could until I crossed swords with Olivia Freneton."

Two hours after Godden's arrival at the Fabrelli villa, he and Jennifer were sitting at a table under a bougainvillea-covered pergola near the clifftop as the sun set behind the villa, the sea ahead of them bathed in a dancing, golden light. Godden had been shown his room and given a tour of the villa while the brief storm Jennifer had predicted refreshed the land before rolling on its way to the south–west of the island.

"What a fabulous location, Jennifer," enthused Godden as he took a sip from his Campari soda. "It's going to be hard for you to drag yourself away from it."

"Not at all," replied Jennifer, stretching out her legs. "I can only have so much of paradise; I need something to stop my brain atrophying." For the time being, she was keeping her Russian studies to herself.

"Excellent," said Godden. He sat up and fixed his eyes on hers, his demeanour now businesslike. Jennifer registered the change with excitement. She wanted nothing more than to get back to work after so long.

"Before we discuss what I've got in mind for you," began Godden, "and why I wanted to discuss it here, well away from the office, why, in fact, I don't want you coming to the office at all, I want to give you some general background.

"The world of high-value art and its collectors is not all it may seem, not all rich benefactors supporting or funding art museums, encouraging young talent and so on. Obviously, and thankfully, a lot of that does exist, but there are many facets to this particular gemstone.

"There are, for example, many collectors whose portfolios are established for purely financial reasons; they have no real interest in art at all. Their objective is to see their investment rise in value; their paintings are just another commodity. I don't have much time for such people, but they are harmless so long as they are honest about how they acquire their paintings and how they sell them. If, as sometimes happens, they fall into the category of benefactors too, then everyone gains.

"But then there are the secretive types, those who want to possess a painting and hide it away from the world, especially one by a famous artist or an old master. This happens a lot with what one might call the newly rich set, in Russia or China, for example. There are all sorts of reasons, fear of theft or damage being one, but another is that some of their works may have been illegally acquired. Sometimes this can be through a sponsored theft from a gallery, but more often than not, it's theft from another private collection, especially one where paintings have also been illegally obtained. You see, the victims of such thefts are in a sticky position: they can't report their loss if what was stolen was itself illegally acquired. It's murky, messy, and played for very high stakes. The annual world value of the market runs into billions, and most of the time the world at large is completely unaware of it.

"Interwoven with all this is the forgery market. Now, you might think for well-known works, forgery wouldn't be much of a problem. After all, everyone knows the Mona Lisa and where it is. It would take not only a remarkable forger but also an amazingly slick con man to persuade someone he had the real Mona Lisa for sale. But famous paintings do get stolen and some are never recovered. If one of those is offered for sale on the black market, it could be the real thing or it could be a forgery. Clearly the potential buyer is in something of a quandary since he can't go to legitimate authorities to have it verified; he has to rely on his own sources, ones he knows he can trust."

Jennifer nodded her enthusiasm. "And of course they can't call on the likes of Ced Fisher to verify the paintings."

"No," agreed Godden, "they can't, as much as they'd like to. Fisher's program has been a game-changer for the legitimate art world, but for players in the shadowy world of high-value art forgery, it's not available."

"I should imagine the people on the forgery side wouldn't want their work to go anywhere near Ced," said Jennifer.

Godden smiled. "Of course not, no. But the potential buyers would love to. This is why use of Fisher's program is now very tightly controlled. In the early days, he could run it from his house, but that's all stopped following a few approaches made to him by some dodgy people. It has now been made public knowledge that the program is carefully protected, access to it requiring the presence and cooperation of at least three people."

Jennifer frowned. "Do you think Ced is in any kind of danger from his program. I mean, of someone kidnapping him, or worse, his family, and forcing him to write another copy."

Godden waited before answering, playing with his glass. Jennifer felt he was weighing up what he could tell her.

Finally he nodded, as if to give himself approval. "Yes," he said, "it is recognised as a potential problem, and although he was resistant to start with, he's now been persuaded to comply with the recommendations of the security people. When was the last time you saw the Fishers?"

"I went to their house a few times last year when I was hunting for information to clear Henry's name. I haven't been back since the injury, clearly, but I speak to Sally from time to time on the phone. She told me some time ago they were moving."

"That was one of the recommendations," said Godden. "Their new place is far easier to monitor. Before they moved in, it was gutted and fitted with some pretty hi-tech security. Beyond that, I'm not in the loop; it's none of the squad's business. But I do know, and this is certainly confidential, that Fisher has some interesting connections in the shadowy world of national security who look after him, so the threat to him and his family is contained. This includes watchers who apparently love the posting since they spend hours running or cycling when he or his wife are out doing the same, mostly without them knowing they are there. It's regarded as excellent training for them, so everyone wins."

Jennifer laughed. "He's a fitness fanatic; they both are, and I expect now Sally has had their second child, she's back in the routine as well. I've been trying to get them to come here, but Ced's always so busy."

"It would be the perfect place for them since your security is pretty top notch."

Godden finished his drink.

"Another one, Paul?" asked Jennifer.

"I'll wait until I've finished my little lecture, I think," said Godden. "Got to keep a clear head. Now, I've given you a very sketchy outline of the art sales and forgery world; there's a lot more in a paper I'll give you later. Makes fascinating bedtime reading."

"Can't wait," replied Jennifer, rubbing her hands together.

"OK," said Godden, "I know you're wondering what my unit gets up to and how we see you fitting in; what your role might be."

Jennifer waited, saying nothing.

"Well," continued Godden, "there are two sides to what we do. The first is the public one, the one that gets talked about, the one described on any documents or websites where we're mentioned. That side deals, among other things, with investigating any thefts or burglaries aimed at paintings, normally high-value ones. It's not a huge caseload, but given who some of the victims are, not all the cases are made public, so there's more to it than meets the eye. The investigations are nuts-and-bolts police work: information gathering exercises requiring legwork, interviews of victims and suspects, as they are for any crime, and in addition we use our extensive network of contacts — owners, dealers, galleries, both in the UK and elsewhere — to look for leads. Developing the types of relationships we need for this takes time, effort and maintenance, and much of my time and that of my chief inspectors is spent on the road keeping these people sweet."

"I can imagine it's a huge amount of work," said Jennifer.

"It is and we can only justify the man hours spent on it because of the importance of the victims we're dealing with. Most of them carry considerable clout and no government wants to be seen dragging its feet or skimping on supporting them. The bean counters hate us, but we carry on regardless of their acquisitive eyes gazing longingly at our budget.

"Fortunately, we've had some high-profile victims whose art we have managed to locate and return in very little time owing entirely to the intelligence networks we've set up. It shuts the finance people up every time."

Godden coughed and looked around. "Actually, Jennifer, if you don't mind, could I get a glass of soda water? All this talking is giving me a thirst."

"Stay where you are," said Jennifer, jumping to her feet. "I'll fetch some from the fridge behind the pool bar."

She returned with the drinks and waited while Godden took a large gulp from his glass.

"Thanks," he said. "Now, where was I? Yes. Our operations are in many ways no different from other crime investigations that rely on intelligence, and they come with the same problems. Take drug investigation units, for example. For some of their large, complex investigations, they will try to get an officer on the inside, gradually gaining the trust of the criminals as they try to work their way deeper and deeper into whatever organisation it is. Clearly this is dangerous work: if they are discovered, it could be fatal. Drugs-related criminals are particularly ruthless."

Jennifer was watching Godden carefully, wondering where he was going with this.

"The problem with that sort of work," he continued, "is you can't just take someone off operations and send him or her under-cover. The criminals aren't stupid; they have their own informants and they know who works where. It would be suicide for a young drugs squad officer to be in HQ operations one day and working undercover the next in the same area. For this reason, undercover officers are normally from elsewhere in the country on someone else's payroll; certainly never on the unit's they are reporting to. They remain invisible to checks, both legitimate and illegal."

His eyes caught Jennifer's as he watched her reaction. He knew her mind would be racing ahead. Was the thought of what he was about to say too daunting for her?

Jennifer held his eyes. "So this is the second part, is it?"

Godden nodded slowly, a wry smile at the corners of his mouth.

"Yes, it is. You see, Jennifer, there are many artists around the world who are extremely good at copying other people's work. Mostly they do it legitimately, that is, they don't even try to claim their paintings are originals. But the unscrupulous side of the art world is always on the lookout for such talent and whenever they find the rare man — and for some reason it nearly always is a man — who is so good his work is indistinguishable from the work he's copying, they will woo him with promises of wealth beyond his dreams. There's a cost, of course; there always is. It's essentially a pact with the devil and once in, there's no escape."

Jennifer was puzzled. "But what's the point of copying some famous old master? Surely there can only be one; you can't have two or even three on the market."

"Ah, but you can. You see it all depends who your buyer is and how greedy he is. And how gullible. Suppose a Caravaggio is stolen, a known one, but one from a private collection. There are plenty to choose from. Once it's stolen, our forger makes the perfect copy. The mastermind behind this then has two choices: he can either return the real painting to the original owner in some contrived circumstance or other, or he can return the fake. His decision will depend on the expertise of the original owner vis-à-vis the buyer. Let's suppose he returns the genuine painting to the original owner. His task now, as the consummate salesman, is to convince the buyer that *he's* the one buying the original while the fake has gone to the owner. If he's successful, the buyer will pay a fortune for it. The mastermind is confident about security since the buyer will only ever keep it for personal display, never admitting he's got it to anyone."

"Wow, sounds a risky undertaking. The forger will have to be good."

"Oh, not just good, he has to be brilliant, an old master five hundred years on."

"And these forgers exist in the UK?"

Godden pursed his lips and leaned his head slightly to one side.

"They do … yes …" he nodded, "but the particular investigation I'm setting up is not centred in the UK."

"Roma?" asked Jennifer, the Italian connection having now crystallised in her mind.

"Firenze," he replied.

Chapter Fifteen

"Diana, you poor dear. I'm so sorry. You must go immediately."

Connie had listened in alarm to Olivia's tale about her aged aunt's unfortunate death in Brussels, her eyes glistening with tears of sympathy. The only aunts she had were hard-as-nails, acquisitive Massachusetts elite, driving their husbands to early graves with their never-ending desire for more wealth. While Connie was as rich as any of them, she had nothing else in common with a single one. Hearing her friend's story about a zany relative for whom she clearly had great affection, she wanted to help as much as she could.

"Let me organise a jet for you," continued Connie, as she reached for her phone and started scrolling through her contacts. "It's the least I can do. You'll be there in three hours or so."

It was Olivia's turn to be alarmed. She wasn't going anywhere near Brussels but Connie couldn't know that. And she most certainly didn't want Connie making any associations between her and England.

She touched Connie's arm. "Thank you, that's the most generous … you really are …"

She let her voice break as she smiled at Connie with all the warmth she could muster. "If my dear aunt hadn't already passed away and I needed to get to her as fast as possible, I'd have jumped at your offer. But it's not so urgent that I have to get to Brussels by this evening. I can get a flight in the morning. I've checked the schedules; there are several every day from both Ciampino and Fiumicino."

"It's your decision, Diana, but if you change your mind, a jet can be arranged in no time at all."

"You're too kind, Connie. I don't know what I've done to deserve such a wonderful friend."

"Come," said Connie, holding out her arms. "Let me give you a hug. Cry on my shoulder if you wish."

Olivia didn't wish. Her eyes flashed in distaste as she looked down over Connie's shoulder while they embraced. This was the closest physical contact they'd had and she had to remind herself not to kill Connie there and then.

"Did you manage to get any sleep, Diana?" asked Connie the following morning at breakfast. "I'm sure I wouldn't have been able to in your position. You should have taken a pill."

"I don't like the things," replied Olivia. "I'd rather not sleep than be knocked out by some drug. But, yes, I think I did drop off eventually. It was all rather fitful though."

The truth was altogether different: she'd slept soundly and when she awoke at five, her thoughts had been entirely focussed on her plans.

"What time's your flight? I'll organise a car from the hotel," continued Connie.

A question asked innocently but one that could have had repercussions if Olivia hadn't already anticipated it and used her innate planning skills. She had chosen a flight to London that left within minutes of one of the Brussels flights. If Connie did by chance check the flight, there would be no time discrepancy to raise any flags.

"It's just after eleven," she replied, not wanting to specify the number of minutes past the hour.

She leaned forward. "Look, Connie, The last thing I want is to leave. I love what we have here and I so appreciate being, well, appreciated. It's not something I'm used to. I don't want the bubble to burst but I really have no choice. I spoke again to my aunt's lawyer last night after I went back to my room and he said he would try his best to get everything settled within two weeks, three at the absolute outside. It's ridiculous, I know, but you know what Brussels and bureaucracy are like."

Connie was dismayed but tried not to show it. She wasn't sure how she was going to manage without Diana for three weeks. "Would it help if I got my team of lawyers onto it? They're very efficient; they could work alongside your man."

Olivia shook her head. "Thank you, but he's an old timer. He's been my aunt's lawyer for ever. I think he'd feel extremely put out if I suggested something like that."

"All right, Diana," conceded Connie, "if that's what it takes, I'll have to live with it. However, please remember, if there's anything I can do to help, anything at all, just contact me."

Olivia reached out to touch Connie's arm. "Thank you, Connie, thank you so much."

"It's purely self-interest," said Connie, pulling a resigned face. "Whatever it takes to get you back quickly works for me."

Olivia knew she was taking an extra risk by flying to and from the UK. However, she had little choice: it would take far too long to make the 2600-mile round trip to Nottingham and back from Rome, even on her BMW. It was around twenty hours of driving each way and when she arrived she needed to be more than fresh; she needed to be at her very best.

Having sent the hotel car on its way, she walked into the terminal at Ciampino airport and headed for the washroom. In the privacy of a cubicle, she folded her now shoulder-length hair into a skullcap and put on a wig of lank, greasy dark brown hair she had prepared specifically for the trip. She was always thankful that her own hair was extremely fine; it made hiding it under wigs very straightforward.

Next she removed the brown, neutral prescription contact lenses she had always worn for Connie's benefit and replaced them with a dull blue pair, far darker than the pale grey-blue of her own pupils.

Following the lenses, a finely crafted gum shield pushed out her top lip and lifted her cheeks, making her chin appear to recede slightly. Lipstick she deliberately applied poorly and a patchy dusting of cheap powder completed the picture. Her features now strongly resembled the woman whose passport she was about to use, a passport she had stolen the day before from a carefully chosen British tourist at Rome's Spanish steps.

She had already checked in online so after leaving her bag at the self-service bag-drop, she headed for security. No problem there; she was carrying nothing remotely illegal or prohibited in her cabin bag.

The final and potentially most difficult hurdle was passport control. Here she was banking on the officer in the booth being bored as he checked the thousandth passport of the day. To help her cause, she stood in front of a far-more-attractive twenty-some-thing blonde in the passport queue. The officer behind the desk dismissed Olivia with a cursory glance, his attention fully on the blonde.

There would be a final check of her passport against her boarding pass at the gate, but the airline staff there were programmed simply to match name against name with only a cursory glance at the photo. It was simple psychology: if the passport and boarding pass names matched and the photo was similar enough, no doubt would raise itself in the checker's brain.

Leaving Italy on a stolen British passport was one thing; entering the UK was another. Olivia couldn't risk the probable greater scrutiny of her face against the photograph in the passport by the UK Border Police, and nor did she wish to risk the ePassport queue, even though the passport she'd stolen had the appropriate chip. But there was a simple solution. Italian nationals are required to carry an official ID card issued by the *comune* in which they live, and these cards can be used to travel anywhere within the EU: no passport is required.

Earlier that week, Olivia had positioned herself at an open-air bar in the Piazza Navona in central Rome and waited until an Italian woman of a similar age to her sat down nearby, hanging her open handbag on the back of her chair. While the woman distracted herself with texting on her phone, Olivia quietly changed tables, reached into the bag and removed the woman's ID card from her purse, the process taking no longer than the time to bend and retrieve the napkin she had deliberately dropped as a smokescreen.

Five minutes later, down a dark alley smelling strongly of garbage, Olivia had climbed a dingy flight of steps to knock quietly on a door, using a prearranged sequence of knocks. Inside, a young drug addict called Mario covered the cost of his habit by forging and counterfeiting ID cards. Olivia handed him the stolen card and a photo-booth shot of herself as Signorina Drab. The Italian ID card has far less built-in security than a state-of-the-art passport, and in a matter of minutes, Olivia's photo had been substituted for the original, the corner suitably embossed with a replica of the appropriate *comune* stamp.

With her new Italian ID in the name of Chiara Terzi, Olivia bought a second ticket for her flight, checked in online and printed out a second boarding pass. She wasn't sure if the UK Border Police would ask to see it or not, but she now had that covered, just in case. They certainly wouldn't know Signora Terzi was registered with the airline as a no-show.

In the event, the friendly-faced officer at the desk at Stansted airport simply looked at the ID card and asked her a question she pretended not to understand.

"Mi dispiace, ma—"

The officer held up a hand to stop what he assumed might become a long flow of excited Italian.

"I asked you how long are you staying in the UK, Ms Terzi," he repeated slowly with exaggerated patience.

She nodded as he spoke, as if processing and translating each word.

"Ah," she cried, pushing her hair behind her ear and smiling, "Due, er, two-a weeks-a."

"Enjoy your stay," he said, handing back the ID card.

Chapter Sixteen

Paul Godden completed the hundred lengths he had set himself, the pace leisurely compared with his normal training session in the cooler, over-chlorinated pool near his office in Canary Wharf. As he towelled himself down, he gazed out over the Tyrrhenian Sea thinking life as a British bobby wasn't all bad.

He had spent the previous evening sitting with Jennifer at an outside dining table explaining the details of the joint operation he was setting up with his opposite number in the Polizia in Rome.

"Massimo Felice is a delightful man, as you might expect a cultured Italian with a love of art to be, even if he is a copper," he said, a twinkle in his eye as he glanced across the table at her.

Martina, the resident cook, had served them one of her signature dishes — coda di rospo alla catanese: breadcrumbed monkfish on a bed of fresh broad beans that reflected her Sicilian ancestry — and Godden, who had decided he'd died and gone to heaven, was now sipping a grappa from one of Pietro Fabrelli's vineyards in the Veneto region of northern Italy.

"Our paths have crossed before in a couple of cases, but this one promises to be rather more complex. It started with a call from Sir Brian Gounder, the self-made squillionaire who thinks that because he's fed a fortune back into the country's coffers the entire British government is at his beck and call, along, of course, with the police, the crown prosecution service, et boring cetera."

"I've heard of him," said Jennifer. "Something of an—"

"Obnoxious little upstart with an ego the size of his bank balance?" suggested Godden.

"That's the one."

"His latest passion is art and, having bought a few daubs, liked them and then got serious about collecting, he now regards himself as an art buff. Fortunately for him, he has a couple of good advisors because otherwise he'd be at risk of squandering millions on junk."

"I'm on the side of the junk," said Jennifer.

"Me too," agreed Godden. "At some point, Sir Brian got into Renaissance art, wanting to buy it wholesale. The idiot was seriously miffed when the Italian government told him he couldn't buy frescos and ship them and the walls they were on to his Northamptonshire estate."

"Arrogant sod," said Jennifer.

Godden smiled. "I'm pleased we're of the same opinion. Anyway, undeterred, he sought out galleries in Italy that specialise in the lesser-known fifteenth- and sixteenth-century artists. With an eye for business, Gounder reckons they will be famous one day and when they are, he'll hit yet another jackpot as museums and foundations beat a path to his door."

Jennifer's laugh was scornful. "Hasn't it occurred to him that if they haven't jumped the big league barrier in five hundred years, it might be a while before they do, if ever?"

"Maybe he's planning to live for a thousand years," replied Godden.

He paused to take another sip of his grappa.

"All went well until he discovered a gallery in Florence well known for acquiring rare and sought-after paintings, and selling them on at outrageous prices. They smoothed the way to Gounder's cheque book by discounting a couple of small portraits, one of which is an exquisite Giovanni di Luca. I was very jealous when I saw it and rather outraged it should be in the hands of someone like Gounder. Do you know his work?"

"Di Luca?" said Jennifer. "Yes, a little. Venetian with a style remarkably similar to Tommaso Perini's."

"I agree," nodded Godden, "especially considering they never met and are unlikely to have seen each other's work."

"Now, what was interesting about the two small portraits was they came with a revolutionary new security tagging technique embedded into the fabric of the canvas, something the gallery developed and patented. The components are sub-microscopic in size, completely invisible to the naked eye and once they are there, impossible to remove. There are thousands of them forming an array that can interact remotely with a detection device that transmits to them. The components in the painting are passive, requiring no power, so there are no batteries to worry about or heat generated by the electronic systems."

Jennifer shook her head in disapproval. "Surely that wouldn't be acceptable for major works. It would be regarded as altering the nature of the painting, potentially compromising it if something unexpected happened to the micro-components in the future. I don't know, leakage, perhaps?"

"Yes, you're right," agreed Godden. "Museums and foundations with priceless works wouldn't touch it, but concerned private collectors think differently. They want to ensure that if there's any attempt at theft of their collection, it's nipped in the bud. And if for some reason a painting is somehow stolen, they want to be sure it can be located wherever it is in the world."

"Impressive," said Jennifer, puckering her lips in reluctant approval.

"Yes, and it might well be the genuine article. But we also think it's the lead for a con."

"Really?"

"Yes. What happened was Gounder was so impressed with his new acquisitions, the theft-proof paintings he'd bought for a song, that he wanted the system for his other far-more-valuable works. Which was exactly what he was supposed to want. The gallery owners of course reluctantly explained that the technique was so sensitive and complicated to apply, it could only be undertaken in their specialist laboratory in their gallery in Florence, the process of inserting the micro-components taking three months for each painting, although they could do several at once."

"I think I see where you're going," said Jennifer, a sparkle in her eyes.

"Yes, during the three months while they were hidden from view in the gallery's laboratory, the paintings were copied by one or more master forgers who could in that time fabricate everything about the painting, all imperfections in the canvas, wear and tear, the lot. The painting itself is the easy part."

"What did they send back to Gounder? A pile of fakes?"

"Oh no, they're too clever for that. He entrusted them with five masterpieces with a total value of around two million pounds, and when the paintings came back, they all passed his scrutiny. It was only when one of his advisors took a careful look that any doubt was raised, and then only about one of them. There was something about it, although he couldn't put his finger on it."

"That good, eh?"

"Yes. Anyhow, Gounder pulled some strings and got Ced Fisher to check the paintings with his magic program. Four duly passed the test, but the fifth, the one his advisor had questioned, a painting by an obscure but sought-after Neapolitan artist that's worth nearly half a million, was a fake. A brilliant one, according to Fisher, but nevertheless a fake."

"What did Gounder do?"

"He hit the gallery with it, who were outraged. They said if it was a fake, it must have been all along and to prove it, they produced a set of photographs taken in Gounder's presence of the paintings before they were shipped from his house to Florence. They were digital images, so the metadata had effectively date-stamped them, and they insisted Fisher examine them. He did, under protest — Ced Fisher doesn't like being ordered around — and lo and behold, the photos showed the painting was a fake all along."

Jennifer shrugged her scepticism. "Metadata can be altered, as Ced will tell you, even the stuff that's supposed to be carved in the original stone of the image. Didn't Gounder have any photos of his own?"

"He did, but the ones of the questioned painting had disappeared. Somehow, someone in the gallery must have arranged it."

"Really? Presumably they must have planted someone in Gounder's organisation."

"That's the assumption, yes," nodded Godden, "but we don't know for sure."

"Who did he buy the paintings from? Surely they were certificated."

"They were and they came from a very reputable source. Unfortunately the expert certifying them is now dead and the photos in the records he left behind are all rather poor quality film shots."

"How convenient. What does Gounder want you to do now?"

Godden laughed. "I think what he wants is for Britain to declare war on Italy. What he actually got from us was a helpless shrug. But then we got a similar report from another collector, a far nicer man who lives in the wilds of Scotland. He's only had one painting security tagged by the gallery, and it's the same story. He was suspicious but not certain. Ced has been called in and certified the fake, but it's a fake from a different hand, so there's no connection with Gounder's fake, and again, the gallery produced its own photographic record taken before the painting was shipped to Florence. And, surprise, surprise, there are no previous digital photographs."

"Does Gounder know about the other case?"

"Heavens, no, he'd be screaming at everyone from the PM downwards. But two cases did give me enough to think about contacting Massimo Felice. Now, what Massimo had to say was most interesting. It seems he has long been suspicious of the gallery — it's called the Galleria Cambroni and is run by a father and son, Maurizio and Ettore — but every time he's tried to mount an operation, he has been told to back off by his superiors. It would appear that the Cambronis are extremely well connected, all the way to the top."

Jennifer was shocked. "Scandalous. Who can you trust if you can't trust your own organisation?"

Godden nodded. "Yes, Massimo muttered darkly about mafia connections as well as political ones. What he wants to do is get someone on the inside, but without his bosses knowing."

Jennifer snorted a laugh. "Huh! You threw that one in very subtly. Presumably you want that someone to be me?"

"That's the idea, Jennifer, yes. When I told Massimo I had an officer who could pass for an Italian and who was an art expert, he was positively salivating. You see, he has no one in his squad he could use who might not be recognised. As he put it, you never know when his director might pay a visit to the gallery to be shown a nicely discounted painting he might just want to buy. The director would be horrified and very embarrassed to find one of his own officers greeting him at the door."

"Embarrassed! Jeez!" Jennifer let out a bark of derision. Then she grinned. "When do I start?"

Godden wanted to hug her, but he masked his delight by reaching for his grappa and taking another sip. "Well, there's quite a bit to put into place, not the least of which is getting you employed there."

Jennifer was puzzled. "Is your Ispettore Felice happy to go ahead on your say so, I mean, that I can pass muster?"

"Very astute of you, Jennifer. No, he quite reasonably wants to talk to you. He's waiting for a call from me so he can confirm a flight tomorrow morning. Is it all right if he comes for lunch? I thought perhaps you could meet him at the airport, get all the chit chat sorted out in the car on the way back."

Godden was considering following up his swim in the pool with a sea swim in the tempting waters lapping onto the Fabrelli beach when he heard voices from the house.

"Paul!" called Jennifer, "We're back."

Godden looked around to see Jennifer showing Massimo Felice onto the terrace that led to the pool. Felice was exactly as Jennifer had expected from Godden's brief description: a little under six feet tall, early forties, immaculately cut hair with a hint of grey peppering the otherwise jet black curls and a lightweight pale grey suit that hung perfectly over his slim frame. Only his dark, brooding eyes hinted at something beyond his urbane outward appearance.

"Paul," said Felice as he strode over to where Godden was standing, his arms outstretched. "How delightful to see you. You look as if you've made yourself at home."

"I could get used to it, Massimo," said Godden as he accepted Felice's kisses on both cheeks. "How was your flight?"

Felice shrugged. "A bus ride; forty-five minutes from Roma, followed by an hour of delightful conversation with Ginevra." He grinned enthusiastically as he dropped his voice, his tone conspiratorial. "Paul, you have made me a very happy man. She is perfect!"

He half turned in time to see Jennifer eyeing him suspiciously.

"Ginevra?" asked Godden.

Felice smiled. "Ginevra Mancini. It will be Ms Cotton's new name; the papers are almost ready. I thought I should use it from the outset so it becomes natural to me."

"Mancini," repeated Godden. "That's a pretty common Italian surname, isn't it?"

Felice waggled his head. "Relatively, yes. But there's no such thing as a really common Italian surname. Even for Rossi, which is the same as your Smith or Jones, there are only a few tens of thousands. But yes, you are right; Mancini is relatively common. We chose it deliberately to make the outcome of any searches by the Cambronis ambiguous."

Jennifer guided them to the table under the pergola. "I'll check with Martina on how lunch is coming along," she said. "Can I get either of you anything? Massimo, an aperitivo?"

Felice sat back and smiled. "So, Ginevra, you speak some English. It sounds good; I think you could almost pass for an Englishwoman!" He turned to Godden, his face now serious. "I must admit, Paul, I was a little nervous about meeting Ginevra, despite knowing her background. You see, like most Italian men, I have a very good ear for accents; it's a game we like to play."

"And?" asked Godden.

Felice sighed and shook his head theatrically, his shoulders shrugging automatically. "What can I say? Ginevra's Italian is better than mine. It has an undercurrent of Milanese, which is to be expected and which we've written into her story, but I would defy anyone not to consider her a native Italian."

He turned his attention to Jennifer, his eyes amused. "What I want to hear more of is your English accent, Ginevra. I'm sure it must have an Italian edge, like mine."

Jennifer put her hands on her hips and eyeballed both men, lapsing into the Nottinghamshire accent she'd learned and used as a police constable in Newark to help her blend in.

"I don't know what you're talking about, Signor Felice, I'm a Nottingham girl, born and bred. And if you two don't make up your minds about what you want to drink, I'll be supping on me own. Now, what's it to be?"

Paul grinned as Felice clapped in delight. "Brava! OK, I'm convinced. Now, you mentioned a Moscato Bianco in the car …"

They lingered over lunch until four. Felice's return flight wasn't until seven that evening, while Godden's to London left half an hour earlier. Talk over lunch was mainly business, although both the policeman and the Italian in Felice wanted to know as much as possible about the villa and Pietro Fabrelli. Jennifer was used to this; she had grown up with it, and she had a set of standard answers that appeared to be comprehensive but in fact revealed only what she wanted to reveal.

Now Jennifer had a clean bill of health, both Godden and Felice were keen to move forward with their plans. Felice explained that Jennifer's new identity papers and all that went with them would be ready by the middle of October, by which time he hoped to have made progress on creating a vacancy for her in the gallery. From his own point of view, Godden wanted Jennifer to undergo some specialist training in basic fieldcraft for officers working undercover and a refresher course in unarmed combat. He esti- mated about a month would be needed to complete everything so

November was agreed upon as a probable starting date, assuming the vacancy in the gallery could be created by then.

Once they had finished discussing business, they all sat back, the men wanting to savour the atmosphere before they left.

"It's a pity you both have to go so soon," said Jennifer, pouring everyone another glass of the chilled Moscato Bianco from one of Pietro's lovingly maintained vineyards, this one on Sardinia's west coast.

"It is." Godden's sigh echoed his regret as he held up his glass to study the wine. "I know Moscato isn't unique to Sardinia, but this vintage is spectacular, don't you agree Massimo?"

"Divine," was all Felice had to say as he savoured the wine.

"You must come again, Paul, bring your wife. You too, Massimo. I'm sorry, I forgot to ask. Are you married?"

Felice's wan smile spoke of the many pressures on him.

"I am, in fact effectively I have three wives."

Jennifer raised her eyebrows, thoughts of multiple divorce flitting through her mind.

"Yes," nodded Felice, his face still radiating subjugation. "Stella, my actual wife, and two control-freak teenage daughters. It's like having three wives."

"Well, next time you both come, you must bring as many wives as you like," laughed Jennifer. "And I'll make sure that Pietro's here. There's nothing he likes more than showing off his wines."

"And there's nothing I'd like more than to sample them," said Godden.

As she waved them off, Jennifer thought about the compliments they had both paid her. She was delighted how positive Felice had been, not only about her language skills but also about her art knowledge — much of the discussion in the car had been about their shared passion for Italian art of all periods. And she was equally thrilled to have Godden's confidence, his faith in her abilities. However, before she got underway with her new role, there were three further hurdles she had to overcome, and the first was arriving the following morning.

Chapter Seventeen

Staying disguised as Chiara Terzi, Olivia took the regular bus to central London and a train to Ashford, in Kent. A ten-minute taxi ride to the small village of Capston-Sur-Marsh left her with a half-mile walk to the caravan site, using a public footpath through farmers' fields rather than the main road.

As she approached the site, she scanned for anything among the vans or near the gaudily painted cabin serving as office and home for Kevin, the site's owner, to indicate a police presence. The image from the caravan's webcam on her phone showed nothing unusual, but just in case, she had also put a low-tech back-up in place. Pulling a pair of binoculars from her bag, she focussed on the curtains on two of the caravan's windows. She had added roller blinds to both windows, their cords attached with thin cotton thread that she trapped in the door jamb as she closed the door to leave. If anyone entered the van, the cotton would be freed and the blinds unroll a few inches — not enough for an intruder to hear or notice, but enough for Olivia to know someone had been there.

Confident that the van had not been disturbed, she walked closer, constantly watching for anything that would constitute suspicious activity.

An inspection of the heavy-duty padlock on the caravan door revealed no sign of tampering, and once she was inside and had double-checked all the security she had put in place, she was satisfied. Her refuge had not been compromised.

She removed the Terzi disguise and replaced it with one she used when at the caravan site: faded jeans, a black vest and well-worn denim jacket, a pair of fake studs to the side of her nose and tattoo transfers to the left side of her neck and her left forearm. This was followed by a wig of short bleached hair, a black baseball cap and several clunky rings on the fingers of both hands along with a number of equally clunky bracelets on both wrists. She needed to look the part for Kevin since, although bone idle and stupid, he would eventually notice her van was now occupied.

"'allo Sadie, didn't 'ear yer bike."

Kevin was slouched in a battered office chair behind the table that served as a reception desk watching a programme on an ancient portable TV that seemed to be picking up mainly static.

"Didn't come on it, did I," replied Olivia in her best Eastenders accent as she carefully studied the overweight fifty-year-old's face for any sign of caution or guilt.

"In the shop, innit," she continued. "Had to come on the bleedin' train. Come to fetch me uvver bike."

"Bugger," nodded Kevin sympathetically as he reached out to thump the top of the television set. "Wot's up wiv it?"

"Gearbox."

"Shit."

"Yeah."

She smiled to herself. Kevin was running out of conversation. He seldom said much to her on the rare occasions she showed up at the site: she was taller by five inches and her whole presence intimidated him. It was the combination of the mirror sunglasses she always wore — he had no idea what her eyes were like; he'd never seen them — and the fact that five years previously when she'd arrived at the site and bought the caravan with a wad of cash, she'd informed him in clear, plain language what his fate would be if ever anyone went near her van, including him. He understood — Sadie Smith wasn't the only dodgy owner at the site, most of them were a bunch of criminals in his opinion, but at least the others were friendly enough. Sadie wasn't, not by any stretch of Kevin's limited imagination.

"Everyfin' been all right 'ere?" asked Olivia, still watching him keenly.

Kevin's eyes stared into her sunglasses, wondering if it was a trick question.

"Yeah," he said, finally, his brow furrowing. "Everyfin's good."

"I'll be in and out for the next few days," said Olivia. "Got some business to attend to. Anyone else around at the moment?" She waved her arm in the general direction of the thirty vans parked at the site.

Kevin shrugged. "Just the usuals, keeping themselves to themselves. Hardly see 'em." He scratched his face, as if trying to remember something. "Oh yeah. 'Arry was down 'ere coupla weeks ago wiv some black tart. Noisy bitch, she was. But they had a big fight and he slung 'er out. Buggered off himself the next day."

Olivia had no idea who Harry was, but he didn't seem to be a problem, and from Kevin's demeanour, she was confident her caravan remained undiscovered. She left him to the ghostly static on his TV and went to check out the Kawasaki locked up in the small shed next to her caravan.

Although she was pleased to find the motorcycle hadn't suffered in the months since she'd stowed it in the shed, in reality, Olivia expected nothing less. It was a sealed, dry space and her pre-storage maintenance had been comprehensive.

She spent the evening reviewing her programme for the next day. She would head for West Bridgford, just across the river Trent from the City of Nottingham, and drive past the flat to check for any signs of activity. Depending on how things looked, she'd make a decision on whether or not to go in. If she felt in any way suspicious, she'd have to find an alternative base in the area. Since she wanted to spend several days there before she rolled out her disposal schedule; a reliable command post was essential.

. . .

Olivia left the caravan site at five thirty the following morning. Although keen to get to Nottingham, there was a task she had to complete first which involved a wide detour and a long day's drive that wouldn't see her at her final destination until early evening.

Steeling herself for eleven hours astride the Kawasaki, much of the journey on motorways, she headed for the M20, turning west towards the M25 to skirt London, from where she followed the M3 until it branched towards Winchester. From there good quality A roads took her all the way to Penzance in Cornwall.

A few miles short of Penzance, Olivia pulled off the main road onto a quiet rural lane with no traffic. At a bend on a rise where she had a good view of any approaching vehicles she stopped the motorcycle, put it on its stand and climbed off to stretch, working her stiff back and neck to ease the tightness in her muscles.

The Kawasaki had two metal panniers, one of which she opened to retrieve a toolkit and a set of fake French number plates. She worked fast in case any traffic appeared, and within a minute she had exchanged the bike's German plates for the French ones. In the other pannier were a red crash helmet and a set of black motorcycling leathers with distinctive pale blue flashes on the arms and legs. She put them on, stowing the white helmet and dull black leathers she had been wearing in the pannier.

Feeling fresh in the new gear, Olivia jumped back on her bike and headed for a café she had passed earlier. There she had lunch and some much needed coffee, after which she hit the road again for the second part of her long journey.

Rush hour traffic with extra speed restrictions on the M5 and M6 near Birmingham slowed Olivia's progress, and it wasn't until eight in the evening that she finally approached the outskirts of Nottingham. Arriving from the south–west, the road took her into the suburb of West Bridgford she was so anxious to visit.

She was tired and sore after so many hours on the road. She longed for a hot shower or better, a soak in a steaming bath, although she doubted the hotel she'd booked ran to baths. But first she couldn't resist taking a look at the lock-up garage and flat that were the first focus of her trip.

Her drive along Rampton Street, the short, uninspiring road

where her flat and lock-up were located, told her only that there appeared to be no activity around the premises, no lights on either in her flat or the ones nearby. The place looked no different from when she had last seen it a year previously.

She turned at the end of the road and looked back down the street, checking every one of the hundred yards ahead of her for cameras on lamp posts, cameras on buildings innocently pointed in the direction of her lock-up or at the windows of her flat, cameras on rooftops. There was nothing.

This was good, encouraging, but was it real? After all, the webcam had failed. She had to get closer, preferably go inside, but for that, she needed to be fresh and not in her motorcycle gear.

She took a deep breath as she stretched, satisfied for now, gunned her Kawasaki and headed for the hotel. When she opened the door to her room and found the bathroom did indeed have a bath, she felt it was a good omen.

As she lay luxuriating in the steaming water, the heat melting the tiredness and stiffness out of her aching body, her mind was still working hard, plotting the next twenty-four hours. Or at least the sixteen hours that would follow the eight hours of sleep she was looking forward to after her bath.

Chapter Eighteen

"Tesoro, this is madness. Total madness. You can't possibly be serious. It's far too dangerous. These are bad men, tesoro, bad men."

Pietro Fabrelli was pacing the floor while gazing imploringly through the massive windows of the villa's huge living room, trying to abstract inspiration from the panoramic view of the Tyrrhenian Sea. Jennifer sat on a large sofa watching him and waiting for the first wave of resistance to pass. She knew he'd come round, as she knew Henry would, and Derek, but Pietro in particular would find it necessary to explore all avenues of potential rejection.

Once Paul Godden had explained his plans for her, Jennifer knew the matter of who could be in the know would be an issue. She had therefore raised it with him immediately, knowing he would resist, and knowing it would be better if he understood her position before heading for his room to sleep on it. He had slept on it, after tossing and turning on it and chewing on it so much his mouth screwed up with the bitter taste. But by the time he emerged for breakfast, he was far more accepting of the situation Jennifer had presented to him.

His first objections had been predictable and understandable.

"This is an undercover operation, Jennifer. You're going to be assuming a different identity, you're going to be Italian, not English; you won't be able to take calls from friends."

Jennifer laughed. "I understand that, Paul, and my friends won't have my number. My friends can be told I'm doing something else entirely, that I'm somewhere else entirely, so my disappearing for a long period of time won't appear odd. But there are certain people, three to be precise, whom I can't fob off with some story to explain why I can't contact them. I simply can't. They won't accept it; they are too much a part of my life. And anyway, I think at least two of them could be useful to the whole scheme."

"How do you figure that?" asked Godden, his tone sceptical. He didn't want outsiders involved, untrained people who weren't police. The whole operation was precarious enough as it was.

"Well," replied Jennifer, trying to keep her voice light, "We need somewhere in Florence for the team monitoring things to stay. Somewhere convenient and comfortable that's in no way connected to either the Italian police or to us. Pietro has such an apartment only ten minutes' walk from the gallery. I'm sure Massimo Felice would appreciate it too, given the problems he's had in the past and given he wants to keep my operation quiet. The apartment's big, comfortable and almost never used. It's not registered in Pietro's name, of course, nor connected to him on paper — all part of dealing with the extortionate Italian taxes, you understand." She held out her arms, her palms upwards and gave an Italian shrug. "This is Italy."

Godden snorted. "You're a police officer, Jennifer, how can you condone tax evasion?"

"It's not evasion; it's perfectly legal. It's simply playing a system so staggeringly complex no one truly understands it, not even the tax man."

She knew how he felt. No foreigner could understand the Italian fixation with taxes and how to avoid them. It was played at all levels of society from the poorest to the richest, and while the system continued to be perceived as punitive instead of constructive, nothing would change.

"The point is, Paul, the apartment's unattributable, anonymous, and there are dozens of good routes I can take to it to ensure

I'm not followed. And I can assure you Pietro won't get in the way. I'll tell him exactly what he can and can't do, the most important of which is to keep away. He'll understand. And he also has good connections in Florence, as he does in every Italian city."

"That's what worries me." Paul was still unconvinced.

Later, as his resistance to Pietro thawed, he asked, "OK, I'm beginning to see why you can't exclude Pietro, but why does Henry Silk need to be in the loop?"

"You mean apart from the fact he's my father, that he calls me almost every day and that he put his career on hold while I got over the worst of my injuries despite having been offered the best parts ever?"

"He's a famous actor, Jennifer. You can't have him sashaying around Florence with you, drinking espresso or aperitivi or what-ever, he'd be recognised instantly and your cover would be blown."

It was Jennifer's turn to snort. "Henry Silk is a master of disguise. Haven't you seen any of his stuff? I can assure you that if he took to sashaying around Florence, firstly, I wouldn't be with him, and secondly he could walk right up to you and you wouldn't recognise him."

"So how do you see him being involved?"

"I don't. I don't want him involved and I'll tell him so. It's not necessary. But I can't just disappear from his radar. I know Henry; he's like me. He would regard finding me as a challenge."

"Even if you told him it could endanger you, that he should keep his distance?"

"Yes, I can tell him that, but I'd have to tell him why. Don't you understand? He would have to know I was safe. It needn't amount to more than a brief, coded text every few days."

"You're a grown woman, Jennifer, a police officer going under cover in a protracted and potentially dangerous operation. You don't need parental interference."

"There won't be any, I can assure you. But Henry's still angry with himself over the Freneton case. He knows she's still a threat and he feels he could have done more."

"He was in prison; how could he have done more?"

"I don't know. He couldn't. He just thinks he could. And now he's not in prison, he certainly won't accept my being out of touch while Freneton's still at large." She paused to take a sip of water.

"Look, Paul," she continued, "I know you can simply order me not to tell Pietro or Henry or Derek anything. I'm just trying to explain that that could be more dangerous, more likely to compromise the operation than if they were told something. If I lay down the ground rules, they'll follow them. I just need to toss them a crumb. Surely this situation must occur in other undercover operations."

Godden shook his head. "Actually, it's not normally much of an issue. Officers going under cover tend to be single, unattached and with average backgrounds. They can disappear off the radar quite easily and keep any concerned parents at bay with the odd phone call where they just say how great everything is, how busy they are, and so on. You're unusual in the scheme of things in that your background is, frankly, privileged and you have concerned parents who, as a result of what happened to you, need constant reassurance about you. Under normal circumstances you wouldn't be a good choice, but you have special talents that are very hard to find. You're a one-off, Jennifer, especially as you're willing to take on the task."

Jennifer took a deep breath; she knew she had won. "I'm more than willing, Paul. It's a very exciting challenge. I really want to be part of it."

———

Pietro had stopped pacing. He turned to face Jennifer, his back to the view, the source of hoped-for inspiration that had failed him.

"Tell me once again, tesoro. Explain it in simple terms I can understand, per piacere. I am just a simple fashion designer; I make pretty dresses for pretty ladies, I don't understand all your complicated police intrigue."

Jennifer found it hard to avoid smiling. Pietro was anything but simple: he was a highly articulate businessman with a razor sharp mind. Nothing and no one in his world deceived Pietro, which was why he was so successful and why he had to know what she was up to. Apart from that, with his connections and understanding of the darker side of Italian business, he would be able to put a slant on it that Godden, as a foreigner, wouldn't come close to appreciating. She had seen Pietro's soft-soap oh-so-humble approach many times before and seen his charm carry it off. To her, it was ridiculously transparent, but all part of the theatre.

"Sit down here next to me," she said, reaching out for his hand and patting the sofa. "Your pacing is making me dizzy."

Pietro obeyed, allowing his face to crumple like a disobedient puppy that has just been told off.

"It's very straightforward," started Jennifer, and summarised the background of the need for the operation, although she held back on the location of the gallery. When she reached the part about the creation of the forgeries taking three months, Pietro queried it.

"That doesn't seem a great deal of time to recreate a master-piece, tesoro. Some of these paintings took years to complete."

Jennifer laughed. "We're not talking about the ceiling of the Sistine Chapel, Pietro, we're talking about relatively small paint-ings. However, I know what you mean: Godden was sceptical too, so he contacted a painter in the Lake District who apparently is as good as it gets when painting in the style of the old masters, a man called John Andrews. Andrews reckons it would take him around three to four months to knock up a copy of a Renaissance-period painting that was a convincing fake. He's bona fide, by the way, beyond reproach, apparently."

Pietro nodded. "I know his work; it's brilliant. In fact, I have one of his portraits. Don't you remember it? It's of a little girl, his daughter I think. It's stunning, breathtaking."

"Of course, the one in the formal dining room in the Milan apartment," said Jennifer. "I didn't make the connection."

"Well, it's modern, tesoro," teased Pietro, "so you don't tend to take so much notice."

Poking her tongue out at him, she continued, telling him about the embedded security created by the gallery.

Pietro was shaking his head. "Beyond my simple brain, tesoro," he said, pulling a face.

Pants on fire, thought Jennifer.

"There's something else you haven't covered," said Pietro once Jennifer had finished. "You say you think the gallery produced a fake of the painting from the Sir Gounder person. I've met him, you know, hideous little man. What are they doing with the original? And what about the copies they will have made of Gounder's other four paintings?"

"There's been no suggestion they did that," replied Jennifer, surprised by his remark.

Pietro laughed. "Listen, tesoro, these men are businessmen. Crooked ones, but businessmen just the same. They have an opportunity to maximise their profits, so why not take it. They have a market somewhere, people who think they are buying originals. China, I suspect, where they know little about art."

"Pietro!"

He looked somewhat shamefaced but defended himself by saying, "European art, I mean, it's outside of their culture, the same as understanding their art is hard for us."

"I'm surprised at you," Jennifer continued to scold.

Pietro ignored her. "What I was going to say is they probably make copies of everything, return some originals to the owners and some fakes. And those they sell on to China or wherever it is, they claim are originals. They are playing both ends off against the middle."

"I agree," said Jennifer, impressed by his assessment. For Pietro, it was a foregone conclusion that the fraudsters would explore every possibility.

"So," said Pietro, getting up from the sofa again — he could seldom sit still for long, "that's the scam, and the British police want you to go and work under cover in the gallery, according to what you told me earlier. Why you in particular? That part you haven't told me yet."

Jennifer pulled a face.

"OK," she said, dropping her voice and looking around. "This part is … sensitive."

Pietro smiled. "It's all right, tesoro, there's no one else here, not in the house anyway. I sent them all away."

"I'm sure you've actually guessed already, Pietro, but if you want me to spell it out, the fraudsters are not in England, they are here in Italy, on the mainland, that is. Their operation uses a very prestigious gallery as a front and it's assumed they have a number of master forgers there or nearby who are turning out the paintings."

Pietro pursed his lips. "I see. They've chosen you because you can pass as an Italian. Where is this gallery? Roma? Firenze? I know many of the galleries in this country since, as you know, I have bought a number of quite expensive paintings myself. I also know the gallery owners, some better than others. Most I should say are entirely honourable men; others … well, I can think of three galleries I wouldn't trust and would certainly never buy a painting from now. So, enlighten me, tesoro."

"Firenze."

Pietro raised his eyebrows and sighed in a way that said he now knew everything.

"Cambroni," he said, shrugging his shoulders, "it has to be. They are the only gallery of any note in Firenze I wouldn't trust. Father and son business. Maurizio, the father, is old now, around seventy. I bought a painting from him about forty years ago, but there was something I didn't like about him even then, and of course, one hears things. And his son, Ettore, I wouldn't trust an inch."

He looked at his stepdaughter in satisfaction. "Am I right?"

"Yes," she laughed, "spot on."

Pietro wasn't laughing. "As I told you earlier when I thought the gallery was in London, these will be bad men; it will be dangerous. And now I know it's in Italy, my concern is even greater. They will have connections, if you know what I mean. I am not happy about this."

Chapter Nineteen

Fully refreshed after an undisturbed eight-hour sleep, Olivia jogged from the hotel near the river Trent, making her way along the river bank to Trent Bridge. Here she crossed the river and headed into West Bridgford.

Her running clothes made her as anonymous as any other jogger: black leggings, dark blue running shoes, a zip-up, tightly fitting dark blue lycra jacket over a sleeveless black top and a slightly oversized dark blue baseball cap with a false chestnut pony-tail falling through the gap in the back. Wrap-around dark glasses and earbuds trailing to a mobile phone strapped to her left upper arm completed the image. Attractive, fit and forgettable.

After passing Trent Bridge Cricket Ground, she left the main road and the morning rush-hour traffic to make her way to Rampton Street. Stopping opposite the entrance door to the flat alongside the large garage doors of her lock-up, she ran on the spot as she pretended to adjust her phone. The street was quiet: no traffic, no pedestrians, no other joggers. Glancing to both ends of the street, she jogged over to the entrance door and pressed the buzzer. She could hear it sounding at the top of the stairs, but there was no follow-up sound of footsteps, just a rapidly fading echo. She pressed the buzzer again as she scanned the street, taking particular note of the buildings opposite. There was nothing. She removed a key from her jacket pocket and quickly let herself in.

She closed the door behind her, her senses on high alert. There was no webcam at street level, but her eyes searched every inch of the wall and ceiling for any changes. She tried the handle of the internal door to the garage. Locked, as she had left it a year ago. A good sign. Unlocking it, she slipped into the garage, standing in the entrance to allow her eyes to adjust to the gloom.

Before switching on the overhead light, she pulled her phone from her sleeve and turned on its torch, moving the beam around the walls and ceiling and large white van. Nothing had changed so she flicked the light switch, which was when she noticed the first sign of disturbance. The cables leading from the van's battery to the trickle charger she had left attached had moved. She had arranged them in a characteristic configuration as they ran from the van across the floor and up to the charger. They no longer followed the same path.

Her senses now tingling, she carefully opened the van's passenger door and peered inside. At first sight, nothing appeared to be out of order, but when she focussed the torch beam onto the steering wheel, letting it glance along the surface, she could see smears in the dust. The wheel had been wiped, swabbed probably. A forensic team had been here. There were more signs of swabbing on the handbrake and the floor, all places she knew there would probably have been traces of blood. Her blood, and therefore her DNA. And even if the traces were not blood, they would have found her DNA from her smeared fingerprints left when she had driven the van without wearing gloves.

Turning to the pocket in the passenger door, she removed the four maps she had carefully placed there the previous year. Road maps of Devon and Cornwall, Somerset, South Wales and Southern Ireland, the Somerset map folded very specifically and reversed in the stack from the others, its front cover facing onto the front cover of the South Wales map. At least that was how she had left them; but they were no longer arranged in the same way. It was quite clear the maps had been removed, opened and examined before being returned to the door pocket.

She nodded, smiling grimly. Her hideaway had been discovered and searched. It was compromised; she shouldn't stay long. But how thorough had the search been? Had her hidden stocks been found?

She closed the van door, locked the internal door to the garage and headed up the stairs to the flat above the lock-up.

The first items to look at, in case she was now broadcasting her presence to a watcher, were the modem and the webcam. There were no lights working on the modem, even though it was still plugged in and switched on. She sniffed at it, immediately registering a smell of char. It had burnt out: the report of lightning strikes had been accurate. So how come the premises had been searched? Coincidence? Who had found it?

As if in answer, the sound of a key in the lock of the main entrance at the bottom of the stairs cut through the silence. She instantly moved to stand behind the bedroom door. She was thankful she'd had the foresight to switch off the garage light and to close and lock the door. Whoever was entering the flat would have no advance warning of her presence.

She heard the intruder try the handle of the internal garage door. Smart. Cautious. Then the more confident sound of footsteps on the stairs. Just one set, and no conversation. Whoever it was, they were alone.

Olivia readied herself for dealing with the intruder. The flat had been discovered; it was probably a patrol or someone from the SCF. How ironic if it turned out to be Bottomley or Thyme. Whoever it was, she was already adjusting her schedule, knowing immediately she would no longer have the luxury of several days to finalise her plans.

Peering through the slight gap she'd left as she stood behind the bedroom door, she waited for the intruder to appear at the top of the stairs. As he did, she almost felt disappointed. It was Peters, the idiot landlord. Wasn't he supposed to be in Australia? He must have returned, paid the flat a visit and when he found it empty and unused, reported it to the police. Perhaps he'd recognised her face on some flyer. Whatever the reason, he was about to pay heavily.

Ever since reporting his suspicions to the police, Clive Peters had been kicking himself. Having been away for two years, he'd completely forgotten about the concealed space in the cupboard below the kitchen sink, a hidey-hole created by a former tenant whom Peters suspected had been dealing drugs.

When the woman he knew as Alice Morton had rented the flat for three years, cash upfront, Peters had been suspicious of her. Another dealer? Nevertheless, as a body-builder himself with advanced qualifications in Thai boxing, he had been impressed by her obvious fitness, and challenged by her coldness. In an attempt to ingratiate himself with her, he had dropped his voice to a conspiratorial whisper and told her about the hiding place. She had ignored him and hardly glanced at the cupboard. But she knew it was there and that was enough for Peters. She might have used it and he wanted to know.

Fortunately for Peters, the police search missed the concealed cupboard, the young forensic officer who looked under the sink not noticing the cupboard's backboard was a foot closer to the doors than in the other cupboards. Now all the tenant's other belongings had been returned, Peters had been itching to check it out.

Knowing the police would be watching the place, he had waited for a few days to get to know their schedule. Confident neither the little round sergeant nor the big black guy would show up before lunchtime, he decided to call in one morning after breakfast.

He parked his car outside the house and headed for the main door. Everything seemed quiet in the flat — the other downstairs door was locked, no sounds from upstairs — so Peters ran up the stairs and walked straight to the kitchen. He opened the doors to the cupboard below the sink and peered in. It was as he remembered: there were no screws, just a plain painted board. Whoever had installed it had mounted a large magnet on the rear side of the board that would engage with another magnet when it was brought up close on the outside, allowing the panel to be pulled away smoothly. The innocent-looking magnet on the fridge door had been left there for precisely that purpose. Peters retrieved it and leaned his hand forward into the cupboard, allowing magnetic attraction to do its work.

Peering into the gloom of the space behind the panel, he could see several packets. He reached in.

The first packet immediately confirmed his suspicions about Alice Morton. It contained passports, ten of them. He flicked through a couple but they didn't interest him. If he had bothered to look more carefully at the personal data pages, he would have discovered that each passport was for a woman of about Alice Morton's age, each of the women bearing a close resemblance to her.

He ducked his head back into the cupboard, reaching farther into the hidden space. As his hand folded around a plastic bag containing something long and thin wrapped in what felt like cotton cloth, the sudden sound of a voice from close behind him made him jump in alarm, his head banging hard against the sink's downpipe.

"Looking for something, Clive? There's no cash, if that's what you're after."

Peters backed out of the cupboard and sprang to his feet. Alice Morton was standing about six feet away from him, a half-smile on her face, her eyes piercing into his.

"No, but the pile of passports is interesting, Morton," he said shifting his weight onto the balls of his feet, ready to pounce. "Or should I call you Freneton? Ex-Superintendent Olivia Freneton. Seems you're in a spot of trouble."

Her eyes didn't leave his for an instant, which is why she didn't notice his right hand exploring the bag it was still gripping. He could feel a handle through the plastic and cloth.

"Well, Superintendent? Murdering bitch Superintendent? Your mates told me all about you, said you were good with your hands. Fast."

He feinted a rapid movement with both hands, but Olivia didn't so much as blink. However, what she did do was notice the packet in Peters' hand as it flashed across her vision.

Her sneering smile hardened. "Knives, Clive. Two very sharp knives."

"What?" he said, frowning.

"In the bag you're holding, the one you picked up from under the sink. It contains two very sharp knives. One of them excellent for throwing, if you know what you're doing. So it won't be much use to you, will it?" she offered sarcastically.

Peters shrugged. "Don't need no knives, not when you've got these," he said, lobbing the packet to one side and starting to lift his fists.

But he had already made his mistake, and Olivia only needed one. As he lobbed the packet away, he had taken his eyes from Olivia's for a fraction of a second. Out of nowhere, a searing, sickening pain enveloped his abdomen as his legs collapsed under him. Olivia's right foot had done its work, crashing into his groin like a piledriver.

Olivia darted forward and seized Peters' right hand from where it was instinctively reaching for his battered testicles. She spun him onto his front, twisting his arm and forcing it up his back.

He was big, but Olivia was strong. Keeping the pressure on the twisted arm, she hauled him to his feet and marched him to the top of the stairs where, before he had time to react, she pushed him hard out into the void of the stairwell. With no opportunity to find his feet, Peters tumbled awkwardly, his head striking a stair corner, the weight of his body dragging him on, still tumbling. His skull hit the concrete floor first, his body following, compressing and twisting his head. His neck broke with a sharp snap.

Olivia stood at the top of the stairs, watching for movement, but she knew he was dead from the lay of his body.

Returning to the kitchen, she picked up the discarded packets of passports and knives, after which she kneeled and reached into the hidden cupboard space to retrieve the pack of explosive charges. She pulled a drawstring cloth bag from her pocket and pushed all the items in. After carefully wiping the surface of the false panel Peters had removed and putting it back in place, she returned the magnet to the fridge door.

She glanced around the room, making sure everything was in

place before carefully descending the stairs, avoiding any points of contact Peters had made with his head and other parts of his body as he fell.

Stepping over the body, she turned and bent to go through his pockets. As she did, a cruel smile of satisfaction spread across her face. Peters' inside jacket pocket contained an envelope stuffed with twenty-pound notes; he must have been collecting back rents from various properties he owned. She made a rough count — around five thousand pounds; a most welcome top-up to her depleted funds.

When she checked his other pockets, she was further delighted to find his car keys. "Thank you, Clive," she said, waving the keys at her landlord's body. "The police won't be looking for your car for quite a while, even if the next patrol comes by fairly soon. I can drive it with impunity, and an anonymous car parked in Thyme's street will be far less noticeable than a motorcycle."

After driving to her hotel, Olivia paced her room for ten minutes revising her schedule. She would undoubtedly be blamed for Peters' death once his body was found, making it necessary to complete what she could of her intended programme that day. Not ideal, but among her many contingency plans there were several scenarios from which she could choose.

She had two objectives remaining: the disposals of Bottomley, Hawkins and Thyme, and searching Thyme's flat for anything that would lead her to Cotton. It was still possible to complete all of these by the end of the day providing all went smoothly.

The logical order for the disposals was Bottomley, Hawkins and Thyme, since Thyme, as a single man, would be less likely to return to his flat early after work. However, the disposals were for later on; right now her priority was finding information on Cotton's whereabouts.

She remained dressed in her jogging gear, but in a small ruck-sack she carried with her, she had a change of clothing, a wig and different dark glasses, just in case.

Driving slowly down Thyme's street, she looked for signs of

activity in the three-storey block that housed his flat. There was nothing.

The twelve flats were all small, one-bedroom units, aimed mainly at the young singles or newly-wed market, although the ground-floor flats with their tiny patches of garden would appeal to retirees.

And it was a retiree, a widow, who let her in. The elderly woman was leaving to walk to the supermarket three streets away as Olivia approached the main door. The woman even held the door for her.

"Thanks so much," enthused Olivia as she looked up from the phone she'd pulled from her pocket. "I'm popping into Derek Thyme's flat for something. He lent me his keys but I forgot the password for the door. I was just about to call him." She held up her phone as proof of her story.

The woman smiled. "Pleased to be of help, dear. It's seven-six-two-six, in case you call by again."

"You're very kind," said Olivia. "Derek told me he had charming neighbours, and now I can see what he meant."

She watched the woman walk the short path to the gate and head off down the street before taking the stairs to Derek's flat on the first floor. Here she paused, sniffing the air, listening for sounds of activity behind the other three front doors. Nothing; no music, TV or radio. Just to be sure, she put her ear to each door and bent down to look underneath for any moving shadows.

Satisfied she was unlikely to be interrupted, she turned her attention to Derek's front door. There were two deadlocks — one clearly new — and a Yale. The Yale would be easy, the work of seconds, but the deadlocks would require a little more. The presence of a new, second lock concerned her. Had Thyme beefed up his security? Was the place alarmed? She might only have time to grab his laptop and run.

Removing a set of picks from her rucksack, Olivia set about the deadlocks. Although they were chunky, impressive-looking devices, their mechanisms proved no barrier to her skills and she had them both open in under thirty seconds. The Yale, as expected, pleaded no contest.

She gently pushed open the door, checking the frame for telltale signs of an alarm trip. There was nothing obvious. From where she stood, she quickly scanned the room. There was only an entry phone, no indication of any alarm. Of course, it may be sophisticated, well hidden and controlled remotely through Thyme's mobile phone. She would have to risk it, but to cover her bases, she checked the kitchen window. It looked out onto a small garden to the rear. Dropping down into it wouldn't be a problem if she needed to leave in a hurry.

Thyme had left his computer on the dining table along with notebooks and papers. Olivia opened the laptop and the screen sprang to life, a box in the centre demanding a password. She hit the return button, just in case no password was required, but the on-screen box shook and the cursor kept flashing.

Luuk, Olivia's fence in Amsterdam, as well as dealing in all types of stolen goods, knew far more than the average mortal about computers and computer security. Knowing his clients often wished to access files on their targets' computers, he had put together a sophisticated program that examined a computer's CPU with a view to discovering all passwords, but particularly the one that opened up the computer from scratch.

Olivia removed a flash drive containing the program from her rucksack and plugged it into one of the laptop's USB ports. Within a few seconds, a panel appeared on the screen, a logo of a ripped-apart heart in its centre along with the word 'Heartbreaker'. A small black panel within the main one filled with rapidly scrolling lines of code.

After only ten seconds, the scrolling stopped and Olivia expected the computer's main home screen to appear. But instead another panel opened flashing the word 'Danger'. Underneath was a short message. 'This computer is protected by highly sophisticated security and cannot be accessed. Remove the drive immediately before any internal systems copy or destroy it, and before any message is transmitted to announce Heartbreaker's attempted intrusion. You have five seconds. Four …'

Olivia snatched the drive from the port, her eyes searching the room for Thyme's modem. Finding it, she tore the power cable from it along with the Internet feed.

She stared at the computer, almost expecting it to say something smug, but all the screen displayed was the original panel demanding a password.

Angered by this setback, she slammed the lid shut and turned her attention to the notebooks. She picked up each in turn, systematically searching through them so it wouldn't be obvious they had been examined. But they were only casebooks: notes and aides memoires, references, cross-references, and summaries, one book for each major case Thyme had worked on or was working on. He was nothing if not thorough, although the ex-senior officer in Olivia was mentally reprimanding him for having such material sitting on his dining table. At the very least the notebooks should be in a safe. Did he even own a safe?

Olivia began a rapid search of the flat for anything else that might contain reference to Cotton. But there was no safe, no other notebooks, no photos. Nothing that made any mention of her.

Taking deep breaths to control her anger, Olivia considered what to do. There was nothing here, which was a huge disappointment. And in case there was a silent alarm or indeed the computer had managed to send a message to someone or something somewhere, she should leave. But before she did, she returned to Thyme's bedroom where, supported on a pair of stands, were two racing bikes: a Cannondale and a Raleigh. She stared at them as she again rethought her day. Although she didn't believe in luck or fate, she seemed to be having more than her fair share of setbacks. If something else went wrong, maybe she wouldn't get a chance to return here later to kill Thyme. Perhaps she should take some action now. OK, it wouldn't guarantee his death, but under the right circumstances …

She pulled a toolkit from her bag and set to work on the bikes.

Chapter Twenty

Henry Silk leaned back in a large, leather armchair, his cupped right hand warming the Armagnac in his brandy goblet, his eyes fixed on his daughter as she nestled comfortably on the sofa opposite him.

"What?" said Jennifer, raising her eyebrows in mock innocence as she pulled her feet more securely under her. She knew she couldn't hold out much longer, but she wanted the questions to come from him.

Henry waited a few seconds before replying. When he spoke, his voice was soft, affectionate.

"Ever since I arrived in this paradise this afternoon you've spent the time using diversionary tactics. We've swum in the pool and the sea, we've walked the gardens where you surprised me with your knowledge of Mediterranean flora, you've reintroduced me to the wonderful Martina in the kitchen with whom I've swapped recipes, although I don't think she thought much of mine, you've even allowed me to take over from Martina to show off my limited culinary skills and you've plied me with the most exquisite wines. Throughout all this, we've talked about anything and everything except what's really on your mind. When are you going to tell me what's going on? Tell me why, if you're going to be working in an art fraud squad, there's a need for such secrecy, why I still won't be able to enjoy the pleasure of taking you to what I regard as the best Italian restaurants in London once you return to England?"

Jennifer shrugged. "You're too modest, Mr Silk. Your culinary skills are anything but limited and you know it. I doubt there's a restaurant anywhere that could better those linguine alle vongole; they were to die for."

Henry dropped his eyes into a squint and put on his best Bronx accent. "Cut the crap, Cotton, and spill the beans."

Jennifer giggled. "OK, boss, you win, but it's no different from before. While I'm over the moon we've found each other, that I have a father who's not only alive and amazing, but also one who is quite a celeb, I still don't want my picture in all the glossies along-side yours. I hate the way these gossip-mongers — to call them journalists insults the professionals in the business — the way they assume they have the right to intrude on anyone's life, that they can plaster your photo everywhere and pepper it with pathetic innuendo."

Henry smiled. "I don't recall seeing you in any of the glossies."

"Exactly. I'm not a celeb and I don't want to be one. It's bril-liant my name and photo have been kept away from the press so far, that they don't know I'm your daughter. I know it hasn't been easy and I'm so very grateful that you and everyone else has kept it quiet. It wouldn't help me if you kept popping up in conversation in everything I do. You know this; we've been through it."

"It will probably come out if Freneton's ever found. She would delight in revealing our connection in court, if she got the chance."

"I know, and because of that, I feel as if I'm living on borrowed time, career-wise. But while I am, I want to maintain the status quo. That's why I haven't taken you up on your offer of letting me live in your house in London once I'm back, which I'd really like to do. I love that house; it's so … you. And I'd love to go out to restau-rants with you, but you know exactly what would happen; I'd be featured as your latest conquest in the tabloids. And when they found the truth, they'd be all over me, and … well, it would place a huge constraint on my effectiveness."

Henry took a sip of his brandy while watching her over the rim of the glass. "Interesting way to express it, Jennifer, but there's more than that, isn't there? I've got to know you very well in the past year, and I know you're holding something back."

She pulled a face. "You'd make a good police officer, or perhaps I'm just transparent."

"I don't think you'd be transparent to anyone else; your inscrutability is impressive, but possibly because we share so many characteristics, I can see through it." He grinned. "You don't know how good that makes me feel."

She laughed. "Perhaps I should take up acting."

"If ever being a plod gets too much, you should think about it."

She straightened her back and lifted her chin. "Jennifer Cotton, star of stage and screen." Sagging back into the sofa, she made a face. "Doesn't quite cut it somehow. I think I'll stick to chasing bad guys."

"So tell me about them," said Henry, "tell me about the bad guys in the art world. Are they really so bad?"

Jennifer nodded. "You better believe it. The bad ones are up to every trick in the book. Crafty as the proverbial cartload."

"And your role?"

She sighed, sitting up again. "This is all highly confidential, Henry. I'd rather not be telling you, but I realise for many reasons I have no choice."

Henry waited, concerned he wasn't going to like what she was about to say.

"There's an investigation under way into a massively high-value art fraud," continued Jennifer. "It involves some brilliant forgers and a lot of super-rich people, some of them innocent victims, although I think I'd also call them gullible, and some of them anything but innocent."

"That doesn't explain your role."

"They want me to go undercover, get on the inside of the gallery that's behind it."

Henry was shaking his head, the concern he'd felt all along now showing on his face.

"I knew there was something you weren't telling me, Jennifer. This sounds really dangerous! And why you, for heavens sake?

You're new to their squad; there must be other police officers who have a good knowledge of art."

Jennifer shrugged, ignoring the rise in his voice. "È facile, signore," she said, holding out her palms. "Parlo italiano."

"This scam is centred in Italy? Now you most certainly do have me worried. Whereabouts?"

She pursed her lips. "Look, Henry, there's only so much I can tell you, you understand that, don't you?"

"Of course I do, but I'd need to know where you are, in case you need me to come running."

"That's exactly what you mustn't do. I'll have excellent support in this; I won't be operating in isolation."

Henry shook his head. "The question 'What could possibly go wrong?' comes to mind. Don't you think a plan B would help? I'm not sure how much confidence I'd have in the Italian police."

"If it were the ordinary cops, I think I'd agree with you. But this is a specialist squad who are dedicated and good. I've met their boss and I was impressed. However, having said that, although he's leading the operation, he's doing it without the blessing of his bosses, for very good reasons."

"Which means, presumably," said Henry, "you are going to be operating in a foreign country without official approval."

"Hardly," disagreed Jennifer. "Massimo Felice, the boss, will take the fall for anything that goes wrong."

Henry was clearly not convinced so Jennifer explained the problems Felice had had with his own organisation.

"Never goes away, does it?" sighed Henry, once she'd finished.

"No," agreed Jennifer. "There are too many powerful people who could end up being embarrassed, people in business, the civil service and in politics."

Henry nodded. "So when your boss told this Felice about you, that you are a UK police officer with mother-tongue Italian, someone who could not only pass for an Italian but who is also something of an art expert, and in addition someone with no connection to the Italian police, he must have thought all his birthdays had come at once."

"Certainly got his attention, yes. He said that by necessity it would be a long slow job since first of all they had to find a way of getting the gallery to give me a job, although he had some ideas on that one. I got the impression a light had come on for him."

Henry gave a rueful nod. "I'm sure it did. A bloody great beacon, more like." He sighed. "No point in my objecting then? You sound as if you're pretty set on the idea. I get the impression you like putting your head on the block."

"It's in my DNA," said Jennifer with a cheesy grin.

"Must be your mother's side," countered Henry, his face dead-pan. "OK, what stage are you at now?"

"Well, as soon as I'm declared fit, I'll head back to England, and while the ID and so on are being set up, I'm undertaking all sorts of training. I've seen the synopsis. It's fascinating, so I won't be kicking my heels."

"And the apartment you're going to be living in once you arrive in London, it's secure? I'm thinking of Freneton now. She seems to pop up out of nowhere."

"It's one of Pietro's and comes with typical Pietro hi-tech security and a live-in housekeeper who could take on an army in unarmed combat and win. I'd hate to be on the wrong side of her. I've known her for several years; she used to work in one of Pietro's houses in Milan. Being Italian and about forty-five, she sees herself as a sort of mother figure, so I imagine she'll be clucking around me given half a chance. I'm not actually sure I'll like all the attention, but it won't be for long. Once I get back to Italy, I'll be on my own in my own place, one that will have had the Pietro makeover too."

Henry raised an eyebrow at her. "Back to Italy? It's a big place, Jennifer."

She sighed. "OK, to Florence. I'll be based in Florence. But I don't want you turning up, seeking me out."

"Don't worry, I can be very discreet. And I am a master of disguise."

"That's what I told Felice."

"And where you'll be living in Florence, it's definitely secure?"

Jennifer nodded. "No question, Pietro will make sure of it.

What about your house in London? You're one of Freneton's targets too."

Henry laughed. "Yes, I know, but most of the time these days I'm in the US now my star has ascended. And as with your flat in Nottingham, Pietro has kindly made my house impenetrable. The security's amazing: micro-cameras everywhere, all movement-triggered, all on independent circuits. I have to move fast when I come home from somewhere or all the alarms go off and I find myself trapped in the vestibule between the main front door and the inner front door."

Jennifer stretched and sighed. "All because of one crazed psychopath. At least the official story is that I've been in the UK all the time. And although there's nothing to suggest to Freneton I'll be working in Italy, that doesn't stop me wondering where the hell she is."

Chapter Twenty-One

After leaving Derek Thyme's flat, Olivia drove back into Nottingham city centre where she parked Peters' car in the Broadmarsh shopping centre car park. She knew the entrance camera would record the car's number plate; it might even take a shot of the driver. She didn't care. She knew the police would soon be searching for her again, and just to rub salt into the wounds she had already inflicted, she intended to become the Olivia Freneton her targets remembered, one with close-cropped, expensively cut dark brown hair. She had just the wig to reproduce how she had looked a year before.

Since she had no further use for the car, she was tempted to look up and smile in case her face was being recorded. Instead, she left the keys in the ignition and walked away. Her evening disposals would see her back on the Kawasaki, parked close to whichever of her targets she was dealing with and ready for a quick getaway should anything go wrong.

As she walked back to her hotel, Olivia thought about that. What could possibly go wrong?

Each of her three disposals were to take place at their respective homes. Both Bottomley and Hawkins were married so their wives would also have to be dealt with in some way. She didn't want to kill the wives — she normally killed women only if they were part of an overall scheme, such as the prostitutes she'd killed in the framing of victims like Henry Silk — instead, she wanted them to suffer by witnessing the deaths of their husbands and having the brutal images etched in their minds for the rest of their lives.

Cotton, of course, was different: she had to die, but normally Olivia's targets were men, and the more men she could dispose of, the better. Her father had taught her that lesson by subjecting her to eight years of abuse until ironically, he provided her with the skills to kill him. His total betrayal of his responsibilities as a single father had warped her mind — Olivia's mother had died when she was born — and very few men she had met since had given her any reason not to think that almost all men were like him. She sometimes wondered if he'd realised what she'd done when his brakes failed and he hurtled to his death, not that he featured often in her thoughts.

At six that evening, Neil Bottomley and Derek Thyme were ready to finish for the day. Both had spent most of the morning and the entire afternoon at their computers checking CCTV footage and stills from security cameras in and around the East Midlands for vehicles involved in a high-value wages snatch that had occurred two weeks previously at a factory in Hucknall, north of Nottingham. It was tedious work requiring a great deal of concentration, and they were tired. Also, for both of them, at the back of their minds was the ongoing possibility that Olivia Freneton might turn up following the failure of her webcam.

Checking Peters' flat was to be Derek's last task for the day; he had tossed a coin with Neil for the duty and lost. Neil was heading straight home and looking forward to a night out with his wife Pam.

Derek was about to switch off his computer when a result he'd been waiting for flagged a message on his screen.

"Bugger," he muttered, stabbing at his keyboard. "I knew I should have turned this thing off two minutes ago."

He called up the file the message related to and started reading the contents. Out of the corner of his eye, he saw Neil putting on his jacket.

"Don't be too long, laddie," said Neil. "Whatever it is can probably wait until the morning. You need to get some beauty sleep."

"Face like that, he'll need to be comatose for a couple of years for it to improve," called someone from across the room.

"Better than looking like a cadaver, Scottie," replied Derek as he carried on scrolling his screen.

"See you in the morning, lads," said Bottomley.

A chorus of 'G'night Sarge' followed him through the door.

Thirty minutes later, Derek had finished all he needed to do. He closed down his computer and locked his notebooks in a drawer. After checking Peters' flat in West Bridgford, he was intending to go for a long bike ride along a Trent towpath.

Neil Bottomley's drive to his home in the village of Southwell took around twenty-five minutes. As he drew up outside the house, he frowned in surprise — his wife's car was occupying the driveway, she must have forgotten about it since normally she'd have put the car in the garage by now.

Strolling from his car towards the front door of his three-bedroom, two-storey semi, he glanced along the road, his attention caught by a large motorcycle parked two doors along next to the gravelled path that led to the rear of the row of houses. The bike had two large panniers either side of the rear wheel. He squinted, trying to read the number plate, but it was too far away in the fading light, although he could make out the blue EU circle and yellow stars. His frown deepened briefly before he remembered his neighbour, Joe Pawton, had been complaining about his teenage daughter's succession of biker boyfriends. Good luck with that, thought Neil, it looks like a serious touring bike.

He shrugged and turned to admire some freshly pruned roses. Roses were a passion for the Bottomleys, their garden a catalogue of varieties, all lovingly tended.

He nodded appreciatively and walked to the front door. Before the Freneton case, the door was always on the latch. The house was in a quiet road in a quiet village; security was hardly ever an issue. But now, with the bitch still out there and knowing how ruthless she could be, Bottomley had insisted to Pam that all the doors to the house remain locked, especially when she was at home alone.

He opened the door with his key and called out to his wife.

"It's me, Pam. The Glorious Tisdale pinks are looking wonderful, Mrs Green Fingers."

"Thanks, darling, I'm in the lounge."

Bottomley froze to the spot, his senses on high alert. Two coded words. One: darling. Pam never, ever, called him darling, so they'd decided long ago to use it as a code for her being in trouble with an intruder. Two: lounge. For Pam, lounges were in pubs; her house had a sitting room. In their prearranged code it meant one thing: Freneton.

Bottomley willed himself to remain cool. He had to summon help but he couldn't use his phone in the hallway in case Freneton heard him.

"Just going upstairs to change, Pammy, won't be a second."

There was a moment's pause, then Pam called out, "Come in here first, darling, I've got something to show you."

Bottomley gulped; he could hear the edge to his wife's voice. Freneton was probably threatening her. Every instinct told him his wife needed him right now, while all his experience said wait, call in.

"Be with you in a mo," he called and bounded up the stairs.

He rushed into their bedroom at the front of the house, punching a speed dial number combination on his phone as he did. The call answered in two rings.

"Neil, I—"

"Boss, she's here, at my house. She's got Pam." Bottomley was speaking in a hushed tone, his hand cupped in front of his mouth. There was no doubt in either man's mind who 'she' was.

Hawkins reacted instantly, knowing the sergeant couldn't stay on the line.

"Got it, Neil. Be there ASAP."

"Tell them no sirens," urged Bottomley, and rang off.

Bottomley slipped off his jacket and tossed it on the bed; he needed to move his arms freely. He looked around for a weapon but there was nothing sensible upstairs. While he was totally against guns and arming the police, it didn't stop him wishing he had one right now. He wondered if Freneton had a gun.

He walked back down the stairs, every step cautious, his eyes searching for some indication that Freneton might have moved position and be waiting for him.

He turned the handle to the living-room door and strolled in, wanting his arrival to appear natural, not giving Freneton any sign her presence was known to him, that he might have summoned help.

"That's bett—" he began, pausing mid-sentence as his eyes fell on Olivia and his wife.

Pam was perched on a sofa, leaning forward, her hands roped at the wrists behind her back. She looked uncomfortable but her eyes were alert, searching her husband's. Olivia stood to one side of the sofa, her right hand clutching a knife that was hovering near Pam's throat. Her smile was hard and victorious. "Neil, how nice to see you. How are the teeth?"

"What the hell? What do you want, Freneton?"

"I should have thought that was fairly obvious, even for a tub of brainless lard like you."

The knife in her hand was one of the two in the bag Peters had pulled out from under the sink in the lock-up; the other was in her belt. She caught Neil's eyes on the weapons and sneered.

"I shouldn't get any ideas, Neil, if I were you," she added, weighing the knife in her hand.

Bottomley held his hands up in submission. "Let's just keep calm, shall we? There's no need for anyone to get hurt."

Olivia's laugh was scornful. "That's where you're wrong, Neil. There's every need. You're on my list, you see. My disposals. I should have finished you off in Harlow Wood when you got in my way, but given you've suffered greatly since, I'm rather pleased I didn't. This little interlude of personal attention will be very pleasurable."

She lifted her right hand threateningly, adjusting her grip on the knife.

His hands still held out from his body, his palms upwards, Bottomley tried to control his breathing. He needed to engage this madwoman in conversation, stall her for long enough for Hawkins' back-up team to arrive.

"OK," he said, speaking slowly and deliberately, "I can understand why I might be among your … what did you call them? Disposals? But there's no need to hurt my wife. She's an innocent. Why should she be on your list? What purpose would it serve hurting her? This is between us, Freneton, the SCF squad and you. Who else—"

"I want to see your phone, Neil," she barked, interrupting him. "Take it out of your pocket and place it on that side table, then move back." She had seen through his desperate attempts at conversation.

"I left it upstairs in the bedroom," lied Bottomley.

"I can see the bulge in your pocket, you idiot," snapped Olivia. "Just do it!"

Bottomley dropped his right arm and put his hand in his pocket, slowly pulling out the phone. He hadn't deleted the call to Hawkins. If Freneton found it, she'd kill him immediately and probably kill Pam as well. He couldn't allow that to happen.

"There," he said. Ignoring Olivia's order, he tossed the phone high in her direction, but to her right, making it difficult to catch with the knife in her hand.

Olivia was fast. In a flash, she transferred the knife to her left hand and had her right hand out to catch the phone.

Pam Bottomley had been waiting for her moment. She was seething. This woman had taken her by surprise, overpowered her and was now threatening her husband's life for the second time. She was determined they wouldn't give in without a fight.

She had been horrified at the injuries Neil had received at Harlow Wood, while at the same time proud of his bravery in facing up to Olivia Freneton.

Ever since the murders of Mike Hurst and the Chinese woman, and the shocking attempt on Derek Thyme's life, Pam had been expecting something to happen. She may be a short, round, middle-aged housewife, overweight like her husband, but she had grit. She had boosted her fitness with twice-weekly sessions at a gym and regular jogs around the village, and she had lain awake for many a night as Neil tossed and turned beside her, his mind torturing him with troubled dreams. During those hours of darkness, she had rehearsed many scenarios, all of them aimed at subduing Olivia Freneton.

As Neil tossed the phone towards Freneton, Pam made her move. She rolled sideways on the sofa, falling onto her back while at the same time she kicked her legs high in the air, aiming at Olivia's right arm.

Bottomley saw Pam react, but wary of the knife now in Olivia's left hand, instead of diving at her, he reached out for a glass vase standing on a bookcase to his right, grabbed it by the neck and threw it hard at Olivia's head.

Distracted by her right hand being kicked and the phone flying past her, Olivia's reaction to the vase was too slow. It crashed into the bridge of her nose and shattered, one of the larger shards adding to the damage by cutting her eyebrow. She staggered backwards as blood welled and flowed down her face, aware of Bottomley now running towards her.

Although her left hand wasn't as good as her right for throwing a knife, she had trained with both, and her left arm was strong. She hurled the knife at him hoping to find his heart, but instead, the knife sank into his left shoulder. It was enough to stop him in his tracks, his right hand clutching at the injury.

In spite of her spinning head, Olivia wanted to finish her work. She reached for the other knife in her belt. Two steps and she could slash his fat throat and leave.

But Bottomley wasn't beaten. To Olivia's surprise, he reached for the handle of the blade sticking out of his shoulder and made to pull it out. He knew the bleeding would increase, that it was a dangerous move. He also knew he had little choice.

Olivia stopped and as she did she heard a thump to her right. Pam had rolled off the sofa and was intending to try to trip her.

The decision-making process took only microseconds. This fight was getting messy and by now Olivia was convinced Bottomley had called for help. She had to leave. Every second counted. Resisting the temptation to kick Pam in the head, she backed away towards the door at the rear of the living room that led to the kitchen.

Wiping blood from her face with the back of her hand and feeling dizzy from the impact of the vase with her head, she turned and ran through the kitchen and out into the back garden, through the back gate and down the path to where she had parked her Kawasaki.

She flipped open a pannier to retrieve her bright red helmet, pulling out a scarf at the same time and folding it into a wad to press on her bleeding eyebrow. With her helmet and visor holding the scarf in place, she fired the engine and revved it loudly. She wanted to be seen, she wanted someone in one of the houses to get a description of the motorcycle, of her, of the panniers.

Out of the corner of her eye, she saw some curtains move in the house opposite the Bottomleys'. It was enough; she kicked the bike into gear and roared off towards the M1 motorway.

When the first of the police patrol cars arrived at the end of the Bottomleys' road, their flashing lights were off, their occupants awaiting orders. As they pulled to a halt, a message came through: Neil Bottomley had called in again; the suspect had escaped. With no more need for caution, the two officers ran from the car towards the Bottomleys' house.

Chapter Twenty-Two

After her dinner with Henry at the villa in Sardinia, Jennifer went to bed late, somewhat light-headed from a few too many glasses of her favourite red. She was pleased to have told her father about her posting to Florence, although from his reaction she was more than a little concerned he would turn up unannounced in some disguise or other while she was working in the gallery.

On her bedside table was the thick file of notes left by Paul Godden. She had been slowly working her way through them, but tonight she knew she wouldn't be receptive to the finer points of art fraud. Instead, she wanted to think back over her evening with Henry. Their meetings were rare enough and she wanted to savour this one as she drifted into sleep.

Half an hour after laying her head on the pillow, her reaction to being jolted awake by a ping from her phone to announce an incoming message was teeth-grinding irritation. Until she realised it was her own fault: she had meant to switch the phone to silent. Who the hell was texting at this hour? She stretched and reached for the offending device, fully intending to turn it off without reading the message.

But she knew in her heart she couldn't; she must at least read what was on the screen. When she saw Derek's name against the two-word text, 'call me', her mind focussed immediately.

She punched the call symbol and waited impatiently for the reply.

"Jen, hi. Sorry for the late hou—"

"Derek! Are you OK? You never contact me this late. What's happened?"

She heard a dry chuckle from the other end. "Stop working yourself up, Jen, I'm fine, believe me. Frustrated, but fine. I just couldn't wait to tell you."

"Why are you frustrated?"

"She's slipped through the net, Jen, last seen heading south west. It was close though. I reckon the sarge nearly had her."

"Freneton?"

"Yes."

"Is Neil OK?"

"Nothing a few stitches won't sort out."

"Oh God! Tell me." She was now fully awake and sitting up on the edge of the bed. She glanced around for a notebook, saw one on a side table across the room and ran over to fetch it. She sat back on the bed, juggling phone, pen and notebook.

"She was waiting for him when he got home from work, holding his wife hostage."

"Pam?"

"He's only got one wife, Jen."

"Is she OK?"

"She's not hurt although she's pretty shaken up. She was very brave, actually; they both were. They'd devised a clever warning system, so as soon as he got through the front door and called out to Pam, Neil knew Freneton was there."

"Good for Neil."

"Yeah, he figured he was on her list, that it was only a matter of time before she showed up."

"You said he was injured."

"Freneton threw a knife at him. Fortunately her aim was off and it went into a fleshy part of his shoulder. A lot of blood but no permanent damage, according to the doctor at A&E when I went to see him.

"And Pam was amazing. Even though her wrists had been

bound behind her back with rope, she managed to roll over on the sofa she was sitting on and kick out at Freneton."

"She was lucky Freneton didn't retaliate."

"Yeah, but they both knew if they submitted or otherwise failed, there was only one outcome: she would have killed them."

"So what happened? Why did she stop?"

"Neil managed to hurt her, injure her. He lobbed a glass vase at her which thumped her on the nose. It broke and glass from it cut her quite deeply, according to Neil. That's when Freneton threw the knife at him."

"Wow!"

"Yeah, and after that she ran. Neil reckons she'd worked out he'd called in, which he had before he went into the living room where Freneton was holding Pam. She'd know there'd be squad cars arriving within minutes. As it is, we reckon she'd only just disappeared when the first car arrived. They saw nothing and headed in to check out the Bottomleys."

"I'm amazed she didn't try to injure Neil more."

"He reckons the vase really shook her; said she looked pretty groggy. He reckons if she hadn't thrown the knife at him, he'd have had her."

"Not so sure about that; she'd have fought like a demon."

"You're right; I think they are extremely lucky. The other thing is they got sight of her as she roared off. She was on a motorcycle with panniers. She was wearing smart leathers, which, of course, the Bottomleys saw close up, and she had a red crash helmet on. There have been a couple of possible sightings and it looks as if she's heading south west."

"Rings a bell."

"The maps in the van, you mean?"

"Yes. How did she look?"

"What do you mean? Healthwise?"

"No, idiot. Hair. It's been a year, Derek. Has she grown her hair or does she still have that cropped, boyish style?"

"Oh, right. That was interesting. Neil said she looked exactly the same as the last time he saw her in Harlow Wood. Same short hair, same slim, athletic build."

"Same colour hair?"

"Yes, but when we asked Pam about it, she said she was pretty sure the hair was a wig."

Jennifer stared out of the window to the moonlit sea, thinking through the information.

"Pam'd notice that, of course, being a woman," she continued. "It's interesting, it sounds as if she'd made herself deliberately look the same as a year ago, whereas she's probably now quite different. You know, grown her hair, styled it differently. Worth getting an artist to come up with a few hairstyles with longer hair, don't you think?"

"I do, yes. In fact Crawford is already on it, as a matter of routine. Anyway, Jen, that's not all. Olivia had a busy day."

"What else did she do?"

"She almost definitely killed Clive Peters, the owner of the lock-up in West Bridgford."

"Peters has been murdered?"

"Yes, although there's an outside chance he fell down the stairs."

"Right, tell me more."

"I mentioned last week when I first told you about Peters we would be checking the flat every day. Well today was my turn and this evening—"

"Wait a minute," interrupted Jennifer, "when you say it was your turn, did you go there on your own?"

"Yes, I—"

"Derek, we discussed this. You should never have gone on your own."

"I called the nick, Jen, just before I went in, and of course, called again almost immediately because as soon as I got through the door from the street, there was Peters' body."

"So you're thinking Peters went there — *alone* — and Freneton was waiting, and, what, pushed him down the stairs? Was there any sign of a fight?"

"No, none."

"That could have been you, Derek."

There was silence from the other end.

"Derek?"

"There's a difference, Jen. Peters wouldn't have been expecting her to be there. She'd have taken him completely by surprise, whereas every time I've been there, I've gone in cautiously. I was ready for her."

"Doesn't make any difference; two of you would always be better. How did Peters die?"

"Broken neck, almost definitely from the fall."

"No other injuries?"

"None visible. And he was a pretty powerful bloke; fit with no flab on him. She must've got quite a drop on him for him not to have fought back."

"Make sure the pathologist examines his testicles. You might remember they are something of a target for Freneton."

"No need to remind me, Jen," said Derek with a grimace, a hand instinctively dropping to protect himself.

Jennifer was tapping her pen onto the cover of the notebook as she thought through everything Derek had told her.

"OK, let's think about her day. How long had Peters been dead?"

"Several hours, according to the pathologist. Reckons it would've been around nine this morning."

"Makes sense. As you said last week, she'd've wanted to know whether the webcam failing was accidental or because it'd been discovered. And although she was probably reassured to find it had burnt out, she must've also worked out the place had been processed by the lab. Freneton's no fool; she'll have left certain things placed in very particular ways. As for Peters, it was probably just bad luck he turned up when he did. I wonder why he went back. Do you think there could've been something hidden there the forensic team missed?"

"It's possible, yeah. Perhaps we should make another search."

"Yes, although if there was something, Freneton will most likely have taken it away, knowing she can't possibly return there again. I wonder where she stayed, assuming she didn't drive up overnight from wherever she's hiding out. Are the hotels in the area being checked?"

"As we speak."

"Good. Now let's think about what she was up to. She didn't go to Nottingham to kill Peters, that was unexpected and possibly buggered her plans, since she'd know he'd be found. She definitely came to kill Neil. I wonder if she intended to target others. You, for instance, and Hawkins."

"Perhaps she's waiting for me."

"Where are you?" cried Jennifer in alarm.

"I've just pulled up in the street along from my flat. Stop worrying, Jen, I told you, there have been sightings of her hot-footing it away from here. And she's injured, remember? Whatever plans she had to occupy the rest of her evening, they've been scuppered."

"Nevertheless, you shouldn't underestimate her," said Jennifer. "Stay on the line as you go in. Make sure everything is as you left it this morning. And don't talk me through it until you're sure she's not there listening."

She heard Derek's keys jangling and, after a long pause, the sound of a key being pushed into a lock followed by a grunt from Derek. After the sound of a key being inserted into another lock, there was another grunt followed by the characteristic sound of a Yale key being pushed home.

After another pause of about a minute, Derek's voice came back on the phone.

"All clear, Jen. She's not here, but I reckon she has been. Someone most certainly has: both deadlocks were unlocked. And a couple of things I placed very deliberately have been moved."

"As well as finding more out about your movements, she'll almost definitely be looking for something to tell her where I am," said Jennifer.

"Yeah," replied Derek, "She's had a look at the computer. Let me call up the login record. Yes, here it is. There was a failed attempt at eleven this morning. That extra security your friend Ced Fisher put on this machine is paying off. She hasn't got past it. The system works, Jen!"

"Presumably there's still nothing on there about me, even if she had got in?" asked Jennifer.

"Nothing at all, as I've told you before. The only record of you is on my phone, which I always have with me."

"You should leave your flat now, Derek, immediately. Check into a hotel. Better still, go to my place in The Park."

"I've told you, Jen, she's long gone, and injured."

"I don't mean that. Your flat is now a crime scene. It needs to be examined and you shouldn't do anything to compromise it."

"Jeez, that's just what I need."

"She's a mass murderer, Derek, a serial killer. I know the chances of her leaving trace evidence are slim, given her forensic knowledge, but a search has to be made. Everything should be checked."

"OK, you win, but I'm knackered, I'll stay near here. There's a place down the road I can use. I'll call you in the morning when the lab's released the flat."

Chapter Twenty-Three

Livid with anger that her plans had been ruined once again, Olivia was nevertheless congratulating herself for taking the trouble to set up the false trail that was now essential for her escape to succeed.

Fighting waves of nausea from the blow to her nose, she headed south down the motorway to the turnoff for the A42. She knew there would be cameras recording her leaving the M1, but she couldn't be certain there would be any more until she reached the M42 a few miles farther on. Once on that road, she needed to run the gauntlet of any traffic police looking for her, be prepared to outrun them. It was important her route pointed to her heading south west, for Cornwall, and the farther she could go in that direction, the more the police would be led along the false trail she'd given them with the maps in her white van.

She felt the adrenaline coursing through her with every mile, the pain of her bruised nose and her dizziness banished as she constantly scanned for any indication of police vehicles. She knew the many cameras on the gantries above the heavily monitored complex of motorways around Birmingham would record her passing. If she could get as far as the M5 and head towards Bristol, even if she then left the motorway, the police would join the dots. Tomorrow would see hundreds of officers scouring the wastes of Cornwall and Devon for her non-existent hideaway, especially once they'd found images of her from her journey north the previous day.

As she passed the turnoff for Worcester, the telltale blue flashing lights of a police car appeared in her right mirror, the vehicle approaching her at high speed. She braced, ready if necessary to turn round into the on-coming traffic and race back along the hard shoulder to the slip road only a few hundred yards behind her. But the car with its siren screaming roared past her to disappear into the distance.

Twenty miles farther on, she saw the same police car, its lights still flashing. It was stopped on the hard shoulder in front of a large Kawasaki with panniers similar to hers. One police officer was searching the rider, who had removed his red helmet and was clearly protesting his innocence; the other police officer was talking earnestly into his radio, his eyes fixed on the innocent motorcyclist.

It was time to quit this particular episode. Two miles on, Olivia took the slip road from the motorway at junction 11a. She knew the road from there past Cirencester to Swindon was a good dual carriageway. At Swindon, she could pick up the M4 and head towards the M25 around London and her caravan in Kent. But first she had to become invisible.

A mile after leaving the M5, she pulled off the main road and headed into the village of Little Witcombe. Here she turned into a quiet lane and in the now near darkness she stopped the Kawasaki.

She had to work fast; this time she didn't want to be spotted. In under two minutes, bolts were removed, both panniers were lying alongside the motorcycle and the German number plates were back in place. To complete her disguise, Olivia took off her red helmet and dark-blue leathers, replacing them with the worn black ones and white crash helmet.

A few yards along from where she had stopped were three large rubbish disposal bins into which she dropped the panniers, the red helmet and discarded jacket and trousers.

Finally, she retrieved a first aid kit from her back-pack and fashioned a crude dressing for the cut to her eyebrow, wincing with pain as she pressed it into place. Back on the bike, she took the

A417 towards for Swindon, an anonymous German tourist of no interest to the police.

Arriving at the site in Kent soon after ten thirty, Olivia stowed the Kawasaki in its shed and did her best to patch herself up. A large blue-black bruise now spread from the bridge of her nose to under both eyes, making her look like a startled panda.

The cut to her eyebrow needed stitches, which right then was out of the question. Instead, Olivia fashioned a butterfly plaster to keep the jagged ends of the cut together and covered the area with another, larger dressing.

She sighed with tiredness as she remembered she was Sadie Smith to Kevin, and wearily pulled off the motorcycle gear. Dressing in Sadie's faded jeans and an old T-shirt, she took the short blond wig from a cupboard and pulled it on, covering most of it with the baseball cap. Opening a drawer, she retrieved some bracelets and rings, but the fake nose stud and transfers were a bridge too far. She slipped on the denim jacket and pulled up its collar, hoping the Kevin wouldn't notice the missing items of her disguise.

She looked around the caravan, fairly sure that once she left, she'd never be back. She gathered together as much as she could of her supplies of identity documents and explosive charges and stuffed them in the holdalls. Clothes she would need later went into a rucksack. Regrettably, she'd lost both her knives, the second one left by mistake outside Bottomley's house when she was applying the scarf to her cut eyebrow. However, she did have all the cash she'd taken from Peters. Five thousand five hundred pounds that would buy her a passage across the channel and, if needs be, get her back to Rome.

"Bugger me, Sadie, what happened to you?"

The insistent banging on Kevin's door had woken him from where he had fallen asleep in front of the television in what passed for his living room, the television there cursed with the same white noise as the one at the reception desk. He nearly fell over in surprise when he saw Sadie Smith standing in the doorway, her face a mess, not wearing her sunglasses and clutching two large holdalls and a rucksack.

She pushed past him.

"Shut the door," she ordered.

"Fall off yer bike, Sadie?" asked Kevin. "You look as if you need to see a quack."

"No time for doctors or 'ospitals, not at the moment," said Olivia, looking around the room with undisguised disgust. "How d'you live in this shithole?"

"Each to his own, Sadie," grinned Kevin. "I think it's rather cozy, meself."

Olivia pushed a pile of papers from a chair onto the floor and sat down. Her head was throbbing despite her having swallowed several strong painkillers. Rubbing her temples with the fingers and thumb of her left hand, she looked up, her eyes piercing into Kevin's. "You still doing runs across the channel?" she asked, her voice menacing.

"What runs, Sadie?" said Kevin, his face all innocence.

"Booze, drugs." She paused, wanting his full attention. "People."

"Dunno what yer talking about," replied Kevin, his eyes unable to meet hers.

"One day when you weren't 'ere, I checked out yer van, my friend. It's cleverly done, although like all these fings, it wouldn't stand too close a look."

She'd lost him. "Whatdya want, Sadie?"

"I want you to get me across the Channel, through the tunnel."

"You in a spot of trouble?" asked Kevin, instinctively sensing a significant exchange of money for his services. "Wot you done?"

"None of yer business. I just need to get out of the country for a while." A very long while, she thought.

Kevin was rubbing his chin, trying to be the cool businessman. "Interesting. Normally it's people wanting to come in this direction. So I've heard, like. Not that I'd know meself."

"Oh stop playing the innocent, Kevin. I know exactly how you operate. Don't waste my time. I need to go now and I need you to take me. I'll pay you a grand up front and anuvver when we get to where I want to go in France. The uvver grand is there, by the way, just in case you're thinking of double-crossing me or reporting me."

"Yeah, I'm likely to do that, Sadie, aren't I," said Kevin, sneering.

He hesitated before taking the plunge.

"And two grand ain't enough."

It was, in fact, more than he'd ever been paid, but he wasn't about to let on.

"It's normally more like five for an emergency exit, as it's known."

It was Olivia's turn to sneer. "Don't be greedy, Kevin. I know what the going rate is and my payment is generous." She scowled at him, but, to his credit, he said nothing.

"OK," she sighed, "I'll make it three. A grand now, the rest once we get there. Now, let's go, I don't 'ave a lot of time."

"You want to go now? Can't it wait til morning? I've 'ad a coupla drinks."

"Make yourself a strong coffee."

She held out her hand. "Gimme the keys to yer van; I want to take a closer look at this chamber, make sure I'm not going to suffocate."

Kevin shuffled over to the cooker and lit the gas under a kettle. "They're on that peg, behind you," he said, pointing.

He paused, plucking up courage before turning to look her in the eye. "If you're serious about this, Sadie, I want all the cash upfront."

Olivia picked up the rucksack. She was in no mood to barter with him. It was only because she needed him that she didn't kill him on the spot. Unfortunately, he was the sort of creep who was required in times of dire emergency; it was probably what kept him alive.

She opened the rucksack and pulled out a wad of notes she'd separated from her main stash when she was still in her caravan.

"Here's the grand," she said, tossing the wad onto the table. "I told yer you'll get the rest once we're in France."

Kevin had chosen his cover well. The signage on his van announced his company to be 'Kevin Maxwell. Racing Bike Specialist'. Under the trendy, urgent letters symbolising speed was a silhouette of a hi-tech bike. If the customs inspectors opened his van, they would find two state-of-the-art bikes loaned to Kevin by a mate who ran a bike shop in Brighton, the fake paperwork indicating he was delivering them to a company in Lille. Behind the carefully positioned bikes on their stands bolted to the van floor was a large tool box spanning the van. On opening it, anyone inspecting it would see a neat tray of gleaming tools laid out in their foam holders. A second tray reinforced the image of quality maintenance. Under the second tray was a void capable of carrying one adult in coffin-like conditions, the air supply just sufficient to prevent suffocation.

The journey through the channel tunnel went without a hitch and three hours after she had banged on Kevin's door at the caravan site, Olivia burst impatiently out of the tool box the moment Kevin removed the trays of tools. They were on a quiet country road outside the town of St Omer, a few miles from Calais.

"Jesus, Kevin, that was worse than any nightmare," she said as she sat down heavily on the box. She was still hungrily sucking in breath, her eyes wide. "It was like being buried alive. And stowing my two bags with me didn't help."

"Yeah, I used to recommend sleeping pills to most of my clients, then one bloke snored so loudly that I thought he'd be heard, so I stopped."

He looked her up and down.

"You look pretty shook up, Sadie. I've got a flask of tea. D'yer want some?"

Olivia glanced up at him. For a man, he was better than she'd given him credit for. He was just a run-of-the-mill petty criminal, nothing dodgy. She was thankful for that. The way she was feeling, she'd have found it hard to fight him off, even if she did tower over him.

"That would be nice, thank you," she said, for a moment forgetting the accent she used when dealing with Kevin.

"You sound very posh all of a sudden," said Kevin with a sideways glance. "Is this the real Sadie Smith?"

"Don't push yer luck," replied Olivia, reverting to the accent Kevin was used to. "Right, I need you to take me to Brussels and then do one more little job for me before we go our separate ways."

"Brussels?" repeated Kevin as he handed her a plastic mug of tea. "I dunno, Sadie …"

Olivia shook her head and took a deep breath of resignation. "It'll be worth an extra five hundred."

On the outskirts of Brussels, Olivia got Kevin to check them into a seedy hotel where the sleepy receptionist was hardly likely to have the latest police notices at his fingertips. Nevertheless, Olivia wound a scarf around her face and kept her head down as she hurried to the stairs.

On entering their dingy room, she headed straight for the bathroom to get the money from her rucksack. She checked her face in the mirror. It was a mess and about to get messier.

"There," she said, as she went back into the room. "Your balance of two thousand."

Kevin took the money and stuffed it into a pocket.

"I thought you said there was an extra five hundred," he said, warily.

"There will be. Like I said, I've got one more job for you. It won't take long."

Kevin said nothing; he had no idea what to expect, and when she told him, he could hardly believe his ears.

"Ever slapped a woman around, Kevin?"

"What? What d'you take me for, Sadie? I don't go around bashing up women. I don't do the physical stuff, and even if I did, it wouldn't include women." He shook his head dismissively. "Nah, I don't care who it is, I'm not into that."

Olivia snorted a laugh, the movement of her skin sending a

dagger of pain through her nose. "I'll wager you'll change your mind when I tell you."

Kevin screwed up his face. This conversation was way outside his comfort zone.

"It's me, Kevin, I want you to knock me around a bit."

"You're bonkers, Sadie. Did somefin' happen to you in that box? Not enough air, or somefin'? I'm not going to knock you about. You'd break my neck."

"I will if you don't, and I'll be the two grand I've just given you better off. Now listen, I'm not going to retaliate, I just want you to slap my face very hard three times. It doesn't matter why, I just want you to do it."

Kevin looked as if he was about to be sick. "Sadie, I—"

"I can see I'm going to have to train you," said Olivia, shaking her head. She turned to pick up a pillow from the bed.

"Right," she said. She pulled the room's one chair from under its tired-looking desk, turned it round so that the seat faced her and the back faced Kevin.

"That's my face," she said, jamming the pillow down onto the top of the backrest. "Whack it as hard as you can. Take a good backswing."

Kevin took a step back, thinking he might just leave.

"Do it, Kevin! Be a man!"

Kevin's hand slapped into the pillow, his eyes full of fear as he waited for Olivia's reaction.

"I asked you to slap it, not tickle it, you wimp. Give it some welly!"

Three slaps later, Olivia still wasn't satisfied.

"You're pathetic, Kevin," she yelled. "So far, I would hardly even have felt those. Imagine you're trying to knock my head off, launch it through that window there."

Kevin took a deep breath, stood straight and twisted his head hard to the right and then the left, his neck vertebrae cracking. He rolled the fingers of his right hand nervously before launching his palm at the pillow, hitting it so hard Olivia almost dropped it.

She smiled. "That's better. Now, do it again."

Kevin's hand smacked across the pillow.

"Good. Again."

On the third slap, Olivia let go of the pillow a fraction of a second before Kevin's hand contacted it and it flew across the room.

"Perfect, Kevin." She flipped the chair and sat down on it, facing him.

"Now do the same to me. You've got three goes."

Although Kevin was now breathing heavily, his eyes still radiated doubt.

Olivia grabbed her rucksack from the bed next to her and pulled out the five hundred pounds she'd separated and tossed them onto the desk.

"There's your money. Now go for it."

The crack of hand on flesh surprised them both. Olivia was sitting on her hands, willing herself not to duck or retaliate, and when the blow came it was far harder than she had anticipated.

"Shit, Kevin. Ow, that hurt," she said shaking her head. "Now, again. Even harder!"

Kevin hit her again and she almost fell off the chair. The room began to spin. "Once more," she groaned, biting her lip in anticipation and lifting her head to receive the blow.

As soon as he'd hit her for the third time, Kevin took a step towards her. "Christ, Sadie, I'm sorry. I—"

"Just bugger off. Right now, before I decide to kill you," mumbled Olivia. "Go on! Take your money and get out!"

Kevin had thought of calling on a contact in Lille and picking up some tablets, a little extra business to add value to the trip, but he was so disturbed by what Sadie had demanded of him he could think of nothing except getting back through the tunnel to Kent as fast as he could.

After leaving Folkestone at six thirty the following morning, he stopped at a roadside cafe to pick up some strong coffee. As he paid, his eye fell on a rack of the early editions of several national newspapers, each of them prominently featuring a photograph of a woman on the front page. Although she looked different in the photo, he was in no doubt about who it was.

'Wanted for murder, attempted murder and grievous bodily harm. Ex-Police Superintendent Olivia Freneton is at large somewhere in the country. If you see this woman, do not approach her under any circumstances. She is armed and dangerous. Call the police hotline at the number below'

Kevin fingered the cash in the inside pocket of his jacket. If he'd known who Sadie was, he'd have tried to get more, although in his heart he knew it wouldn't have worked; she would probably have killed him and stolen his van. He read through the accompanying article listing Olivia's crimes. He grinned, appreciating the opportunity that presented itself: there was no way she'd be back and her Kawasaki was still at the site, as was her caravan. They would be worth quite a bit.

Chapter Twenty-Four

Henry Silk dabbed at his lips with a starched napkin, leaned back into the hardwood dining chair at the poolside table and sighed with satisfaction.

"I'm thinking of getting married again," he said, with a nonchalance that took Jennifer by surprise.

"You're what! Who's going to put up with your crazy schedule now that the acting world has finally recognised your talent?"

Henry shrugged. "Martina," he said, as if the answer should be all too obvious.

"Martina?" Jennifer frowned as she tilted her head in question. "Who's Martina? Do I know her?"

Henry waved his hand casually in the direction of the villa. "Martina," he said.

"Our housekeeper? That's all very sudden. Did you have a secret midnight tryst? Does her husband know about your plans?"

"Her husband is a minor detail, Jennifer. And as for a tryst, that would be far too vulgar for someone like Martina. No, I've decided that after last night's dinner, this morning's breakfast and now this quite exquisite lunch, I can't possibly live without her. She's a culinary goddess, blessed with gifts ordinary mortals can't possibly aspire to. Certainly not the ones who run the studio canteens in Hollywood."

"Idiot."

"I'm serious," replied Henry, although a twinkle had now appeared in his eyes. "How do you expect me to leave this afternoon, to return to the real world knowing such perfection is being created daily here on this magical island?"

"Well, you can't have her. I'll send you food parcels."

"You're too cruel. How can you be so mean to your father? I'm your flesh and blood."

"Good impersonation of an ageing thespian; you should have been wearing a large floppy hat and a pink silk scarf."

"Raspberry, dahling, crushed raspberry."

"Silly old fart. D'yer want a cup o' Nescaff before yer go?" sneered Jennifer in her best East Midlands accent.

Henry's response was a theatrical shudder. "What has the police force done to you? I fear there's no hope. Actually a glass of that grappa would go down well; I've got hours of sitting on a plane ahead of me."

"I don't envy you that," said Jennifer, pulling a face. "But I'm so pleased you came. We see far too little of each other."

"Thank heavens for Skype," said Henry, now back to his normal, less theatrical voice. "At least I can monitor your progress from afar."

"Yes, it's brilliant," agreed Jennifer. "Although there'll never be anything quite like sitting in the same room with each other."

"Or racing each other round the point," added Henry, his arm waving in the direction of the sea and the bay below the terrace where they had swum once again that morning. "Of course, I had to hold back to let you win. Positive reinforcement is all part of the recovery process."

"Huh!" Jennifer was dismissive. "I'm fully recovered, thank you. You should know that I was only in first gear. I—"

She was interrupted by a ping from her phone. Another incoming text. As she glanced at the screen, her banter with Henry was immediately forgotten. The message was from Derek. 'Call me ASAP'.

"God, what's happened now?" Jennifer's voice was filled with a sudden tension as she hit Derek's name in her favourites list. "Sorry, Henry, I think this is important."

The call answered in two rings.

"Derek! Wha—"

"Jen, thanks. I … sorry, I'm … a bit spooked."

"What's happened? You sound more than spooked; where are you?"

She looked up and caught Henry's eye, realising as she did that she was gripping her phone so hard she was in danger of breaking it.

"Jen, listen, I'm fine. I just needed to talk to you."

"Well, you don't sound fine. Look, Henry's here, OK if I put this on speaker?"

"Of course. Hi, Henry, how's paradise?"

"Blissful, as always, Derek. Listen, has something happened?"

"Yes, well, that is, no, nothing actually happened in the end. What she was planning didn't work."

"She?" said Henry, cautiously.

"Freneton," replied Derek.

"It wasn't a bomb under your car, was it?" asked Jennifer. "You've continued checking, like I insisted?"

"Every time it's left somewhere potentially vulnerable, yes. No, it wasn't my car, it was my bikes."

"She put bombs on your bikes?"

"Don't be daft, Jen, of course she didn't. She cut part way through the brake cables of both bikes so that if I applied the brakes hard, like in an emergency, the cables would snap and I'd have no brakes. I could've gone slamming into the side of a bus, or worse. That's what's spooked me."

"So how did you find out?"

"I always check the brakes before I head out for a ride, before I even get on the bike. It's just something I do, more I think to remind myself which is the front brake than anything else."

"You find it that hard to remember?"

"It wouldn't be," said Derek patiently, shaking his head at her remark, "but I've got two bikes. One is British made and the other was shipped over here from the US by the bloke I bought it from. The brakes are the other way round there. It's important to know so you don't hit the rear brake too hard."

"Makes sense."

"Praise indeed, DC Cotton. So, anyway, each time before I get on, I pull on the brake levers very hard, and this time both cables snapped. When I looked at them, they had been cut through."

"And you're sure it's Freneton?"

"Well, she didn't leave a note." He frowned as something occurred to him. "Actually, thinking about it, she did. The lab techs who were here earlier found a couple of her fingerprints. And the bikes were indoors in my flat, not out on the street."

"Fingerprints? Really?"

"Yeah, she must be getting careless."

"That I doubt," said Jennifer, shaking her head. "More likely she's just waving two fingers at everyone."

"Bitch," muttered Derek.

Jennifer looked over towards Henry to see him nodding in agreement.

"Derek," he said, "Jennifer told me this morning about what happened yesterday. Are the police any closer to finding her?"

"Not that I've heard, no," replied Derek. "They've got traffic camera images from last night that are almost definitely her. She can be seen heading down the M42 towards Birmingham, and then briefly on the M5, after which she disappears. There are no more sightings yet from further south. Nevertheless, it all still points to her heading for somewhere like Cornwall or Devon."

"Why not South Wales?" asked Jennifer. "One of the maps in the van was South Wales, wasn't it?"

"Could be," agreed Derek. "But two of the lads have been trawling through traffic cams from a couple of days ago. They've got some rapid ID system to speed up the search. Anyway, they found the same motorcycle heading north up the M5 and then tracked it back in time to find out where it had been. The earliest image they have is not far outside Penzance in Cornwall."

"Same bike? Same leathers?" Jennifer's mind was whirring.

"Yes."

"So they'll be looking for similar sightings from down there in the last few weeks."

"Months, probably," added Derek.

"I wonder why the sightings of her from last night stopped once she'd hit the M5," said Jennifer quietly, more to herself than the others. It was Henry who suggested a reason.

"Maybe she came off the motorway to use A roads, knowing there would be less likelihood of being stopped or recorded on some CCTV."

"Yes," agreed Jennifer, "that works. And so does the possibility that the whole thing is a decoy, that she's set up an elaborate plan to make us think she's in the South West when in reality she's somewhere else."

"Was she put on the stop list at the UK borders?" asked Henry.

"She's been on it for a year," said Derek. "Although it's not likely to make much difference. She's a master of disguise, as we know from when she tried to screw you."

"Jennifer said she's injured," added Henry. "Her face must be pretty bruised and she has a deep cut over her eye."

"That extra information has been given out to border police, yes," said Derek. "They'll pull everyone with any facial injuries out of the lines and check them out."

Henry took a reflective deep breath and sat back in his chair. He glanced over to Jennifer.

"What are you thinking, Jennifer? You've gone very quiet. I can almost hear the grey cells whirring."

Jennifer smiled at him and touched his arm affectionately.

"I was thinking about the maps in the van. It seems rather sloppy for Olivia. And who uses maps these days when there's the same information, often better information, in apps on phones? I think there's a strong chance all the searching in Cornwall and Devon today and on subsequent days will draw a blank. She's not there. If she were, I don't think she'd be leading us by the nose. My guess is she went off into some village, changed the look of the bike by perhaps removing the panniers, maybe even giving it a quick spray job. She could have changed the plates too."

Henry was nodding in agreement. "Crash helmet as well. She'd know the police were looking for a particular colour, so she could have had a spare in the pannier."

"Maybe even spare leathers," suggested Derek.

Jennifer pulled a face. "Bugger. That means she's effectively disappeared again while watching us waste huge amounts of resources on the pointless exercise of scouring the countryside."

"She'd be running a big risk in the long term if she tried to continue operating in the UK," said Henry. "From what you were telling me last night, she'd be strapped for cash and forever running the risk of being spotted. Going abroad is by far the safer option. Does she speak any foreign languages?"

"Nothing on her record that I can recall," said Jennifer.

"You're right," added Derek. "I was looking at her file the other day for something. There's nothing there about language skills."

Jennifer checked the time on the phone. Henry had to leave soon in order to make his flight. She caught his eye and tapped her wrist. He checked his watch. "Half an hour," he said, quietly.

Jennifer turned her attention back to the call.

"How are you feeling, Derek?" she asked.

"I'm fine, Jen, thanks. It has really helped talking it through with you both. I'd better go, I'm supposed to be at work."

"I'm sure Hawkins will understand," said Jennifer. "Is Crawford a reasonable man?"

"Yes, he's good, and bright too."

"Well, remember we could be entirely wrong about Freneton. She could be fooling us all and living in Nottingham, just waiting for her chance. Don't skimp on the checks, Derek. Under the car et cetera, and before you fall through your front door at night, look for any signs that someone is there. And remind Hawkins he was probably next on the list after Neil. Maybe you too. Perhaps she was planning a triple whammy."

"Thanks, Jen. I'll hold that thought and store it up for my next nightmare."

Chapter Twenty-Five

Connie Fairbright jolted from a deep sleep as her subconscious worked out the shrill tone of her mobile was reality and not part of her dream of floating in fields of sunflowers. She tumbled from the bed and staggered in confusion to the coffee table where she'd left the phone the evening before.

As she rubbed her eyes and let them focus on the screen, she registered two things: the time — 4.30 in the morning — and the caller's name.

"Diana! What's happened? Are you all right? It's the middle of the night. I—"

"Connie." Olivia's voice was a whispered croak that she had no need of faking. Her jaw was aching from the three vicious slaps she had demanded from Kevin.

"Diana! You sound hurt. Are you injured? Has there been an accident?"

Olivia waited before answering to allow Connie to continue to work up her state of panic.

Speaking slowly, her sentences in fragments, she said, "Connie. I'm hurt. Don't worry, it's not … life-threatening. I was beaten up. I thought … at first … it was a mugging. But now I'm … I'm not sure … although I have been robbed."

"Beaten up! Where are you, Diana? Are you still in Brussels? Have you called the police?"

"It was the police who did it."

"The police beat you up?"

"They weren't in uniform, but I'm pretty sure they were police, yes."

"Why? What possible motive could the police have in hurting you?"

"I don't know. I was walking back to my hotel, from my lawyer's office. I took a short cut. I was stupid. Through a dark and rather dodgy area. They grabbed me from behind. Took me completely by surprise."

"And they've hurt you. How badly?"

Olivia waited, letting her heavy breathing sound before she sobbed her reply.

"They punched me hard on the nose. It hurts like hell; I think it's broken. And then they slapped me around. One of them must have been wearing a ring because my eyebrow's cut. My face is a mess, Connie." She let the sobs mingle with a series of shuddering breaths. "I don't know what to do. I'm afraid to go out in case they're waiting somewhere."

"Do they know where you're staying?"

"I don't know. I'm frightened, Connie. One of them held me by the arms, really hard, from behind while the other one twisted my face in all directions."

"What were they doing?"

"I don't know. It was … it was as if he was examining a horse. I wondered if they were into kidnapping. You know, for some eastern bloc cartel who want women with very precise specifications."

"You mean like white slavery?"

"Yes. No. I don't know. Maybe. I'm confused. All I know is I was desperate to escape and when the one holding me relaxed his grip, I kicked the other one hard in the balls."

"Good for you, Diana."

"Not really; he was wild. That's when I was grabbed again and the one I'd kicked beat me. Then they ran off."

"What makes you think they were police?"

"When they first grabbed me, the one who did all the talking flashed me what looked like a warrant card. Said something about the gendarmerie."

"Probably fake. I think you should report it."

Olivia turned on more sobbing. "I just want to get out of here, Connie. But I can't; I've got no money. They took what I have from my bag. Cards as well. Fortunately, earlier on I brought my aunt's things back to the hotel from the lawyer's office. And the stupid thing is I needn't have come here at all. When I went back to his office this evening, the lawyer told me he'd finished everything. He even said he could actually have sent the papers and my aunt's stuff by courier for me to sign. I was livid. I yelled at him and stormed out. That's when this happened."

"OK, Diana, just give me the address and I'll get up there immediately. I'll fly up. If I rattle a few cages I could be airborne within an hour. Just stay put in your room, bolt the door, put a chairback under the handle and wait for me. I'll bring a doctor and a nurse; the hotel has them on call."

Olivia waited impatiently, drumming her fingers on the bed. Finally, after four hours, her phone rang.

"Diana, it's me. We've just arrived at your hotel. It's a real dump. Why are you staying in a place like this?"

"It was convenient and I stayed here once before, many years ago. My memories of it were better than what it's become. I'll open the door for you. I'm on the first floor, room 14."

Olivia sat on the edge of the bed and waited. She heard footsteps running up the stairs followed by an urgent knock on the door.

"Come in," she croaked. "It's open."

Connie burst into the room followed by two other women, one in a nurse's uniform, the other a duty doctor from the hotel in Rome.

"Oh my god, Diana, you poor dear! Let me look at you," cried Connie.

She sat on the bed and threw her arms around Olivia, who allowed her head to sink into Connie's shoulder.

"Dottoressa," called Connie, turning her head towards the two women.

The doctor stepped forward and took Olivia's wrist to check her pulse, after which she put a hand under Olivia's chin to lift her head and shone a torch into her eyes. She nodded and studied the marks and bruises on Olivia's face, gently peeling off the plaster Olivia had put on her eyebrow.

"Did they hit you anywhere else, signora?" she asked Olivia. "On your body?"

Olivia shook her head. "Only my face," she replied through a succession of sobs.

"Good," said the doctor. "You appear to have a slight concussion; I'll give you something for the pain; it will only take a few minutes to start taking effect. In the meantime, we'll clean you up and put a temporary dressing on your eyebrow. It needs stitching but I'd rather do it in my surgery back in Rome. When we're there, I'll also give you a full examination, just to be sure."

"Thank you," said Olivia. She turned her head to Connie. "Thank you, Connie. I can never repay your kindness. I thought they were going to kill me. I—"

"Don't try to talk, Diana," said Connie softly. "The important thing now is that you're in safe hands. Let's get you out of this terrible place. Can you walk? If not there's a wheelchair in the van outside."

"I'll be fine if I can lean on you," said Olivia as she turned to allow the nurse to swab her face.

While the doctor continued with her examination, Connie busied herself with pulling Olivia's few clothes from the wardrobes and drawers and packing everything back into the rucksack Olivia had hastily pulled them from a few hours earlier. Olivia continued with the suffering victim part while carefully watching Connie's every move, looking for any indication that she might be suspicious. She needn't have worried: Connie had swallowed the tale completely, her concern radiating through her actions. She simply wanted to get her friend back to the safety of Rome and the hotel. She hardly glanced at the two holdalls in which Olivia had stowed everything she didn't want seen, both sealed with substantial padlocks.

After a further fifteen minutes of unwanted attention, Olivia was declared fit enough to travel. Flanked by Connie and the doctor, with the nurse bringing up the rear with all the bags, Olivia allowed herself to be escorted carefully to the street, where the luxury minivan was ready to carry them to the waiting jet.

Chapter Twenty-Six

Jennifer Cotton skipped down the stairs of her flat in Nottingham's exclusive Park district, pulled open the front door and turned to call out to Derek.

"Come on, Thyme! I thought you were an Olympic athlete. Surely I haven't worn you out."

"You're joking, Cotton," yelled Derek as he bounded down three steps at a time, landing next to her with a thump.

"A half-hour tumble in the hay has just warmed me up," he said, kissing her on the cheek before heading for the door.

"Oi!" she yelled. She grabbed his arm and pulled him back to her, throwing her arms around his neck and pulling his face to hers. "I want more than a peck on the cheek."

"You're insatiable, Cotton," he grinned.

Too late, he realised her ploy was to turn their entwined bodies so she was closer to the door.

"Hey!" he called, but she was gone, racing for the gate.

"Close the front door!" she yelled as she pulled on the gate handle. "And make sure this one's shut too," she added as she pounded along the road.

There was a bang as the gate slammed into place and a slap of running shoes on tarmac as Derek sprinted after her.

"I must give you my notes on cheating, Cotton," he said, easing alongside her with his comfortable stride. "Tricks like that would get you banned from every meet in the country."

"Gotta have some advantage," she laughed as they ran towards Newcastle Circus, the larger of the two tree-lined roundabouts in The Park.

Jennifer stopped by a gate at the top end of the circus. "You go clockwise; I'll go anticlockwise. Three circuits and you take the outside when we pass. OK?"

Derek frowned and looked around. "Where's my chair?"

"What?"

"I'll need somewhere to sit and wait once I've finished. I'll be so far ahead of you."

"Huh!" cried Jennifer, tossing her head as she sprinted off.

Ninety seconds later, Jennifer completed her third loop to find Derek leaning casually against the gate.

"Lose your way?" he asked.

"You only did two," she countered.

"Actually it was four. That blur was me in overdrive."

"Yeah right, Thyme. Come on, we'll head towards the Castle then loop around the top roads."

Since returning to England in late September and starting her full-time training with the Art Fraud Squad, Jennifer had spent every weekend in Nottingham. In spite of the luxury of the villa on the cliffs overlooking the Tyrrhenian Sea, she had missed the tree-lined seclusion of The Park and the comfort of her flat with its spacious, high-ceilinged rooms and carefully chosen furniture, perfect for long lazy weekend days. She had also missed Derek.

Derek had met Jennifer at Heathrow. She had been feeling strangely nervous about returning, and about being met. For the last three months, they had spoken almost daily on the phone and on Skype, but throughout the flight she had questioned whether the magic she'd felt back in June would still be there. Was it real or had it all been an illusion brought on by the spell of Sardinia, the lapping waters and the perfumed breezes?

Derek's grin as she appeared immediately dispelled any

thoughts she'd had of doubts on his side, and when she felt his arms fold around her and her face snuggled into his neck, she knew nothing had changed.

However, the banter was strangely missing as they drove up the M1 motorway. It had been nearly a year and England looked strange, different. It wasn't just the light or the muted shades of green of the woodland, hedgerows and fields when compared with the vivid Italian landscapes; everything seemed alien, foreign, and incredibly busy. She felt like an observer rather than a participant, strangely out of place.

"That's why I want to get to the flat," she said as she tried to explain her feelings to Derek. "I need the feel of my own stuff, familiar surroundings. I've really missed it."

She turned, putting her hand softly on his arm. "I've missed you too, Derek, more than I thought was possible."

She raised her eyes to his. "Sorry, I shouldn't have said that."

He grinned. "Why not? You always say it like it is."

He reached over and stroked her hair.

"Missed you as well, Cotton."

Later, extracting herself from the duvet and their tangle of legs, Jennifer sat up and laughed. "Christ, Thyme, two minutes in a place and you've turned it into a tip."

He reached out and took her arm, pulling her down on top of him.

"You know what you said about not being able to keep our hands off each other …"

"I don't remember saying that," she said, nuzzling his neck.

"Pants on fire, as you're fond of saying."

"I'm not wearing any," she giggled.

On that first, long weekend, they had hardly left Jennifer's flat, except for a brief visit to Beeston for Derek to show Jennifer what he was now starting to call his country residence, since it was twenty minutes out of town rather than two.

"I'm trying to look at this place from Freneton's eyes," said Jennifer, once Derek had given her a tour. "She'll have stood here, near the door, worrying about hidden alarm systems, wondering when you might show up, wondering where to start searching for any information you might have on me, and hoping that you haven't taken your computer into work with you."

Derek shook his head. "No, she'd remember that's not allowed. We can only use the official desktops or authorised tablets. Nothing personal. The DCS is very rigid on that."

"You could have chucked it into your car for safekeeping."

"But I didn't, and she found it. I'd love to have seen the frustration on her face when the security Ced installed cut in."

Jennifer smiled. "Yes, it's great to have a friend like Ced in tow. What he doesn't know about computing isn't worth knowing."

"Yeah," agreed Derek, "he's a total genius. He was appalled when I called and told him about what Freneton had done to my bikes. I'm glad he and his family are completely off Freneton's radar."

"Have you upgraded your locks since she broke in?" asked Jennifer.

"They were already upgraded. The locksmith reckoned they were the best."

"Well, either she's exceptionally good at picking locks or your locksmith's rubbish. I'll get Pietro's guys onto it."

As Derek drew a breath to object, she cut him off. "No objections. I insist. You can pay the bill so there's no acceptance of favours. I know it's unlikely she'll come back any time soon, but I want to be reassured that when I'm not around to hold your hand, you won't have any unpleasant surprises waiting for you when you come home. And you must look into getting somewhere to garage your car. It's too vulnerable out on the street. Look what she did to Hurst's. It was all way too easy."

Derek held up his hands in submission. "OK, boss, you win. And I agree, you're right. I can't trust the old dears downstairs not to let her into the building, so the locks have got to be good."

He took her hand. "Now, I don't think you paid enough attention to the bedroom."

Having assigned Jennifer to work undercover for his specialist unit in the Art Fraud Squad, Paul Godden was determined she maintain a low profile. Secrecy was essential and although he trusted his officers completely, his main offices in the large police complex near Canary Wharf were far too public for his liking. Not only were many other police formations housed in the building, there was some public access, and certain art dealers had the annoying habit of dropping in uninvited on the pretext of having some useful snippet of information for the squad. If Jennifer were seen there, she would be bound to attract attention. Godden knew that several of his successful cases had ruffled feathers among the more unscrupulous dealers, particularly those who dealt with high-value sales of paintings of dubious origin. They had eyes at all the auctions, checking on any new faces whose connections appeared blurred; they wanted to know precisely who could be trusted and who might arrest them. For Paul Godden, anonymity for certain of his officers was paramount, Jennifer included.

For this reason, on her return from Sardinia, Jennifer had spent her weekdays training in a palatial house set in large grounds in Surrey, a specialist training centre used by both the security services and the police, whose activities were hidden from the outside world by high walls. It was here she met up with Nicole Turner, a specialist in interviewing and behavioural techniques she had previously spoken to at length on Skype while still in Sardinia. Turner was an expert at crafting young officers into playing the roles demanded of them while undercover, ensuring their natural tendency towards acting like police officers was well hidden. Jennifer wondered who she actually worked for; certainly it wasn't the Art Fraud Squad as she'd originally thought.

After six weeks, Jennifer was ready. She had covered all she needed to with the added bonus of getting up to scratch with her unarmed combat skills. While she thought there would be little need for these in the refined world of art galleries, she was more than grateful for the opportunity — for as long as her nemesis, Olivia Freneton, was still at large, a burrowing worm of worry would be forever present at the back of her mind.

Her normal practice on arriving at the Surrey house every morning at eight from Pietro's apartment in Wimbledon was to warm up for the day with a run through the grounds with one of the resident physical trainers.

The mid-November morning was verging on frosty, a lacklustre sun making little headway in penetrating the mist rolling in from the Downs to the south. Both Jennifer and Jim Smith, her companion that morning, were in full track suits and insulated ski hats, their breath billowing away in clouds as they sprinted from the woods towards the house at the end of their session. Arriving at the main door, Jim pulled it open, moving aside to let Jennifer through.

"Thanks, Jim," she panted, peeling off her scarf as the warmth of the entrance hall set her skin tingling. "That got the circulation going."

"Always a pleasure, Jennifer," replied Jim. "Now, you should get in a hot shower to keep those muscles nice and warm."

"You betcha," she said, turning towards the corridor that led to the changing rooms.

"DC Cotton," called one of the two receptionists. "Got a message for you."

Jennifer broke her stride and walked over to the desk.

The woman smiled at her. "Superintendent Godden called to say he's on his way down from London. Asked you to meet him in the cafeteria at nine thirty."

"Thanks, Siobhán," said Jennifer, her mind now full of expectation. She had been waiting for Godden to get in touch for over a week, knowing that things were starting to fall into place in Florence.

"As you know, Jennifer," said Godden as he settled in the uncomfortable plastic chair in a quiet corner of the cafeteria, "while you've been completing your briefing down here, Massimo Felice has been preparing the way for your potential placement in the Cambroni gallery in Florence. For that, a vacancy in the gallery for new staff was required. Massimo told me he'd handle it and his plan is now moving forward.

"Basically, there are two admin assistants in the gallery. One is a lady in her early sixties, Maria Renzo, who isn't in the best of health. In fact she's been taking more and more time off owing to sickness. Although we haven't ascertained exactly what she does in the gallery, we do know she's been with them for more than thirty years, so she must be at the heart of much that goes on there. There's not a lot can be done about her, given her history, but it should be safe to assume that she'll continue to be absent from the gallery quite often.

"Now the other assistant is altogether different. She, to quote Felice, is an arrogant bitch of thirty-one called Gabriella Panella whose uncle got her the job a few years ago through connections with the elder Cambroni. She's known to be disliked by the gallery staff and losing her job will not cause her any pain since her family's rich. Apparently they find her equally obnoxious; they just wanted to get her out of their hair. Felice has come up with a scheme to set her up, which should be happening in the next day or so. Panella has a penchant for expensive clothes and accessories that are way beyond her salary. She's often in exclusive Florentine fashion stores where she loves to throw her weight around because her uncle is important. Felice has a female officer tailing her who, when Panella next goes shopping in a particular store, will lift a couple of very expensive scarves from the display and pop them into Panella's bag. Since the scarves are tagged, an alarm will sound when she tries to leave the shop. The store in question always calls the police in shoplifting cases and has a policy of pressing charges. The local police will try to dissuade them, given Panella's connections, but the store will insist. There's also a tipped-off local journalist who'll arrive on the scene and the outcome will be a minor scandal for the family. This will give the gallery an excuse to sack her since they won't want to be associated with any adverse publicity.

"So, Jennifer, your name, or more precisely Ginevra Mancini's name, is now with the exclusive recruiting agency the gallery uses on the rare occasions it needs their services. Your superb qualifications should ensure that you'll get an interview."

In spite of this being the news she had been waiting for, Jennifer was still shocked. "So it's all falling into place. When do I leave?"

Godden pulled an envelope from his pocket. "Here's your ticket for a flight later this afternoon. You're travelling on your ordinary British passport, which we'll then store for you at the safe house. Your apartment, rented in Ginevra Mancini's name, is all set up, as you know. Once you're there, you'll be contacted by Felice or one of his squad. Sorry it's short notice."

Jennifer nodded. "Yes, even though I was expecting it, it's still a surprise. This is presumably why you insisted on my having a bag here packed and ready."

"Exactly."

Godden checked his watch. "Now, we still have some time and I need to brief you on a couple of important matters that have arisen since we last spoke."

Jennifer took a deep breath. "Wow, it's really happening."

Godden grinned. "Yes, Jennifer, it is. OK, I want to give you a heads-up on what we've got so far about how the gallery is organised."

He sat back, crossing his legs. "Basically, there are three parts, so far as we can see. The first, the public part, for want of a better phrase, is located on the first floor of the building up a flight of internal stairs that lead only to the gallery. Here collections of mainly modern paintings are exhibited for sale. They generally feature the work of well-known artists, but even for this public shop front, casual tourists and other visitors are discouraged by the presence of a large African security guard posted on the street-level door. If he doesn't like the look of anyone, he refuses to let them in. The clientele tend to be moneyed Italians — Florentines mainly — and rich foreigners who are either old clients or who have introductions from previous clients. The main reason there is a public gallery at all is that there have been several high value sales over the years to walk-ins who for whatever reason chose not to make an appointment. Business is business.

"The second part of the gallery is more private and accessible only by invitation or appointment. This we know is on an upper floor accessed only through the first-floor gallery and some more internal stairs or a lift, also internal. This private gallery is for well-heeled clients who wish to remain anonymous or who do not wish to mix with people they don't know. These clients, as far as we can ascertain, are basically honest collectors who want to have access to valuable paintings that have come onto the market either through sale or because they are the latest works of a highly sought-after living talent. This happens in various ways in top-end galleries in this country too, as you now know from your briefings. OK so far?"

Jennifer nodded. "All sounds straightforward enough. I should assume that if they take me on, it would be in what you're calling the public part of the gallery until either I've earned their trust or perhaps dire necessity requires me to be in the more private areas."

Godden smiled. "Exactly, and to that end, Ms Renzo's ill health might just be encouraged if we can find a way. However, you don't need to concern yourself with that."

"I don't think I want to," said Jennifer, raising her eyebrows. "You said there are three parts to the gallery."

"Yes, and perhaps more. The entire building is owned by the Cambronis and being several hundred years old, is something of a labyrinth. We're pretty sure there is a third, extremely private inner sanctum on the top floor just below the roof. From the building plans it seems to be quite separate from the main gallery and is probably accessed by a lift from a discreetly placed door on a side street that leads into a secure lobby. Neither we nor Felice have been able to get anywhere with that except for observing who enters and leaves. You must also remember that since this is an old building, there are very likely hidden passageways and possibly even back stairs that are not on the plans.

"Now, what is also interesting is that Felice's information indicates the artists the gallery uses to produce forgeries have a studio somewhere in the building, possibly also in this top floor private sanctum. And somewhere in the building there's also what's been referred to as their laboratory for installing the security microchips. We don't know how many forgers there are, but from Ced Fisher's results and the observations of Felice's team, we know there are at least two. Their guise will be as restorers. It's the forgers who are the final point I want to raise with you."

Jennifer gave Godden a suspicious look. "If they are elderly and set in their ways, I don't think I'll be their type," she said, her face deadpan. "However, if one or more of them is young, cool and good-looking, I assume you're thinking of a honeytrap."

Godden laughed, shaking his head. "No, far too risky. If you, as a newly employed assistant in the gallery, start dating one of their master forgers, they will immediately be suspicious. It could be dangerous for you. You're trying to blend in there, not be under the spotlight."

Jennifer smiled to herself. Could be dangerous for the forger too, she mused, thinking of Derek.

"So one of them is young, cool and handsome?"

"Yes," said Godden. "One of the two we know of is. He's a thirty-year-old called Tonino Varinelli. He was a brilliant student at art college but that was ten years ago and since then he's gone off the radar. He's had no further connection with the art world or with his former fellow students. Any information you can find out about him and his colleague or colleagues will be very useful. Something that Fisher could analyse would be ideal since that would link the fakes to the gallery."

"Someone's taken a look at where he lives, presumably."

Godden shook his head. "Lives with his mother who never leaves the apartment. Felice hasn't been able to get close. Not that there's likely to be anything lying around there; these people are too good for that."

"Not even an early work la mamma has hanging on the wall?" mused Jennifer. "Anyway," she added, "it could all take a while, given that it's bound to take some time before I can build up trust."

Godden agreed. "Operations like this can't be hurried. No, what we need, as was in the briefing papers we discussed last time I was here, is to catch the Cambronis in the act of moving some fakes to somewhere else rather than back to the owner of the original painting, or even better, transporting genuine works they should no longer have on their books. By that I mean they've given a fake back to the collector who thought he'd had security installed in his genuine painting."

"I'll keep a careful record of anything and everything and get it to the safe house."

"Of course, and remember, they're going to be watching you. They will almost definitely have internal security cameras which could be trained on you. We also strongly suspect that once they've taken you on, someone will visit your apartment when you're not there to look for anything to indicate you're not who you say you are."

Jennifer smiled. "Everything's in place, all Ginevra's memories, mementos and so on. And don't forget the apartment is now bugged with two or three micro-cameras in every room, movement triggered, so if someone does take a look around, I'll know."

"Yes, the additional security courtesy of your stepfather is first rate. We can't normally justify installing it in an operative's apartment, so it's a real added bonus.

"Now, Jennifer, before I send you on your way, I want to remind you that your safety in this operation is of the utmost importance; nothing justifies compromising it. You've been instructed and briefed on all the exit strategies. Remember, they are in place for your protection. If you get any indication that you are suspected in any way, you must not hesitate to follow your training and abort your placement in the gallery."

Jennifer smiled, although rather than reassure her, Godden's words brought home the fact that for most of the time, she would be on her own.

"Thank you, Paul. I won't let you down. I know how much is resting on this and I want it to succeed as much as anyone. Don't worry, I won't take risks and I won't do anything stupid."

Chapter Twenty-Seven

Olivia spent the day of her return to Rome from Brussels allowing the doctor to examine her, stitch and dress the cut to her eyebrow and tend to her other injuries. And even though she hated every moment, she also allowed Connie to cluck around her, ministering to her every need.

As her face moved through various shades of unattractive yellow and purple, she was pleased she'd gone the extra mile of Kevin's beating: every time Connie looked at her, which was almost constantly, the sympathy in her eyes increased. If Connie had felt close to her friend before the fictitious departure to Brussels, her conviction now of wanting her to be a long-term companion was total.

The morning after their return, Olivia was making notes on her secret computer when her phone pinged with a text from Connie.

'Are you awake? Is it too early to call by?'

Olivia had slept well, exhausted by the activity of the previous two days, particularly the self-orchestrated beating and the nightmare three hours hidden in the tomb-like confines of Kevin's toolbox, the latter requiring every ounce of her self-control not to have screamed for release.

But all that was now history; she had the future to plan and had been up for two hours gathering her thoughts and revising her strategies.

'Give me 5m' she typed in reply, getting up to stow her computer and notebook in the safe before mussing up her hair in preparation for Connie's arrival.

"I've ordered you some coffee, Diana, I hope you don't mind," said Connie once she'd ushered Olivia back to her bed and sat herself down on the end. "Don't worry about the staff, I'll collect it at the door. We'll keep you cloistered away until the worst of the bruising's gone. I don't want rumours that we've had a fight."

She gave a nervous laugh as Olivia responded with a half smile.

If we'd been fighting, thought Olivia, you'd be in the mortuary by now.

"Yes," she said, "I'll be wearing large dark glasses and an excess of powder for a few days if I need to go out."

"Are you up to breakfast?"

Olivia was ravenous but thought it better to suffer it until lunchtime.

"Just a little toast, I think," she said, easing her back with exaggerated care into a more comfortable position. "And perhaps some plain yoghurt."

After reaching for the room phone and placing the order, Connie returned to the bedside.

"Gosh, I'm sorry, Diana. My stomach's ruling my head as usual. How are you feeling? Did those sleeping pills the doctor gave you allow you some rest? You poor thing. I can't begin to imagine what you've been through. Are you ready to talk about it yet?"

Olivia had thrown the pills away, never wanting to be in a position where she couldn't snap awake at a moment's notice. She set her face with a pained expression. "Actually, Connie, I think I'd rather forget all about it. Put it down to a bad experience owing largely to my own stupidity for being in the wrong place at the wrong time."

"Why do you think they attacked you? Were they trying to kidnap you?"

Olivia shook her head. "I've been thinking through what I can piece together of it. It all happened so fast, you understand. I reckon it was a case of mistaken identity. They were expecting someone else whom I happened to resemble so they grabbed me. They must have quickly realised they'd got the wrong person so they let me go."

"Then why beat you up? It seems horribly sadistic."

"Maybe it was a warning or maybe they were the kind of men who like beating women. Who knows? Whatever the reason, it's over and I want to forget it."

She reached out to touch Connie's arm. "I'm sorry to have been so much trouble, Connie. I don't know what I'd have done if I'd not had you to call."

Connie placed her hand on top of Olivia's. "It was the least I could do for my dearest friend," she said, smiling. "What's important now is to get you on the road to recovery. The doctor says while the redness to your face should start to fade in a day or two, the bruising on and around your nose will take longer. What worries me is how it's affected you psychologically, emotionally. Did you have nightmares last night? Do you think perhaps some trauma therapy would be a good idea?"

Olivia found it difficult not to laugh in Connie's face. The last thing she wanted was some analyst getting inside her head. It would be unhealthy territory for anyone who tried, and the more they probed, the more Olivia would need to kill them.

"I'm a big girl, Connie, I don't think I'll be suffering any long-term effects."

Over the next weeks, Olivia was pleased to see Connie's reliance on her increasing. Once the stitches were out of her eyebrow and the swelling to her nose had subsided, the range of Connie's expectations of her friend began to increase beyond what they had been before the Brussels incident. Connie was now consulting her on just about every non-investment-related aspect of her life, even seeking her advice on her clothes, which was ridiculous given Connie's far better sense of fashion. Olivia was rapidly becoming indispensable.

During her 'convalescence', Olivia also reflected long and hard over her UK disposal strategy. She had to assume that her caravan bolthole had disappeared along with the West Bridgford garage and flat. She now had no refuge in the UK to which she could head to plan any future exercise and much as it pained her, she reluctantly made the decision to put the outstanding disposals on hold until some unspecified time in the future. Her strategy now must be to get ever closer to Connie, to win her trust and gain access to her wealth. Connie's money would become her number one priority, her motivator.

However, no matter how much closer the pair became, Connie kept all matters relating to her wealth totally to herself. Money was merely something she had; how it was managed back in the States was only vaguely hinted at. Her dealings with the highly-paid advisers and financial managers employed to deal with her vast portfolio were conducted twice a week after lunch behind the closed doors of her suite. Olivia was never invited.

Olivia knew the numbers were huge; she had long since researched Connie and her dead husband online, extracting what snippets were released to the financial press. She was realistic enough to accept that she would never be likely to gain direct access to large amounts of Connie's cash, so another way would have to be sought. There were several possibilities, all of which involved theft and therefore would have to be perfectly timed, since once the deed was done, there would be no going back. The obvious target would be the works of art Connie had proposed buying on many occasions, but so far, her collection remained only in her head, her prevarication on moving forward endlessly frustrating.

The weeks dragged for Olivia, the time made more difficult by her having to play the sweet Diana to Connie, a dear friend with all the answers, never ruffled, never bored, always kind, attentive and supportive. Olivia gave vent to her frustration with intensive sessions in the gym where she would stretch her finely tuned muscles to the limit. She took particular pleasure in boxing and kick boxing training where she frequently made even the most seasoned of instructors cower. When this wasn't enough and the tension in her head threatened to bubble over, she would take herself off late at night to the seediest and darkest back streets of Rome where she would deliberately allow herself to be followed and accosted by a mugger unaware of what he was taking on. If he was lucky, the mugger would be left a pummelled mess of flesh and broken bones in a gutter; the unlucky ones became just more statistics in the unsolved murder list, assumed to be victims of mob retribution.

Finally, three months after the Brussels incident, light appeared at the end of Olivia's tunnel of impatience, and when it appeared it offered far more possibilities than she had expected.

The request came out of nowhere one morning at breakfast. When Olivia made her way to the terrace, she was surprised to find Connie already there sipping her coffee and working her way through what was now a far-more-comprehensible Corriere Della Sera. The wary Mario broke cover to appear at the table in time to pull out Olivia's chair and spread her napkin, immediately removing himself lest he upset la Signora Fairbright.

Connie poured Olivia a coffee and sat back, a smile on her face radiating excitement.

"You're looking very pleased with yourself this morning, Connie," said Olivia, reaching for her cup and raising a quizzical eyebrow.

"I've been thinking, Diana, plotting," said Connie, sitting upright and placing both hands on her thighs as she leaned forward towards her friend. "I'm ready to take my plan to the next stage and I'm afraid, as usual, that I'm going to be asking for your help in sorting something out."

Hardly able to contain her avarice as a number of ideas flashed through her mind, Olivia allowed a knowing smile to spread across her face, "You mean you want to start your art collection? You feel ready?"

Connie clapped her hands, immediately confusing Mario who shot to attention before working out he wasn't being summoned.

"Yes! Exactly! I know I've talked and talked about it until your eyes drooped with boredom—"

"Never, Connie!" protested Olivia, laughing as she said it. "It's a wonderful project."

"Isn't it just?" Connie reached out and squeezed her friend's arm. "Anyway, I've been privileged, thanks to you, to have had the benefit of Alessandro's brilliant teaching for several months now, and I've been stuffed full of just about everything Cesare Contorni has to offer for far longer. No, that's not fair. If I remained his student for the next ten years, I think he would still find new artists and their work to delight me with. However, although I want to carry on the lessons with Alessandro, I think I'm ready to cut down on Cesare's to, say, a couple a week, to free up some time. You see, I think I'm ready to start exploring the world of galleries and salesrooms without being ripped off at every turn."

"That's wonderful, Connie, I wondered when you would want to move forward. It's a very exciting thought. So, how can I help? Do you want me to make a shortlist of reputable galleries here in Rome?"

Connie shook her head. "As far as Rome is concerned, I'm already familiar with all the galleries I would consider using. What I'd like you to do is look at some elsewhere. Florence would be a good place to start. Or Siena perhaps?"

"It would be a pleasure," said Olivia. "I'll get on to it this morning while you're with Alessandro."

She studied Connie's face, letting her own register amusement.

"That's not all though, is it? I know that scheming look, Connie Fairbright; you're hatching another plot."

"Gosh, am I that transparent?"

"Only in a good way."

Connie squeezed Olivia's arm again. "I want to move out of Rome."

Olivia pursed her lips and nodded. "Why not? Where do you want to go? Florence? Siena? Bologna?"

"No, not to a city. You see, if my plans work out, I'm going to be acquiring some pretty valuable pieces over the next year or two." She looked around and let her voice drop. "To the tune of several million dollars," she mouthed, the words hardly even a whisper. "I'll need to store them somewhere."

"Too right," agreed Olivia. She couldn't believe where this might be going. "A very secure vault comes to mind."

"That's the point, Diana; that's exactly what I don't want to do. If I buy all these wonderful works, I'll want to look at them. Every day. Have them on show, for me that is." She smiled. "For us, I mean, if that's what you still want."

Olivia said nothing, letting what she hoped was an affectionate enough smile speak for her.

"Don't you want to be in a city?" she asked. "What about security? Wouldn't it be easier to burglarproof a house in a city rather than a villa in, I don't know, Tuscany, for example?"

Connie was shaking her head. "Not with the sort of security I have in mind. There'd be little difference, and any advantage that being in a city might confer, such as the police being closer, would be totally outweighed by all the advantages of being in the country."

"Heavens," said Olivia. "I think you mean it."

"I sure do, honey. You see I'm no novice at this. The house where we lived in Massachusetts was hardly urban. It was on huge grounds and Brad had installed just about every security device known to man. If a mosquito landed on the lawn at night, it would set alarms off."

Olivia laughed. "And you think you can get the same here."

Connie nodded. "Almost definitely, and if I can't, I'll import it from the States."

"So that's another little task for me to research for you?"

"Actually, Diana, no, it's not; the security aspect, I mean. I have good contacts in the States who are very well connected internationally in the security world. They are real experts. And, with respect, you probably don't know too much about it."

Olivia gave a nod to indicate agreement. What her face didn't register was her amusement at the irony of the situation. Police Superintendent Olivia Freneton had made a specialist study of innumerable security systems and been briefed by the top specialists from the UK defence agencies. She had probably forgotten more about security systems than Connie's people would ever learn, not that she would be telling Connie.

"So what would you like me to do?"

"Find me a villa."

Connie's expectations of a villa were ambitious. Its condition didn't matter since she would be implementing a major renovation. What was important was its size and location. It had to be large, with rooms that could be reliably climate controlled to protect the paintings she intended to buy; it should be set on at least twenty hectares of land, more if possible, land that could be well fenced to keep out hunters, walkers and foragers as well as potential burglars, and it needed to be relatively remote, not easily visible, either from a distance or even from its entrance gate.

Olivia pulled out a notebook and together the two women compiled a detailed shortlist of requirements.

"What sort of time frame are we looking at?" asked Olivia, tapping her notebook with her pen.

Connie pulled a face. "Well, this *is* Italy, so even if we can find the right property soon, the bureaucracy together with the building work to bring it up to spec could take a year. But hey, we might be lucky and find it takes less. Wouldn't that be marvellous?"

"So ideally, late summer next year?"

Connie's face lit up. "Do you think that's doable? Gosh, it would be so wonderful. I mean, this hotel is magnificent and my suite beautiful. But it's still a hotel. Much longer and I think I'll be climbing the walls."

"If you want to get out of here sooner, you could always consider renting somewhere," suggested Olivia. "In fact, that would be a good idea once you've settled on a property to buy. If you rented in the same area, you could keep an eye on progress, be on hand for any decisions that needed to be made."

"Diana, you're brilliant," enthused Connie. "And your mention of Tuscany, a place where I know I'd love to live, fills me with excitement. I'd like you to start your search there."

.   .   .

Olivia hadn't just casually mentioned Tuscany; once Connie had expressed her wish to buy a villa, she decided it was the only location. Her own small farmhouse — her secret refuge and centre of operations until she'd met Connie — was in the wilds of Tuscany and it would be far more convenient if Connie's proposed villa were relatively nearby.

Nestled in the hills beyond the Val di Chio about fifteen miles from the medieval town of Castiglion Fiorentino, south of the city of Arezzo, Olivia's farmhouse was on a remote, seldom-used track that went nowhere. She knew of several luxury properties within a twenty-mile radius along with many others in varying states of disrepair. One of them would be bound to fit the bill.

Chapter Twenty-Eight

MARCH – MAY 2016

Maurizio Cambroni shuffled from the internal lift into the private second-floor gallery as fast as his failing legs and leather slippers would allow.

"My dear Contessa," he called, his lisping Florentine tones overlaid with a whistle of age, "a thousand apologies; a million. I was detained downstairs with a demanding client, you understand how it is, and I failed to notice the time."

The Contessa De Santi waved a parchment hand in his direction, the expertly cut carats of her several rings catching the light.

"Slow down, Maurizio, or you'll have a heart attack. Surely you know you are supposed to take it easy at your time of life."

Jennifer suppressed a smile as she looked at the filigree of lines etched into the ageing contessa's face. She was every bit as old as Maurizio Cambroni, if not several years his senior.

"You needn't have concerned yourself, you know," continued the contessa, "your Signorina Mancini has been charming her way to my chequebook on your behalf. If she continues to weave her spell, I'll be in danger of frittering away what's left of the late Conte's fortune on these miracles of creativity."

She waved the bejewelled hand at the array of paintings on the gallery wall.

"You've excelled yourself, you old crook. A collection of exquisite and rare Rondinos and an even more exquisite young lady to sell them for you. You must be raking it in; I trust you'll give me my usual discount."

Cambroni's palms turned outwards instinctively as he shrugged his acquiescence.

"You are taking the entire collection?" He was hardly able to hide the disbelief in his voice.

"All five," said the contessa, with a dismissive toss of her head. "One for each of my great grandchildren. Not that they'll be allowed anywhere near them until many years after I've gone. But they'll have gained in value by then. Pay for their education."

She turned to Jennifer. "My account with these rogues goes back so far, my dear Ginevra, that I doubt your parents were born, let alone you. Such a lovely name, always liked it. Contact my office, they'll sort everything out."

She held out a regal hand.

"Now, perhaps you'd be so kind as to escort me to the lift. We can continue our little chat on the way down. My car's waiting in the street."

"Little chat?" asked Maurizio Cambroni, raising a silver eyebrow. Jennifer had returned to the gallery and was heading for the accounts office.

She stopped and walked over to him, smiling. "A rather one-sided chat, Signor Cambroni. The contessa was telling me all about the lovers she's taken since the conte died."

"Hah!" barked Cambroni scornfully. "Her imagination is considerably more athletic than her body. She's eighty-six, you know."

Jennifer nodded. "She told me. She's very proud of it."

The corners of Cambroni's mouth lifted in what passed with him for a smile. "You've done well today, Ginevra. Extremely well. The old girl normally ends up buying what I reserve for her, but it always takes several visits and endless haggling. I've never known her buy on a first viewing. Excellent work. There'll be a good bonus coming your way, I promise you."

"Thank you, signore," said Jennifer, her deferential tone hiding her indifference to the payment. As an undercover police officer, any payments she received for anything, including the salary from the gallery, would eventually end up in the Metropolitan Police coffers, not her own. All she was permitted to receive was her normal salary plus a special duties allowance.

———

Jennifer's comfortable and relaxed relationship with the Cambroni's, Ettore in particular, was in sharp contrast to how she had felt during her early days at the gallery, four months previously.

Following a probing interview, the pair had accepted her as the most qualified by far of the three candidates for the vacant post, after which they kept their distance, leaving her training to the ailing Maria Renzo while they cautiously awaited reports from the two faceless investigators assigned to follow her and to examine her apartment while she was at the gallery.

Renzo herself was guarded in her acceptance after her experience with the dreadful Gabriella Panella. However, within a few days, Jennifer had charmed the woman with her knowledge and with the refined Milanese manners she could turn on when required.

The first note of a thaw from the Cambronis came two days after the team of watchers sequestered in Pietro's Florence apartment reported to Jennifer that her apartment had been searched. Although a professional job from the two Cambroni investigators, they failed to notice the carefully hidden array of micro surveillance cameras: the team had watched the entire operation as it happened. The outcome, reported back to the Cambronis by the senior of the investigators, was as it had been planned. Ginevra Mancini was a studious young woman with a love of art. She had all the normal photographs and mementos from her youth and childhood, with nostalgic shots of her now-dead parents. Her wardrobe indicated nothing wild or extreme in her leisure activities, while her music collection was a mainstream selection of classics and casual, inoffensive pop. She didn't smoke, there was no alcohol and there were no drugs hidden anywhere. All in all, she was exactly what the gallery wanted: a conservative young lady with no ostentation. They simply needed reassurance.

Nevertheless, the Cambronis were taking no chances. Jennifer's apartment was searched twice more in the next three weeks and the investigators continued to follow her. However, rather than being concerned by the attention, Jennifer welcomed it as an opportunity to fine-tune her tradecraft.

Her first real conversation with the elder Cambroni was the day after the third search of her apartment.

"I seem to remember you saying in your interview that you have only recently moved to your present address, signorina. How are you getting on?"

"Very well, thank you, signore. I like the apartment a lot. It's large, airy, and surprisingly quiet. And it's so convenient for the gallery."

"What about security? This city is not without its burglaries."

"It's not bad, although the locks are all ancient. I don't know how good they are."

"I know an excellent locksmith if you want one. He could update your apartment's main door lock; give you peace of mind."

And give you a spare key, thought Jennifer, although her face registered no reaction to Cambroni's unsubtle suggestion.

"How kind of you, signore. Thank you so much."

Two months on and the thaw had continued. In the 'public' part of the gallery, sales were up for both walk-in and existing clients, all of whom were impressed by Jennifer's knowledge and professionalism. She was careful to avoid expressing any interest in the other areas of the gallery, although she took a careful note of clients who were whisked directly to the upper floors. On the one occasion she mentioned recognising a well-known politician to Maria Renzo, she was put severely in her place.

"Ginevra, under no circumstances do we talk about anyone who visits the gallery, you never know who's listening. That applies both inside its walls and outside, where such indiscretion is absolutely forbidden. And," she added in a discreet whisper, "never let

Signor Maurizio or Signor Ettore hear you making such comments."

Jennifer's first sight of the private gallery was forced on the Cambronis in late April by a long-time client, an ageing Italian movie star known for both his womanising and his connections with the underworld. Sergio Gianpietro Zaccaro was being escorted by Ettore Cambroni through the first floor gallery to the internal lift when his eyes fell on Jennifer who was working at a desk about thirty yards away.

"Ettore!" cried Zaccaro, marching down the gallery to the confusion of Cambroni, "You have employed an angel to work here? Why didn't you tell me?"

Cambroni was too slow to prevent the actor gliding up to Jennifer, taking her hand and pressing it to his lips.

"Bella signorina," he gushed, his face and bad breath far too close for Jennifer's liking. "I am in awe. You eclipse the normally unrivalled beauty of the enchanting paintings on this gallery's walls."

He lifted her hand and kissed it again. "Let me introduce myself. I am Sergio Gianpietro Zaccaro." He paused, giving her time to be impressed before turning to Ettore Cambroni. "My dear friend, I insist this goddess be my guide to the collection you have waiting for me. Come, signorina, take my arm, escort me upstairs to show me what they have prepared."

Jennifer glanced at Ettore Cambroni. His face was set in disapproval, but he was in no position to refuse. The actor had money and was prepared to spend it. He let the gushing continue as they took the lift to the next floor.

Knowing the gallery's security cameras were probably following her every move, Jennifer had never ventured this far, given she'd been told it was out of bounds for her. She therefore had no idea what to expect. What she found was a modestly decorated space, smaller than the gallery below, the natural light from the high windows muted by plain curtains, the works on display lit by well-placed, unobtrusive spots. As Ettore Cambroni switched on some supplementary lights, Jennifer took in the twenty paintings on display, five of which she recognised immediately.

She guided Zaccaro towards them. "As I'm sure Signor Cambroni has told you, signore, these portraits by Philippe Laurent are very special and their sale a rare opportunity. You are familiar with his work?" As she spoke, she glanced at Cambroni, noting with amusement the look of total surprise on his face.

"They are new to me, bella," said the actor. "When were they painted? They are divine."

Zaccaro matched every one of Jennifer's steps, ensuring their shoulders remained touching.

"Laurent worked mainly in Marseille in the late seventeenth century," replied Jennifer, quickly noting each work as she tried to ignore the invasion of her space. "Mainly portraits like these. He had a wonderful touch."

"I particularly like this one," said Zaccaro, pointing across Jennifer's body and letting his hand brush lightly over her breasts. "What do you think?" he added, his tone radiating innocence.

I think I'd like to break your arm, thought Jennifer, but instead, we'll just take you to the cleaners.

"It's lovely," she said, as she moved away from his reach. "However, this one on the right is far better. Look at the brushwork. It stands out from the rest, wouldn't you agree?"

Zaccaro didn't have a clue but he was prepared to be led. "Indubitably," he declared as he turned to Cambroni. "That one, Ettore, I'll definitely take that one and let you know about the others."

"I'm intrigued to know why you chose that particular portrait over the others, Ginevra," said Ettore Cambroni once the sale was complete and Zaccaro had been sent on his way, disappointed not to have a dinner appointment with Jennifer.

"It's quite simple, signore," said Jennifer with a careful nonchalance. "I strongly suspect it's a fake, and yet the price is the same as the others, which I'm sure are genuine. He's paid way over the odds for it, which is all he deserves after his groping."

"A fake?" Cambroni affected surprise although he knew full well. "How could you tell?"

"There's just something about it," she said. "A freshness the others don't have."

She shrugged self-deprecatingly. "I could be wrong of course; I'm no expert."

"I'll have it checked," said Cambroni. "If it is, it's slipped through the net. However, I'm impressed by your knowledge, Ginevra, very impressed."

Jennifer smiled to herself. It had been a stroke of luck. The original of the Laurent in question was owned by Pietro Fabrelli and was hanging in the living room of the villa in Sardinia. Jennifer had seen and admired it every day for months.

In early May, Jennifer's campaign to win over the Cambronis took another significant step forward when Ettore Cambroni summoned her on an internal phone to go to the upper gallery to keep an eye on two clients while he made preparations for them elsewhere.

"Of course, signore," said Jennifer, putting down the catalogue she was reading and hurrying to the stairs. She was puzzled. No one had passed through the main gallery on the way to the private gallery on the floor above, so whoever the clients were, they must have accessed it through stairs or a lift she was unaware of. And Cambroni's mention of another location, 'elsewhere' as he put it, was the first direct reference she had heard to further hidden galleries or studios Massimo Felice had suspected were in the building.

She hurried up to the private gallery where she found Cambroni talking to two large, squarely built men in black suits, their faces both set in permanent snarls. Their whole demeanour spelt mob, but not the Italian one. One of the pair, dripping in gold bracelets and rings, was clearly the boss. His minder was trying to work his way through Cambroni's attempt to simplify his Italian. They all turned as Jennifer came in, the visitors' eyes unsubtly roaming her body.

"Ah, Ginevra," said Cambroni. "These two gentlemen are from Moscow. Perhaps you could speak English to them, answer any questions they have about these paintings while I check things for them upstairs."

As he walked past her, his voice dropped to a whisper.

"Watch them like a hawk," he said, shifting into a strong Florentine dialect the Russians would never understand even if they spoke some Italian. "Make sure they don't steal anything; I don't trust them an inch."

Jennifer turned to the Russians, who were still undressing her with their eyes.

"Is there anything I can get you, signori?" she said, in English. "Some coffee or tea. Perhaps I can tell you something about these landscapes." She took a step forward and pointed to the display which comprised five modernistic Florentine cityscapes.

"You can get on that table and spread your legs," the shorter, rougher looking man drawled in Russian, his mouth a lascivious snarl. "I'll soften you up for my boss; he likes them warm and moist."

Jennifer fought to control her anger; it was imperative that they didn't know she understood.

The boss waved a dismissive hand. "You can keep her, Vasili, she's far too bony. I don't want splinters. And her tits are too small, nothing to get my hands round."

He turned away, seemingly more interested in the paintings. There was a silence as the first man continued to stare at Jennifer, his black eyes malevolent.

Jennifer held her breath. She could almost smell his lust. She was sure she could put up a good fight if they went for her, but their sheer size and weight was intimidating. One good strike from that handful of rings could do her serious damage.

The man snorted and turned to his boss. "You're right, I'd probably snap her in two. And we don't want to upset that twat Cambroni, not with the pile of paintings he has waiting for us."

The senior man chuckled harshly as he cracked his knuckles.

"You know, the security's not up to much here. Just that ape on the door. We could get the boys to call in another day, take him out, have their fun with this one, then go through the place, take the good stuff."

He turned towards Jennifer and frowned. She was making a point of looking towards the CCTV. She glanced at him and smiled. "Sorry, while you were talking, I was checking the security cameras are all responding; it's one of my responsibilities. Is there something I can do for you?"

Hearing a door open, she spun round.

"Thank you, Ginevra," said Cambroni as he strode towards them. "I'll take it from here."

Jennifer walked up to him, intercepting his path. "I think it might be better if I accompany you, signore," she said, her voice a barely audible whisper.

Cambroni shook his head. "I don't think so, Ginevra, I'll—"

"I speak Russian, signore," she interrupted. "And I can assure you, they mean trouble."

Once the Russians had left, Jennifer was summoned to Cambroni senior's office along with Ettore. The old man looked pained as he struggled with conflicting emotions. While he was angry that Jennifer had seen so much, he was at the same time delighted to have learned the Russians' plans. His main interest now was ensuring the Russians were beaten at their own game. Ginevra Mancini could always be dealt with later if they decided she was a risk.

"You are sure about what you heard, signorina?" he said to Jennifer.

"Quite sure, signore. They made no attempt to disguise what they were saying since they assumed none of us understood. They want to have a quite valuable Russian painting tagged with your security system, but they plan to send a fake version and when it's returned, accuse you of substituting the real one with a fake. After that, they intend to leverage what they called your dishonesty by taking control of your reputation among the other newly rich businessmen in Russia, many of whom are old-style crooks. They'll keep quiet so long as you provide them with valuable paintings at bargain prices."

"Blackmail," spat the old man, his face screwed in anger. "They don't know who they are dealing with."

"They are playing it carefully, Babbo," said the younger Cambroni. "They want us to go to Moscow to show us the real painting so we know we've seen the real thing, and then swap it for a fake before it's sent here."

The old man stared at his son as his mind processed the problem. "We need the genuine painting to come here," he muttered.

"May I make a suggestion, signori?" asked Jennifer.

Both men turned their heads to her.

She took a breath. Two hours earlier, as far as these men were concerned she knew nothing about the forgery side of their operation. Now here she was offering advice on how to go forward.

"When I was in the workshop on the top floor," she said, "I met two of your, um, restorers."

She looked for any reaction, but their faces were impassive.

"The younger one, Tonino, was demonstrating the security tagging to the Russians, although he was careful to keep what he told them to a bare outline. I know this because I was translating what he said into English for them."

"Good," muttered Ettore. "The less they know the better."

"It occurred to me, signori," continued Jennifer, "that if Tonino went with you as your security expert, when they show you the genuine painting, he could examine it closely in front of them, make a great play of it, in fact, and once he's sure that it is the genuine article, before they could stop him, he could spray the back of the canvas with a watered-down version of the tagging medium. He can claim he's doing it for security while the painting is being shipped. He can even demonstrate it using the geotagging software on a laptop. Once that's done, they won't be able to swap the painting since any fake won't be tagged. They'll have to ship the genuine painting here."

Maurizio Cambroni placed his elbows on the desk in front of him and leaned his chin into his hands, his eyes darting as he thought through the proposal. He nodded. "A good suggestion,

Ginevra. Clever. You're a clever girl. However, you've left one thing out. No, two things."

Jennifer waited, knowing she wasn't expected to speak.

"Firstly, you must go too, signorina. To Moscow. These men are not to be trusted. You will be our ears when our eyes aren't enough. You will listen like you listened earlier and learn anything and everything they might be planning. It's important in case they come up with some way of foiling the plan. We know they are stupid enough to discuss their ideas in front of you."

He raised his eyes from the desk to Jennifer's.

"You don't look too pleased with my idea."

"Oh no, signore, I think it's a good idea. It's just that I don't like those men. They are brutes and made lewd comments about me to each other. I don't want to be alone with them."

Maurizio Cambroni smiled for the first time. "If that's all you're worried about, it can be taken care of. I'll send along two people to accompany you at all times. You'll never be alone. And at night, one of them will stay on guard outside your room."

"Thank you, signore, thank you so much. You are too kind."

"You're a valuable asset, Ginevra, and those men are depraved pigs. They have no respect for women, which disgusts me. Now, the second thing. What do you think will happen once we get the genuine painting back here?"

"Happen?"

"Yes, happen. I have no intention of giving it back to them. What they'll get back will be indistinguishable from the genuine article and it will be properly tagged. But it won't be the one they gave us."

As his eyes bored into Jennifer's, she saw a different light in them, an emptiness, devoid of all warmth. She felt she was now looking at the real Maurizio Cambroni, not the gallery façade.

"You have come a long way with us in a short time," he rasped. Even his voice was darker. "It was not intended to be like this; you were not meant to learn as much as you have learned. Today, you have seen another part of the gallery, a secret part. You are not stupid, Ginevra, so I have no doubt that you understand what goes on there."

He paused, watching as Jennifer opened her mouth to speak. But she thought better of it and simply nodded.

"You are wise not to deny it, signorina," continued the elder Cambroni, "wise beyond your years. I hope you are wise enough to understand that what you have seen and what you now know is utterly and completely secret. You are to tell no one, discuss it with no one outside these walls, take no personal advantage from it. Whether you like it or not, you are now part of us, a privileged part. Very few outsiders gain this level of knowledge about our organisation.

"And with this knowledge, there is responsibility, an allegiance. Your loyalty will bring its own rewards, I can assure you, substantial rewards. Rewards that should make you happy enough to want to stay forever. That is important because I think you understand that you can never leave. I have made myself clear?"

Jennifer suppressed a gulp.

"Yes, signore, you have. Very clear."

"He said that? He threatened you so overtly? And then you went to Russia?"

Jennifer had returned from her trip to Moscow and was sitting in the safety of Pietro's apartment along with Paul Godden, Massimo Felice and three of the team. Godden was shocked by her account.

Jennifer nodded. She had been worried about coming to the apartment, worried that the Cambronis' surveillance of her would have been stepped up. They were nothing if not cautious.

She had signalled her concern to the team who dispatched two people to shadow her to check she wasn't being followed. Her route was complicated, weaving in and out of the back streets of Florence, jumping in a taxi, stopping it before her declared destination and disappearing down yet another side street. After an hour of this, she felt sure she had not been followed and a message on her phone from one of the team confirmed it.

She sat back in her chair. "Yes, Russia. It was something of a surprise."

"Thank heavens we made a good job of your passport," commented Felice.

"And the trip went well?" said Godden.

"Completely to plan. Tonino was amazing."

"That's Tonino Varinelli, the youngest of the forgers?"

"Yes. He's absolutely brilliant. And very sweet. I've got to know him quite well and—"

"Jennifer," interrupted Godden, "I thought we agreed this wasn't a good idea."

She chuckled. "Don't worry, Paul, he has no interest in me beyond simple friendship; he's gay. He's no more pleased about the hold the Cambronis have on him than I am. It didn't dawn on him to start with; I think the security of the money was all he saw. However, now he's realised that for the rest of his life he's going to be working in the shadows, never to have his skill as an artist recognised, he's not so happy. He knows the consequences of trying to break free, and he knows the consequences of painting anything outside of the gallery. The Cambronis have absolutely forbidden it."

"Can't expect anything else," said Godden. "Far too much of a risk for them."

Jennifer's eyes were smiling as she glanced from one of the group to the next.

"But …?" said Felice.

"He has a lover, a secret one because although the Cambronis know he's gay, they want to vet anyone he gets close to. And his lover is not someone they would like. Too extrovert for their tastes."

"And …"

"He showed me a picture of him."

"Do we know him?"

"No, Massimo, you don't, at least I doubt you do."

"A picture," said Godden. "Do you mean an actual picture, not a photo?"

"Yes, a small painting. He showed it to me."

"Any chance we could get our hands on it?"

Jennifer shook her head. "None whatsoever. The Cambronis have his apartment searched periodically as well, so he guards the painting very carefully."

"So why are you telling us?"

Jennifer opened her bag. "Because he has also painted one of me."

She pulled out a roll of paper about six inches long, unrolled it and held it up to display a brilliant acrylic sketch of her.

"I thought it might be a suitable candidate for Ced Fisher's magic program."

Paul Godden clapped his hands in delight.

"DC Cotton, you're a genius!"

"All part of the service, guv'nor." said Jennifer.

Chapter Twenty-Nine

Olivia Freneton stood on the large first-floor balcony of the rented Villa Luisa set in the hills to the west of the Val di Chiana that had been her and Connie Fairbright's home for the past eight months. It was seven in the evening and although the June sun had only just sunk behind the villa, the east-facing balcony had been bathed in cool shadow for the last hour. Olivia took a sip from her glass of spring water as she enjoyed her favourite spot and favourite time of day. She would stand here most evenings if Connie hadn't returned, soaking up the view across the nearby town of Monte San Savino and the valley beyond to where, several miles away, Castiglion Fiorentino sat near the foot of a range of rugged hills. And hidden from view in those hills was Connie's huge new project, the Villa Brillante, now in its final stages of renovation.

The villa had been carefully chosen by Olivia from several within thirty miles of her own far-more-modest farmhouse. It ticked all Connie's boxes, making her decision easy. The price had been irrelevant, although Connie still insisted that Olivia drive a hard bargain — it was a matter of principle to her.

Connie had no intention of letting it be known that once the villa was finished it would contain a collection of paintings worth many millions of dollars, paintings dating from her beloved Renaissance. Most would be portraits, because she adored portraits, and many would have been painted within a hundred-mile radius of her villa. The names of the artists she was actively buying might not roll off the tongue quite as easily as Michelangelo, Giotto or Della Francesca, but the thought that during their lives they had gazed across similar views to those she would be gazing across once the Villa Brillante was finished, visited the same towns, enjoyed the same wines and even witnessed similar pageantry during the many festas still celebrated in the region, filled her with a sense of belonging, a oneness with life five hundred years before.

While she understood that to exclude her neighbours would be foolish and would set her apart from the community, she was also well aware that her precious canvases needed protection, and to achieve that protection she was fitting out three windowless rooms within the villa that would be sealed against the environment, hidden climate-controlled rooms where she and her dear companion Diana could enjoy the wonders displayed on the walls. For the parts of the villa where visitors would be allowed, paintings displayed there would be far less valuable, nothing that anyone would be tempted to steal.

Not that giving into temptation once she moved in would be of much use to any would-be thief. Long before anything of value was reached in the house, long before the house was even reached at all, a symphony of alarms would be alerting both the surrounding countryside and Connie's armed-response security company, while floodlights turned night into day and an array of hidden cameras delivered gigabytes of imagery to dedicated servers as evidence against the intruder.

But that day was still at least two months off. While the modifications to the building were complete and the new wiring in place, much of the sophisticated electronics, the backups, the fail-safe devices, and indeed the solar energy installation courtesy of which Connie intended the villa to be totally off the grid were yet to be finished.

Entrusted with ensuring that nothing slipped behind schedule, Olivia was tasked with overseeing progress, and now things were moving apace, she needed to visit the Villa Brillante site almost daily. In anticipation of this, Connie had leased a luxurious upmarket Audi hatchback for Olivia's use when they moved to the area from Rome — Connie knew nothing of Olivia's stolen Golf now rotting quietly in a garage yard in Castiglion Fiorentino.

Her frequent visits to the site enabled Olivia to give the leering squad of Eastern-European workers the sharp end of her tongue; a necessary release for her continuing frustration with not having completed her disposals in England, although as in most of her confrontations with men, she had to be careful not to let her anger run riot. Visiting the villa also meant she could spend time at her farmhouse checking that everything was in perfect working order should she need to leave in a hurry. She had a small stock of explosive packs hidden away in a secure cellar and she worried that they might deteriorate. However, the house was dry, its walls thick, and as long as she kept everything properly sealed and packaged, nothing seemed to be suffering.

Above all, the daily chores meant she didn't have to accompany Connie on her endless trips to galleries in Tuscany and Umbria, or on her increasing forays further afield. Connie's driver would whisk her in air-conditioned, leather-upholstered luxury to the nearby galleries, but for her more distant trips, she had been making use of the services of a private airline based in Perugia who would pick her up at the small airport in Arezzo. It meant she could cover a wider area and usually still be home the same day to regale Olivia with tales of new portraits found, new purchases, sometimes new artists, and an ever-increasing list of eccentric gallery owners, all of whom were charmed by her now impressive command of Italian.

Twice a week, both Connie and Olivia would head to Rome for their three-hour language lessons and Connie's three-hour art lesson from Cesare Contorni. While in Rome they still based themselves in the same five-star hotel where Connie retained a suite for her exclusive use should she decide to stay the night. As always, lunch was taken on the terrace, weather permitting, to the continued torture of Mario, the waiter.

Connie had widened Cesare Contorni's terms of reference to include that of advisor on Renaissance paintings she had either discovered or been offered by a number of galleries. Her knowledge in the field had increased immensely over the months and she could now reel off a list of more than fifty lesser-known artists who had been active during the fifteenth and sixteenth centuries, often recognising previously unseen works by them. Signor Contorni was justifiably proud of his pupil, his eyes glowing with delight when he watched her in action in a gallery. Olivia, by contrast, spent much of the time stifling yawns of boredom.

While in Rome, Contorni would frequently join them for lunch, spending the time advising Connie on what he knew of galleries elsewhere in Italy. Somewhat suspicious of his motives, Olivia felt he was probably angling for a few trips, especially now Connie was fond of flying around the country. However, even she had to admit that whatever Contorni's motives, he was of great help in Connie's decision-making process, and on more than one occasion he had saved her a considerable amount of money by quietly pointing out that the portrait she had just fallen in love with was a modern fake.

"Actually, Connie, I have no problem with fakes," Contorni would explain. "A painting should be appreciated for what it is, not because this artist or that one painted it. If you like it, buy it, but don't pay more than it is worth. And of course no fake is worth much more than the value of the canvas and the paints, plus perhaps a little extra for the efforts of the artist."

Connie and Olivia both laughed at his position.

"Only a little extra, Cesare?" asked Connie. "Surely the man's time is worth something."

Contorni shook his head, his hooded eyes full of sadness at human folly. "You must remember, Connie, that many of these forgers are artists of great talent. If they spent their time developing their own style and producing originals instead of copies, then of course their time should be considered more seriously, and their skill. Copying is what students do when they are learning. They copy the works of the great masters to learn from them. That doesn't mean they should spend the rest of their lives copying."

"Easily said, Cesare," commented Olivia, "but it's a cut-throat world out there, one that's full of highly talented artists. Getting noticed is difficult, and the patronage system of hundreds of years ago is not so common these days. I can fully understand why these people are doing what they're doing."

Contorni bowed his head in submission. The signora Diana was right, in principle, and anyway he was wary of her. There was always something about her tone and the look in her eye he found chilling. She was so different from Connie, who was charming, if a little naïve.

It was during a lunch with Contorni that Connie asked if he knew of the Cambroni gallery in Florence.

"I have heard of it, yes, but I have never been there. It is rather out of my league and I believe it is a gallery that does not encourage casual browsing. Having said that, it has a reputation for acquiring some very valuable paintings. Not so much the period that interests you though, Connie, they are normally more modern. Why do you ask?"

"I visited it last week. You're right, I had to call to make an appointment, otherwise I'm not sure I would have been allowed in. The huge African man they have on the door is rather intimidating. However, once I'd got past that barrier, the young lady who showed me around was utterly charming, and was quite happy for me to speak Italian even though her English was remarkably fluent, with just the trace of an accent."

Olivia laughed. "You're getting quite superior about other people's language skills, Connie. It's unusual to hear a native Italian speaker who doesn't betray an accent when speaking English. You know, hanging on final consonants and so on."

Connie smiled. "I suppose I am, but believe me, this girl was good. However, I digress. What was interesting wasn't so much the paintings, although there were a couple I fell in love with they are reserving for me, no, what took my attention was a tagging system for paintings the gallery has developed. The signorina — what was her name? yes, Mancini — she was telling me that although it's expensive, the gallery claims it's the most secure and reliable system in the world. Apparently once it's installed, the painting can be traced anywhere on the planet. And it's impossible to remove."

"Installed in the painting?" Contorni's tone reflected his horror. "Unacceptable, Connie. Such a scheme would be totally invasive. You cannot compromise valuable works of art in such a way."

Connie laughed. "Don't be so conservative, Cesare; it might be a very good system."

Contorni continued to grunt his disapproval, but Connie wasn't deterred.

"Apparently," she continued, "it involves some sort of sub-microscopic technology that's embedded in the canvas. I can see why museums might not be interested in it, in fact the signorina mentioned that it's aimed more at the private collector than museums and state galleries. And I have to think about my collection. I want to know that if ever a thief manages to get as far as my paintings and remove them, they will be traceable no matter where they go."

She glanced at Contorni whose face still looked as if he had just eaten a lemon.

"Cesare, Signorina Mancini said that if I was interested, she could arrange an appointment for me to see the gallery owner who would demonstrate it to me. And as it happens, starting next week, there is a new exhibition and sale of Renaissance portraitists at the gallery. I want you to come with me to Florence; you too Diana. We can kill two birds with one stone. What's on sale will be perfect for enhancing my collection, and at the same time, we can review this tagging system with a view to incorporating it into my existing collection and everything I buy in the future. It's a very exciting prospect."

Chapter Thirty

Jennifer yawned as she touched the red button on her phone's screen to end the call. It was ten thirty in the evening and after a busy day at the gallery eavesdropping on more Russians for the Cambronis, and two long Skype calls, one to Henry and the other to Derek, she was ready for some sleep.

She was still yawning as she headed for the bathroom to brush her teeth when the phone pinged again to signal an incoming text. Displayed on the screen was what appeared to be a rambling advertisement from a telemarketing company, but crucially within the text were five consecutive key words that gave Jennifer the real meaning behind it: an instruction from Paul Godden to go immediately to the watchers' apartment.

She sighed. It was late, she was tired and she knew that even if whatever Godden wanted to discuss only took five minutes, with the convoluted route she was committed to take to ensure she wasn't being followed, both on the way to the apartment and on her return, she wouldn't be in bed until at least two in the morning.

However, she knew better than to take shortcuts — especially as a couple of Felice's watchers were probably keeping an eye on her just in case — and it wasn't until nearly an hour after the text message arrived that she was standing in front of the entry phone's video camera tapping the prearranged sequence of knocks onto the apartment door to indicate she was alone and under no threat.

The door opened and she walked in to find Paul Godden and Massimo Felice sitting opposite each other on two large sofas, both men looking very pleased with themselves.

"Jennifer," said Godden as he stood. "Sorry for the late hour but a little while ago I got some good news that enables us to move forward significantly."

Jennifer sat in an armchair, glancing at Felice as she did. There was a large box file open on a coffee table in front of him and a couple of documents from it balanced on his knees. His grin as he looked at her was triumphant.

"You both look like you've won the lottery," said Jennifer. "It better be good if I'm losing my beauty sleep over it."

"It is, Jennifer," said Godden. "More than good."

She waited, watching while Godden opened up a folder he was holding.

"We've had the results back from the tests Ced Fisher performed on Varinelli's painting of you," said Godden. "And they're positive. The artist has the same style signature as the artist who painted the forgery reported to us by the Scottish collector."

Felice leaned forward. "This clinches it, Jennifer. It's definite proof that the gallery is crooked. The Cambronis should be going down for a long time. Obviously we've got to play it carefully, get everything just right before we raid the place, but I can tell you it will be soon."

Jennifer sat back, smiling. "That's brilliant. What's your plan now?"

"Well," said Felice, "the first thing we need to decide is what happens to you. It's important for your protection that the Cambronis don't suspect you. We're dealing with well-connected, dangerous people, and you've penetrated the heart of their organisation. They will want revenge if they discover the truth about you."

"You're not suggesting I disappear right now, are you?" said Jennifer.

Godden shook his head. "No, we're not. We've been discussing it and we reckon on balance it would be better if you're picked up with the rest of the employees. There will be bail posted, probably for everyone. There's not much we can do about that. And that's the dangerous time. We can easily get the charges against you dropped later, although to do that we'll probably have to drop the charges against Signora Renzo as well."

"What about the forgers?" asked Jennifer. "I told you Varinelli is out of his depth. Can't something be done for him?"

Felice scratched his chin. "We'll have to see. He has definitely broken the law so it depends on the public prosecutor and the court."

Jennifer stared at the box file as she thought through the conversation, a niggling doubt teasing her.

"Are you sure there's enough?" she asked, finally. She looked up to see indignation registered on both men's faces. "To prosecute them, I mean," she added, hurriedly.

"Of course," snapped Godden, suddenly irritated. "Do you see a problem with it?"

"Well, the issue of the painting being a fake has already been addressed by the gallery. There's no proof that the painting supplied to the Scot wasn't a fake all along."

"But Jennifer," objected Godden. "We now have Ced's results. The painting was produced by Varinelli."

"Isn't there a danger," countered Jennifer, "that the Cambronis will say he painted it elsewhere, that it's nothing to do with them if they happen to employ a rogue painter? In other words, use Varinelli as the fall guy and walk away."

Godden was shaking his head. "We'll undoubtedly find other fakes by Varinelli and the other forgers the Cambronis employ when we raid the gallery."

"Sure," agreed Jennifer, "but they are just paintings in the gallery. No claims have been made about them. The Cambronis could say they have an arrangement with, I don't know, shops and other galleries that specialise in copies of famous paintings. With the right lawyer, it could all appear completely innocent."

"And there's no doubt their lawyers will be top notch," said Felice, looking concerned.

"What we need," said Jennifer, "is a waterproof chain of evidence connecting the fake paintings to the gallery. We need to catch them as they're being shipped. And that's something of a problem since it would involve the buyers, most of whom wouldn't be interested in cooperating with the police, given they are probably crooks themselves."

She paused to think through her argument before continuing. "No, we need a bona fide buyer whom the gallery is cheating big time."

"I felt good about all this until you arrived, Jennifer," muttered Godden. "Now it all seems to have slipped away again."

Jennifer laughed. "It's not the end of the world, but neither is it the end of the case. We need that little bit more to make it watertight. Actually, there's been a new client at the gallery recently whom I've met and like. I think she's totally honest and I know the Cambronis are intending to cheat her with security-tagged fakes."

Felice was shaking his head. "I can see your point, Jennifer, but surely there must be good evidence from the records the gallery is bound to have. They can't keep all their transactions only in their heads."

"You're right," agreed Jennifer, "they don't and there are plenty of records. But for older swindles, before the tagging started, the fakes are all deniable, even if we can link them to the gallery, or at least to the forgers. For the tagged pictures, the Cambronis will have a harder time denying their involvement since it's their system."

"Then we should go ahead," said Felice.

"Well, you're the boss and it's your call," said Jennifer, "But I don't agree. There are too many holes. We need to catch them in the act. Now, I happen to know that the Russians' paintings — the Russians I went to see in Moscow — are almost ready. What I mean is that the tagging is done and the fake that Varinelli is preparing from the genuine painting we conned the Russians into providing is almost finished. With those and the con they're setting up for the American woman—"

"American woman?"

"Yes, the woman I mentioned. She's a rich American widow. The Cambronis have already sold her a couple of genuine paintings and are eager to sell her a lot more. Some will be top quality and totally bona fide, some won't."

"Who is she, this rich widow?" asked Felice.

"Her name is Connie Fairbright. Her late husband was the billionaire Brad Fairbright of Fairbright International fame."

Chapter Thirty-One

Olivia Freneton sat alongside Connie Fairbright in the rear of the black limousine as the gleaming vehicle cruised at 150 km/h along the A1 autostrada in the direction of Florence. Her jaw was set and her eyes behind her large dark glasses glared angrily at the back of Cesare Contorni's head. She was there under sufferance largely because Connie had insisted, and Olivia hated being told what to do. Meanwhile, Connie was bubbling with an enthusiastic glee that Olivia found nauseating.

"This is such an exciting day, Diana," gushed Connie for the fifth time in an hour. "I have a good feeling about this gallery. I think this trip will mark a big step forward in the establishment of my collection. A watershed, don't you agree?"

She turned and put a hand on Olivia's arm. "It's what we've been working towards; Signor Cambroni and Signorina Mancini were both exceptionally helpful. Not only am I confident that Cesare will be most impressed by their knowledge, I'm also sure you will be too. Signorina Mancini is such a dear; a real gem."

Olivia remained silent. She was trying to tune in to Contorni's conversation with the driver from his position in the front passenger seat. However, their muted tones and use of Roman dialect were making it virtually incomprehensible.

She felt Connie's hand squeeze her arm. "Are you feeling unwell, Diana? You're very quiet."

Olivia regulated her breathing. For two pins she could strangle this woman with her bare hands. Patience, she thought, patience. It won't be long now until I'm free of all this.

"Just a slight headache, Connie," she lied. "I've never suffered from them before, but since … Brussels," — she paused for dramatic effect — "they've become something of a problem." She pulled a brave smile to show Connie what a trooper she was. "It's nothing serious. I'm sure it'll soon be gone. Now, tell me, how come someone as young as you say this Signorina Mancini is knows so much about Renaissance art?"

"She said she specialised in the period during her university studies. Spent some time at a college in London, which is presumably why her English is so good."

Olivia didn't care. She had been meticulously reviewing her situation in the past weeks, revising plans, making new ones, working through the contingencies and applying all her brilliant skills to bringing this operation to a satisfactory conclusion. With her purchases over the past few months, Connie's art collection was now substantial; it just needed the final boost that the Florence gallery might well give it. And the sooner Olivia judged the portfolio of paintings to be valuable enough, the sooner she could relieve Connie of it, along with her life.

However, there was a concern flagging itself in her mind. The tagging system. Was it going to slow things down? Was she going to have to wait for months while it was applied to whatever Connie bought from the Cambronis?

Ideally, of course, she didn't want anything tagged. Ideally she would convince Connie that tagging was just icing on the cake, superfluous to requirements given the nature of the villa's security system. Tagged, a painting was traceable. If she couldn't talk Connie out of tagging, she at least needed her to take possession of the paintings first with a plan to release them in batches for tagging later. That would give Olivia the opportunity to pounce, kill Connie and disappear with the untagged paintings.

What had also helped move Olivia's plans forward was Connie's decision to give her access to the collection, which for the time being was housed in a huge safe Connie had installed in their rented villa.

"I think it's important, Diana." Connie had explained. "If something were to happen to me, I want the way to be smooth for the paintings to be accessible, retrievable. I don't want them tied up in probate for years while lawyers argue over their value. It's very important to me that the charities named in my will have access to the money that will be realised from their sale as soon as possible, not years in the future. I know you'd organise that so well, Diana," she said, squeezing Olivia's arm in what had become a frequent expression of her affection.

It was the realisation that she could simply walk into the study and walk out with Connie's collection that had focussed Olivia's thoughts. The contents just needed to be worth it and the timing perfect. For Olivia, that would pose no problem: she had total confidence in her own planning skills.

The limousine purred to a halt outside the gallery door and Thompson, the huge doorman, emerged to escort them, his welcome in stark contrast to his first meeting with Connie.

As the party of three passed through the doors, Ettore Cambroni came rushing down the stairs.

"Ah, Signora Fairbright, how delightful to see you again," he said, taking Connie's proffered right hand in both of his as tenderly as if it were priceless porcelain. "My entire gallery is at your service; your every wish our deepest pleasure to fulfil."

He leaned forward conspiratorially. "I know you will not be disappointed with what we have to show you today, signora; it is a collection without parallel in recent years. We feel privileged to have the honour of assembling such a collection. It is … ottima."

He turned his eyes towards Olivia. "And this must be the friend you told us was coming. Signora … Fitchley? Did I pronounce your name correctly?"

Grovelling toad, thought Olivia.

"Perfectly," she said, dismissing him with the slightest of nods.

As a consummate criminal, Ettore Cambroni prided himself on

being able to judge a person's character with a minimum of verbal and physical signals. His life had depended on his judgement on several occasions. Without making it obvious, he studied Olivia's face for clues, but with her deadpan expression and many of her features obscured by a designer scarf, huge dark glasses and more make-up than was fashionable, he found even his powers challenged. There was something rather theatrical about the woman, like a fugitive from the cinema of the sixties. But it was more than fashion, there was a darkness about her that set alarms screeching inside his head. And what concerned him most, more than just fashion, more than her looks and stance, was the tone of the one word she had spoken. Behind it were freezing chasms of ice, a hostile terrain raising hackles on the back of his neck.

Trying hard to quench his concerns for the present, Cambroni turned to Cesare Contorni.

"Signor Contorni," he said, all obsequiousness once again. "I believe I have not had the pleasure. It is always a delight to welcome another expert in our noble endeavours." He took Contorni's right hand and shook it vigorously.

Continuing to hold Contorni's hand, he circled his left arm around the bemused Roman and guided the party towards the lift.

"Before I introduce you to the wonderful works I have assembled for you, Signora Fairbright, may I offer you all some refreshment? You must be thirsty after your journey."

Connie shook her head. "Maybe later, Signor Cambroni. For now, I can't wait another second to see these paintings. None of us can."

She glanced at Olivia, hoping for support, only to find she was staring straight ahead, apparently oblivious of the conversation.

The lift took them to the first floor gallery, the limit of its capabilities. As the party walked into the main 'public' gallery, Connie asked after Signorina Mancini, surprised to find she wasn't waiting for them.

Ettore Cambroni waved an arm along the gallery to where, some thirty yards away, Jennifer was standing with her back to the group, deep in conversation with two wealthy Dutch clients who had come to view.

"She'll join us as soon as she can, signora," reassured Cambroni as he glanced again at the mysterious and aloof Signora Fitchley.

The party headed for the internal lift that would take them to the upper gallery. Once there, Connie took one look along the carefully arranged display of fifteenth- and sixteenth-century portraits and gasped. Thoughts of meeting Signorina Mancini were put to the back of her mind, replaced with a total focus on the works before her.

"Oh my heavens, Signor Cambroni," she said, clasping her hands in front of her in delight, "these are exquisite. How clever of you to have anticipated my tastes so precisely. I want you to tell me everything about each one."

Cambroni tilted his head in deference and walked her towards the first of the paintings, noting as he did the scrutiny Contorni was already giving each work. He had anticipated this, although he had never heard of Contorni, and he was pleased with himself for displaying a full set of genuine portraits for the rich American; the substitutions with the copies produced by Varinelli and his colleagues would come later. However, what puzzled him and distracted him slightly from his normally effortless delivery of information was the almost complete lack of response to the paintings shown by Signora Fitchley, her reaction to the works in total contrast to both Connie and Contorni. He began to wonder if she was more of a bodyguard to the rich American than an interested party, muscle rather than brain. Now that he looked at her more closely, he saw that she carried no excess weight, that her movements were smooth and athletic. That would certainly explain it. He should have realised: Fitchley was the Fairbright woman's version of Thompson. He gave a mental nod as he relaxed into his main routine. His mistake was easy to explain: the mob would never give such responsibility to a woman. Ever. It wasn't the way things were done, so the explanation had eluded him. How strange these foreigners were.

Given the detailed and excited scrutiny Connie gave every painting, with a seemingly endless set of questions, together with the interest she showed in the tagging process Cambroni demonstrated with great pride, the viewing took longer than anticipated. Cambroni had arranged to take the party to lunch at his favourite restaurant, Il Latini, a few streets away, and as the morning wore on, he was concerned that the popular tourist destination would be filling up. For while his table was assured — a corner position in one of the smaller rooms he always reserved — he wanted to ensure his guests had the best attention.

Returning finally to the main floor, an elated Connie was deep in conversation with Cesare Contorni about several points she'd noticed. She was thrilled that his general impression of the paintings was more than positive, his main concern only the huge amount of money that Connie would be spending if, as he suspected she might, she bought the entire collection. Turning into the public gallery, Connie held up a hand to Contorni.

"Excuse me, Cesare, we'll continue this in a moment. I want to say hello to Signorina Mancini. I was rather hoping that she would have joined us, but I can see she's still busy with those people down there. I hope she's had as successful a morning as our Signor Cambroni."

She smiled and walked off in Jennifer's direction.

Sensing Connie was going to take at least several more minutes, Olivia turned to Ettore Cambroni.

"Signore, is there a bathroom here I can use?"

"Of course, Signora Fitchley. It is 'signora' isn't it?" he said, still interested in learning more about this enigmatic woman.

"Actually, it's signorina, but at my age I take no exception to 'signora'," replied Olivia. "It is normally how I am addressed."

"Thank you for your cordiality," replied Cambroni, translating his formal Italian rather awkwardly. "The bathroom is that way." He pointed back to the corridor. "Turn right and then immediately left through the swing door."

Following the instructions, Olivia pushed her way through the swing doors. To the left along the short corridor she could see a door marked 'Bagno', to the right another door that was half open. She peered in and saw the security control room for the gallery, a bank of monitors linked to a number of CCTV cameras displaying high-resolution images of various rooms on both the first and second floors, as well as the corridors and main entrance, where she could see Thompson lurking. There was no one in the room so she walked forward to study the system in more detail. She glanced at the first floor images, the gallery just along the way, where on monitor 1-C she saw Connie as she passed close to a security camera. There was no sound, but as Connie's image passed, she was clearly calling out a friendly greeting. On the next monitor, 1-D, was the group of three people Olivia had seen in the distance from the doorway to the first floor gallery. One of them, who must be Signorina Mancini, had her back to the camera and was turning in response to Connie's greeting.

Olivia moved closer to the monitor, interested to get a look at the brilliant young lady Connie had been describing. As she did and the young woman's face appeared large on the screen, Olivia froze in her tracks, her eyes wide in disbelief. The young woman was the main target of her vendetta in the UK. She was looking directly at Jennifer Cotton.

Chapter Thirty-Two

Olivia Freneton looked around anxiously to check there was no one behind her — a guard returning from a break perhaps, or another employee. Satisfied she was alone, she turned again to the bank of monitors, her mind already racing through various courses of action.

She stared in continuing disbelief at the image on the screen 1-D. DC Cotton. What the hell was she doing here? The girl was clearly comfortable in her surroundings so she must have been working in the gallery for some time and have the confidence of the Cambronis. Was there a possibility that the injuries Olivia had inflicted on her had proved too incapacitating for her to continue on active service? Had they condemned her to a desk job if she stayed in the police? Olivia studied Jennifer's movements on the screen as she spoke firstly to Connie and was then introduced to Cesare Contorni. She didn't look incapacitated in any way; she looked to be bounding with energy. So she must be a plant, a police officer working under cover.

Olivia thought back to what she knew about Cotton, to the file she'd studied on her during the disciplinary inquiry into her conduct over not revealing that her father was Henry Silk. Yes, that was it. She'd been brought up in Italy so it was only natural she would speak fluent Italian. And she'd studied art! Of course she had. Olivia nodded, her face grim. What a gift Cotton must have

been for the authorities. Clever, articulate, fluent Italian and knowledgeable enough in the field of art to work as a sales assistant in a
prestigious gallery. Then the final piece of the puzzle slipped into
place. Her name. According to Connie, she was called Ginevra
Mancini. If she had left the police and was genuinely working as a
sales assistant, why would she change her name? She obviously
wanted the Cambronis to think she was Italian. And yes, Connie
had commented on her slight accent when she spoke English. Her
whole presence in the gallery was a façade.

The question now was what to do about it. When was she
going to kill her? She studied Jennifer's face, her animation as she
talked to Connie and Contorni, the ease with which she brought
her other clients into the conversation, perhaps using Connie to
help soften them towards a decision over a purchase. Certainly
Connie's endless enthusiasm combined with her recently gained
knowledge of Renaissance art could only help the process.

Olivia felt her nostrils flaring involuntarily as the thrill of the
chase consumed her. She had dreamed of this moment, dreamed
of the time when she finally caught up with Cotton, dreamed of
the time when she'd have her helpless in front of her as she slowly,
meticulously, put her to death. But the girl had been so incredibly
elusive that Olivia certainly hadn't dreamed of her being presented
on a plate.

She walked quickly back into the small corridor. It was imperative that Cotton remain unaware of her presence, imperative there
was no introduction. Cotton was nobody's fool; she'd see through
Olivia's make-up, dark glasses and Gucci scarf in an instant. She
stopped as a thought struck her. What would Cotton do with that
information? She certainly couldn't announce to the Cambronis or
indeed to Connie that they had a wanted criminal in their midst.
That would blow her own cover immediately. More likely she
would have a phone with a number of coded text messages ready
to send, one of which would call in the troops.

Olivia slipped quietly into the first floor gallery, almost
bumping into Contorni as she did.

"Ah, Diana, there you are. Connie was wondering about you.
She'd like to introduce Signorina Mancini to you."

He turned, as if to escort Olivia down the gallery.

"Actually, Cesare," whispered Olivia conspiratorially as she rubbed her forehead with the fingers and thumb of her right hand, "I've still got that damned headache. There's something about the atmosphere in this gallery, a sort of cloying stickiness to the air. Don't you feel it? If I don't get some fresh air immediately, I think I'll throw up, which would be rather embarrassing for all of us. Would you mind giving Connie and the others my apologies and tell her I'll meet you all outside?"

Without waiting for the surprised Contorni's reply, Olivia turned and made her way quickly to the stairs, disappearing from view just as Connie turned her head in question to Contorni.

Olivia brushed past the bowing Thompson and hurried into the street. She glanced around, taking in doorways, windows and parked cars. What would whoever was controlling Cotton have in place? How close was her backup? She looked upwards, checking windows overlooking the gallery entrance. There were too many and they could all hide a surveillance team with no difficulty at all. She needed to get out of sight. Where was the damned car? Then she saw it, parked about fifty yards along the street, deep in the shadow of a building. She hurried over and banged on the windscreen, jolting the dozing driver into life.

Settling in the rear seat, she instructed the driver to stay where he was. She needed to be out of the sun and out of sight.

As she waited, Olivia thought again about her strategy. She was angry since this development had taken her by surprise, had taken at least a layer of control from her, probably a number of layers. But as she regulated her breathing, she realised that as long as Cotton remained unaware of her existence, nothing had changed. She simply needed to ensure that the guileless Connie hadn't contrived a meeting, perhaps invited Cotton to lunch, although it wasn't Connie's place to do so. Lunch was supposed to be on Ettore Cambroni. However, she couldn't remain in the car in case Cotton emerged from the building alongside Connie.

She opened the door and slid out, making sure the movement was minimal and well in the shade.

"Tell Signora Fairbright I've gone for a walk," she instructed the driver. "I won't be long and she has my number."

Without waiting for his answer, Olivia slipped along the cobbled street, staying in the shadows. There was a small leather shop about thirty yards along that would have a reasonable view of the gallery entrance. Before she went in, she stepped into the shade of another entrance to check the windows on upper floors near to her in case anyone was straining a neck trying to see where she had gone. She also watched doorways for anyone leaving in a hurry, hoping to follow her. But there was no one. She took a deep breath. It would appear she hadn't been noticed.

She crossed into the leather shop where she was immediately greeted by a smartly dressed, middle-aged woman. Summoning up her best Diana persona, Olivia smiled at the woman and asked to look around.

"Of course, signora, please take your time. We have only the best Florentine leatherwork in this store, straight from our exclusive artigiani."

"Thank you," said Olivia, picking up a bag while keeping her attention focussed on the gallery entrance, "the craftsmanship is impressive."

After five minutes of browsing, picking up and putting down belts, bags, purses and shoes, Olivia eventually saw Connie walk from the gallery, her arm held by the fawning Ettore Cambroni. Contorni followed, but much to Olivia's relief, there was no sign of Cotton.

The limousine driver had the car alongside Connie almost before she'd had the time to look up the street. Olivia thanked the shopkeeper and hurried back along the street to the car, climbing in through the offside door just before Connie got in from the street side, followed by Cambroni. Contorni, as was his habit, settled himself in the front passenger seat.

"Diana!" exclaimed Connie. "There you are. I was worried. How are you feeling? Are you up for lunch? Signor Cambroni tells me that the restaurant he wants to show us is one of the best in Florence."

"Thank you, Connie, I'm fine now. I don't know what came over me. I just had to get some air." She forced a laugh. "I think all those amazing portraits made me giddy."

"They are rather special, aren't they," beamed Connie. "And I am so going to enjoy seeing every one of them in the third gallery at the villa."

"Every one of them! Connie Fairbright, does your love of art know no bounds?"

"Every single one," giggled Connie. "I simply couldn't resist. Signor Cambroni has agreed to hang on to them until all the tagging is in place, then we'll have a very exclusive opening ceremony for the third gallery."

It was not what Olivia wanted to hear.

"Actually, Connie, do you think that's the best idea? From what I understand of Signor Cambroni's tagging system, each painting requires many weeks of intensive work. The collection you've just bought could take as much as a couple of years before it's ready. Are you sure you want to be without all those paintings for so long?"

Connie frowned at the thought. "This is why you are absolutely indispensable, my dear Diana. I hadn't thought about it like that. Of course I couldn't be without them for that length of time, not now I've experienced them close up. It's going to be hard enough waiting until the villa is finished."

"And that's only one short month away now, Connie. Can you believe it?" said Olivia. "Why don't we arrange for the bulk of today's purchases to be shipped to the villa, leaving a couple for the gallery to work on. What do you think, Signor Cambroni? Would you agree with that?"

Ettore Cambroni didn't care. One way or the other and at one time or another, Signora Fairbright's collection was going to be replaced with totally convincing forgeries while the originals would disappear into Russia and China.

While they were talking, the limousine was quietly taking them the few streets to Il Latini, a traditional Florentine restaurant in a narrow side street close to the Arno.

"It was a pity you weren't feeling well, Diana," said Connie, "I should so like you to have met Signorina Mancini."

Olivia's mouth formed a smile, but behind her dark glasses, her eyes shone with malevolent delight. "There will be other exhibitions, other collections to tempt you, Connie. I'm sure Signor Cambroni will be inviting you to another private showing before long. And as for Signorina Mancini, I'm sure our paths will cross very soon."

Chapter Thirty-Three

The discovery of Jennifer Cotton working in the Cambroni gallery was a game-changer for Olivia, a development even she had not considered. As she sat in the car with Connie and Contorni after lunch while it sped back towards their rented villa in the hills near Monte San Savino, she tuned out from Connie's chatter as she mentally sifted through a succession of new plans aimed at taking full advantage of this new and exciting situation.

She had been tempted to make some excuse for staying in Florence, to wait around near the gallery and follow Cotton when she finished work, but that would have been foolish, precipitous, and may have aroused suspicion. To think that she had almost not gone with Connie and Contorni to Florence at all that morning; she certainly had only accompanied them reluctantly on Connie's insistence. As it was, she had been lucky; it could have worked out very differently if an unwitting Connie had introduced her to Cotton in the gallery. That would have been interesting. How would Cotton have reacted? she wondered. To have seen the look on her face would almost have been worth it.

No, this was a better outcome and she must capitalise on her good fortune.

As she stared at the blur of passing traffic, she became aware of Connie's voice penetrating her thoughts.

"Don't you think so, Diana? Diana?"

Olivia clenched her teeth, groaning inwardly.

She forced a pained smile. "Er, sorry, Connie, I was miles away. This damned headache, I can't seem to shake it off."

Connie squeezed her arm. "It was nothing, dear, just twitter. Have you taken something for it, your headache? Perhaps you should see a doctor. You can't be too careful with headaches, you know."

"Acqua, Diana," said Contorni as he turned from his position in the front passenger seat and passed her a bottle. "Water. You should drink plenty of it. Best thing for a headache. You are probably dehydrated."

Olivia took a swig from the bottle. "I expect you're right, Cesare," she said, continuing her role play. "This summer heat can be horribly draining."

She put the bottle into the door pocket, leaned back and closed her eyes.

"Would you mind if I just took a little doze, Connie," she said, quietly. She was desperate to get back to her train of thought, to revise and review her plans.

"Of course not," said Connie, "I might just do the same myself. It's been an exhilarating day and I suddenly feel quite tired."

Olivia sighed, nodding in agreement. Her mind was already back on track, no longer distracted by her employer's drivel. An idea was forming, developing fast like a time-lapse sequence of a plant growing from a seed. She had been increasingly concerned that her plan to steal the bulk of Connie's paintings once the woman had been killed, whilst a good one, still had a potential flaw in that it shouldn't be the only route to getting access to Connie's fortune. As it stood, the success of the plan hinged on Olivia being able to sell the paintings to her contact in Amsterdam. She knew her profit should be substantial even if she didn't get anything like the market value. But would it be substantial enough? Did her fence have the contacts himself? Were such high-value paintings out of his league? It was a potentially dangerous situation since by the time Olivia got the collection to Amsterdam, her fence would have seen the news, have heard that a rich American woman had been killed and her valuable art collection was missing. He would know Olivia was involved and he would use that knowledge to beat down the amount he was willing to pay her.

But now, quite unexpectedly, a gift from the gods had arrived. Jennifer Cotton. Once Olivia had captured her and locked her away in the cellar of her farmhouse, she could use her to force Connie to transfer a large sum of cash to an account Olivia had set up in the Caymans. It was so simple, so elegant. Transfer the money or sit and watch as Olivia subjected Cotton to excruciating pain while threatening to kill her.

She smiled to herself. She would, of course, kill her anyway. In fact, they would both die, once Olivia was sure the transfer had been effected.

Her first course of action must be to abduct Cotton and take her to the farmhouse. For that she needed time alone in Florence to follow the girl, find out where she lived and seize her. In her mind she ran through Connie's agenda for the next week. There were a couple of local visits to catch up with gallery owners she'd got to know. Although trips of no more than a few hours, there would be time enough for Olivia to head up to the villa site to check on construction progress and to continue to her own farm-house to set up her cellar for her anticipated guest. The cellar had been a masterstroke. Designed principally to stop any intruder getting in and finding her stock of explosives, detonators, weapons, documents and disguises, once secured, the rooms were equally impossible to get out of. And Cotton could scream and yell as much as she liked; there would be no one nearby to hear her.

For her drive to Florence, Olivia needed Connie to be away for longer. And in five days' time, there was the perfect opportunity. Connie had plans to go to Naples on an overnight trip, two nights possibly if the promised collections proved good enough. Of course, she wanted both Contorni and Olivia to go with her, but Olivia had the headache excuse mastered, switching it on and off as required.

The following few days saw Olivia impatient with anticipation. Finally, on the morning of Connie's departure for Naples as she sat in the shuttered darkness of her room, she knew she was ready. She had visited her house twice to fine-tune her set-up for Cotton and now she was waiting for Connie, her excuse ready to be rolled out once again. As expected, there was soon a gentle tapping on the door.

"Diana? Are you awake? Is everything OK?"

Olivia waited, lying back on the bed, her palms covering her eyes. She heard the door open.

"Diana? Oh dear, you're still in bed."

Olivia stirred and groaned softly. "Connie, I'm so sorry; I don't think I'll be able to go anywhere today. I took some tablets an hour ago, but this headache just won't shift."

She felt Connie's hand on her brow. "I don't think you're running a temperature, but I still think I should call the doctor; these headaches are becoming just too frequent. In any event, I'll postpone the trip. I can't leave you here like this."

Olivia reached out and took Connie's hand. "No Connie, you mustn't. All the agents are lined up; it would be a terrible waste. And you know that some of the paintings are only available for a very limited time. You don't want to miss this opportunity; there are some fine works listed."

"Your health is more important, Diana, I'm sure they'll understand."

Olivia shook her head, wincing as she did. "Connie, these are difficult men, proud men." She dropped her voice to an emphatic whisper. "Neapolitan men. They think differently, live by different rules. They're not used to selling directly to women, not even if they are rich. They would see your not keeping your appointment just because your PA was ill as a slight. They might well withdraw their collections. You don't want that."

She waited, letting Connie wrestle with her conscience. She knew how much Connie wanted the paintings on offer, and there was more than a grain of truth in what she had said: the gallery owners in Naples were hard to deal with. They were closed, suspicious men, unused to forthright American women who didn't know their place. Contorni had helped to smooth the path, but even he, as a Roman, was an outsider, never to be completely trusted.

Eventually Connie sighed, her resignation clear. "I know you're right, Diana, and I know how hard you and Cesare have worked to set up these meetings. But let me at least call the doctor."

Olivia patted her hand. The last thing she wanted was to be waiting around for some doctor. "Let's give it another day; I'm sure the pills will cut in soon. If I'm no better when you get back, I'll see a doctor, I promise. But please don't hurry back on my account. As I've tried to explain before, some of these men can't be rushed. Let Cesare take the pulse of the meetings. If the trip needs more time, let it happen. I'll be fine."

She forced a smile. "Now, off you go; Cesare will be waiting. You know how much he loves his flights in a private jet; they appeal to his sense of self-importance."

Olivia gave them fifteen minutes before getting showered and ready. It was the maid's day off and she was alone in the villa, so there was no one to tell tales.

Two days before at her house, she had taken a small handgun fitted with a silencer from one of the safes built into the walls of the smaller of the two cellars. She retrieved it now from where she had hidden it in her wardrobe and buried it in her handbag.

After parking her car at the Santa Maria Novella Station in Florence an hour later, she walked through several back streets to the Cambroni gallery, pleased to see Thompson the doorman in his usual place as she passed on the opposite side of the street. He didn't look up — passers-by were of no interest to him — and even if he had seen her, with her wig of short blonde hair, large sunglasses, jeans and short waist-length jacket, she bore little resemblance to the woman he had met with Signora Fairbright a few days before.

Olivia was waiting for lunchtime when she knew the gallery would close, and she was hoping that Jennifer Cotton would oblige her by going home for lunch. Or perhaps she would be meeting her minders. That would be interesting.

At one precisely, the door to the street swung open and Jennifer emerged alongside Ettore Cambroni. When the pair started to walk in the same direction, Olivia was concerned that they might be going to lunch together. But then they stopped, exchanged a few words and Cambroni headed off in the general direction of the Ponte Vecchio while Jennifer strode away in the opposite direction. Olivia smiled to herself; she needed Cotton to be alone.

Keeping her distance, Olivia followed Jennifer, acutely aware of the need for caution. The girl had probably been trained in stealth techniques, her antennae fine-tuned to detect anyone trailing her. However, the spring in Cotton's step seemed to say otherwise. There was an urgency about her pace, as if she were about to meet someone special, and there were no sudden changes of direction, pauses in doorways or shows of studying a shop window. Who could it be? A lover, perhaps? Whatever the reason, Olivia could see no evident caution in Cotton's march through the back streets to her apartment building a few minutes from the gallery. From the shadows a hundred yards distant, Olivia saw the girl punch in a code and disappear through the entrance door. She hurried along the narrow side street, hugging the shadows until she was outside the entrance. There was an array of buzzers alongside name panels for the occupants of the six floors. And on the fourth, the one in which she was interested. 4A Mancini.

Olivia looked along the street. Thirty yards from the entrance to Cotton's apartment building was a wider section to the narrow street where an old building had been demolished and its replacement set back from the street, giving up just enough space to park a car. The space was empty. Olivia turned in the direction of the Santa Maria Novella station car park and hurried off.

Chapter Thirty-Four

On the day of Connie's visit to the gallery with Olivia and Cesare Contorni, Jennifer had been disappointed to be told that instead of accompanying Connie Fairbright around the collection of Renaissance portraits Ettore Cambroni had acquired, she was to work her charms on a Dutch couple who had called that morning to request a viewing. For Cambroni, mention by the couple of a rich Belgian widow from Antwerp who had spent a small fortune in the gallery over the years was temptation enough. If, as they insisted, this couple were good friends of hers, they must also be loaded.

"Find out their tastes, Ginevra," instructed Cambroni, "show them whatever we have. Retrieve paintings from the vault if necessary. But don't let them leave without spending some good money, or at the very least, committing themselves heavily. Whatever they like, we can accommodate them, as you know."

"I assume, signore, that since they are new customers, they are restricted to seeing the first floor gallery only."

"Yes, we can't be too careful, even if they appear to be genuinely wealthy. And we have Signora Fairbright and her party arriving this morning as well. She seems to be the sort of person who expects exclusivity; I don't think she would appreciate having to share her space with others."

His rare smile was artful as he tilted his head to Jennifer, who thought the unusual distortion of his normally severe features made him look like a hungry python.

"I know I can rely on you, Ginevra."

"Thank you, signore."

The Dutch couple had proved demanding, wanting to know every smallest detail of the provenance of each of the paintings that interested them. Their knowledge was broad and Jennifer found herself wondering if she should recommend to the Cambronis that it might be risky to substitute any of the paintings they were looking at with fakes. But then she remembered why she was there, what the police hoped to achieve. Maybe this couple was exactly the break the team needed to expose the Cambronis for what they were. In the meantime she would continue as instructed by Ettore Cambroni and let the deals evolve.

When Connie took the time to seek Jennifer out, it created a few moments of light relief after an hour of heavy discussion. The Dutch couple too seemed to appreciate the short distraction. Connie mentioned her companion, as she had on her previous visit to the gallery, and dispatched Cesare to find her. When he came back empty-handed, Jennifer glanced along the gallery just as Olivia was heading for the stairs, her back to the gallery. As her eyes fell on her, something distant in the deep recesses of her brain sparked, but the spark was weak, gone as quickly as it came, and before she could link the image with any other information buried in her memory, the woman had disappeared.

Joining Connie for lunch was out of the question. The Dutch couple had made their own arrangements and insisted Jennifer go with them. As a result, Jennifer didn't pursue the spark, and it didn't seem important enough for her to check the CCTV records to see if the woman was shown.

The Dutch couple returned to the gallery for the next four days wanting more and more information before, on the fifth day, they finally purchased a stunning portrait of a young Florentine street urchin by the eighteenth century French painter Pierre Labreche. Jennifer had coveted the painting for some time and had been hatching a plan to persuade Pietro to buy it. However, a sale was a sale and the Dutch couple were thrilled with their purchase.

Jennifer declined their offer to join them for lunch; she was intending to spend an hour at her flat on a Skype call to Derek who was currently involved in a case that saw him spending many long evenings and nights staking out the East Midlands headquarters of a criminal network employing under-age Eastern European girls in a pornography and prostitution racket. His only opportunity for calls was therefore limited to lunchtimes, soon after he woke up following his night shift.

Shortly before one o'clock, Ettore Cambroni indicated it was time to close the gallery until it reopened at four, and Jennifer hurried through the narrow cobbled Florentine streets that led to her apartment. At least for this apartment she had no need to take the diversionary tactics required for visiting the watchers and she was eager to speak to Derek.

Rather than wait for the ancient lift, she ran up the stairs to her fourth floor apartment and headed directly for the vacuum cleaner and her hidden mobile phone, the one she used for communicating with Felice and Godden beyond coded texts on her ordinary phone, and for calls to Derek and Henry. The phone was sealed in a ziplock pouch inside the dust bag.

"Yo, babe!" cried Derek as their call connected and they could see each other. With fibre-optic connections at both ends, the image was crisp, vividly clear and free of pixelation. "How's it going?"

"You're looking at the Cambroni gallery's sales assistant of the year. I've just pulled off another big-bucks sale to enrich their very dodgy coffers."

"I thought you were the only sales assistant."

"I am, effectively, since Maria is at work so little now, but that doesn't mean my brilliance isn't appreciated."

"What about your modesty? Are they impressed by that too?"

"You betcha; they love me. Can't believe their luck."

"It's going to be a bit of a rude awakening then. Are you any closer to your endgame?"

"Top secret, dear boy, you never know who's listening."

"Bollocks, Moneypenny. This is 007 you're talking to."

"Then you should understand the need for caution. But yes, I think we're getting close. I've got another meeting this evening with the team and we're going to discuss strategy."

"So by this time next week you could be back in Nottingham?"

"I suppose it's a possibility; I hadn't really thought of it like that. I doubt it though, the paperwork will be horrible once this part's over. And there are all the previous sales to follow up on."

"Surely the Italians will field that for their end, and Godden for yours. After all, he's only interested in the UK connection."

"You reckon? I've a strong feeling that yours truly will be hauled in to push paper, so a week might be a tad ambitious."

"Weekends?"

"What are they?"

"Days allocated since the dawn of man for relaxation."

"Interesting concept, but relaxation wasn't what I had in mind once I'm back in my flat in The Park."

"Really? Are you still bent on pounding the streets and frightening dog walkers with your racing bike?"

"That would be outside my flat. What I'm thinking of inside is far more energetic."

"Can't think what you're on about, DC Cotton. I guess you'll just have to show me."

"Use your imagination. Right, it's your turn to tell me how you're getting on. How are the midnight trysts?"

"Mind-numbing, to tell the truth. The info is developing at snail's pace."

"There must be something to divert my mind from thoughts of selling paintings."

"OK," said Derek, dropping his voice. "Here's how it sits."

He spent the next twenty minutes giving details of his case, although as always, he avoided mentioning any names or locations despite his total confidence in the security system Ced Fisher had installed in both his and Jennifer's phones.

After another exchange of nonsense about the SCF office in Nottingham, Derek announced that he had to get to work. "Sitting around all night in a draughty derelict building may sound like a plum posting, but like you, I still have the paperwork to attend to," he said. "What are you up to now? Back to the grind?"

"Actually, I'm going to get an hour's shuteye. The siesta really is a most civilised practice, especially when tonight's session promises to be lengthy."

They rang off. Jennifer put the phone back in the vacuum cleaner's dust bag and headed for the bedroom, setting the alarm on her ordinary phone to ensure she'd be back to work on time.

At three thirty, refreshed after her nap, she was ready to face any afternoon customers. Boosted as always by her call to Derek, she set the apartment's security and CCTV, locked the door and skipped down the stairs.

Outside in the narrow, deserted street, the only sound was the click of her heels echoing from the cobbles and the ancient stones of the surrounding buildings. Thirty yards from the entrance to her building, a large Audi hatchback occupied the spot where the street briefly widened, but this was normal; the space was often used by one or other of the nearby residents during siesta time, and Jennifer took little notice of the car now parked there beyond noting that the tailgate was open and a jack was sitting on the street. As she walked past the car, she heard footsteps behind her and a voice say, "Mi scusi, signorina."

Jennifer sensed from the accent that the woman speaking was a foreigner, but in Florence that was hardly unusual. She turned and was confronted with the barrel of a small, silenced handgun pointing at her chest. Automatically half raising her hands, she looked up from the gun to the face of the person holding it. As she took in the woman's features, she gasped, a cold shiver of fear raking her spine.

"Freneton," she whispered, her heart racing.

The spark she had felt briefly in the gallery days before rekindled, this time stronger as she fitted the pieces together.

"You were at the gallery. What are you up to?"

"Time for chit-chat later, Cotton, assuming I can contain my enthusiasm to kill you."

She pointed towards the car with the gun. "Get into the back," she snarled, "before I change my mind. I can assure you that nothing would give me greater pleasure than shooting you here and now. But as it happens, you are temporarily more useful to me alive."

She took a step forward, but still remained too far out of range for Jennifer to make a move.

"I won't say it again, Cotton. Get in."

Jennifer walked slowly to the rear of the car and stopped.

"In!" growled Olivia through clenched teeth.

Jennifer reluctantly climbed into the luggage area and made to turn around, her eyes scanning the surrounding buildings for any sign of someone emerging.

Olivia was gesticulating with the gun.

"Lie down with your back to me. Foetal position. Hands to your face."

Jennifer lay down and no sooner had she turned away than she felt the sharp jab of a needle in her neck. Briefly her head was a vortex of jagged light spinning out of control, after which there was silence and blackness.

Chapter Thirty-Five

At three thirty the following morning, Derek Thyme's head was nodding slowly, the long hours of tedium starting to take their toll. For the last four hours there had been no activity in the building opposite that was the focus of his interest, but less and less of his attention, and in spite of several strong coffees, he was struggling to keep awake.

When the phone in his pocket vibrated with a message, he assumed it was Pete Harding, his replacement in the boring stake-out duties, texting to say he was on his way.

Derek pulled out the phone, his witty response to what would doubtless be the usual crude comment already half-formed in his head. He had the brightness turned down to prevent the screen lighting up the room like a beacon and revealing his presence to anyone outside who happened to be looking his way. Holding the phone low under the table where he was sitting he peered at the screen to see the first part of the message.

There was only one line. As he read it, Derek snapped awake with a start.

'Urgent. Call me ASAP. Godden'

He stared in disbelief at the screen. What had happened? It must be something serious for Godden to get in touch at this hour. He felt his breathing increase and his gut tighten as various possibilities flooded his mind, all of them unthinkable. Jen. Something had happened to her. He checked the time, willing Pete Harding to be early for once. He had to call Godden but he and his team weren't allowed to talk beyond whispers in the observation room; that could only happen in the back room.

In the early days of the stake-out there had always been two of them on duty, so one or the other could always cross the hallway to call in any urgent information without compromising the operation. But as one uneventful week gave way to the next, the bosses had scrutinised the budgets and decreed that one officer per shift would do. If he needed to leave his post for a bathroom break or to make a cup of coffee, he could turn on the video surveillance camera and leave the room, so long as the absence wasn't for more than a few minutes.

Derek checked the video camera focus, pressed the record button and zoomed out to make sure the field of view covered all he could see with his naked eye, after which he rushed from the room, hitting Godden's name in his contacts list as he did.

Godden answered immediately.

"Derek, thanks for calling back so quickly."

"Sir, it's the middle of the night. What's happened?"

"It's Jennifer, Derek, we've lost track of her. When was the last time you spoke?"

"Yesterday. Lunchtime," Derek could feel a pulse suddenly pounding in his head. "We had a Skype call," he added. He could almost taste the tension in his voice.

"Time exactly?"

"Er …" Derek shook his head. He had to focus. "Just a moment, I'll check."

Derek took the phone from his ear and pressed a few buttons.

"Twelve sixteen until twelve forty-nine. That's UK time."

"Nothing since?"

"No. Sir, please, what's happened? What do you know?"

There was a long sigh from Godden.

"We know a number of things. We know she turned off her apartment's alarm around one thirteen our time when she arrived home, and then clearly she called you immediately. We also know she turned it back on at three thirty, after which she's recorded on the CCTV leaving the apartment. Since then, there's been no sign of her."

"How did she look? On the CCTV, I mean."

"She looked fine; not under any duress. No telling glances at the camera."

"Have you checked her second phone to see if she made any other calls on it? It's in the apartment."

"We haven't located it. Presumably it's well hidden."

"It's in the dust bag of the vacuum cleaner, in a poly bag."

"She should have told me that. I'll get someone onto it."

Derek heard the snap of Godden's fingers as he said "Vacuum cleaner. Dust bag."

"You're in the apartment now?"

"Yes, we've been here for the last four hours. You see, the first indication we had that something was wrong was when Jennifer didn't turn up for a meeting at the safe house. She was due to arrive at ten. She's always punctual, never been more than a few minutes late, so even by ten fifteen we were starting to wonder. I sent a couple of coded texts but there was no reply, so I used an app the techies have developed for calling her ordinary phone that will tell me whether it's switched on or off without ringing the phone itself. And her phone is off."

"She'd never turn her phone off," insisted Derek, "and she's obsessive about keeping it charged; it couldn't be out of juice."

Derek's head was pulsing with questions. "Do you know if she returned to the gallery? Have they suddenly got suspicious of her?"

"Difficult to say. Obviously it has to be a distinct possibility. As you know, we can't just walk in there. Apart from anything else, the warrant to do that will have to be delicately handled, given the Cambronis' connections. We could lose the whole case. However, we are watching every known exit from the building."

"What about her phone records?" said Derek. "Presumably calls to her phone are logged. If the Cambronis aren't involved in her disappearance, wouldn't they try to call her? And wouldn't that show up?"

"It would, yes, and we're on to the phone company. But this is

Italy, Derek; we're not likely to get an answer until later on this morning, at the earliest."

"Shit."

"Yes, but you have to remember that if these people are good, they'd make those calls anyway knowing they wouldn't be answered, to cover their backs."

"You think they're that good?"

"We have to assume so."

Godden flipped through a book on a table in front of him as he considered how to phrase what he wanted to say next.

"Derek, your conversation with Jennifer. What did she say about her progress?"

"Well, she was careful, as she always is, no names and so on. She indicated that things were coming to a head, that she thought you'd be in a position to raid the place very soon. There was nothing else apart from her saying she was positive about the meeting you had scheduled for last night; she said it should define the way forward."

"Did she say anything about Olivia Freneton?"

"Freneton? No. Why? Do you think she's involved?"

"She might be, yes, but it's all a bit puzzling."

"You think she's tracked Jennifer down?" Derek was gripping his phone tightly, his voice punching out the questions. "What do you mean, 'puzzling'?"

"Freneton has been in Jennifer's apartment, but it was after Jennifer left yesterday afternoon. The CCTV tripped, as it's designed to do. Recorded her whole visit."

"In Jen's apartment!" He realised he was almost shouting. "Sorry," he said, lowering his voice. "You're sure it's her?"

"Yes, we ran the facials through recognition software. Even though she was in disguise, there's no doubt it's her."

"Do you think Freneton located Jen, searched her apartment then went to the gallery and perhaps somehow grabbed her after she left in the evening?"

"That's what we're thinking, yes. Something along those lines."

"How long after Jennifer left to go back to the gallery did Freneton arrive?"

"Only a few minutes."

"So she must have been watching the apartment, too much of a coincidence otherwise. But, just a minute, that doesn't make sense. If Freneton had located her, seen her go into the apartment, with her lock-picking skills, she could have at least accessed the building. We know that Jen's on her hit list. Why didn't she just wait and attack her when she left the apartment? Or force her way in? Freneton's mad enough to go for the heavy approach on the grounds she'd probably win."

"You could be right," agreed Godden. "On the other hand, if Freneton knows where Jennifer works, and perhaps has even worked out that she's undercover, it's possible that she sees some advantage in not hurting her, for the present anyway, although what that advantage might be, I can't say."

"In that case, Freneton must also have some connection with the gallery. Have Felice's people recorded her visiting the place?"

"Too early to say, I'm afraid. There's a lot of footage and it will take a while to go through it. And Freneton may not be in the same disguise as yesterday."

"Did she find anything in the apartment?"

"No. I'm pleased to say that all the precautions worked, even against someone with Freneton's knowledge of security. From her actions, she didn't appear to spot the micro-cameras, which is the point of them of course, and like us, she didn't find Jennifer's hidden phone. She did find her computer, but gave up trying to access it after a couple of minutes. Your friend Ced Fisher is very good, you know."

"Yes," replied Derek. "He put the same stuff on mine and that defeated Freneton too."

He scowled at the impenetrable darkness of the grimy street outside the back room window, the ghostly outlines of nearby buildings giving him no inspiration as he frantically trawled his mind for sensible questions.

"In your previous meetings," he continued, "has Jen mentioned anyone in particular? Clearly she hasn't seen Freneton at the gallery, but, I don't know, has some client featured in her thinking?"

"There was one she mentioned at our last meeting," replied Godden, "A Connie Fairbright."

"Never heard of her."

"No, neither had I. Seems she's the rich widow of someone called Brad Fairbright. Jennifer said that she's been buying paintings by the cartload and that the Cambronis intend to palm her off with fakes."

"Is she in Florence? Could Freneton have anything to do with her?"

"Good questions, Derek, but I'm afraid I don't have the answers. We were leaving it to Jennifer to give us the heads-up on when the Cambronis were ready to action their deception. I'm pretty sure that Felice hasn't followed up on Fairbright. However, I can assure you that first thing in the morning that will change; we'll get onto it immediately. Maybe Freneton's latched onto her in some way and is planning a con of her own."

"Yes," agreed Derek. "One of the things we've always discussed about Freneton is her source of funds. She's not rich and she must have cash-flow problems. You could be right about their connection."

"I hope I am, but from what I understand about Freneton, she's nobody's fool. And with her years of police experience, she'll be second-guessing every move we make. We'll have to act fast."

"Yeah, and now we know she's involved in some way and has been spotted in Florence, the SCF will want to be involved. I'll report to Mr Hawkins, the CSP, first thing, if that's OK."

"Of course," replied Godden, "it's essential that he's briefed as soon as possible."

Derek hesitated as he weighed up how to phrase his next thought.

He took a breath. "Sir, would there be any objection if I ask the CSP if I can join you in Florence?"

"Only if you keep calling me 'sir', Derek. It's Paul, I hope you can get used to that; I had the same problem with Jennifer when we first met. No, I'd welcome you out here, and anyone else with a detailed knowledge of how Freneton operates."

"That's great, thank you, si… er, Paul. What about Henry Silk?

And for that matter, Pietro Fabrelli. Do you want me to contact them?"

"I've been wondering about that. I know both of them will want to drop whatever they're doing and come to Florence, which is all very well given that Jennifer's well-being is of the utmost importance, our number one priority, but I have to look at the bigger picture and consider the operation. I haven't met Silk, but from what I've heard, he's sensible enough. However, I worry about how someone with Fabrelli's resources and contacts will react; I don't want him blundering in and trying to take over. How well do you know him?"

"I met him a few times when I was convalescing at the villa in Sardinia," replied Derek. "We got on well. I'll talk to him, persuade him to hold back, leave it to the pros. He'll be as worried as hell, like I am, but he won't want to risk doing anything behind our backs that could potentially hurt Jen."

Chapter Thirty-Six

At six thirty, three hours after Godden's call, Derek risked the wrath of Pete Hawkins by phoning him at home, hoping the man was an early riser. He was, and despite his gruff, off-hand demeanour, he was wise enough to understand that a detective constable would not be calling him at such an unsocial hour if it wasn't important.

"Get on a bloody plane as soon as you can, laddie," yelled Hawkins once Derek had briefed him. "Why did you wait so long to call me? Where's your initiative? You've already wasted three hours. Are you going to need anyone else?"

"Er, can I call you on that once I've arrived, sir?"

"Yes. I was thinking about the people who knew Freneton best. Of course, two of them are dead and another is Cotton. You're probably the next on the list, apart from me. Listen, laddie, where are you?"

"At home, sir."

"Packed and ready to go?"

"Yes, sir."

"Right, there'll be a squad car arriving within minutes, as soon as I've called in. He'll take you to Birmingham; it's the nearest sensible airport now East Midlands is all bloody budget rubbish."

"Sir, I've checked the flights and I've missed the only non-stop one to Rome from Birmingham already. And anyway, if I want to get to Florence as quickly as possible, a direct flight would be better. There's a service from London City. I know it's further to drive, but I'd be better off flying from there."

Derek winced as the displeasure of Hawkins' grunt pounded his ear.

"Do whatever it takes, Thyme, and report to me as soon as you arrive and know something. I want hourly updates."

Derek hadn't been idle in the three hours between Godden's call and his conversation with Pete Hawkins. First, he had called Henry Silk, hoping there might be evening flights direct to Rome from Los Angeles. There were none, but it didn't matter.

"Henry, it's Derek. Sorry if I've interrupted something, but it's important."

"You've interrupted nothing except my attempts at sleeping."

"Sleeping? Isn't it the early evening there?"

"Where?"

"Los Angeles."

"In Los Angeles, it is, yes, but I'm in London. I flew in yesterday morning. I've got a break in filming. What's up?"

As Derek explained, Henry was already grabbing a bag and throwing things in it.

"Christ, Derek, that's …" was all Henry could manage once Derek had finished.

He took a deep breath. "Look, I'll get the first flight I can. I'll probably be there before you, or we could even be on the same flight. I assume you'll be going from City Airport."

"Yes, the eleven o'clock flight."

"I'll book that one too. See you there."

After Henry, Derek had called Pietro Fabrelli, knowing he was an early riser. But he too wasn't where Derek had expected.

"Madonna, Derek," gasped Pietro, "that's …. Listen, I'm in China, in Pechino, at a huge fashion show. I'll drop everything and jump on the next plane, but I probably won't get back until tomorrow or even the next day. However, Chiara, my PA in Milano is in the office as usual. Anything you need, Derek: people, access to anywhere, contacts, anything at all; you must call her. I'll tell her to give you everything you want. And if there's any sort of ransom demand …"

"Actually, Pietro, it's really important that the whole approach to this is softly softly. It requires great delicacy."

He heard Pietro snort. "I hear what you say, Derek, and I promise I won't go blundering in. However, I must say I find it most reassuring that you British Bobbies are involved. I don't wish to be disparaging about my countrymen, but—"

"I can assure you, Pietro," interrupted Derek, "that Massimo Felice is a very professional and competent officer. From what I've seen, not all your police are like the idiots in Montalbano."

"I hope you're right," muttered Pietro.

By four that afternoon, Derek and Henry were in yet another of Pietro's apartments in Florence, one he reserved for important overseas contacts in the fashion world. With insight that impressed the police officer in Derek, he had called back to suggest its use rather than meeting up in the safe house apartment.

"I know that Felice and his people have been taking great care to keep their use of that address secret," said Pietro, "and I know their current operation is still ongoing. If the people targeted in that operation are nothing to do with Jennifer's disappearance, we don't want to ruffle the waters, do we?"

Derek smiled to himself at Pietro's metaphor confusion.

"That's brilliant, Pietro, thank you. I'll tell Paul Godden we can use it as a base."

"Not just a base, Derek; stay there too. There's no need for a hotel. It's got four bedrooms and Chiara can organise food; anything you want."

Twenty minutes after Derek and Henry arrived at the apartment, Paul Godden pressed the buzzer at the street-level entrance. He was accompanied by a young female officer from Felice's squad, Martina Bianchelli, who had been assigned to him to smooth away any problems he might encounter when not with Felice. Her slight build and ready smile that lit up her already attractive face didn't fool Derek for a moment. He could see from her overall stance and economy of movement that she was more than capable of defending herself or subduing an unwilling suspect.

While Signorina Bianchelli settled herself by the window to watch the street three floors below, Godden introduced himself to both men — he'd spoken to Derek several times on the phone but they had never met — and invited them to join him on the sofas surrounding an expensive and exclusive all-glass coffee table.

"Delighted to meet you at last, Henry," said Godden, ever the gentleman. "Of course, having seen you on the screen many times, I feel as if I know you."

"Occupational hazard," said Henry, with a smile. "Now, please, Paul, do you have any good news for us?"

"No, I'm afraid not," said Paul, pulling a face. "We still haven't located Constance Fairbright. It seems she values her privacy and can afford to screen herself behind layers of her organisation. Almost everything she does is through another name. We've contacted her HQ in Boston who were cagey, to say the least, even when we cut up through the layers to a Vice President, whatever that means."

"Just a title," said Henry. "Often not as important as you might think."

"Maybe, but this person, a quite aggressive lawyer representing Fairbright, absolutely refused to give a number for her and even maintained that the only address he had in Italy was the Hotel Barchester in Rome. As you may know, that's possibly the most exclusive and expensive hotel in the city, and Fairbright keeps their largest suite on a permanent booking."

"I can't believe that, can you?" said Derek, frowning. "The bit about not having another address, I mean."

"No, I can't," agreed Godden. "We've got onto our US counterparts who will be trying their luck today, but Fairbright has committed no crime and nor is she missing, apparently, so her company is under no obligation to play ball."

"What about the hotel?" asked Henry. "They must have something; can't they be leaned on?"

"They've been a little more forthcoming. It would appear that they genuinely don't have a contact address for Connie Fairbright. However, they did tell us of a Cesare Contorni who has been instructing her in Renaissance art — we're still trying to find him — and an Alessandro Rossi, who is a language tutor. Unfortunately, Alessandro Rossi is a very common name, so we haven't located him yet either."

"And Freneton?" said Derek. "Has she been seen at the hotel?"

"Oh yes, they were in no doubt about that. Until Fairbright moved out a few months ago, Freneton had been living there on her tab, everything paid for. We showed our file photos to various members of staff there and they all agree she's the woman they know as Diana Fitchley. Their reserve disappeared when the conversation moved to her. I don't think a single one of them liked her at all."

"Hardly surprising," muttered Derek.

Godden was about to continue when his phone rang. He answered, listened, thanked the caller and rang off.

"They've found the right Alessandro Rossi," he said, smiling. "Unfortunately he has no other address for Fairbright, although he did say she was renting a villa in Tuscany while the villa she's buying, also in Tuscany, is being renovated."

Henry sat back on his sofa, sighing. "Tuscany's huge," he said. "She could be anywhere."

"It is," agreed Godden, "but given what she's buying is probably pretty grand, if we trawl the bigger estate agents, perhaps we'll strike lucky."

"Don't hold your breath," said Henry, shaking his head, "Even the one-man-band agents will take on big properties given half a chance. And agents like that are two a penny."

"Well, we have to start somewhere, and Felice's drafted in some extra hands to call every architect, design studio and geometra they can find in Tuscany."

"Geometra?" asked Derek.

Henry leaned forward to explain. "They're a cross between a surveyor, engineer, estate agent and general middle man. You can't do without one in any property deal; they have all the contacts.

With luck, if the names of both Fitchley and Fairbright are floated around, someone might have heard of them."

"All we can hope for at the moment," said Godden.

"Have other dealers apart from the Cambronis been contacted?" asked Derek. "We know that Fairbright is buying up paintings."

"Yes, and it's turning into quite a list. The problem for Felice is that it's all being done in the context of the Cambroni gallery and the investigation there, which is something he's trying not to advertise, as you know. So he can't just call in huge extra resources without questions being asked; he doesn't want the wrong people hearing about it."

Henry shook his head in disgust.

"Talking of resources," he said, "if this Fairbright person has spent liberally at various galleries, surely one or more of them must have some details of the woman. Credit card information and so on."

"Not necessarily," said Godden. "All we've had so far is from a couple of galleries in Rome that sold to her. When it came to payment, the money all came directly from an account in the US. That's all they had. As I said, this woman likes her privacy and she can afford to pay for it.

"However, on the positive side, we do now know that Freneton works for Fairbright and that she most likely intends to relieve her of some of her money, and we also know that both women went recently to the Cambroni gallery where Freneton must have recognised Jennifer. Unfortunately, it would appear that Jennifer didn't see her."

"So having stumbled across Jen," added Derek, "once she'd got over the surprise, she must have followed her, discovered where she lives and somehow, somewhere, abducted her."

"Do you think the gallery is involved?" asked Henry. "Could Freneton have tipped them off about Jennifer?"

Godden shook his head. "You know, I doubt it," he said. "She'd be in great danger of blowing her own cover. I mean, she could hardly admit she was once a UK police officer and had recognised Jennifer as one of her former subordinates."

"Who she tried very hard to kill," snarled Derek.

"Exactly," agreed Godden. "No, in my view she's snatched Jennifer and taken her somewhere that Fairbright doesn't know about."

Henry's voice was quiet and reflective as he spoke more to himself than the others.

"The question is where the bitch has taken her and how she intends to use her."

He was already making his own plans which he had no intention of sharing with anyone.

Chapter Thirty-Seven

From nowhere a pounding headache hit Jennifer like a punch in the face as she snapped into consciousness. She groaned and rolled onto her side, the sudden movement creating a tornado of nausea that stretched her stomach in all directions. She clenched her jaw to combat the bile in her throat, trying to breathe deeply through her nose.

She opened her eyes and immediately regretted it as the dazzling light ten feet above her head added to the torture of what felt like a band of metal crushing her brain.

A violent shiver pulsed through her body. The thin, hard mattress she was lying on offered little insulation from the cold stone floor beneath it, and, while unconscious, she had kicked away the single sheet that had been thrown over her.

Her hands were free and she pushed herself up into a sitting position. That was when she discovered her legs were shackled together at the ankles. She must have been moving on the bed during her dreamless sleep: her tights were in shreds around the bands of the metal shackles.

She squinted, forcing her eyes to focus, and looked around the room. It was about fifteen feet square, high-ceilinged with broad wooden beams and a powerful, central light bulb way out of reach. A small metal table against the wall opposite the mattress appeared to be bolted to the concrete floor. The wooden chair next to it was not. There was a plastic jug of water on the table, a single plastic beaker and what looked like chocolate bars. She pushed her tongue through her lips, her throat felt parched, but the overriding demands of her bladder were starting to consume her.

To her left was a doorway with no door. Was that the edge of a wash basin? A bathroom?

She turned, pushed herself up onto all fours and then tried to stand, but the nausea returned sending her stomach and head into orbit around each other. Gritting her teeth, she tried again and this time, by reaching out to the stone wall for support, she managed to stand.

She took a breath, turned towards the doorway and, still using the wall for support, shuffled forwards, the eighteen-inch chain connecting the shackles preventing her from walking properly.

The room was indeed a bathroom and she almost cried with joy as she stumbled the three small steps to the toilet.

Standing up after peeing, she pressed the button on the wall-mounted cistern. As she did, the nausea returned, triumphant and sensing victory. Her stomach gave up the fight and she just managed to spin around and kneel on the floor before she vomited.

Five minutes later she was sitting at the table drinking her third beaker of water and munching on an energy bar. Feeling a thousand times better than when she woke up, she took another look at her surroundings. As well as the table and chair, the mattress and discarded sheet, there was a thin duvet on the floor near the mattress, but nothing else. The room itself had a concrete floor and rendered walls painted white. The stock of food on the table — mainly energy and chocolate bars and a large slab of cheese — was enough to feed her for a few days. Water was available from the bathroom. A forbidding-looking metal door was located in the centre of the wall opposite the bathroom, with a small inspection panel set in it at head height.

She stared at the stock of food, puzzled. How long was she

going to be kept here? But right at that moment, the answer to that question was secondary to her hunger. She unwrapped another energy bar and broke off a lump of cheese, washing them down with more water.

Her senses now back on full alert, she looked down at herself. Her clothes were the pencil skirt, jacket and blouse she had been wearing when Freneton ordered her into the car.

Freneton! It all came flooding back. She had been waiting for her outside the apartment, armed with a gun. The bitch had some nerve. True, the apartment block where Jennifer had been living for the past few months was in a quiet back street, but there was occasional traffic, including prowling Polizia patrol cars. It could have all gone horribly wrong for her. What would she have done then? Shot Jennifer and run? Whatever: it hadn't gone wrong and now here she was. A prisoner. How long ago was that? A day? Two days? More? No, it couldn't be too long since she hadn't soiled herself and she'd woken up needing to pee. Ten hours? Twelve tops, she reckoned. Which made it now sometime in the middle of the night. However, since she hadn't been wearing a watch and there were no windows, there was no way of telling whether it was night or day.

She shuffled back to the bathroom and this time noticed that as well as a hand-towel, there was a larger bath sheet. She looked up and saw a shower head high on the wall, a tap at waist level to control the water. There was only one pipe so the water for the shower had to be cold, and like so many basic Italian bathrooms, there was no shower pan; everything around just got wet.

Again the thought: how long was Freneton intending to keep her here?

She made her way back into the room and over to the metal door. The small panel, about a foot by nine inches, looked as if it could either be slid or pulled open from the outside. An inspection panel to check Jennifer was well away from the door before opening it, the hole large enough for Freneton to be able to see the entire room.

She pushed and pulled at the panel, but it wouldn't move.

Sitting back down on the mattress, Jennifer leaned forward to examine the shackles around her ankles. She pulled a rueful face as she registered their strength. There was no way she would be able to pick the lock or break them. Same with the chain, which was made of heavy-duty steel links.

She reached out to grab the duvet, folding it to form a large backrest, and settled against the wall, her legs stretched out ahead of her as she tried to remember every moment of her brief encounter with Freneton.

And it had been brief. A couple of words of foreign-accented Italian, a silencer thrust at her chest, barked instructions and then oblivion.

What had Freneton been wearing? How did she look? Was she confident or nervous? In control or on the edge? However she appeared, the abduction was well planned and confidently executed.

She shut her eyes to think. What was her hair like? It was short and blonde. Not the colour Jennifer remembered. A wig?

And her clothes. She had a vague impression of jeans and a short jacket.

She leaned her head back against the wall and sighed. She would presumably find out the answers to these thoughts when Freneton appeared from behind the panel in the door. Clearly with the food and facilities, and the fact she wasn't bound hand and foot, Freneton wanted to keep her alive. She hadn't left her to starve to death.

The thought made her shudder as she considered the alternative. Being the crazed psychopath she was, Freneton would want to witness every moment of Jennifer's death, would want to be in complete control of it. She'd more or less said as much in the past.

She let her eyes wander around the room, taking in as much detail as she could, anything that might trigger a thought as to what Freneton was intending. She studied the ceiling. The large rough-cut beams had smaller cross-beams running above them at right angles, those beams in turn supporting terracotta tiles. Standard old-style construction. The single light had a cable running to it from the side of the room, but the position of the light in relation to the beams meant that the recesses were poorly lit. She peered into the corners and that was when she saw the tiny camera, well hidden in the half darkness. So Freneton was using more than just the hatch to observe her; she could watch her any time she chose. What about the bathroom? Jennifer stood and shuffled back there, this time searching the ceiling recesses and quickly finding the second camera.

She pulled a face. No hiding place, even when she was on the loo or braving the cold water to take a shower. The thought didn't please her.

However, what was still puzzling her was why Freneton was keeping her alive. What had she to offer? What was her value?

She returned to the mattress and lay down. Convinced it was the middle of the night, she decided she might as well try to get some proper sleep, not the drug-induced variety. She grabbed the duvet and pulled it over her, covering her head in an attempt to shield her eyes from the harsh light.

After several hours of tossing and turning, Jennifer finally fell into a deep sleep troubled with many tortured dreams, all of them featuring a demented Freneton chasing her, threatening her, attacking her with a huge knife, binding her, lifting her protesting body over a bridge parapet and letting it fall into the depths of an endless chasm.

She awoke with a start as the metal panel in the door clanged open. She pushed away the duvet and stared into the darkness beyond the open panel. A pair of eyes was watching her. Freneton's eyes.

"You may sit up, Cotton, but don't attempt to stand. When I enter the room you are to stay exactly where you are. And just to let you know, since you'll no doubt be thinking you might over-power me, I have a taser, and I won't hesitate to use it."

Jennifer sat up, leaned against the wall and waited. After ten seconds a bolt was pulled and the door swung open.

Olivia Freneton took a step into the room and stopped.

"And remember, I am also taller, stronger and more ruthless than you, so if you do decide to go for it, keep in mind that I'd enjoy inflicting pain on you," she said, her eyes piercing into Jennifer's.

"What do you want from me?" said Jennifer, her eyes fixed on Freneton's.

Freneton's smile was malevolent. "For now, just your living, breathing and conscious body." Her eyes narrowed. "Conscious is very important."

"I don't understand," said Jennifer.

"All in good time, Cotton. You'll soon be up to speed. Now, a little housekeeping, just so you know the score. Firstly, you are in one of the rooms in the cantina, the cellar of an old farmhouse. But it's no ordinary room; I had it reinforced to make escape impossible. Secondly, the farmhouse is mine. It's deep in the woods, at least three miles from the nearest building, a house that is anyway currently empty."

"And that interests me because …?" said Jennifer trying to sound flippant in an attempt to get under Freneton's skin.

"I'm telling you," snapped Freneton, "simply to inform you that there's no future in yelling and screaming. There's no one within earshot and since the house is some distance from the fence, even if someone were to come as far as the gate to this property, there's no way you would be heard. I've tested it."

She dropped her voice, but made no attempt to hide the threat. "There will be plenty of opportunity to exercise your lungs in due course."

Jennifer shrugged her indifference.

"What about the food? A few rubbish bars and some cheese aren't going to last long."

"I'm not anticipating that you'll be here long," replied Olivia. "If it turns out otherwise, I'll replenish the stocks."

"And if you're arrested and don't tell the police about this place?"

"Then I suppose you'll die of starvation. Not actually what I have in mind for you but in the unlikely event of my being picked up, it would give me solace to think of you sitting here getting weaker by the hour."

Jennifer stared at her. How did this crazed bitch get so far in the police force? She was completely unhinged. However, she said nothing in response to Freneton's taunting. She wasn't going to give her the satisfaction of their exchange becoming a conversation. She was still mulling over how Freneton had discovered her. It had to have been at the gallery, although she doubted the Cambronis were involved. If they had suspected Jennifer at all, they would have had ways of getting rid of her that would not require the involvement of a crazy English woman. But what had she been doing at the gallery? As she continued to search Freneton's eyes, the pieces suddenly fell into place.

"It was Connie Fairbright, wasn't it?" said Jennifer, "It has to be. She's rich, widowed, likes the good things in life. You're operating some sort of con on her, aren't you? You're after her money. Well, good luck with that. She's nobody's fool."

As she was speaking, she was checking every nuance of Freneton's face for a reaction, for an indication that she'd guessed it right. She only had limited experience of interviewing suspects, but she'd also read all there was to read on the subject and experimented with many role plays at police training school. She was good at it, considerably better than average, and she could tell she'd guessed correctly with Freneton.

"You were at the gallery last week with Fairbright and that fawning Roman art expert, weren't you? She said there was someone she wanted me to meet. That would have been interesting since you can't have known in advance I was there. You were the person who rushed out of the gallery claiming you needed some air."

She noted the fire in Freneton's eyes and was determined to continue, to push the woman. "Did you spot me on the CCTV? That must have given you a surprise."

Freneton's smile was cold. "It did, but not for long. I couldn't believe my luck; still can't. To have you served up on a plate, Cotton, was more than I could have hoped for. Oh, and in case you think I overlooked your phone, I didn't. I switched it off immediately and as soon as I reached somewhere more remote, I smashed it to pieces. So no cavalry, I'm afraid."

"I shouldn't expect anything less," replied Jennifer with a shrug, hoping her disappointment didn't show.

Still watching her captor's every movement, Jennifer was hoping Freneton would move close enough for her to throw herself at her, to inflict some sort of injury. If there was a whisker of a chance, she'd go for it, although she knew that from a sitting position it would be almost impossible, especially with the shackles. But Freneton was good; she was keeping just out of range, almost as if she were tempting Jennifer to try something. Then she took Jennifer by surprise.

"Stand up!" she ordered.

"What?" Jennifer couldn't believe it; she'd have a far better chance from a standing position.

"You heard me. Do it!"

Jennifer swung herself onto her knees and pushed herself up, keeping Freneton in view out of the corner of an eye.

She stood and faced her. They were about ten feet apart so she made to take a slight step forward.

"No you don't," said Freneton, moving back to maintain the distance between them. "Stay exactly where you are!"

She reached behind her to take something from her belt.

"Do you think I'm simple, Cotton? Don't you know I can read every twitch of your face, every movement of every muscle? Are you so stupid that you don't realise that everything registers in your eyes and hands? Your body language has been screaming your intentions at me. I almost let you have a go since I should have enjoyed retaliating. But instead, I thought I'd give you a demonstration, a taste of things to come, particularly if you try to resist me, a tiny example of the pain you are going to be suffering in the very near future."

She brought her hand round in front of her and to Jennifer's horror, she saw it was holding a taser.

"Freneton! No! There's no need to—"

The protest stopped abruptly as Olivia squeezed the button to fire the taser. Two electrodes shot across the room hitting Jennifer's chest, delivering over a thousand volts to her body. Her voluntary muscle control incapacitated, she collapsed onto the bed, stunned.

Before Jennifer had a chance to recover, Freneton clipped the taser gun back onto her belt, turned on her heel and left the room. The door slammed shut and the bolt was thrown.

As Jennifer slowly lifted herself back into a sitting position, still reeling from the shock, the room was plunged into blackness as somewhere outside Freneton threw the light switch.

Chapter Thirty-Eight

As she drove from her farmhouse to Connie's villa restoration project, Olivia Freneton felt invigorated, her senses finely tuned and ready for action. Finally after months of waiting while she put up with the damn woman's gushing nonsense, she could launch her plan.

She had never had a fixed timetable for what would happen when; it all depended on how things fell into place with the paintings Connie stored in the safe at the rented villa. As they were intended to augment the large sums Olivia was about to extort from Connie, there needed to be enough of them to make stealing them worthwhile.

And now there were more than enough, too many in fact. With Connie's various purchases over the past months and the delivery of a further sixteen paintings from the Cambroni gallery, there was a haul worth close to ten million dollars. But she couldn't take them all, much as she would like to. They were masterpieces, they had to be treated with care. She wasn't an opportunist art thief willing to cut a priceless painting from its frame, roll it up and run. On the contrary, she had no desire to damage what she intended to steal, which meant that each of her chosen portraits would have to remain on its stretcher and be carefully packed. That in itself limited the number she could handle. She would choose the twenty most valuable; a number she could store in large suitcases in her car. Once on her way, her revised plan was to sell them one by one, negotiate the best deals, and not necessarily through the creep in Amsterdam; she could do better than that. She would have time — there would be no urgent need for the money from the paintings; it was icing on the cake.

The visit to the Cambroni gallery had certainly proved to be a profitable day out. As well as the paintings, Jennifer Cotton had unexpectedly surfaced, prompting Olivia to implement her plan while completing the disposal she had dreamt of ever since escaping from Harlow Wood.

Jennifer Cotton. She still couldn't believe her luck. The girl was now locked away in the cantina of her farmhouse, the room she had prepared as a precaution, another of her brilliant contingency plans. It had the basic necessities of food, water, sanitation and somewhere to sleep. She could watch any captive's every move remotely and punish them where necessary by depriving them of light. It was escape proof and essentially soundproof.

However, for Cotton, the long-term was irrelevant; she would only be in the cantina for another twenty-four hours before Olivia moved her to her final resting place, and during that time, the girl could enjoy the disorientation of total darkness along with the terrifying knowledge that her death was imminent. When Olivia picked her up the next day, her defences would be compromised.

In the meantime, she had work to do. The Villa Brillante was still a busy building site with a squad of ten workmen, a geometra in daily attendance and security guards. To implement her plan, they all had to go.

The guard on the gate had little enough to do given the remoteness of the villa's location, however, having been subjected to Olivia's wrath on two occasions for trivial lapses, he knew better than to shirk his duty. By now he knew the sound of her car as it approached on the winding track and as always was standing to attention as he waved her in. She ignored him and drove over to the caravan that served as the site office for Carlo Menci, Connie's surly geometra. Olivia disliked the man intensely; if she had been calling the shots she would have sacked him months ago. But Connie liked him, and Connie paid the bills.

As she pulled open the caravan door and walked in, she sniffed the air.

"You've been smoking in here again, Menci," she said by way of greeting. "How many times do you have to be told?"

Menci shrugged. "This is a stressful job, signora, every day there are so many decisions to make. And the labourers, they are lazy. And the suppliers … What can I do?"

"You can go outside if you have to smoke, that's what you can do!" barked Olivia. "Now, I want to know if there are any crucial operations planned for the next three days that can't be put on hold."

Menci stared at her in incomprehension. "Er, no, I don't think so," he said cautiously. "The parquet flooring has been delivered, and the fittings for the main bathroom. The kitchen tiling is complete and the artigiano in Monte San Savino says the kitchen will be ready for installation in ten days' time. The drainage system was completed yesterday and most of the bathrooms are now working."

He lifted his shoulders to indicate his total puzzlement. "Signora, why should you want to interrupt things at this stage when for so long you have been pushing me to work faster?"

"It's not me," snapped Olivia, her voice all disapproval. "It's Signora Fairbright. She called me this morning to say she needs to spend time here alone. She feels the development of the house is at a critical stage, and now so much of the main structure is in place, she wants to move around it unhindered by any construction noise or worker's chatter. She says she must have the silence these woods will bestow on the site once everything is finished. Only then can she envision the villa in its final form and complete her plans for the interior decoration. You must understand, Menci, that she is an extremely sensitive person."

Menci pulled a face. These foreigners were crazy. "As long as la Signora understands it will cause delays—"

"Of course she understands," interrupted Olivia. "And she

accepts it. It's only three days and if there's a problem, you and the men can work overtime."

"And the watchmen, signora? I assume they must stay."

"No, I said the signora wants total privacy. That means no one is to be here, not even on the outside of the fence. I want you to issue immediate instructions to everyone to finish what they are doing and then leave. That includes the watchmen. I'll return here later this afternoon to check that everything is ready for Signora Fairbright's visit, which will start tomorrow. Then you can give me all the keys and leave yourself. I'll call you to say when the work can recommence. Until then, I don't want you or any of the workmen, guards or anyone else anywhere near the place."

By six thirty that evening Olivia had completed her task list. Everything was now ready for Jennifer's installation the next morning followed by implementation of her plan the day after.

She had returned to the site two hours earlier, satisfied herself that the only person remaining was Menci, taken all his keys and sent him on his way. In case he decided to return in spite of instructions, she not only secured the metal gate to the site with the existing padlock but also added her own extra padlock to it, one for which only she had a key.

To complete her check, she paced the perimeter of the entire temporary fence that had been erected inside the main wall surrounding the twenty hectares of land comprising the estate. The fence had been installed to add security while the house was under renovation; once the main wall had been upgraded and fitted with state-of-the-art security devices, the temporary fence would be removed. But for now, it was important that it was as strong as the day she had overseen its installation.

She next checked the landline in the caravan to make sure the Internet was working. It was essential to her plans for relieving Connie of some of her fortune.

Her final task for the afternoon was to prepare the room in which Jennifer was going to be held until her death in two days' time. She had chosen one of the large first floor bedrooms — presently just four walls, two radiators and some construction mess. What it lacked, for Olivia's purposes, was sufficient flammable material.

After fetching a metal-framed office chair from the caravan and chaining its frame to one of the radiator pipes in the room she had chosen for Jennifer, she spent thirty minutes locating and moving piles of discarded wood and card from packing materials stacked and awaiting collection near the gate. As well as arranging it around the room where it would burn readily once ignited, she placed some near the chair. She wanted to be sure that Jennifer didn't pass out from smoke inhalation prior to burning to death; she wanted her to feel the flames, like a witch or heretic at the stake in the middle ages.

She stood back to admire her handiwork. It looked good, and with the aid of some accelerant and a timing device to set it remotely, all it now lacked was the star of the show. That omission would be rectified the following morning.

On returning to the rented villa near Monte San Savino, Olivia called Connie to make sure she hadn't extended her stay in Naples. She had already called after breakfast, but with Connie, things could change on a whim and Connie's presence was essential to Olivia's plan.

"No, Diana, nothing's changed," said Connie when she answered the phone. "The jet is still booked for four thirty tomorrow afternoon, so I should be back with you by seven at the latest. We're landing in Rome on the way to drop off Cesare, but that will only add a small amount of time to the journey."

"Excellent," replied Olivia, pleased to hear that Contorni wasn't going to be a factor she had to allow for. "I just wanted to be sure so I can arrange dinner. How did it go today? Any new acquisitions?"

She heard a giggle from Connie, the type of giggle Connie gave after spending a lot of money.

"I can't wait to show you, Diana," she enthused. "I've picked up five of the most amazing paintings, all portraits of little aristocratic Neapolitan girls from the sixteenth century. They are absolutely divine. Even Cesare was getting excited when he saw them and you know how dour he can be in the face of highly priced paintings."

"You're bringing them home?"

"Of course! I couldn't possibly have left them behind. Apart from anything else they are paid for; the transfer went through immediately while I was in the gallery. These places might look as if they're still somewhere in the nineteenth century, but when it comes to technology for payment, they're entirely up to speed. Better than the dealers in Tuscany even."

"Quite a payload in your jet, then," said Olivia, trying to sound jokey but wanting to know values.

"Oh yes. A little over two million. That's why I use private transportation to go everywhere: no undesirables on board. Listen, Diana, I've got to rush. I'm getting ready to take Cesare out to dinner. He's been told of a wonderful place on Capri; we've got a rather smart boat taking us over there. I told you you should have come."

"Oh, I've been having some fun of my own up at the villa. I think you'll approve," replied Olivia.

"Ooh, tell me more."

"You'll have to wait, Connie. It'll be too late tomorrow evening so we'll head over there the next day after breakfast."

"It sounds very mysterious," said Connie, "I'm intrigued. I'd come back earlier if I could, but I've got to sort out today's purchases and there are two more galleries Cesare wants me to see. So my haul could be even larger."

"You are incorrigible, Connie Fairbright!" admonished Olivia, forcing a congenial laugh. "And anyway, there's no point in coming earlier. What I've got planned won't be completely ready until the day after tomorrow, so enjoy your last day in Naples."

And your last complete day on earth, she thought, as she ended the call.

Chapter Thirty-Nine

Olivia Freneton's attempts at disorienting Jennifer were less successful than intended. Jennifer was little bothered by darkness and her exploration of the room earlier when it was lit had given her all the confidence she needed to move about it freely. Of more concern to her was the taser: having been subjected to its debilitating effect once, she had no desire to repeat the experience. As is often the case with physical violence, the threat of it was as terrifying as the implementation.

Still unnerved by the weapon, she wound herself up in the duvet and lay on the thin mattress. Although she doubted Freneton would be back for a while, she was determined to stay awake and listen for her return, to be ready to give the appearance of being more confused than she was. Anything that might potentially blur Freneton's focus.

Her wait was a long one, and she eventually submitted to more sleep. But finally, in the total silence of the house, she heard the faint crunch of gravel outside as Freneton's car drew up. She waited, breathing gently, slowly, trying hard to ignore the cacophony of her beating heart.

Descending the stairs to the room next to where she was holding Jennifer, Olivia focussed her attention on the computer monitor where the CCTV feed from the cell was displayed. She wanted to watch her captive's reaction as she switched on the lights. What she saw was Jennifer shielding her eyes with both hands before clasping her head tightly and shaking it.

"It's too bright!" she yelled. "Please, I can't stand it."

Olivia opened the metal door and stood in the doorway, saying nothing as she waited for Jennifer's eyes to adjust to the light.

"May I sit up?" whispered Jennifer as she looked up, her eyelids scrunched together.

"No, you can kneel and sit back on your heels,"

Jennifer did as she was told and only then looked more carefully at Freneton.

"Oh God!" she exclaimed when she saw the taser in Olivia's hand. "No more, please."

"It's entirely up to you, Cotton. Do what I say and I won't zap you. Piss me off and I'll whack you with the full charge, not the low one I gave you yesterday."

She pulled a pair of metal handcuffs from her jacket pocket and tossed them onto the floor in front of Jennifer.

"Here, clip one half of those onto your right wrist then hold your arms out wide and turn round so you're facing away from me."

Jennifer complied but before she had finished turning, Olivia had grabbed her right hand, twisted her arm up her back and forced her to lie face down. Reaching for her other hand, she handcuffed her prisoner's wrists together in one smooth movement.

Grabbing the handcuff links, Olivia roughly pulled Jennifer to a standing position and moved back two paces, out of reach.

"We're going for a drive, Cotton. Get moving."

"Where are we going?" replied Jennifer, allowing her voice to sound strained, nervous.

"To your friend Connie Fairbright's magnificent villa. Now, move it!"

Jennifer shuffled slowly forward, labouring her movements. As she passed through the doorway, she was sizing up the open metal door, wondering if she could dive at it and kick it shut in Freneton's face.

However, the ever-watchful Olivia didn't miss the slight move-ment of Jennifer's head. "Don't even think about it Cotton. I've got the taser aimed right at you. If I have to use it, I'll drag you up the stairs by your feet, making sure you're bouncing on your face. That won't do your pretty looks much good, or your teeth."

When they got to the car, Olivia popped the tailgate and told Jennifer to lean into the car. Grabbing the shackles on Jennifers' ankles, Olivia then hauled her in.

"I'm not going to inject you this time," she said, "but in case you're thinking of kicking and screaming, the roads we're driving along are very quiet, just the odd tractor. So save your energy."

After throwing a blanket over Jennifer, she slammed the tail gate shut, locked up the house and drove off.

Olivia pulled up in front of the temporary gates at the Villa Bril-lante and got out. She looked through the mesh to the site to check if any of the workers had turned up despite her instructions. There was no one: the locks on the gates were exactly as she had left them the previous evening and there had been no cars parked anywhere along the two miles of gravelled track leading to the villa.

She unlocked the gates and drove through, stopping again to lock them behind her.

The villa was set on a natural plateau on a moderately steep west-facing hillside, with wild oak woods above, below and on both sides. The only way it could be overlooked from the front would be to use a high-powered telescope from a hill across the wide valley below. As for the other three sides, the trees here were particularly dense, so anyone wanting to spy would need to be close. Nevertheless, Olivia waited, watched and listened for any unnatural noises, any sudden squawks and concerned calls from the many magpies and hoopoes patrolling the woods. There was nothing.

As she dragged the dishevelled Jennifer from the car, Olivia slipped on some mud, giving her captive the slimmest of chances to attack her. Ready for any opportunity, Jennifer took it, but Olivia was too fast and too nimble. Back on her feet, she slapped Jennifer hard around the face, once to stop her in her tracks, and twice more to hurt her.

Jennifer sank to her knees, dizzy from the blows, blood dripping from her nose.

"Don't try that again, Cotton, or I'll break your arms." snarled Olivia.

She grabbed the handcuffs and pulled Jennifer's arms up high behind her.

"All right, Freneton!" screamed Jennifer, as she squirmed and wriggled, her shoulder sockets electric with pain. "You've made your point, you sadistic bitch. I can walk without your help."

"Through there and up the stairs, then turn left," said Olivia, pushing her towards the villa's main doors.

Taking care not to trip on the chains, Jennifer hauled herself up the stairs and turned into a wide corridor with several rooms leading off it.

"All the way to the end," barked Olivia. She was two steps behind her. "And don't forget the taser in my hand."

As soon as she saw the piles of wood and card scattered around the room, Jennifer understood what Olivia had in mind. She stopped in the doorway, fear overwhelming her, strength draining from her legs.

Olivia prodded her in the back with the taser.

"Impressive, don't you think?" she gloated. "And all for you. It's carefully laid to minimise the smoke. There'll just be plenty of flame and heat. Imagine how painful that will be. Now get over to that chair and sit down." She pointed to the office chair she had previously chained to the radiator pipe.

In response, Jennifer turned, trying to face Olivia, but all she saw were the taser terminals thrust into her face.

"I'm sorely tempted to discharge this taser directly into your eyes, Cotton, just to see the effect. Do you want to be my guinea pig?"

Jennifer could feel her pulse racing, every nerve in her body on edge, waiting, but there was no opportunity to act without the retaliation being severe.

She shuffled over to the chair and sat as she had been instructed.

Olivia moved behind her and looped a strong chain around the links connecting the handcuffs, and, using a padlock, she secured the two ends together around the backrest support, binding Jennifer tightly to the chair.

She stood back to admire her handiwork. Cotton was completely secure: it would take heavy-duty bolt cutters to free her from those chains. There was certainly no way she would be able to free herself. She checked the time: twelve thirty. Plenty of time to return to the rented villa and wait for Connie's return. And tomorrow? Tomorrow her months of conditioning and manipulating Connie Fairbright, her months of putting up with her drivel, her months of fine-tuning Connie's life to her own purposes, would all come to fruition. She would walk away richer than she'd ever imagined, leaving the bodies of her victims behind her.

Olivia cupped a hand under Jennifer's chin, confident for the first time there would be no retaliation. She studied her bruised and bloodied face. Her right eye was swollen and half closed from the slap; her nose still bleeding slightly. She had been intending to slap her a few more times, but on inspecting her handiwork, she decided that the message written on Jennifer's face was strong enough to induce Connie to comply with her demands. Any sign of resistance from Connie and Olivia would enhance Jennifer's pain. It was a perfect plan.

Chapter Forty

When Connie returned that evening, Olivia was determined to limit how much time she'd spend listening to the endless tales of galleries, dealers, new artists discovered and paintings bought. While it was their last night together and she should grit her teeth and be patient, her plan was now underway and she was finding it hard to maintain her guise of the enthusiastic companion. She had had enough and wanted the seclusion of her room to run over all her plans one final time.

She allowed Connie an hour of non-stop tales, culminating with her proudly displaying the five portraits she had brought back with her. Olivia made all the right noises and agreed on their excellence — although all she could really see in them were dollar signs — after which she feigned a headache and went to her room, leaving Connie to store the paintings in the safe.

The following morning when she came down, Olivia was surprised to find Connie already up and sitting on the balcony nursing a mug of coffee.

"You're up early, Connie. Have you had any breakfast?"

Connie turned to her, studying her face. She took a breath and smiled. "No, I was waiting for you. I don't actually think I want much; I just want to get up to the villa. I'm intrigued to know what you've been up to."

Olivia forced an enigmatic smile that hid her unease. Connie sounded different, her voice thicker, and even though she had smiled, it was only with her mouth; her eyes were saying something else.

"All in good time," she said at last, trying as ever to keep the upper hand over her employer. "Now my head's stopped thumping, I'm rather hungry. I feel like some eggs; sure you won't join me?"

It was going to be a long day and she wasn't sure when she'd next get the chance to eat.

"Just some yoghurt and grains, I think. And of course, another coffee," replied Connie, standing.

Olivia reached out and took her mug. "I'll fetch it. Why don't you stay here and enjoy this wonderful morning? The sun's glorious."

But Connie didn't sit down. "I think I'll take my shower," she said. "I won't be long."

When Connie walked into the kitchen after her shower, Olivia was at the breakfast bar with a plate of scrambled eggs, a mug of steaming coffee next to her. But her mind was elsewhere as she reflected on the day ahead, possibly the most important day of her life. If things went as she expected — and why shouldn't they given her meticulous planning? — it should be the most lucrative day of her life as well.

She looked up as Connie's footsteps interrupted her thoughts.

"There you are," she said, reaching over to press the button on the coffee maker. "Are you sure you won't have some?" She pointed with her fork to the plate.

"Quite sure, Diana, thanks," said Connie, as she waited in front of the coffee maker while it filled her mug.

To Olivia's finely tuned ear, Connie still sounded distracted. She needed to lighten her mood.

"I was thinking again about the paintings you brought back

from Naples," she said. "In my lay opinion, they're among the finest in your collection."

Connie smiled but said nothing.

"What's the grand total now?" persisted Olivia. "It must be close to fifty. Am I right?"

Connie nodded. "Something like that, yes." She frowned. "Do you think it's too many? Am I being foolish, or greedy, perhaps?"

Olivia smiled reassuringly. Was guilt the cause of Connie's preoccupation?

"Not at all, Connie, I think you've created a wonderful collection. You have the means to do so, and if it gives you pleasure, why shouldn't you? If you're worried about no one else having the opportunity to view them, you can always lend some to state galleries around the world."

Connie nodded slowly. "You know, that's a good idea. It would help widen the exposure of these wonderful artists. There are so many that are either overlooked or totally forgotten."

To Olivia, Connie's eyes were warmer this time. Maybe her off-the-cuff reply had lifted her out of her mood. She hoped so; she wanted the impact of her surprise to be as profound as possible.

She was further reassured when Connie stood and put her hands on her hips.

"OK, Diana," she said, "I don't think I can wait any longer. Either you're going to have to tell me what you've done at the villa, or show me,".

Olivia laughed. "Telling you would spoil it. Let's get ready and head up there."

By the time they were climbing into the car, Connie seemed to be back to her normal self. Olivia sighed inwardly; the stupid bitch could be capricious at times, she thought, but there was no point in worrying further about it; that was just the way she was. In any event, there would soon be no reason to concern herself over Connie ever again.

As they drove through the gate, Connie was again talking excitedly about her paintings, which ones would go where, how best to arrange them. Olivia was hardly listening; the paintings were never going to get as far as the villa.

.   .   .

Connie was still in full flood when Olivia drew the car to a halt in front of the gates of the Villa Brillante.

"Why are the gates locked?" exclaimed Connie in surprise. "Is nobody working here today?"

Olivia smiled at her. "It's all part of the surprise. I gave everyone the day off. It will be better without them."

"Really?" questioned Connie, her voice echoing her alarm.

"Yes, really," said Olivia. "Relax; I've been so looking forward to this. It's going to be such fun."

Connie was still uncertain.

"What about the guards? Surely they should still be here, with all the valuable materials in the house. Wasn't that the whole point of the guards?"

"Of course it was, Connie. And it still is. They'll be back this evening," lied Olivia. "I doubt word has got round in such a short time that they aren't here. And anyway, the gates are locked."

She got out of the car to release the padlocks.

Connie's eyes roamed the site. It seemed so empty without the builders, and she could think of no reason why they shouldn't be there. What was Diana up to? Her feeling of unease returned.

"Diana—" she started as Olivia got back into the car. But Olivia cut her off.

"Nearly there, Connie, you won't have to wait much longer. I can't wait to see your face." She patted Connie's arm and smiled as she drove through the gates and up to the villa's main door.

"Oh, we have a door," said Connie, distracted by progress she didn't know about.

"We have, yes, with a handle and a lock," said Olivia, holding up a key.

"A locked door isn't much use when there's no glass in the windows," commented Connie.

"Glass scheduled for next week," countered Olivia, "together with work starting on the main boundary wall and the real gates."

"Fortress Fairbright," said Connie.

"It's what you wanted."

"It's what's necessary," replied Connie as she opened her door and stepped out of the car.

"Come on, I can't wait any longer," she added, but the earlier fire in her voice had died again.

"Once more with enthusiasm?" said Olivia. "I've been planning this for ages."

She recoiled slightly as Connie gave her a long, cold look. There was no humour in her eyes, none of the eager anticipation she had been expecting. Had she guessed what was happening? She couldn't possibly have since if she knew, she most certainly wouldn't be there.

She waited, feeling more tension than she had anticipated, when suddenly Connie surprised her by smiling and holding out her hand.

"Sorry, Diana, I'm just in a strange mood. Take no notice of me. Show me your surprise; I'm mystified as to what it can be."

Olivia kept hold of Connie's hand and walked her to the main door. She stopped to turn the key in the lock, pushed open the door and stood back.

"After you, signora," she said, curtseying. "After all, you are the lady of the house."

Connie walked into the entrance hall and looked around. Apart from more building supplies stacked on the floor, not much had changed since she was last there. She turned to Olivia to find her holding her arm out towards the stairs.

"Upstairs, Connie, that's where the fun starts."

Connie walked up the stairs and stopped at the landing.

"That way," said Olivia from immediately behind her as she pointed left down the corridor. "Stop at the end by the door."

"That's one of the guest bedrooms," said Connie as she walked towards the door.

"Right," agreed Olivia, "Now, I'm going to open the door, but before I do, I want you to close your eyes. No peeping, OK?"

Connie glanced back at Olivia, her smile still tinged with hesitancy. "You're enjoying this, aren't you?" she said.

"More than you could possibly imagine," said Olivia, forcing her own smile, knowing it was the final time she'd have to do it.

"Now, eyes closed. Good. I'll take you by the hand and lead you in."

She turned the handle and pushed the door wide open. She wanted to check on Cotton before she guided Connie into the room.

Her features hardened as Jennifer looked up. There was some disturbance of the chains and the chair where she had been trying in vain to free herself, but mainly there was desperation in her eyes as well as pain. The tight gag round her mouth was making breathing difficult.

Olivia took Connie's hand and walked her five steps into the room.

"OK, stop there," she said. "I want to introduce you to somebody. You can open your eyes now."

Connie opened her eyes, gasping as she saw Jennifer bound and gagged in front of her.

"Connie Fairbright, meet Jennifer Cotton, or as you know her, Ginevra Mancini. Jennifer is my guarantor."

Connie turned her head to Olivia, the expression on her face a mixture of horror and incomprehension.

"What in—"

She was stopped mid-sentence as Olivia slapped her face viciously, the slap followed immediately by another, and then, as her legs gave way and she sank to her knees, a third.

Before Connie could react, Olivia had taken her hands, pulled them round behind her and handcuffed them with a pair of cuffs she had left on a pile of wood near the door.

"Diana!" screamed Connie, her mouth and nose bleeding.

Olivia's face had transformed from genial friend to cold-hearted killer.

"That, Connie dear, is just a taste of what Jennifer will feel if you don't cooperate. As you can see from the blood on her face, I softened her up a little yesterday. It's looking rather bland now it's dry; I think I should freshen it up, don't you?"

To demonstrate her point, she walked over to Jennifer and slapped her hard round the face, immediately opening up the wound in her nose.

"Diana! Stop it!" screeched Connie. "What do you want? I don't understand. What's this all about? Are you mad?"

Olivia turned to her, the malevolence in her eyes filling Connie with fear.

"No, Connie dear, I'm not mad. I'm clever and calculating, but not mad. Although if I stayed much longer in your company I might go mad. Do you know what it's been like all these months having to put up with you, with your gushing, your privileged crap, your simpering enthusiasm for everything, your gullibility? I've earned everything you are about to give me, make no mistake about it."

"What ... what the hell are you talking about? We've been friends, confidantes. What's got into you?"

"God, you're so naïve," spat Olivia. "You sit on your gilded throne thinking all the world is yours at your bidding."

She stopped abruptly, not wanting to be distracted by a rant. There was much to be done.

"To answer your question," she continued, "what's got into me is your wealth. I want some of it. Not all of it, in fact what I want is trivial compared to what you're worth, but it will be enough for me to disappear and live in comfort for the rest of my life."

"Haven't I paid you well enough? I've been more than generous. You had nothing before you started working for me." Connie was indignant.

"You think that was enough?" barked Olivia. "Why the hell do you think I sought you out? For your sweet, sickly, small-town personality?"

She sneered at the incredulity on Connie's face.

"I targeted you, you stupid bitch, and I've had a hard time not breaking your pathetic neck every single day."

While she was talking, she had walked over to a bag in the corner of the room and removed a pair of heavy-duty hiking boots. She kicked off her shoes and put on the boots.

Smiling, Olivia then turned her attention towards Jennifer, rejoicing in the fear reflected in the girl's eyes. She strode over to her, grabbed hold of the chair back and one of the chains binding Jennifer and toppled the chair onto its side. Jennifer grunted through the gag as her head hit the floor. Olivia walked slowly around the fallen chair until Jennifer was facing her, took a step towards her and launched a kick into her gut.

"Stop it! Stop it!" screamed Connie. "You can have whatever you want! Just stop hurting her!"

Olivia turned back to Connie. "Of course, my dear. I just wanted you to be sure of the consequences of disobeying me; I needed you to witness them first-hand."

She grabbed Connie's handcuffs and hauled her to her feet.

"Right now, we're going to the caravan. We have some work to do online; we're going to connect to your bank. It won't take long and then I'll be out of your hair. And remember that DC Cotton — did you know she's a police officer? — remember she's here and she'll be punished with increasing severity for every delay, every resistance you put up. And I'll drag you back here to watch. Are we clear?"

"Y…yes," stuttered Connie as she looked back helplessly at Jennifer's motionless body.

"Fifty million dollars is too much," gasped Connie as she recoiled from a vicious slap from Olivia.

"There's no point in resisting, Connie. This isn't a negotiation," snarled Olivia.

"I'm not resisting; I'm telling you it's more than the limit!" yelled Connie through a blur of tears she was trying desperately to blink away. "Although it's my money, there are safeguards. I can't just transfer that amount without a detailed discussion with my finance people. A limit was set up for situations exactly like this."

They were in the caravan with Connie sitting in front of the computer. Olivia had freed her hands but made it clear that she wouldn't hesitate to inflict more pain if Connie tried anything.

Olivia searched her eyes. In spite of the terror in Connie's voice, or perhaps because of it, it sounded like the truth.

"How much can you transfer?"

"Twenty, max."

"Twenty? It's not enough."

"It's the best I can do, and beating me, torturing me or even killing me won't change it. I'd give you more if I could, believe me. Anything to stop you hurting that girl again."

Olivia sighed. She had been fairly sure that twenty million would be the limit from a discussion she'd had with Connie in more relaxed circumstances some months earlier. She just needed to be sure. With the additional profit from the sales of the paintings she'd be picking up shortly from the safe in the rented villa, she'd have plenty.

"Do it!" she instructed.

"I have to make a call," said Connie.

"Why?"

"Because that's the way it works. I don't deal with some high-street bank, you know. Mine is a private organisation that exists for a very few clients. It's … different. I have to speak to a certain person to authorise the transfer. It's not difficult, and there will be no problems, but it has to be done that way."

Olivia knew she had no choice. "If you give any indication of the circumstances, scream for help, anything, I'll forego the money and break your neck. Do you understand?" said Olivia, thrusting her face at Connie's.

Connie nodded, pulling back as far as she dared.

Olivia called up Skype. "Do it!" she ordered.

Connie didn't move. "Diana," she said, gulping her words, "I need to be calmer. May I have some water? Please?"

Olivia grabbed a bottle from a table in the corner of the caravan and handed it to her, balling her hands threateningly into fists as she waited.

Connie finished the water and took a deep breath. "Thank you," she said, "I'm ready. Where is the money going?"

Olivia handed her a piece of paper.

"Who are you calling?" she said. "What name?"

"His name is Charlie Lisscombe. He's my account director."

"OK," nodded Olivia.

Connie dialled and waited as the call connected. There was a slight echo as a female voice answered.

"Mr Lisscombe's office. How may I help?"

"Hello. This is Constance Fairbright. May I speak with Mr Lisscombe?"

"Of course. Please hold."

There was a click and a confident voice boomed down the line.

"Connie, how are you? What can I do for you?"

"Hi Charlie. I'm good, thanks. Sorry to bother you. I need to make an urgent cash transfer."

"Of course, Connie. How much?"

"Twenty million."

"Top limit, huh?"

"That's still OK, isn't it?"

"Of course. As per our regulations. Where's it going?"

"The Cayman Islands," replied Connie and she read out the details.

Lisscombe read back the information. When he'd finished, he added, "Listen, Connie, as you know, under the new rules I have to send you a text with a code number that you read back to me. Do you have your cell there?"

"Yes," replied Connie, reaching into her jacket pocket.

A few seconds later, the phone buzzed. "Two seven six, three one eight," read Connie as she held up the phone to show Olivia.

"On the button, Connie. That's all done. Anything else I can do for you?"

"Nothing, thank you, Charlie. Have a nice day."

She hit the red button on the screen and sat back.

"There," she said. "You have your money. Can you please let that poor girl go now?"

By way of reply, Olivia grabbed Connie's right hand, hauled her into a standing position and twisted her arm up her back. In two seconds she was handcuffed again and Olivia was pushing her to the back of the caravan.

"Sit there," she said, indicating a battered armchair. Connie hesitated. Olivia shoved her hard, making her fall awkwardly onto the chair.

"Don't move," she said as she focussed her attention onto the computer.

She typed fast, calling up her bank in the Cayman Islands and checking her account. After typing several instructions, she punched the return key and stood up.

"Your man is right. It's all there. Thank you, Connie, your bequest is much appreciated."

"Bequest?" said Connie as she tried to turn into a sitting position. "What do you mean?"

Olivia laughed loudly.

"Oh, Connie, my dear," she cackled. "Do you honestly think I could let you go free after all that's happened this morning? No way! You'd have your hounds on me in a flash. At least with what I have planned, I'll maximise my chances of getting away. It's all been carefully and meticulously calculated, you see."

"You scheming bitch!" yelled Connie. "You'll never get away with it."

Olivia laughed again.

"Yes, I will. You see, I've been getting away with it for years. I'm simply too good for them. I'll be out of the country by this evening, by which time you'll be long dead, along with your little friend in the villa."

"Why, Diana? Why?"

"It's a long story, Connie, far too long to relate now, and why bother. However, in spite of your rudeness, I have decided to repay your generosity by making your death painless, unlike Jennifer Cotton's. She will feel every flame as it works its way towards her, hear her skin blistering as she screams. It's all she deserves for the trouble she's given me. But you," she said, walking up to the armchair where she had flung Connie, "I'm going to knock you out for a while with a little injection. Nothing too strong, just enough to keep you quiet for a couple of hours while I sort things out at the villa and get on my way."

"Diana," pleaded Connie, "There's no need for any of this. We can work something out. More money. As much as you want. A new identity; I'm sure it can be arranged."

Olivia snorted a cynical laugh. "Already done, my dear, already done. I agree that more money would be good, but I'll get by. Now, let me explain what's going to happen."

She bent down to reach into a cupboard next to her and carefully retrieved a rectangular plastic box of about twelve inches by ten. She placed it on the table near the computer and turned to Connie.

"In that box is your passport to oblivion. It's a bomb that will go off in about two hours' time, about ten minutes after a similar but smaller device sets a fire in front of Jennifer Cotton. This one will destroy the caravan and you with it; it will be completely painless, I can assure you, although I suppose the anticipation won't be fun if you've come round before then. You see, I'm hoping you'll at least hear the device go off in the house and know that as you listen, Jennifer will be dying."

"You are completely and utterly mad. May you rot in hell," snarled Connie as she tried to get out of the chair.

"Tut, tut, Connie. Not trying to escape, are you?" said Olivia. She took a step forward and punched Connie full in the face, knocking her out.

She hauled her out of the armchair and sat her slumped body onto an office chair. Taking a length of rope from a cupboard, she tied Connie's ankles together and fed the rope around the chair to the handcuffs, effectively hog-tying her to the chair.

She stood back and considered Connie's unconscious form. She'd hit her hard; it would be a while before she came round. Her attitude towards her ex-employer was hardening. When she woke up, she could sit and watch the minutes ticking away until her death. She would forego the injection, Signora Fairbright didn't deserve such compassion.

Olivia's final chore at the villa was to set the other explosive device. She retrieved it from where she had left it during her preparations the previous evening and carried it into the room she now regarded as the Jennifer Cotton pyre.

"Recovered from my little kick, Cotton? You know, for two pins, I'd finish the job I started that night in Harlow Wood by methodically crushing your skull. I have the boots for it."

She placed the bomb amongst the paper and wood scattered around the room before walking back to Jennifer to stand over her.

"It's tempting, Cotton, believe me. What's stopping me is the knowledge that the fire in here will be slow, full of flame and extremely hot. I'll be thinking about you. In fact, I'd very much like to watch, but needs must, I'm afraid. I have to be elsewhere."

She turned and walked out of the room, down the stairs and out of the villa. Her work done, she climbed into her car and drove away from the Villa Brillante without a backward glance.

Chapter Forty-One

Olivia took the most direct route across the Val di Chiana, using mainly minor roads to return to the rented Villa Luisa. She'd driven the roads a hundred times, knew where she could speed and where she must take care. She didn't want some over-enthusiastic carabiniere or polizia officer stopping her and, because she was a woman, insisting on trying to charm her while unsubtly letting his eyes explore her body — on two separate occasions now she'd been invited for dinner while at a routine roadside check. She snorted her derision: these dullards had to occupy themselves with something since there was little crime in the area. Then she smiled in satisfaction. All that's about to change, she thought.

As she turned onto the narrow single-track road leading to the villa, she pressed the remote on her dashboard and the gates swung open. She parked by the main entrance and ran indoors.

She had packed the previous evening after Connie had gone to bed, after which she had made her way quietly to the large study on the ground floor where she walked directly over to the massive safe Connie used to store her art collection. The thing weighed a ton, literally, so the chances of its being stolen were zero. It had been a nightmare to install. Connie had initially insisted it should be in a small room next to her bedroom, but there was no easy way to get it upstairs. So a compromise was struck and the ground-floor study agreed upon.

For Olivia, the most important feature of the safe was not so much that it had one of the most advanced locking mechanisms available, making it almost impossible to break into, it was simply that Connie had shared the combination with her. And it had been at Connie's insistence.

During that previous evening, Olivia had wanted to be sure the paintings were ready for stowing the following day into the extra-large rigid suitcases she had prepared for them. There would be a need for her to work fast when she returned to the villa after setting the bombs that would eliminate the distractions of Connie Fair-bright and Jennifer Cotton from her life. Ah, DC Cotton, how sweet that would be!

In the darkness of the study, she had silently turned the dials on the safe door. There were two and the sequence had to be carefully followed. She had practised and practised when Connie was away, so now the operation was swift and automatic to her.

She had turned the main handle and the door swung open. She shone the torch from her phone onto the contents of the safe, checking the labels, making sure they were stacked and ready. She touched the edge of the nearest one, smiling as she did. With her cherry-picked selection in her possession, her future was secured. Satisfied that all was well, Olivia had closed the safe, made sure it was locked, and quietly made her way back to her room.

As she ran up the stairs from her car, Olivia once again checked the time. Thirty-five minutes had elapsed since she set the timers; the first bomb would go off in an hour and fifteen minutes. She only needed ten minutes at the villa to get her bags and the paint-ings, another five minutes to change the number plates on her Audi to a German set, then she would be off, heading for the French border at Ventimiglia. From there she would drive to Lyon and fly out of Europe.

In her bedroom, she opened the large wardrobe and reached through the hanging clothes to where her two small bags were hidden at the back. She grabbed them and took them to the car where she stacked them in the footwell of the front passenger seat — she needed all the luggage space in the rear for the paintings. Returning to her room, she retrieved the five empty suitcases also hidden in the wardrobe and, in two journeys, carried them down to the study. She opened all five on the floor and walked over to the safe.

In the same practised operation she had used hours earlier, she spun the dials clockwise and anticlockwise according to the well-rehearsed sequence. After positioning the final number, she grabbed the large handle and turned it.

Except she didn't. The handle wouldn't move.

Surprised to have made a mistake after so much practice, she ran through the sequence again and grabbed the handle. Again it wouldn't turn. Had she made a mistake twice? This had never happened before.

She repeated the sequence for the third time, now turning the dials slowly and carefully, ensuring she made no error. And still the safe wouldn't open. She stared at it in disbelief until realisation dawned. For some reason, Connie had changed the combination without telling her.

Olivia clenched her jaw as she considered her options. Had Connie found out about her? No, impossible. She wouldn't have played ball that morning. Had she changed the sequence and simply forgotten to tell her? More likely; Connie could be forgetful. And given she was forgetful, she had a habit of writing things down. Olivia smiled. The new combination would almost certainly be in Connie's bedroom in one of the drawers of her dressing table. That's where she kept everything.

She rushed to the bedroom and began searching. She pulled out every drawer, tore out the contents of the wardrobes, lifted the mattress and up-ended several handbags. There was nothing. She stopped, surrounded by the wreck of Connie's room. How much of a setback was it? The paintings were worth upwards of ten million dollars. It was a substantial loss but at least she had the twenty million Connie had transferred earlier; she had checked and it was there in her bank.

Or was it? Had Connie somehow double-crossed her? Was that possible? She grabbed her phone and hit an app for her Cayman Islands bank. The Internet was good and the connection was made immediately. She punched in a password and then another to display her account balance. The twenty million was no longer there. She scrolled down, an unfamiliar feeling of panic creeping over her. Underneath her latest account transactions was another table: 'Transfers to be cleared'. There was one item in the table itself. A sum of twenty million dollars, against which was written 'Transfer frozen'.

The realisation of what had happened and its consequences slammed into her brain. There were no paintings and there was no money. Nothing. She had nothing and she had just killed two people for it. She checked her watch. In forty-five minutes, the first bomb would go off. It would take thirty-five to get back to the villa. She had time to get to Connie and beat the combination out of her, make her watch Cotton writhe and twist in her death throes if necessary. Anything, it didn't matter. She had to salvage something.

She charged down the stairs and into the car, sending a shower of gravel across the driveway as she accelerated through the gate. This time she didn't care about police officers; she'd mow them down if need be. Her entire focus was on getting to the villa as quickly as possible. Twice she risked ending up in a ditch as she overtook slow-moving and over-wide tractors that were going sedately about their business with no interest in whether they were holding anyone up. Twice she left their drivers gesticulating wildly at what was suicidal recklessness, even by Italian driving standards.

Thirty-one minutes after leaving the Villa Luisa, Olivia screeched to a halt outside the Villa Brillante. She had only a few minutes until Jennifer Cotton was toast; a few more until an exploding caravan would reduce Connie to dust.

She ran to the caravan and opened the door. The bomb was still where she had left it but instead of Connie sitting at the table tied to an office chair, there was no one, not even the chair. She checked the time on the bomb. Fifteen minutes to go.

She rushed outside, her eyes narrowing as she saw the office chair lying on its side beyond the caravan. She turned towards the villa and saw a second chair and some chains. Her nostrils now flared with anger, she sprinted through the open villa door, up the stairs and charged along the corridor to the room where she had left Cotton. But as she had already guessed, Cotton had gone. Only the broken and distorted water pipe remained, smashed with something heavy. She stood frozen to the spot, her mind reeling with a whirlwind of fragmented images, thoughts and ideas, but nothing tangible coalesced. She had allowed for none of this in her planning; there were no contingencies to draw on.

She walked over to the small bomb that was about to set this room alight and checked the numbers counting down on the timer. One minute. She had one minute to get out.

Slowly, not rushing in the least, Olivia Freneton walked along the corridor, down the stairs and out of the main door, closing it behind her. She got into her car, reversed up and drove out through the gate just as the bomb upstairs in the villa detonated. It wasn't a huge flash, not as big as the one from the caravan would be. She saw it in her mirror but it hardly registered. Her eyes were fixed ahead as she accelerated down the track. There was now only one thing dominating her mind.

Revenge.

Chapter Forty-Two

The previous day, around the time Olivia Freneton returned to her house to drag Jennifer from the cellar and transfer her to the Villa Brillante site, a smartly dressed man of around sixty had pressed the buzzer of the door to the ground-floor entrance of the Cambroni gallery. Thompson was on hand, as always, to check the stranger's bona fides.

For Thompson, the grey-haired distinguished-looking types were always a challenge. He was streetwise enough to know that many a conman would use this character — straight-backed, military bearing, polished brogues — but that didn't mean everyone dressed that way was a conman. However, with no appointment, Thompson felt duty bound to erect some barriers, to make the person justify his need to enter the gallery.

Nevertheless, politeness, as ever, was a necessity.

"May I help you, signore?"

The answer may have come back in fluent Italian, but after several years in Italy, Thompson had developed a good ear: the man was a foreigner. An American, he guessed.

"I sincerely hope you can, young man, yes," replied Henry Silk, peering through his small rimless spectacles. "I wish to speak with Signor Ettore Cambroni."

"Is Signor Cambroni expecting you, signore?"

"Not exactly, no. But it is most urgent, I can assure you. Would you mind giving him my name?"

"I'll need to check if he's in yet," said Thompson, pulling a mobile phone from his pocket. "What name is it, signore?"

"Mancini. Oscar Mancini," replied Henry. He frowned, his features radiating concern and a certain anguish. "Could you please tell him I need to speak with my daughter? It really is most urgent."

Henry saw the name register in Thompson's eyes before the man turned to make his call. While he waited, he checked his reflection in one of the large mirrors in the lobby. The trim moustache and grey wig aged him about ten years, the swept-back curls adding an impression of Italian ancestry, while the silk cravat and herringbone tweed jacket announced that the fashion he was clearly slave to was stuck back in the nineteen sixties.

"Signor Cambroni would be pleased to see you, signore," said Thompson as he pocketed his phone. "If you would like to follow me …"

"Signor … Mancini?" Ettore Cambroni hurried through the first-floor gallery to where Thompson and Henry had just emerged from the lift, his face a mixture of concern and doubt.

"Yes," said Henry, allowing an inflection of refined Bostonian to colour his Italian accent. "Oscar Mancini. And you are Signor Ettore Cambroni, I presume?"

"Indeed," agreed Ettore. "How may I help you, signore?"

Henry let his eyes scan the gallery as if he were looking for someone.

"I need to speak with my daughter, Signor Cambroni. Her name is Ginevra Mancini. I believe she works here."

His eyes had stopped roaming and were now firmly fixed on Ettore Cambroni's while he watched for any reaction.

"You are Ginevra's father?" Ettore Cambroni's face still registered his disbelief.

"I am, yes. You see, my wife Martina, Ginevra's mother, is seriously ill. It was all rather sudden. Just a few days ago she was as right as rain, and now she's fighting for her life. I hope it's not inconvenient, Signor Cambroni; Ginevra will be needing a few days off. You see, my wife's in a clinic, in Milan."

"I, er, Ginevra has never really talked about her parents, about you. She told us she was from Milan, of course, and even if she hadn't, we'd have known from her accent. But you, signore, you are …"

Henry allowed a gentle, understanding smile.

"I'm from the US. Met my wife while I was here with a military mission, we fell in love and the rest, well … I've lived here now for nearly thirty years, although I regret to say I still struggle with your wonderful language."

It was Ettore's turn for an understanding smile.

"On the contrary, signore, your Italian is excellent. I think I am just a little surprised to learn that Ginevra has an American father. It would help explain her English of course, which is perfect."

"She's a girl of many talents, Signor Cambroni. Never ceases to amaze me."

Henry was confident that the gallery owner had swallowed the bait, but just to be sure, he took his phone from his jacket, hit a couple of buttons and turned the screen towards Cambroni. "Here's Ginevra with her mother just last summer."

He peered over the phone, staring sadly at the photograph, which was of Jennifer and Martina the cook at the Fabrelli villa in Sardinia. Martina was dressed up to go out for the evening, looking every bit as if she could be Jennifer's mother.

"The fickle finger of fate, signore," sighed Henry.

Ettore's face was now distraught.

"I am afraid I have some difficult news, Signor Mancini," he said. "Jennifer isn't here."

"She's not? Is it her day off? She isn't at her apartment. I called by there and when there was no answer, I let myself in — I have a key — just in case she was sleeping off a heavy night out or some such thing."

He gave Cambroni an indulgent father's smile, but Cambroni's face retained its serious expression. The Ginevra he knew didn't have heavy nights out.

"No, it's not her day off. She's missing."

"Missing?" Henry almost shouted the word. "What do you mean 'missing'?"

"I can't explain it, signore. She went for lunch two days ago at the usual time of one o'clock, and she didn't return. She hasn't been seen since."

"Did she call?"

"No, signore, and she's not answering her phone."

"That's right, she isn't. I've been trying too. Did she, I mean, was she upset about anything? Boyfriend trouble?"

"Nothing I nor anyone else here is aware of, no. She seemed in excellent spirits before she left for lunch. In fact, she's been nothing but a delight since she started working here. And an exceptional salesperson. All our clients appreciate her knowledge of art, and she's also managed to charm some of our more difficult ones."

He shook his head in a world-weary way. "The Russians, you know, they are not always easy. It is so fortunate that Ginevra speaks Russian; it has smoothed what might well have otherwise been rough waters on a number of occasions."

Henry hid his surprise. He'd had no idea that Jennifer spoke Russian.

"Have you informed the police about her disappearance?"

"No, not yet," replied Cambroni, his face deadpan. The idea of informing the police about anything was anathema to him. "I thought I'd give it a couple of days. I'm aware that no matter how stable and sensible young women can appear, there's often a crisis bubbling under the surface. They can be very unpredictable."

Old chauvinist, thought Henry.

"I couldn't agree more, Signor Cambroni," he said. "Ginevra certainly had her moments growing up. But these days, she's nothing if not composed and well adjusted." He frowned, wringing his hands. "After what you have told me, I'm now very concerned."

He looked around the gallery to the paintings lining the walls, wondering how many had been produced on site.

"I was speaking on the phone to Ginevra only a few days ago, just before her mother was taken ill. She was telling me about her work and how much she was enjoying it. She was also telling me about some of the clients. Discreetly, of course, no names were mentioned. She said that what she appreciates more than anything is dealing with a knowledgeable client. Do you know if she has become particularly friendly with any of them?"

Cambroni was shaking his head. "I don't think so; I certainly wouldn't encourage it. Once that happens, clients always expect larger discounts. However, there was a lady, an American in fact, with whom we've been dealing recently. She seemed most taken with Ginevra. But I can't imagine how that could be linked with her disappearance."

"I agree; it seems most unlikely. I think Ginevra mentioned that client to me. Is she the one with a passion for Renaissance portraits?"

"Signora Fairbright, yes. A very wealthy woman. I should say she is one of the best clients we've ever had. Interestingly, Ginevra wasn't dealing with her when she was here last time; she was busy with some other people. However, Signora Fairbright did stop to talk to her."

Henry nodded, as if this was all valuable news to him.

"Do you think it might be worth giving Signora Fairbright a call, in case Ginevra's been in touch with her? I know it's a long shot but …"

Cambroni was shaking his head again, and this time his shoulders lifted automatically in resignation. "I agree it would be worth calling but unfortunately Signora Fairbright is a very private person. She left no number. She handles everything through her personal assistant, Signora Fitchley. A most, er, disagreeable woman, I regret to say. I have a number for her, although she didn't answer yesterday when I tried to call her."

He reached into his pocket and pulled out a phone. "I could try again," he said, punching some numbers. He waited, checked the signal strength, and waited some more.

"No answer, I'm afraid, and no voicemail. I imagine her phone is turned off."

"Not much of a PA then," said Henry. "Have you any idea where they're staying? Presumably it's a hotel here in Florence?"

"Neither lady gave me any indication. In fact, even though

Signora Fairbright bought a number of paintings, rather than leaving an address for delivery, she insisted on sending a car for their collection."

"She really does value her privacy," said Henry, the dismay sounding in his voice.

"Precisely," agreed Cambroni.

Then he raised his eyes, a light in them telling Henry he had more information.

"However," he continued, "there was a gentleman with them, a Roman called Cesare Contorni, claiming to be an Italian art expert, although I'm not so convinced about his expertise. He was a little more forthcoming, discreetly, of course. Out of the ladies' hearing, he told me they are staying in a rented villa in Monte San Savino. Do you know where that is?"

"A little south of Arezzo, isn't it?"

"Exactly. It seems Signora Fairbright has bought a substantial villa that she is presently renovating. A massive project according to Contorni, who is rather proud of being in the lady's employ and not shy to brag about it."

"Is that villa there too, in Monte San Savino?"

"No, he said it is in the hills behind the town of Castiglion Fiorentino, above the Val di Chio. Somewhere rather remote."

"I know the area vaguely," lied Henry, who knew it well after having spent a number of holidays there. He let his forehead furrow with worry as he added an extra edge of concern to his voice. "Contorni didn't give you the names of the villas by any chance, did he? I'd like to speak with Signora Fairbright, even if it's only to rule out any connection with Ginevra's disappearance."

Cambroni nodded, persuaded by Henry's performance. He knew precisely what the villas were called — he knew the where-abouts of all his rich clients and their paintings in case he had need of them in the future; Connie's were no exception. Not impressed by her secrecy, he had, as a matter of course, had Connie's car followed when it arrived to pick up the paintings, instructing his driver to find out the names of both the villa under renovation and the villa Connie was renting. However, he wasn't going to give

Ginevra's father any insight into his criminal ways; he would use Contorni.

"As it happens, he did," said Cambroni. 'What I mean is that it slipped out in his conversation; I don't think he meant to tell me. The rented villa, the one in Monte San Savino, is called the Villa Luisa while the one under renovation is the Villa Brillante."

"I'll start with the one in Monte San Savino, the Villa Luisa," said Henry, elated that he had made progress. "It should be easy enough to find. I'm most grateful to you, Signor Cambroni."

"Prego, Signor Mancini," replied Cambroni.

He hesitated slightly before adding, "Signore, I am now also very concerned for Ginevra's welfare. Would it be an imposition to ask if you could keep me informed of any progress you make? A phone call, perhaps?" He handed Henry a card.

"I'll let you know immediately I know anything," said Henry with a reassuring smile. "Thank you again."

Chapter Forty-Three

Henry hurried back to the apartment to change. Derek had left much earlier, long before Henry put on his disguise, and was now at the safe house with Godden and Felice where Felice's team were scouring the Internet and calling all possible sources for anything that might help them find Connie Fairbright.

Henry had made the excuse to Derek that while he would join them later, he couldn't just sit around waiting.

"I have to do something, even if it's just walking the streets for inspiration."

As he removed his disguise and dressed in jeans, T-shirt and a light jacket, Henry knew he should be calling the team with the information Ettore Cambroni had given him. He even picked up his phone and highlighted Derek's number. But he hesitated, his finger hovering over the number.

His concern was that although he had no doubt Freneton was holding Jennifer captive somewhere in the woods beyond Castiglion Fiorentino, the psychopath was also working for Fair-bright. It was likely therefore that Jennifer had been left alone. However, if large numbers of Felice's officers descended on Monte San Savino searching for the Villa Luisa, or started scouring the woods for the Villa Brillante, Freneton might be alerted by the activity and return to wherever she was holding Jennifer and kill her.

By contrast, one man making the same search would be less noticeable. It was a risk and he knew that the rest of the team would be incensed, but he had a gut feeling that it was the best way. And maybe by searching now, he could shortcut the team's actions, enabling them to move directly to the right location. It was his daughter's life at stake; he was strung tight with worry.

He laced up the heavy-duty hiking boots he had bought that morning and reached into his bag for his mobile charger — he couldn't risk his phone dying on him. The final thing to arrange before leaving was transport, a rental. He called several companies until he found one that had a four-by-four available for immediate delivery to the apartment.

After forty-five minutes, Henry was on his way, following the satnav's directions to the A1 autostrada to head south to the small hill town of Monte San Savino. An hour after his departure, he was parked in a car park outside the town walls. Rather than resort to asking at the local carabiniere headquarters, or a tourist information office, he decided to search the Internet for the Villa Luisa using the sites of local letting agents. He discovered three who still had the property listed in spite of the villa's long-term rental to Connie. As a bonus, all the listings carried photographs of the main exterior views and several of the interior rooms. One even had directions. The villa, which was set in six acres of well-fenced wooded hillside, was more substantial than Henry had expected. Considering this and its extensive grounds, it probably had staff. Getting in unnoticed might prove difficult.

He was not so lucky with his search for the Villa Brillante. There was nothing in the area, although there were several others listed around the country. The name was possibly one that Connie Fairbright had given her new house, and so any listing would be under another name, if indeed it were listed at all.

Before driving the several miles west from Monte San Savino to the Villa Luisa, Henry checked out the satellite view on his phone. He could see what appeared to be a narrow surfaced road winding about three hundred yards from the main road to the villa's boundary walls. There were no other properties nearby, just dense woodland.

The road leading out of the town was quiet and once it started to climb, the only traffic Henry saw was a tractor heading in the opposite direction. He drove past the turning leading to the villa's gates and found a spot to leave the car. Doubling back on foot, he set off into the woods about a hundred yards short of the turning, not wanting to be seen by any cars arriving or leaving. However, he quickly found that making his way through the trees was slow going so he walked down to the narrow road, ready to dive for cover if he heard any cars approaching.

He knew from the satellite image that the road curved sharply to the right before stopping at the main gate. At the curve, he slipped into the trees for cover in case the gates opened, although thanks to EU regulations, he knew he would be warned: a light above the gate post was ready to flash when the gates were triggered and there would be an accompanying siren.

Peering through the trees, he could see both the imposing wrought iron gates and the equally imposing six-foot-high wall running away from both sides of the gate posts, its top edge fringed with an old and irregular coating of jagged glass and what was clearly a more recent addition of coiled razor wire. Since the drive on the other side of the gates curved to the left, he couldn't see more than a glimpse of the villa itself so he decided to hike around the perimeter. Perhaps there would be a spot where he could climb the wall.

At this point he began to wonder about other forms of security and whether there were cameras or alarms — in any of the movies he'd been in, the hero would by now have been dancing across trip-wires and cutting feeds to CCTV. The real world of the Tuscan countryside was rather different: there was nothing to indicate any electronic security that Henry could see as he made his way around the outside of the wall. He shrugged and hoped his observations were correct, particularly as he had just spotted an old wooden gate in the wall that he might be able to force open.

The gate was chestnut: solid and heavy with no keyhole, just a latch lever. Henry assumed it would be padlocked on the inside. As he reached out to try the latch lever, he heard voices on the other side of the wall as a bolt on the gate was pulled. He darted into the trees for cover, crouching down behind some heather just as the gate swung open and a middle-aged man emerged dressed in overalls and working boots. The man turned his head back and called out, "Beppe, it's lunchtime. Hurry up!"

"Arrivo, arrivo!" called someone from inside the gate, and a younger man wandered out, his eyes fixed on his smartphone.

He pulled the gate shut behind him and spat out a string of dialect that Henry could just work out was a complaint about the phone signal. He thrust the phone into his pocket in disgust and trotted off after his workmate.

As soon as they were out of sight, Henry walked quietly up to the gate and pushed on it. It swung open. In a moment he was in and closing the gate, surprised to find there was no lock, just a bar that slid into a thick staple to prevent it from being opened from the outside.

The formal grounds near the villa were in total contrast to the woods outside. A variety of trees and shrubs spread out in front of him in a carefully crafted and maintained garden that was more English than Italian. Beds of several varieties of elaeagnus, phlomis and ornamental broom vied for position with floral clusters of lavenders and cotoneaster, some overshadowed by linden trees, others by walnut and chestnut, the expansive lawns in between the beds a vivid, weedless green that spoke of meticulous attention and frequent watering.

Henry made his way around the edge of the grounds, staying close to the perimeter wall until he could see the front of the villa and the gravelled driveway outside the main door. There were no cars. He pulled a pair of binoculars from his jacket and panned them around the windows. He could see no one, no signs of any activity. Was Jennifer imprisoned somewhere here? He doubted it unless Connie Fairbright was in on the abduction, which seemed unlikely. And what about the staff? He had seen two gardeners; there were probably cleaners and a cook.

It seemed to Henry that in the absence of both Freneton and Connie Fairbright, his best chance of finding the location of the

Villa Brillante was from any papers that might be in this villa. Perhaps there were plans the women consulted, estimates, schedules of work.

He decided to move around to the rear of the villa where the views looked out over the Val Di Chiana. As he made his way, keeping behind as much of the shrubbery as he could, he heard the siren from the gate followed by the sound of tyres on gravel. He stopped, ducked down and trained his binoculars onto the drive. A large dark blue Audi hatchback swept into view and skidded to a halt in front of the main door of the villa. He froze as he saw the woman who stepped out of the car. Olivia Freneton. There was no mistaking her in spite of a different hairstyle and clothes. Images, no more than fragments, flashed through his mind: a hotel room, his arrest, his daughter the police officer questioning him long before either of them knew of their relationship, his remand at the prison in Derbyshire, the almost successful attempt on his life. Here in front of him was the woman who not only had tried to kill him but also Jennifer and Derek; the woman who had succeeded in killing several others. A ruthless psychopath on another killing spree, and once again the target was his daughter. This woman had to be stopped.

He found himself standing, moving forward. He wanted to strangle her with his bare hands. He stopped. She was looking his way. Had she seen him? Heard something? Surely not, he was too well hidden.

Olivia Freneton turned back to the villa and walked towards the main door. Henry took a deep breath. This was not the time. If he did kill her, he might never learn where she had Jennifer imprisoned. And the crazed woman was never likely to tell him no matter how much he tried to beat it out of her.

He decided to stick to his first idea of checking out the rear of the property.

As he followed the wall round, a large balcony on the first floor came into view, and standing on the balcony taking in the view was Freneton. She was speaking on the phone while pacing up and down, but she was too far away for him to hear any of her conversation.

After finishing her call, she returned indoors briefly before returning with a book. It was a warm, sunny afternoon and Henry watched, still suppressing his anger, as she stretched out on a lounger to read.

He checked his watch, wondering when the gardeners would return from their lunch break — he didn't want to be caught in the grounds. He decided to return to the woods outside the villa wall and wait for any car that came or went. If Freneton drove away, he would follow her.

But she didn't leave the villa. The only further activity that afternoon was when a van turned up to collect the two gardeners at the end of their shift. As the shadows got longer, Henry began to accept that he was probably going to be spending the night in the woods. At some point he was going to have to call Derek and spin him something. He was still reluctant to pass on what he had discovered in case Derek or Godden or one of the Italian police officers took it upon themselves to arrest Freneton while they could. That would only potentially risk Jennifer's life. Henry had to know where she was before he called in the troops.

He was getting hungry and despite the hot summer weather, he knew the night might be cooler; he needed to return to his car for supplies and if there was a phone signal, which there wasn't in the woods, he would call Derek.

Before leaving the apartment that morning, he had raided the fridge and thrown a wedge of pecorino cheese, some prosciutto and a length of salami into his bag. He had also picked up a woollen jumper.

As he munched on some salami and cheese, washing it down with water from the courtesy bottles the rental company had put in the car, he thought through his story for Derek. Once he was satisfied with it, he pulled his phone from his jacket pocket and checked the signal. There were three bars.

"Derek, hi, it's Henry."

"Henry! Where have you been? I've been trying your number but I keep being told you're unavailable. At least I think that's what the Italian operator said."

"Sorry, Derek. I've been out and about and much of the time in the countryside where the signal is rubbish."

"What are you doing in the countryside? I thought you said you were pacing the streets of Florence."

"I was, and by chance I passed a gallery where I bought some paintings years ago. I'd forgotten all about it but I couldn't help wondering if stumbling across it was, I don't know, predestined, especially when the owner still remembered me."

"You've been talking to too many Hollywood woo-woos," commented Derek.

"Maybe," replied Henry, still developing his story. "Anyway, when I asked the owner if anyone fitting Connie Fairbright's description had visited the gallery, she thought they might have done. She didn't have a name, but since she did have an address, I thought I'd check it out, even though I didn't hold out much hope."

"Bugger. Why didn't you call it in? Felice would have happily sent one of his people; they're champing at the bit to do something."

"I know and I'm sorry. You see, the woman was American, so I felt I could help. I was clutching at straws. As I said this morning, I'd go crazy if I were just sitting around all day, waiting for news. I take there hasn't been any."

"No, nothing. So, where are you now?"

"I'm in Bologna."

"Bologna? Where's that?"

"It's about sixty miles north of Florence, up the autostrada. I rented a car."

"And I take it the woman wasn't Connie Fairbright."

"No, she wasn't. A pleasant enough lady, rather bemused when I spun her a tale, but not Fairbright. However, while I was here, I thought I'd check out some of the larger galleries in the city." He paused before adding, "No joy, I'm afraid."

"So, what time will you be back?"

"I won't, not tonight anyway. I'm knackered and rather emotionally drained after today. I've booked into a hotel. Look, Derek, my phone is almost out of juice. I need to find some way of charging it. I'll see you tomorrow."

"OK, Henry, I'll call you if there's anything. And listen, if you find any other leads, please, let us know immediately."

At seven fifteen, nearly an hour after Henry had established himself at a vantage point in the woods that gave him a view of the villa's gates, he heard a car approaching from the main road. As it neared the gates, the siren sounded, telling him that someone in the car must have a controller. He focussed his binoculars on the rear windows, but the heavily tinted glass prevented him from seeing inside. However, given the car was a top-of-the-range Lexus, he was sure the passenger was Connie Fairbright returning from wherever she'd been. A few minutes later his suspicions were more or less confirmed as the car returned. The driver's arm was now dangling through the open window, a cigarette in his fingers as he tapped his hand to the beat of the now-blaring stereo. His shift was clearly over for the day.

Before darkness fell completely, Henry returned to the gate in the wall only to find it shut and bolted from the inside. He looked up at the forbidding glass and razor wire. As far as he had seen, it continued unbroken around the wall; his hopes of getting closer to the villa and maybe overhearing plans were coming to nothing.

At six the following morning, Henry was awoken abruptly from a fitful and uncomfortable sleep by a loud snort worryingly close to his right ear. Without moving, he opened his eyes. At the edge of his vision, he could just make out the snout of a large wild boar that had come across him while snuffling its way through the woods, foraging for food. Henry slowly turned his head towards the boar, the animal's short but solid-looking tusks gaining his full attention. The boar's tiny black eyes stared unblinkingly at him, its breath visible in the morning air. Even though it was only six feet away, Henry reckoned that at about four hundred pounds it could hurt him badly if it decided to charge. He decided to act cool. Shutting his eyes, he turned his head away. After several endless seconds, he heard another snort and the sound of the beast trotting away. Henry opened his eyes again just in time to see the boar's rear end disappear into the undergrowth.

He counted the seconds for a full minute to make sure the boar wasn't returning with any of his friends, after which he stretched and stood. Every muscle ached. As he worked his neck, he hoped there would be no more nights like that, especially now he'd met one of the neighbours.

He reached into his jacket pocket and retrieved his breakfast — more cheese, prosciutto and salami, all of which tasted more than good. On checking his phone, which he had put to silent the previous evening, he found there were no messages, just a pile of irrelevant emails from his agent. He was surprised anything had come through at all, given the lack of signal. He shivered. He needed to warm up, get a few of the rising sun's rays. He made his way to where he had parked his car and soaked up the welcome warmth coming his way across the valley.

By ten, Henry was beginning to think that the day was going to be uneventful; the only activity had been the arrival of the van with the gardeners an hour earlier. At some stage he was going to have to call Derek and bring him up to speed. He was starting to feel out of his depth and increasingly worried that rather than helping Jennifer, he might be endangering her further.

Unable to keep still any longer, he paced behind the cover of the trees, making sure he made no noise. Ten more minutes, he thought, I'll give them ten more minutes before I call Derek.

After nine minutes, the siren sounded, the gates swung open and the dark blue Audi emerged from the gravel onto the tarmac. Henry could see two figures inside: Connie Fairbright in the passenger seat, chatting animatedly, while a stony-faced Olivia Freneton was driving.

As soon as the car passed, Henry ran at full tilt through the woods, no longer worried about the noise of his footfall. He dived into his car, managed not to fumble over the keys and seat belt, fired the engine, cursed himself for leaving the car facing the wrong way and steamed off in pursuit of the Audi. He knew this was his only chance; there must be no question of him losing it.

Chapter Forty-Four

It helped that Henry knew the area; it gave him the confidence not to follow too closely. When Olivia Freneton's car descended past Monte San Savino and drove east across the Val di Chiana towards Castiglion Fiorentino, Henry felt sure their final destination would be in the hills above the Val di Chio.

What he did not yet know was which side of the valley they would head for; there were many well-appointed villas with considerable acreages of land on both sides, some fully restored, others ripe for restoration. The Villa Brillante could be any one of them. As he followed at a distance, just keeping the Audi in view, he hoped it wouldn't be necessary to drive up through the town itself. The approach roads were narrow and he would have to get far closer to avoid losing the car, which would in turn run the risk of Freneton noticing the continuing presence of his large black four-by-four in her rear-view mirror.

When Freneton's car turned right onto the main road below the town and continued south, Henry was four cars behind and now increasingly sure the town would be bypassed. He was right. The Audi drove on as far as some traffic lights, turning left onto the road that meandered down the centre of the Val di Chio.

Henry allowed the distance between the cars to increase — his view along the road was good and if Freneton turned off, he would see it. However, the car continued on to the end of the valley where at Polvano the road curved to the right, twisting sharply back on itself as it began to climb through a series of hairpin bends. It was now important for Henry to close the gap a little — he couldn't afford to miss seeing where Freneton turned off.

The Audi continued to climb, appearing and disappearing from view with every bend. About halfway up the hill, the number of bends increased as the terrain became steeper, and the car was out of sight for longer and longer. Henry glanced along every narrow road or track he passed for any indication that a vehicle had just passed along any of them. There was nothing.

Towards the top of the climb, the road straightened out as it traversed the pass before heading down into the next valley. Here the descent was more gradual and the road straighter. As the downhill part of the road came into view, Henry expected to see the Audi in the distance. He frowned as a twinge of panic twisted his gut: the road was empty. He floored the accelerator and the four-by-four lurched forward, its large engine responding with a roar. How could they have disappeared? He knew that about a half a mile farther on his view of the descending road would enable him to see well ahead, certainly far enough to know whether the Audi was still on the road or not. When he reached that point, he pulled up and jumped out of his car, running to the edge to improve his field of vision. There was nothing; not a car in sight. It must have turned off and left no trace.

"Shit!" he yelled and rushed back to the car. He quickly called up the maps on his phone, found his position and checked how many side roads, surfaced or not, were shown from where he had last seen the Audi. There were six and Freneton could have taken any one of them. He changed the view to satellite, hoping to see the sort of property he was expecting Villa Brillante to be. There were four possibilities on four different narrow roads and he would need to check each of them. His problem was that he didn't want to drive up to the properties in case his presence was noticed, or worse, he met Freneton coming the other way. He would have to leave the car at the head of each of the side roads and go on foot.

He hit the throttle and sped along the road to where the first of the side roads disappeared off into the trees. He checked the satellite view again and estimated the house he could see was four or five hundred yards along. Leaving the car on a grassy patch just before the turning, he jumped out and hit the road running. Although the narrow road leading into the woods had a paved surface of broken, ancient tarmac, there was no evidence of recent use, no damage to the low-hanging branches from passing delivery trucks. It didn't feel right.

He sprinted to where he had seen a bend on the map, rounded the curve and there were the gates of a villa in front of him. They were shut. Some twenty yards beyond them was a house that was clearly unoccupied — its shutters were closed, there were piles of wind-blown leaves against the main door and a pool beyond the house was covered in a green tarpaulin. With no sign of any construction work and no Audi, this could not be the villa. He turned and sprinted back to the car.

Gulping air, he threw himself in to the driver's seat, gunned the engine and screamed off before screeching to a halt near the next turning.

The road was unpaved but in good condition, the house several hundred yards along it. Henry was panting heavily by the time he got close, and again disappointed. This time, although the gates were closed, all the shutters were open and voices of laughing children rolled up the slope from a pool hidden from view behind the house. A holiday let.

Fifteen breathless minutes later, he had eliminated the third house and was jogging — sprinting was now beyond him — back to his car. There was one possibility remaining. He checked the satellite view again and found the house, and as he did, he realised he should have gone there first. It was clearly a larger property than the others and there were extensive grounds, the entrance located around two miles along the winding, unsurfaced road.

He checked the time. Since losing the Audi, he estimated he had spent forty-five minutes on his search. Forty-five valuable minutes was a long time for Freneton to be on the loose. He cursed himself for his arrogance, He should have called Derek. If nothing else, the access roads could have been blocked to prevent Freneton escaping; there were only two or three options for leaving the valley.

The turning he was looking for was on a tight bend. Any car taking it would disappear quickly, which is why he hadn't noticed Freneton had gone that way. He stopped a couple of hundred yards above the turning, pulling onto the grass at the edge of the road. His breathing was almost back to normal. However, the thought of jogging another two miles with the possibility of a violent confrontation with Freneton at the end was daunting.

He got out of the car and headed towards the turning. He was still about fifty yards from it when he heard a vehicle driving fast through the woods towards him. He stepped into the cover of some trees and waited. He glanced at his four-by-four, reassuring himself that it wouldn't be visible unless the approaching car turned uphill.

As he looked back, the dark blue Audi appeared, braked to allow the driver to check the road, and then roared off down the hill. Henry had a clear view of the driver. It was Olivia Freneton, and she was alone.

Before the sound of the disappearing Audi's engine had completely faded, Henry was back in his car and accelerating towards the turning. He skidded hard left and roared along the narrow road. Fifty yards down, the crumbling tarmac disappeared and the surface became rough gravel, potholed and damaged by the endless succession of builder's trucks that had been torturing it in the past months. Stones and dust flew from the loose surface, the car sliding round every bend.

The temporary gates of the building site appeared in front of him, and they were open. He skidded to a halt between the site-office caravan and the main house and leapt out of the car. The site was eerily quiet, with no signs of any activity, no workers or workers' vehicles. Ignoring the caravan, he turned to the house. The main door was closed but even if it was locked, access would be easy through the glassless window spaces.

He was about to run towards the house when he heard a woman's voice calling out. "Diana! Have you come back? Please, it doesn't have to be like this!" The sound was coming from the caravan. He stopped and turned, which was when he noticed the caravan door was open. "Diana, for pity's sake!"

Bursting through the caravan door, Henry was aware of two things simultaneously. The first was a woman bound to an office chair, her face bruised and bleeding, one eye swollen and almost closed; the second was that on a table immediately in front of her was what looked like a bomb sitting in a plastic food container.

The woman looked up at him, her eyes terrified.

"It's OK," he said. "You're safe. Freneton's gone. You're Constance Fairbright, right?"

"Yes." Connie's reply was scarcely coherent as the relief she felt swamped her emotions.

Henry made his way around the table, taking great care not to jog it, his eyes warily watching the bomb. He could now see a timer counting down what he hoped were minutes rather than seconds. One look at the bindings and chains around Connie's wrists made him realise that trying to free her, with a bomb sitting inches away, would be too dangerous. He bent and spread his arms around the chair, tilting it towards him and hauling it and Connie as high as he could manage.

"Keep as still as you can," he said. "We don't want to knock that thing over."

He manoeuvred her feet around the table and carried the chair to the caravan door. Here he had to put it down since the doorway was too narrow. With his back to the door, he leaned over both Connie and the chair, grabbed the chair seat and hauled it through the doorway. Stepping backwards, he misjudged the distance to the ground, missed his footing and fell heavily, taking the chair and Connie with him.

"Shit," he said, winded by an armrest digging into his stomach. "Are you OK?"

"I'd be a whole lot better if you could stand the chair upright," grunted Connie. "Better still, free me from the damn thing."

"Let me get you farther away from the caravan first," said Henry. "I don't know when that bomb is going to blow."

He stood, pulled the chair onto its wheels and dragged it towards the house, putting the car between it and the caravan.

"Listen, I don't know who you are, but thank you," said Connie as soon as the chair stopped bumping. "I feel safer now with the car in the way."

"You'll be even safer once I can get this lot undone," said Henry, bending to pull at the knots in the rope.

"No, I'm fine!" Connie was shaking her head fiercely. "You must get into the house. Ginevra's in there and she's in a far worse state than I am."

"Jennifer?" cried Henry. "Where is she?"

"She's upstairs, turn left and go to the end. Diana put a load of waste in there; a fire could start at any moment."

Henry raced to the house, flung open the door and charged up the stairs. All that registered as he ran into the bedroom at the end of the corridor was his daughter lying helpless on the floor, her face covered in blood and her body bound to a toppled chair.

Her eyes came to life as they lifted towards him. She pushed her chin forwards as she made a noise through the tape binding her mouth. Henry bent down and carefully unwound the tape.

"Henry," she gasped.

"It's OK," said Henry stroking her face.

She shook her head. "No," she said, gulping the words, "It's not. There's a bomb over there, set to cause a fire and burn this place, and I'm chained to a radiator pipe."

Henry stood and walked towards the bomb.

"No, Henry!" cried Jennifer. "This isn't the movies. Leave it!"

Henry stopped. "You're right," he said. "I need to get you out of here."

He turned his attention to the chain connecting the chair to the pipe running from the radiator into the floor. He pulled at it and realised that it wasn't going to break easily.

"How long?" he said, nodding towards the bomb.

"Don't know," said Jennifer. "Soon."

"I need something heavy," said Henry, making a decision and running for the door.

Outside the house, he searched through a pile of tools near the fence and picked up a spade. It was the largest item he could see, although he doubted it would be strong enough. He was about to run back when he spied a sledgehammer with a head shaped for splitting logs. He threw away the spade and grabbed the sledge-hammer's handle. Lifting it, he estimated it weighed about five kilo-grams; enough to do some damage.

Back in the room, Henry moved Jennifer as clear of the radi-ator as he could before taking a swing at the short vertical pipe. The pipe dented but remained intact. However, a dent was progress.

It took seven hard blows to sever the pipe, and when it broke, water briefly spurted up into Henry's face. Ignoring it, he pulled the chain free of the pipe.

"I'll do the rest outside," he said, pushing Jennifer and the chair towards the door. At the top of the stairs, he put his arms round Jennifer and the chair and, trying not to stumble, hurried down to the main door.

As he lay Jennifer on the ground, she called over to Connie.

"Are you all right?" she said. "Did she hurt you?"

"Not as much as you, Ginevra. God, I'm pleased to see you."

She turned her head to Henry. "Who are you, knight in shining armour?"

"I'm Jennifer's father. Henry," he said as he hauled a large flat stone into position under the chains, intending to attack them with the sledgehammer.

"Well, Henry, I suggest if you could undo these ropes and free me from this chair, I can probably swing my legs through my arms and get my hands in front of me. Even though they're handcuffed, I might be able to help you."

Henry was more intent on freeing Jennifer but a glance into her eyes told him Connie's idea was a good one.

It was, and with Connie's help keeping things in place as Henry swung the sledgehammer, the chain connecting Jennifer's arm and legs was soon removed, together with the one binding her to the chair.

With some difficulty, given the cuffs linking her ankles, Jennifer also manoeuvred her legs through her arms. She stretched out her legs, relieved to have the relative freedom. However, the kick to her stomach had hurt her, as well as the slaps to her face. She didn't try to stand.

"Maybe I can break that chain on your handcuffs," said Henry to Connie, pointing at her hands.

Connie shook her head. "All due respect, Henry, if you miss, I could lose a hand. And anyway, we've got to get out of here right now."

"Why?" said Henry. "You don't think Freneton's coming back, do you?"

"Well, apart from the bomb we're still rather close to," she said, glancing towards the caravan, "if by Freneton you mean Diana, yes I do think she's coming back, in fact, I'm sure of it. And she's going to be more than after our blood, she'll be madder than a wet hen. Help us into your car and I'll explain as you drive. But we must get moving."

Henry lifted Jennifer and carried her to the rear seat of the four-by-four.

"I can walk, if you give me your arm," said Connie as he ran back to her.

"So why do you think Freneton's coming back?" asked Henry as he drove the car back through the Val di Chio.

"Because she's ended up empty-handed. No money and no paintings."

She explained how her call to her private bank had followed a prearranged conversation designed to alert the bank she was under duress.

"No one calls Charles Lisscombe 'Charlie', ever. He hates it, so we agreed that if I called him that, it was part of a coded sequence that would be followed by him asking if the limit was twenty million and my agreeing with that. In reality there's no limit, so now he knew what he should do. The bank has mechanisms in the software and agreements with most banks to make it seem as if the recipient's bank account has been credited, so when it's checked, the money appears to be in the account. However, it isn't; it's a phantom, and after it's been checked once online by the shyster behind it, the sum disappears. In fact it never left my account."

"Impressive stuff," said Henry.

"In my position, you can't be too careful, especially since I don't surround myself with security personnel."

"Surely they don't leave it there," said Jennifer, from the rear seat. "They must inform the authorities."

"Of course, although first the bank's own IT people will be on it, trying to trace the call. With Skype calls, while it's not difficult to trace the country, locating the computer's IP takes some time. I should imagine by now they are getting close, but it wouldn't have been close enough to save our lives."

"You said something about paintings," said Henry.

"Yes, I've recently bought quite a few, as Ginevra knows."

"It's Jennifer," said Jennifer. "Jennifer Cotton."

"Yes, of course. Diana, or whatever her name is, said you're a police officer."

"UK police, yes," said Jennifer. "And her name *is* Diana. She's Diana Olivia Freneton. She was once a police officer as well. Quite a senior one."

"You astound me," said Connie.

"I'm astounded myself every time I think about it," replied Jennifer bitterly.

"To think I trusted her," continued Connie, "thought she was a dear friend. I'd become suspicious of her lately, but I had no idea she was intending to kill me. She must be one disturbed lady."

As she tugged at a pack of tissues in her pocket with her hand-cuffed hands, her phone fell out onto the seat. She stared at it in frustration. "To think that thing was in my pocket all the time and I couldn't reach it."

"Paintings?" persisted Henry.

Connie looked up from the phone. "Why do you look familiar, Henry?"

"I'll tell you if you tell me about the paintings," said Henry.

"Deal. OK, the paintings I have in my possession I keep in a large safe at the villa I'm renting. I gave Diana the combination so if anything happened to me, there would be easy access. Stupid or what! But recently she's been acting strangely. She's been remote and humourless and since she works for me, I didn't like it. However, I thought perhaps it was me, so I didn't do anything about it. Then when I got back from Naples last night with five more paintings, she was distracted. She said she'd got another one of her wretched headaches. Later, during the night I woke up and thought I heard something. I walked around the villa and found the study door was slightly ajar. I peered in and saw Diana with the safe open checking the packs of paintings. It worried me, of course, but I was stupid. I didn't want to confront her right then because I wanted to know what the surprise was up at the villa she'd been teasing me with, gullible idiot that I am. However, once she'd gone back to bed, I changed the combination. So if she's back there now trying to get the paintings, she can't. And if she's checked her account again, she'll know she doesn't have the money either."

"Wet hen won't come close," muttered Jennifer.

They turned on to the north–south road running below Castiglion Fiorentino.

"Listen," said Henry, "where do you think we should go? I'm thinking the Villa Luisa might not be a good choice. Actually I'm thinking that both of you should see a doctor."

"Later," said Jennifer. "Look, Henry, why isn't Derek with you? How come you're on your own?"

Henry pulled a sheepish face. "Derek doesn't know where I am. I didn't tell him."

"What! You've got a bunch of police officers who presumably are looking for us and when you found out where we were you didn't tell them?"

"Jennifer, sweetheart, it all happened so fast. I only found out where you were when I followed Freneton and Connie this morning. There was no opportunity to call Derek."

"Well, we'd better call him now," snapped Jennifer. "Both houses need checking, especially the one we've just come from so it doesn't burn down. And right now, Freneton is still at large. She can't be allowed to escape again. Pass me your phone, Henry."

Chapter Forty-Five

An hour later, they were in an upmarket agriturismo a few miles south of Castiglion Fiorentino. Once a working farm with accommodation for tourists who wanted to experience rural Italy, the Villa Incantata di Chiana now comprised lovingly tended vineyards, twelve luxuriously appointed two-bedroom chalets each with its own private plunge pool, and a restaurant with a cordon bleu chef, all set in serene surroundings and all at central London prices to discourage any riffraff.

The owner, Francesco Aleotti, was an old friend of Pietro Fabrelli, who had finally arrived at the safe house from Beijing two hours earlier. Discouraged by the apparent lack of progress, Pietro appeared to Derek to be about to mobilise every police officer in Tuscany and perhaps even the army.

However, as soon as he received the welcome news that Jennifer was safe, Pietro changed tack and swung into action with seasoned panache. Within minutes, having established where Jennifer and Henry were, the agriturismo was organised, directions given and a doctor on her way along with an ambulance in case Jennifer needed hospital treatment. When he realised the other person involved was Connie Fairbright, whom he had met some years previously at a gala dinner in New York, Pietro summoned a second doctor so that the rich widow wasn't kept waiting. And somehow he also raised a locksmith to remove the shackles and handcuffs from both women.

After that, he rounded up all parties relevant to the ongoing operation — Paul Godden, who was apoplectic at Henry's cavalier behaviour, an uncharacteristically sullen Massimo Felice worried about his operation at the gallery, Derek Thyme and four of Felice's team — and herded them into a mix of police vehicles and his limousine.

As they screamed down the A1 autostrada with police vehicles front and rear of the convoy, their blue lights flashing and sirens wailing, Pietro spent ten minutes on the phone to Jennifer being reassured that apart from the black eyes both she and Connie had sustained, other injuries were minor, and another ten minutes cross-examining both doctors in case Jennifer was understating anything. The rest of the journey was spent with Pietro smooth-talking Derek, Godden and Felice into accepting that Henry's actions had been for the best.

"Imagine, gentlemen, how wretched you would feel if Henry had taken time to call you and been delayed by, say, ten minutes. In that time the bombs might have detonated. As it is, both Jennifer and Signora Fairbright are alive and well. It was unorthodox, I grant you, but brave, so very brave."

While the acceptance was limited, they at least agreed to hold off any further interrogation of Henry until the dust had settled. And when they arrived and saw a cleaned-up and patched-up Jennifer, in fresh clothes the agriturismo owner had organised, fall into Derek's arms, and an equally cleaned-up Connie Fairbright gushing over Henry's heroism, positions softened further. They weren't quite ready for absolution, but it could now be put on the agenda.

Nevertheless, there was the nagging question of Olivia Freneton.

"What do we know and what can we assume?" asked Paul Godden as they settled in a conference room amid plates of nibbles, panini and crostate, jugs of tea and coffee and bottles of ice-cold spring water.

Felice answered for the team now searching the area.

"Firstly," he said, "the news from the Villa Brillante is that although the site-office caravan was severely damaged when the bomb in it exploded, the damage to the villa itself was minor, confined in fact to the room where the bomb set the fire. There was little flammable material beyond what was in the room, and the fire quickly burnt itself out."

"Thank you, Massimo," said Connie, reaching over to touch Felice's arm, "that's a great relief." Turning to Henry, she added, "And thanks to my Hollywood hero, I wasn't still in the caravan."

Jennifer smiled to herself. She couldn't remember ever seeing Henry blush.

"Now," continued Felice. "Olivia Freneton. From what Jennifer has told us, she has a house no more than half an hour from the Villa Brillante. We have put a compass in the map and made a generous circle, but unfortunately, even though we are assuming her house will be remote and we can ignore villages, there are still more than a hundred possibilities for its location. I have six teams combing the area as we speak." He paused, his shoulders sagging, his face indicating his concern. "You must understand, it is difficult countryside and covering all the possibilities will take time. Apart from anything else, each team must be three officers since if they come across the right house, Freneton might come out shooting. We know she has at least one gun and we know she is ruthless; each and every property must be approached with extreme caution."

"I think," commented Jennifer, "that wherever this house is, she won't stay there long. She was a police officer, remember, she knows what will happen and how it will happen." She turned to Connie. "Has she ever said anything about any other property, maybe not even in Italy?"

Connie shook her head. "She never once even mentioned the place she kept you in," she replied. "She must have gone there when I was away visiting galleries."

"Vehicles?" asked Godden.

"She was using a dark blue Audi hatchback, one of the large models," said Jennifer. "Although I somehow doubt she'll continue to use it, unless she has no choice. Of course, once the house is found, we'll know, since if the car's there, she must have something else."

"There'll need to be a careful examination of the ground, then," said Godden, nodding his thanks to Connie. "Tyre tracks or disturbances to gravel might tell us something about the size of any vehicle, and whether it has two wheels or four."

He turned to Felice. "Your teams can be relied on for this, Massimo?"

Felice offered a noncommittal shrug. "I'll call in, just to have them reminded." He stood and left the room, pressing buttons on his phone as he did.

"If she still is using the car," continued Jennifer, "she will probably have changed the number plates. Which means it might not even have Italian plates any more. Would it be worth issuing an order for all Audis of that type to be pulled over to check the driver?"

"Certainly worth it in this area," agreed Godden. "For my money, I think she'll be around here. She'll be angry and perhaps careless as a result. She might be facing a future with almost no funds and nowhere to hide. If that's the case, she'll want her revenge and want it soon."

"I agree about the revenge part," said Jennifer, "but her planning is incredible. I think she'll have somewhere else to go. Failure must always be one of the options she plans for which means there'll be some sort of allowance for it."

The door to the conference room opened and a far-happier-looking Massimo Felice rejoined them.

"Good news?" asked Henry.

"Yes," said Felice, the smile spreading from his eyes to his mouth, "two pieces of very good news."

He looked around to ensure he had their attention.

"The house has been found," he said. "It's roughly where we predicted as being the most likely spot. Freneton isn't there but the Audi is. So it would appear Jennifer was correct; she must have some other form of transport. Right now the place has been sealed and a forensic team is on its way. So there's no point in any of us going there today. However, I think tomorrow morning we shall be able to see it."

He turned to Connie. "The same applies to your villa, Signora Fairbright," he added.

Jennifer put her face in her hands and sighed. "So she's still out there, still one step ahead. She'll assume the house will be discovered so she'll have taken anything she needed from it. Nevertheless, the house was hers — she told me — it will be quite a loss."

She looked up at Felice. "What's the other thing? The gallery?"

"Right first time, Jennifer," said Felice. "The gallery. The team in Florence tasked with watching the gallery noticed there has been a considerable increase in activity at the rear doors, the ones we think access a lift that goes to a workshop."

"What sort of activity?" asked Godden.

"Paintings in and paintings out. Mostly out. It looks as if there's a wholesale movement. Perhaps they are changing locations, replacing paintings, or perhaps they suspect something and are taking precautions. In any event, I've authorised my number two to obtain a search warrant. We are going in," — he glanced at his watch — "in two hours' time." He picked up the briefcase he had brought with him. "Paul," he said, turning to Godden, "you will want to be a part of this, I'm sure."

"Absolutely," agreed Godden, standing. "It's a pity Jennifer can't be, especially after all her groundwork."

"I don't see why not," objected Jennifer.

"Jennifer," said Godden. "You've been abducted, chained, drugged, beaten and left to die. Your face is still swollen and one eye half closed, and on top of all that, you probably haven't slept for more than forty-eight hours. That's why. Your work at the gallery is done and the advantage of your not going in is that with luck, the Cambronis will never know of your involvement."

"It will come out in the trial, surely," said Jennifer.

"Perhaps," said Felice, "perhaps not. It depends how cooperative they are."

"I agree absolutely that Jennifer shouldn't go," said Pietro, nodding. Then with a helpless shrug of his shoulders, he pulled a face. "But Ispettore, do not ever think they will cooperate; they are mafia."

Chapter Forty-Six

Olivia Freneton locked the gates to her house for what she assumed would be the last time, slipped her BMW motorcycle into gear and drove away. The path from her house led onto a minor road that descended into the Morra valley. At the bottom of the hill she could turn one of two ways: right towards the Val di Chio, where she knew by now there would be intense police activity, or left along the valley towards the town of Trestina in Umbria. A different province, a different local police force that with luck would be a few steps behind the search in Tuscany.

She turned left, her temporary destination a small hotel on the outskirts of Città di Castello, part of a low-end chain where she knew her stolen Irish passport would not be questioned; she was just another tourist. She would only be there for a few hours, time enough to fine-tune her revised plans before implementing them. After that, she would disappear from Italy. Another country, another con. It wasn't what she'd hoped for, worked hard for, and before she left, the retribution would be as sweet as it was essential.

Two hours earlier as she drove the Audi away from the fire she assumed would be spreading through the Villa Brillante, her normal clarity of vision had for once been blurred and fragmented, her mind a tempest of wild and irrational thoughts as she gripped the steering wheel in frustration. She had been outwitted. Failure owing to unforeseen, unpredictable circumstances was always a possibility; this was far worse, this was humiliation. It was an unacceptable outcome and one for which Connie Fairbright and Jennifer Cotton would pay heavily.

As she negotiated the torturous bends and poor surface of the road leading in the direction of her house, she forced herself to breathe deeply in an attempt to relax her mind and body, to release the tension knotting every ounce of her being. She knew she must focus, cut through the fog of disappointment. There was no time for reflection, not yet, and no place for anger. Anger was destructive, unworthy of her. She had much to do in a short time; her full attention was required.

She swung the car from the road onto the rough, gravelled track that led through the woods to her house, the tyres hard-pushed to maintain a grip. Bouncing and drifting round the bends, Olivia finally smiled, her frustration now supplanted by satisfaction as she thought of her trump card, one that none of the fools trying to bring her down would anticipate: she had the means to locate Connie Fairbright.

She jumped from the car and ran into the house, her mind back on track. Time was short; the search for her would be gaining momentum. Gathering the essentials for her escape was systematic and efficient. Within five minutes, she had packed the clothes, shoes and personal items she needed into a rucksack which she placed by the front door.

Retrieving the bombs, timers and remote controls for the detonators took slightly longer, care in handling always a priority. She stowed them in a separate, well-cushioned bag, one that sat in a reinforced pannier behind the rear seat of her motorcycle.

Next came her disguises, one of which she had to apply now before she left — she needed to appear totally different from the woman the police were looking for. After fifteen minutes of skilfully padding her cheeks and gums, applying make-up, inserting green-tinted contact lenses and setting and combing her raven-haired wig

in place, she was every bit the colleen described in the Irish passport she was intending to use.

The disguises had been kept in her safe along with the cash she
had been accumulating over the past few months. A little over ten
thousand euros. She stared briefly at the money before zipping it
into an inside pocket of the small rucksack she wore on her back.
Not much after so many months of scheming, which is why her last
piece of preparation was so important, but at least she'd be leaving
this country knowing her disposal schedule had been fulfilled.

She reached into the safe to withdraw the final item. A custom-
modified mobile phone, one for which she had paid a high price to
her contact in Amsterdam. She switched it on, waited for it to
connect and called up the specialised app displayed on the screen,
the only app installed on the device. A map appeared followed by a
flashing beacon. Connie Fairbright, or at least Connie Fairbright's
phone, which given the woman was never far from it meant they
were one and the same thing.

Included in her purchase in Amsterdam had been a micro-
scopic transmitter that within weeks of befriending Connie, she
had installed in Connie's phone. Extremely difficult to detect and
always on even when the phone was switched off, it gave Olivia the
ability to know Connie's whereabouts anywhere in the world
simply by consulting her purpose-built device. And now that device
was telling her Connie was in an agriturismo called the Villa Incantata di Chiana about ten miles from the hill town of Cortona.
Olivia called up the agriturismo on Google and scanned the information. She smiled; it was perfect. Exclusive and no doubt self-
assured in its security, probably with an added police presence to
guarantee the safety of the special guests it was housing that
evening — there was nothing more reassuring than knowing that
no one was going to break in. Which Olivia had no intention of
doing.

In the seclusion of her room in the hotel in Città di Castello, Olivia
retrieved her modified phone and once again checked Connie's

location. It hadn't changed, which more or less guaranteed she would remain there. It was the logical thing to do given both Connie and Jennifer Cotton would require medical attention and rest. Keep the driving down to a minimum and lick your wounds.

How typical of Connie to have discovered one of the priciest and most exclusive places in the area, thought Olivia, a cloud of regret hardening her features as she briefly remembered the twenty million dollars Connie had cheated her out of. Enjoy the comfort while you can, Connie, you only have a few hours to live.

She checked the time; she needed to make a reservation. She hoped Connie hadn't block-booked all the rooms to prevent the arrival of any more guests. She hadn't, and although Francesco Aleotti had looked over the night's bookings and found he had six vacant chalets, since the villa almost never received last-minute enquiries — its prohibitive prices unacceptable to casual tourists — he hadn't thought to tell his receptionist not to accept any more.

When the lady with the soft-spoken Dublin accent called with a tale of having stayed with her husband the previous year in the Chalet Fiorentina, the receptionist's only worry was whether she might cause offence when she informed the caller that the chalet was occupied that evening and would an alternative, the Chalet Veneziana, be acceptable? The booking was made and the receptionist told by the guest she would be arriving rather late, probably around ten.

The young carabiniere officer stationed at the closed gates of the Villa Incantata had the presence of mind to ask the soft-spoken woman on the large motorcycle that drew up in front of him to remove her crash helmet so he could take a better look at her face. Olivia was prepared to break his neck and run amok in the agriturismo if he appeared to be suspicious, but he merely smiled and chatted a little in broken English about the bike before opening the gate for her.

She drove to the reception building and parked, appreciating as ever the reticence of her bike's liquid-cooled engine to make much more than a whisper of noise. Her eyes scanning every corner, every door, she walked up to the reception desk and introduced herself.

If the receptionist was surprised to find her new client wearing motorcycle leathers, she was well trained enough not to show it.

"Signora Murphy," she said, standing and offering her hand. "Buona sera. Our apologies for the police presence at the gate; we have a vip staying here tonight."

Olivia wondered what a vip was until she remembered that Italians always treated initial letter abbreviations as acronyms.

"No problem," she said, emphasising her Irish accent even more than she had on the phone. "He was a handsome young fella; we had quite a chat."

When Olivia explained that owing to her bag being stolen the previous day in Rome she couldn't offer a credit card and asked if it would be acceptable to pay in advance in cash, the receptionist was again unfazed, as if such problems occurred every day. She exchanged a chalet key for five hundred euros and gave Olivia directions.

"Oh, and the bar's through there, if you want a nightcap," she said, pointing to Olivia's left. "Or perhaps you are hungry. I can ask the kitchen to prepare something if you wish."

"I'm fine, thank you," said Olivia, turning her head in the direction of the bar. "I just need to get some sleep. It's been a tiring couple of days."

She almost ran through the exit door and once it had closed she stopped and put her back to the wall, her heart beating unusually fast. Although she had shown no sign to the receptionist, when she glanced through the door into the bar, she had been looking straight at Jennifer, Derek, Connie and Henry seated at a table, deep in conversation.

Olivia was relieved to find that her chalet was some thirty yards from its nearest neighbour, a chalet that itself appeared to be unoccupied. She scanned the site, getting her bearings and trying to work out which of the chalets were occupied by the unexpected bonus of the four targets now sitting in the bar. In her room she found a layout of the agriturismo on the door among the fire safety information. Chalet Fiorentina, which she knew was occupied, and the adjacent Chalet Senese, were well apart from other chalets; she would check those first.

She turned out the lights and crept from the door, staying in the shadows as she made her way in the direction of the chalets. A large black four-by-four was parked outside the Chalet Fiorentina. She stopped and stared at it as images sparked in her mind. It looked familiar. Then she remembered that she had seen either this car or an identical one several times in her rear-view mirror that morning as she was driving Connie from the Villa Luisa to the Villa Brillante. The driver had been good; not once had he come close enough to arouse suspicion, but now she thought about it she realised he had been there for most of the journey. The driver must have been Henry Silk, who must have been staking out the Villa Luisa. Had Thyme been with him? She doubted it, since as a police officer, he would have had others in tow. So Silk had been operating on his own. Olivia smiled to herself. How fortunate! If he had told Thyme what he'd found out, she would almost definitely have been caught. And now they would all pay for that error.

First, however, she would need to know who was staying where. Perhaps Connie was staying in a separate chalet, which would make her an easy target. With luck she could dispose of them one by one. She looked around, found a spot where the discreet path lighting did not penetrate and slipped over to it. She didn't have to wait long. After only ten minutes, her four targets emerged from the main buildings and walked towards the two chalets. Thyme's arm was around Cotton, and from the way she was snuggled comfortably into his shoulder, they had to be a couple. An interesting development, thought Olivia. Perhaps she could arrange things so that Thyme watched his girlfriend die.

The two of them disappeared into the Chalet Senese while Silk and Connie walked on to the Fiorentina. Silk unlocked the door and they both went in, the lights going on behind the closed curtains. Another interesting development? thought Olivia, or was it just that Connie would be frightened on her own? Either way, the relationship was going to be short-lived.

Olivia waited in the darkness for a further twenty minutes until the lights in both chalets had been out for some time before returning to her own chalet, stopping at her motorcycle to retrieve the well-padded bag from the pannier behind the rear seat. She had decided to follow her original plan since the presence of two of her quarry in each chalet could raise difficulties, even if she walked in and shot them.

For the following two hours she sat and watched from her window, checking for any security patrols. There were none; the owners must be relying on the carabiniere on the gate, and perhaps one or two others at other gates to the property.

Satisfied she could now operate unobserved, she left her chalet and hurried over to where Henry's four-by-four was parked, walking on the grass to avoid disturbing any gravel. In a repeat of her actions in the car park in the Lake District the previous year shortly before Mike Hurst's car had launched itself into the freezing reservoir, she bent down, reached up into the engine compartment and placed the magnetic case of the small remotely detonated bomb at the heart of the vehicle's hydraulic system.

The whole operation took seconds, and within two minutes Olivia was back in her room setting her alarm for six in the morning. She was determined to get a few hours' sleep; tomorrow was going to be a busy day, starting with the fulfilling adrenaline rush of witnessing the destruction of her four principal disposals.

Olivia was almost certain the party would return to the Villa Brillante the following morning — Connie would want to see the fire damage first-hand. However, in case there were other plans, she couldn't stray too far from the agriturismo to wait for them.

She left at seven and hid her BMW and herself in among some trees a few hundred yards along the road leading from the Villa Incantata to the main road. Her wait proved to be a long one, and after three hours she was beginning to worry that perhaps there was another exit from the agriturismo she had somehow overlooked.

However, after a further ten minutes, she heard a toot as a car passed through the gate. A carabiniere car appeared followed by Henry's four-by-four. A police escort, she thought. They must be nervous.

Olivia watched the cars drive past before starting her motorcycle, not that its engine would have been heard. She settled on the seat, ensured that the correct detonating device was at hand in her jacket pocket, kicked the bike into gear and set off. When the convoy turned left along the main road towards Castiglion Fiorentino and signalled right at the traffic lights before the town, she knew she had guessed correctly: they were heading for the villa.

She eased back as she followed the road through the Val di Chio, knowing, as Henry had the previous day, she would be able to see the convoy at some distance. She was amused to see that the police vehicle was already some way ahead of Henry's car, way too far for a responsible convoy leader, but given the driver was a young Italian police officer it would be ridiculous to even consider the idea of him driving slowly. When they reached the end of the valley and the road began to rise, there would be no way the driver would have the four-by-four in view in his mirror; he would be at least two bends ahead.

And it was one of those bends that Olivia had in mind for her grand finale, the second of the switchbacks on the steeper part of the hill, a point where the road curved sharply to the left after a straighter, flatter section of some hundred and fifty yards where it was natural to hit the throttle. At that point, there was normally a length of crash barrier to help prevent any out-of-control vehicle from careering over the edge. However, she had seen the previous day that the barrier was missing, damaged by some incident in the past week and not repaired, just a flimsy wooden structure put temporarily in its place. It couldn't have been more perfectly situated since beyond the bend the hillside fell steeply away almost a hundred feet onto a rocky patch below where the ground had collapsed years ago, long before the track above it had been reinforced into the present road. The drop was almost sheer, a hazard now made more dangerous by the absence of a proper barrier.

As Olivia drove towards the end of the valley, she could see the police vehicle climbing, now at least three bends ahead, the driver enjoying slinging the car around the road, safe in the assumption that the driver of the following car knew where he was going.

The four-by-four rounded the first of the bends and started to climb, at which point Olivia accelerated to shorten the distance between them. She wanted Henry, who was driving, to see her bike in his mirror moments before she struck; she wanted her presence to raise doubt in his mind; she wanted his fears to increase before she made them come true.

As the four-by-four continued up the hill, Olivia closed in further to ensure that as she rounded the corner onto the last fateful stretch, she was only thirty yards behind. Just as she expected, the four-by-four increased its speed on the relatively straight and flat section. She twisted the BMW's throttle, quickly closing the gap between them. She wanted to pass the car, wanted them to realise who she was before they met their end. She put her left hand into her jacket pocket and pulled out the remote control, skilfully steering the bike with her right hand as she drew alongside the car. She flipped up her visor and turned her head towards the occupants, laughing as she saw the horrified look on Cotton's face and the utter terror on Connie's. She glanced ahead, the corner was about fifty feet away; Silk would be about to touch the brake and turn the wheel to the left. She pulled ahead of the four-by-four, held up her left hand so they could all see the remote, and pressed the button. The bomb buried deep in the hydraulic system detonated, blowing it apart.

Chapter Forty-Seven

The previous day while Jennifer and Connie were being examined by their respective doctors at the Villa Incantata, Henry had been making his own assessment of the agriturismo. He had already been assured on the phone by Paul Godden that a police presence on the perimeter was guaranteed: one patrol car was stationed at the main gate and another at a smaller, rear service entrance used by farm vehicles and delivery trucks, a gate that was normally kept locked.

However, they were going to be spending the night there and Henry wanted to be sure of his ground. Olivia Freneton was out there somewhere and although he couldn't imagine how she would know where they were, he was sufficiently impressed by the woman's abilities not to discount the possibility of her finding them. In fact, he thought it safer to assume she did know, and to make the appropriate arrangements.

After inspecting the fence, which was high and electrified to prevent people and wild animals from entering the grounds, Henry felt more comfortable. With police officers at the gates, Freneton should find it impossible to get in without being spotted.

What Henry didn't bargain for was Freneton having the sheer gall to make a booking and thereby enter the grounds legitimately. He had checked with Francesco Aleotti about occupancy and been told there were guests in three other chalets, clients he knew well who kept themselves to themselves.

"There are nine other chalets, Signor Silk," he said. "They are all at your disposal should you need them."

"Thanks," said Henry, "I'm not sure if Pietro or our police friends will be staying. For the three of us and Signorina Cotton's, er, fidanzato, when he arrives, we require at least two chalets, maybe three. I need to talk to Signora Fairbright."

Later in the afternoon, once Godden and Felice had left along with Pietro — who had declared he was overcome with jet lag and needed his personal masseur to coax his aching muscles back to life — Henry took Connie to one side.

"Er, Connie," he said, hesitantly, "I don't want you to take this the wrong way, but you've had one hell of an ordeal as well as the shock of discovering that you employed a homicidal maniac—"

Connie put a hand on his arm, smiling with more than a hint of coquettishness as she interrupted him.

"Your good deeds know no bounds, Sir Galahad. You're right, my nerves are shredded and the thought of being alone in one of these chalets, even with a strong police presence, is more than I can bear. You were going to suggest, I think, that since the chalets have two bedrooms, we should share?"

"It would give me peace of mind too," said Henry. "I'd only spend the night watching for intruders."

"Are you sure you don't want to stand guard outside your daughter's chalet?"

Henry laughed. "I think Derek is more than capable of looking after Jennifer, which leaves me free to man the barricades in the Chalet Fiorentina."

"We'll make sure the powder's dry, Trooper Silk," said Connie, saluting him.

Henry suggested that they all go to bed early — he was in need of sleep after an uncomfortable night leaning against a tree in the woods outside the Villa Luisa. Jennifer and Connie both disagreed, preferring instead to take a nap now and meet for a light supper and some drinks around nine.

"If I bed down for the night now," said Jennifer, "I'll be up again at three, in spite of all the aches and pains. A doze followed by a nightcap should ensure that we'll all sleep through."

It was a good idea in theory, and it worked for Derek and Jennifer in their chalet and for Connie in the Chalet Fiorentina, relaxed in the knowledge that Henry was only a few feet away. Henry, however, was anything but relaxed, in spite of his performance of being calm. Once Connie had gone into her room, he turned out all the lights and stared through the window. He could see the nearby Chalet Senese along the track and the four-by-four parked about twenty feet away on the gravel in front of his chalet, but the rest of the Villa Incantata's spacious grounds were invisible in the darkness.

And yet his senses were on full alert. He sighed, pulled an upright chair close to the window and sat, watching and waiting. Quite what for, he didn't know, but having rescued Jennifer and Connie once, he didn't want to be found wanting if Freneton was out there.

By two, he was beginning to nod as the tiredness permeating his body tried to take over from his still-active brain when he saw something, a movement in the shadows. The tiredness instantly banished, he instinctively ducked slightly. As he stared at the spot, a figure darted forward, the movements urgent, deliberate, the position crouched. Henry watched, motionless, straining his eyes to see if it was Freneton. All he could make out was that the person was tall, and from the manner of the movements probably a woman. It had to be her. What was she doing? If she tried to break in, she'd make a hell of a noise. Henry had booby-trapped the door: if someone did defeat the lock and open it, a couple of glass tumblers would break on the floor.

He reached for his phone, about to call Derek, when he remembered that the light from the screen might attract attention. He peered into the darkness. The figure was now crouched down by the car's offside front wheel and reaching up into the engine compartment behind it. Henry watched in a mixture of fear and fascination. What was she doing? Then he remembered the conversations he had had with Jennifer about the murder of her ex-boss the previous year. She was planting a bomb.

In seconds, the figure had retreated into the darkness and the night was once again still. Henry was tempted to rush out of the door and go after her. But something stopped him. He thought about what he had seen, what she had done. He ran through it again and again in his mind and what stood out apart from the planting of the bomb was what the figure had been wearing, or rather, not wearing. There was no mask, no headgear, no jacket; just lightweight clothing, a thin jumper and jeans, both black to reduce the chances of being seen, but otherwise not clothing she would wear if she had broken in from outside. She must be staying at the agriturismo. Henry shook his head at the thought. She was right there in front of their noses. How could that possibly have happened? She must have arrived late, and to have got past the police officer at the gate, she must have had a story. She had made a reservation. He sat back in shock and no little admiration.

OK, he thought, what is she planning? She'd planted a bomb in his car, a bomb that might be on a timer, but that ran the risk of their not being in the car when it exploded. No, it had to be the same scenario that the police had reconstructed for the Hurst murder: she would follow and set off the bomb at a precise moment and location.

He took a deep breath, wondering what his next move should be.

After forcing himself to wait for an hour, Henry listened at Connie's door where he could hear her breathing gently and regularly as she slept, and slipped out of the chalet door to his car. Finding the bomb proved to be easier than he'd imagined and he quickly found himself crouched on the gravel, the bomb in his hands.

He stood and quietly walked into the darkness, following the direction he had seen Freneton take. Fifty yards along the track another chalet slowly became visible, and in front of it, a large

BMW motorcycle. He thought again about the Hurst murder; the bike had to be Freneton's. And he thought too as he had the previous day about Freneton's attempts to kill him, the cold-hearted remorselessness of her actions, her total indifference to the lives of others. And it wasn't just him, she had tried hard to kill Jennifer, his beloved daughter, and Derek, Neil Bottomley, and who knew how many others. Here in Italy she had tried again and almost succeeded, adding Connie to her list of potential victims. Connie, who had put her trust in him to protect her, Connie who was sleeping peacefully back in the chalet. He looked down at the bomb in his hand. With this, she had intended to kill all four of them at once. Would it never end? If she slipped away following the failure of this bomb to kill them, she would surely return again and again until she either succeeded or was caught. He made a decision and walked quietly over to the motorcycle.

The following morning at seven, Henry awoke in his bed with a start and was immediately surprised to find Connie's head nestled into his shoulder.

"Connie, I—"

"Shh," she replied, "it's early. Go back to sleep."

"But—"

"I woke up, it was pitch dark and I was terrified," whispered Connie. "I'm sorry, I didn't think you'd mind."

"Er, no, of course I don't. It's, well …" He grinned. "It looks like dreams really do come true."

"That's a totally corny line, Mr Silk. Do you honestly expect me to believe you?"

She turned towards him and reached up to kiss him lightly on the lips.

"Mind you, you delivered it very well, and, you know, it's not a bad thought. I'm sure no one's going to be worrying about break-fast just yet."

"Breakfast couldn't be farther from my mind," said Henry as he pulled her closer.

.   .   .

It was almost nine before the four of them were settled at the breakfast table. Jennifer and Derek had arrived first, a few minutes ahead of Connie and Henry. Jennifer took one look at the expressions on their faces and understood immediately. She glanced at Derek, wanting to share her amusement, but he was busy with his full English. ·

As they relaxed with their coffee, Henry's phone rang. He answered, listening for a moment before handing it to Jennifer.

"It's Paul," he said. "He wants to speak to you."

Jennifer took the phone, listening, nodding and throwing in the occasional, "Good," "Wow!" and "Cool!" before asking whether he knew if they could go to the Villa Brillante yet.

"Yes!" she said to the others as she closed the call. "The Cambronis are in custody along with three artists Felice's squad found in the hidden studio on the third floor, the one I could never get close to. And guess what they found there?" she added triumphantly.

"A pile of not-so-old masters?" suggested Connie.

"Exactly, Connie, exactly. Caught in the act. Old with new and a shipment intercepted at the airport."

"I think I'll have to get everything I've bought checked out," added Connie ruefully.

"I must introduce you to Ced Fisher," said Jennifer.

"Who's he?"

"He's a genius. You might have heard about his amazing style-signature computer program?"

"That guy," said Connie. "Yes, I have, but I didn't have a name. Is he a friend?"

"He and his wife; they are two of the loveliest people."

Connie reached out and touched Jennifer's arm with one hand and Henry's with the other. "It's an ill wind," she said, happily. "I feel as if I've fallen on my feet in spite of Diana Fitchley's best efforts."

Henry touched her hand with his and smiled.

"Listen," he said, standing. "I just want to check something with reception, then we should be on our way. I'm sure you want to see how bad the damage is to your place, Connie."

He walked out of the dining room and headed for the reception desk.

"Buongiorno, Signor Silk," said the girl dreamily, her eyes star-struck.

"Hi," replied Henry, grinning at her. "I was wondering. Last night. Was there another guest staying, one who arrived rather late? On a motorcycle?"

"Yes, signore, a Signora Murphy, an Irish lady."

"Is she still here?"

"No, she left early this morning. Around seven."

"Has she been here before?"

"She said she had, with her husband, last year. However, when I checked the records after she left, I could find nothing in the name of Murphy."

"Strange," said Henry.

"Yes," she replied. "And she paid in cash, which is most unusual."

When Henry returned to the breakfast table, Derek was stabbing angrily at his phone, finishing a call.

"Bugger," he said.

"What's up?" asked Henry.

"That was Crawford, my DI from the SCF in Nottingham. He's taken it upon himself to fly out here to follow up on Jennifer. 'On the ground' as he put it. Apparently Hawkins is baying for Freneton's blood."

"Where is he now, your DI?"

"On a train from Florence to Arezzo. It seems he turned up on Paul Godden's doorstep. Godden wasn't over-impressed so he put him on a train and at the same time arranged for a car to pick me up from here and go to Arezzo to meet him. Bloody idiot, Crawford, I mean. There's no need at all for him to stick his oar in. I was going to report to Hawkins this morning; I must admit I forgot last night."

"Perfectly understandable," said Henry.

"I'll call him from the car," said Derek. "I'll bring him straight to the villa, if that's OK."

————————

The explosion was more forceful than Henry had anticipated, although as soon as he saw Olivia Freneton hold up the remote control, he was expecting it. What surprised him was how the motorcycle jumped forward as it accelerated and careered through the wooden barrier at the bend — Olivia had involuntarily twisted the throttle as the explosion from beneath her lifted the bike. She had reacted fast, jamming on the brakes with her right hand and right foot. But there were no brakes, the explosion had destroyed them. As Henry brought the car to a halt, the bike disappeared over the edge and was gone.

"Oh my God, what happened?" screamed Connie as she grabbed Henry's arm.

The police officer in Jennifer cut in. She released her seat belt from where she was sitting in the rear of the car, threw open the door and ran to the edge of the cliff. Below, on the rocks, she could see the twisted remains of the BMW and lying beyond it, a motionless Olivia Freneton.

She turned to the car, expecting to see Henry following her, but he was still sitting in the driver's seat holding the distraught Connie.

Jennifer turned back and peered down the cliff, looking for outcrops of rock that would give her footholds on the way down the almost sheer surface. She began cautiously, checking every rock for firmness, quickly gaining confidence in the surface as she descended.

It took her no longer than a minute to reach Olivia's shattered body. She was lying face up across a large jagged rock, her arms outstretched, her right leg below the knee deformed to an unnatural angle.

Jennifer knelt beside her and took her left wrist to check her pulse. It was weak but regular. She was alive.

Although the visor of her helmet had been ripped off, the helmet itself was intact. Jennifer looked along the twisted body and shook her head. Surely she couldn't survive for long.

There was a sharp intake of breath and Olivia's eyes flickered open, her pupils immediately fixing on Jennifer's.

"Cotton," she whispered, her voice hardly audible. "I can't move; I need help."

Jennifer sat on her heels, trying to assess the damage.

"Flex your hand," she said. "Can you ball your fingers?"

She took Olivia's left hand. The arm felt limp; the bones shattered. There was no movement in the hand.

"My arm's smashed, you idiot. I think my back's broken. I can't move anything."

"What happened?" said Jennifer, surprised at the cold and clinical sound of her voice.

"If you honestly don't know, then ask Silk."

"You were intending to kill all three of us with your bomb," said Jennifer.

"Wrong. I was intending to kill all four of you."

"Derek isn't with us, so once again, he has slipped through your fingers. That makes three, Freneton. Three times you've tried to kill him in the most violent way, and three times you've failed."

She was expecting a reaction, but Olivia's face was as steely hard as ever. It occurred to Jennifer that the woman was probably feeling no pain, that her injuries were so bad her nervous system had shut out all response.

"You have the luck of the devil, Cotton, but one day …"

"Dream on, Freneton, there won't be a one day. This is it. You're going to die, here on this rock. A successful suicide, balance of the mind disturbed. You couldn't stand the failure and you snapped."

"You think this is the end, Cotton?" Olivia was trying desperately to lift her head, trying to force her arms to react and grab at the girl. But nothing happened.

"You're a police officer, DC Cotton. It's your duty to help me, your duty to call emergency services, call a helicopter to medevac me. It's your duty. Did you learn nothing from your training? You know that a fundamental role of a police officer is to render all possible help to the public, to protect them from danger. You must help me, Cotton. Now!"

To Olivia's ears, she was shouting her orders, but in reality her voice was little more than a slight disturbance to the air. Jennifer had to lean close to hear anything.

"You're right, Freneton," she said. "It is my duty to protect the public from danger. And I've never come across anything or anybody more dangerous than you."

She leaned forward and reached one arm under the crash helmet, lifting Olivia's head from the rock on which it was resting. Her other grasped the front of the helmet.

"Cotton, I—"

There was a crack as Jennifer twisted the crash helmet sharply to the right. She let go, allowing it to fall, and looked down at the now lifeless body. Olivia's pale eyes were still open, staring sightlessly. Jennifer reached out and closed them with her fingers.

She started as she heard another crack, this one from footfall on a shifting loose rock. She turned her head to see Henry making his way towards her.

"I take it she's dead," he said. "Surely she couldn't have survived a crash like that."

"Yes," replied Jennifer quietly as she stood and stepped away from the body, "she is."

She held out her arms and he took her in his, her head pressing into his shoulder.

"It's over," he heard her whisper.

Henry gently kissed her hair. "Did she say anything?"

Jennifer pushed her face harder into his shoulder, not wanting to move.

Finally she sighed and shook her head. "No, nothing. She was dead."

Henry nodded, understanding. Separating himself from her arms, he knelt next to Olivia's body. He took some tissues from a packet in his pocket and wiped the surface of the crash helmet.

"Can't be too careful," he said, his eyes catching Jennifer's.

She held his gaze for a few moments before her face relaxed.

"I hope you were as thorough with the bomb," she replied, holding out a hand to help him up. "Come on, let's get back to your new girlfriend."

"Yes," said Henry. "Let's do that."

Acknowledgments

As with my previous books, this novel could not have been completed without the brilliant help and encouragement of many people.

Once again, two of my former colleagues in the world of forensic science, Dr Bob Bramley and Dr Sheilah Hamilton, have scrutinised the text for scientific and procedural accuracy. My heartfelt thanks go to you both.

Anne Mensini, Sanford Foster and Luci de Norwall Cornish read early drafts, raising many salient points about the plot as well as helping to fine tune my grammar and style. I can't thank you all enough.

Thanks are also due to my son-in-law, Simon O'Reilly — the fastest copy editor in the East — for his eagle eye.

A number of others have also kindly read through the book in draft form and all were very positive and helpful in their comments. Thanks go to my sister Jill Pemberton, my stepdaughter Zoe O'Reilly, Wendy Bearns, Jill Harrison and Cedric Harben, and of course to my wife Gail who has once again been a sounding board for ideas, a critical and constructive reviewer of drafts, and an enthusiastic supporter of the project.

I have designed my own cover once again, and there were, as ever, several versions on the way as it progressed from my original idea to its present form. Many thanks for comments and suggestions to Gail, Daniel, Zoe, Ben, Kim and Lea.

Finally, I am indebted to my two professionals: Linda Davy for her usual incisive proofreading and Susanna Moles for a wonderfully detailed copy edit. You have both made a profound difference; thank you!

Afterword

I hope very much that you enjoyed reading this book as much as I enjoyed writing it. If you did, I should be extremely grateful if you could spend a few moments posting a review on Amazon or Goodreads (or both!). It needn't be long; one word will do — preferably a favourable one! Genuine reviews, however short, are worth a lot.

And equally as important, please recommend Remorseless to your relatives, friends and colleagues. While word of mouth is very helpful to the cause of any author, it is particularly so for self-published authors for whom marketing is that much harder. If you tell a few people about this book or any of my other books, and they in turn others, the word will spread.

You can find more information about all my books and other book-related stuff on my website at davidgeorgeclarke.com. If you are on FaceBook, Instagram, Twitter and/or Goodreads, I'm there too:

facebook.com/davidgeorgeclarkeauthor

twitter.com/clarkefiction

instagram.com/clarkefiction

goodreads.com/davidgeorgeclarke

About the Author

After more than thirty years as a forensic scientist, most of which were spent in Hong Kong, David Clarke retired to the more bucolic pastures of Tuscany where, after dabbling in art restoration, he took up full-time novel writing. Drawing on his experiences in the scientific investigation of numerous serious crimes, he has written the The Dust of Centuries series, the Cotton & Silk thriller series and An Imperfect Revenge.

He now spends his time mainly in Tuscany, Italy and Phuket, Thailand.

AN IMPERFECT REVENGE

Scan now for your FREE audiobook

If you would like to listen to a free audiobook version of AN IMPERFECT REVENGE read by the author, scanning the QR code above with the camera on your phone will take you to a link to sign up to the clarkeFiction newsletter and download the file. You will also be guided to the BookFunnel app for listening to the book.

Synopsis of An Imperfect Revenge

On assignment to review Villa Brocanti, an up-market agriturismo resort in Tuscany, travel writer Evie Lorrigan explores the dense forest surrounding the Brocanti estate and finds the boarded-up ruin of a palatial villa.

Her journalistic antennae piqued, she breaks in and what she finds is chilling. Prevented from leaving by doors with no handles closing behind her, she has little choice but to make her way through one room after another, each one decorated with extraordinary trompe l'oeil paintings. Lured onwards and upwards, she finally becomes trapped in an attic room with the gruesome remains of a man from a bygone era.

And no one knows she is there…

Enjoy!

A Final Word

Do you have kids or grandchildren, a favourite godson or goddaughter, a class of kids you teach or support in some way? My wife Gail is an author and illustrator who has published ten beautifully illustrated children's books. They are written in rhyme that children from 4–9 years just love reading or having read to them.

Patrick's Birthday Message
Searching for Skye — An Arctic Tern Adventure
Cosmos the Curious Whale
The Chameleon Who Couldn't Change Colour
Sharks — Our Ocean Guardians
[The Shark Guardian Series Book I]
Jed's Big Adventure
[The Shark Guardian Series Book II]
Mischief At The Waterhole
Ndotto — An Elephant Rescue Story
Dormouse Snoremouse
Meerkat's Exciting Adventure

You can find more details on Gail's website and YouTube channel:

www.gailclarkeauthor.com
www.youtube.com/c/gailclarkeauthor

Printed in Great Britain
by Amazon

70406131R00220